ADORA...

Bertrice Small creates cover-to-cover passion . . . a keen sense of history and suspense.

Publishers Weekly

Small's fans know what to expect . . . a good story.

Library Journal

Adora is the finest of classic historical romance. Small's sharp sense of history elevates her books to another level of historical fiction where intrigue, romance, sexuality and accurate historical details share the stage.

Romantic Times

BERTRICE SMALL

Adora

This book is lovingly dedicated to my mother, Doris Steen Williams, who, like Adora, always knew who she was.

Adora
by Bertrice Small

Copyright © 1980 by Bertrice Small

ISBN 13: 978-1-58160-500-5

Printed in the United States of America

Published by Romance Book Classics, a division of
Paladin Enterprises, Inc.
Gunbarrel Tech Center
7077 Winchester Circle
Boulder, Colorado 80301 USA
+1.303.443.7250

Direct inquiries and/or orders to the above address.

Visit our Web site at www.romancebookclassics.com

Contents

PROLOGUE

Constantinople

1341 to 1346

IT WAS EARLY MORNING, AND THE MISTS, LIKE SHREDDED gray gauze, hung over the still waters of the Golden Horn. The city of Constantine slept, unaware that its emperor was dead.

A lone figure—unchallenged by the guards—left the Imperial Palace and made his way across the vast, green park behind the Senate. The man who walked so purposefully towards the Mangana Palace was John Cantacuzene, for the last thirteen years the actual ruler of the crumbling Byzantine Empire. Behind John was Andronicus III, already lying in his funeral bier.

Charming Andronicus had been inadvertently responsible for the murder of his younger brother and the subsequent early death of his own father. He had been forced to overthrow his furious grandfather, Andronicus II. The old man had sworn to kill him. In becoming emperor, Andronicus had been fully aided by his very good friend, John Cantacuzene one of Byzantium's most brilliant minds.

But Andronicus III, once he had gained his heart's desire, found that he preferred hunting, festivals, and beautiful women to the burdens of state. Those dull matters he left to his trusted friend, Chancellor John Cantacuzene. The chancellor worked hard. The government ran smoothly. The emperor's every desire was gratified.

The emperor's mother, Xenia-Marie, and his wife, Anna of Savoy, distrusted John Cantacuzene. They knew the chancellor was ambitious. Andronicus, however, refused to dismiss the friend who had served him so well.

But now Andronicus was dead, and his heir was barely eleven years old. The royal family had triumphed over John Cantacuzene by obtaining a deathbed signature from Andronicus appointing the Empress Anna sole regent for the boy emperor. There would be civil war. John Cantacuzene did not intend for the child's vengeful Italian mother and her priests to rule the empire.

First, however, John had to get his own family to safety. The empress would not stop at murder. But then, smiled John, neither would he.

His older son, fifteen-year-old John, would remain with him. Matthew, at six, could be placed in sanctuary at the monastery attached to the Church of St. Andrew, near the Gate of Pege. His second wife, Zoe, his daughters, and his niece would all go to convents. John could trust the devout Anna not to violate religious sanctuary.

His first wife, Marie of Bursa, had died when their eldest daughter, Sophia, was barely three, and little John was five. He had mourned her for a year and then married a Greek princess, Zoe of Macedonia. Ten months later, Helena, now eight, had been born—followed eighteen months after by his younger son, and two years later by his youngest daughter, Theadora, now four-and-a-half. There had been twin sons, dead a year later in an epidemic. Zoe was again with child.

Entering the Mangana Palace, he hurried to his apartments and was met by his manservant, Leo.

"He is dead, my lord?"

"Yes," John answered. "A few minutes ago. Take Matthew to St Andrew's—immediately. I will wake my lady and the girls." He hurried to. the women's wing of the apartment, startling the eunuch guards who dozed by the doors.

"Say good-bye to Matthew, my love," he told Zoe, "Leo is taking him to St. Andrew's now."

This was not the time for prolonged discussion. Moving on to the bedchamber shared by Sophia and Eudoxia, he shook them awake. "Get dressed. The emperor is dead. You go to St. Mary's in Blanchernae for safety."

Sophia stretched languidly, her nightshift slipping to reveal a plump golden breast. She shook her jet black hair back, and her red mouth pouted. She reminded him more of her mother each day. If he couldn't marry her off right now, then a convent was the best place for her.

"Oh, Father! Why must we go to a convent? With a civil war there will be so many handsome soldiers about!"

He didn't stop to argue, but neither did he miss the look of lust in her eye. "You both have five minutes," he said sternly, moving quickly to his other daughters' bedchamber. Here he stopped, allowing himself the pleasure of viewing his two younger girls in sleep.

His lovely Helena was so like Zoe, with her sunshine blond hair and sky-blue eyes. Eventually, she would marry the boy emperor who was Andronicus's heir.

Little Theadora slept with her thumb in her mouth,

the sweet line of her innocent little body visible through the thin cotton shift. She was his mysterious one. He often marveled that, of all his children, she was the one with his quick, intuitive mind. Though barely out of babyhood, Theadora seemed much older. Her features were delicate, as his mother's had been: she would grow into an extraordinary beauty. Her coloring was unique in this family. Her skin was like heavy cream, her cheeks faintly touched with a soft apricot pink. Her hair was dark, the color of rich polished wood, and it gleamed with golden lights. Outrageously long, dark lashes tipped in gold hid Theadora's amazing eyes—eyes that changed from amethyst to deep purple. He was suddenly startled to find those eyes open and upon him.

"What is it, Papa?"

He smiled down at her. "Nothing to fear, chick. The emperor has died, and you, Helena, and your mother are going to St. Barbara's for a while."

"Will there be war, Papa?"

Again she startled him, and he surprised himself by answering plainly. "Yes, Theadora. The empress got a deathbed signature. She is sole regent."

The child nodded. "I'll wake Helena, Papa. Have we much time?"

"Just time to dress," he said. He left the room shaking his head at her quick grasp of the situation. If only she'd been a boy!

Theadora Cantacuzene rose from her bed. Calmly pouring water into a basin, she washed her face and hands. She then slipped a simple green tunic dress over her shift and. pulled a pair of outdoor boots over her little feet. Refilling the basin with fresh water, she lay out a pink tunic and another pair of boots.

"Helena," she called. "Helena, wake up!"

Helena opened her beautiful blue eyes and looked at her little sister irritably. "It is barely dawn, brat. Why do you wake me?"

"The emperor is dead! We go to St. Barbara's with mother. Get dressed, or you'll be left behind for old Xenia-Marie's torture chamber!"

Helena scrambled out of bed. "Where are you going?" she shrieked.

"To find mother. You had better hurry,. Helena!" Theadora found her mother bidding Matthew good-bye outside the palace. She and her brother were but two years apart and had always been close. Now they clung to each other, and Matthew whispered, "I am afraid, Thea. What will happen to us?"

"Nothing," she soothed him. Lord, he was such a gentle boy, she thought. "Father puts us with the church for safety. We'll be back together again soon. Besides, it should be fun for you—escaping from all us women!"

He took heart from her words and, hugging her, turned back to their mother. He kissed her, mounted his horse, and rode manfully off, with Leo close behind.

Next to go were Sophia and Eudoxia, escorted—to their delight—by a troop of Cantacuzene's household guards. The girls preened and giggled, deliberately bumping the young soldiers, rubbing their bobbing breasts against young male arms and backs. Zoe spoke sharply to them. They gave her sour looks, but they obeyed. She was a good stepmother, more liberal than most, and both girls knew it.

John Cantacuzene would escort his wife and two younger daughters. He had cleverly scattered his family in various locations, the better to conceal their whereabouts. Matthew's monastery was near the Gate of the Pege at the western end of the city. Sophia and Eudoxia's convent was near the Blanchernae Gate in the northeast part of the city. Zoe and the little ones would be at St. Barbara's on the Lycus River, outside the old wall of Constantine, near the Fifth Military Gate.

John helped his pregnant wife to settle beside Theadora and Helena in their litter. It was almost dawn, and rainbow colors sifted through the gray and gold clouds, dappling the waters of the Golden Horn.

"It's the most beautiful city in the world!" sighed Theadora. "I never want to live anywhere else."

Zoe smiled at her little daughter. "You might have to, Thea. Someday you could be wed to a prince whose home is elsewhere. Then you would have to leave here."

"I would sooner die!" declared the child passionately. Zoe smiled again Theadora might have her father's brilliant mind, but she was still a mere female. Sooner or later she would learn to accept that. Someday she would meet a man and then, thought Zoe, the city would matter very little.

They passed St. Theodosia, and though still in the city the landscape became more suburban with comfortable looking villas built amid lovely landscaped gardens. They crossed over the bridge that spanned the river Lycus, and left the Triumphal Way to follow an unpaved dirt road. After a mile or so, another right turn took them up to the great bronze gates set within the whitewashed brick walls of St. Barbara's Convent. Entering, they were met by the Reverend Mother Thamar. Kneeling, John Cantacuzene kissed the ring on the thin, aristocratic hand extended to him.

"I ask unlimited sanctuary for my wife, my daughters, and my unborn child," he requested formally.

"Sanctuary is granted, my lord," answered the tall, austere woman.

He rose, helping Zoe from the litter, he introduced her. At the sight of the children, Mother Thamar's face softened.

"My daughters, Princess Helena and Princess Theadora," John said quietly.

So, thought the nun. *That* is how it is going to be! Well, his family has a right to those titles, though they have rarely used them.

Taking his wife aside, John Cantacuzene spoke quietly with her for a few moments, then kissed her tenderly. Then he spoke with his daughters.

"If I am a princess," asked Helena, "then I must marry a prince. Mustn't I, father?"

"You are a princess, my pet, but I mean for you to be an empress some day."

Helena's blue eyes widened. Then she asked, "And shall Thea be an empress also?"

"I have not yet chosen a husband for Theadora."

Helena shot her little sister a triumphant look. "Why not marry her to the Grand Turk, father? Maybe he likes purple eyes!"

"I would never marry that old infidel," exclaimed Theadora. "Besides, father would never do anything to make me unhappy. And that certainly would!"

"You would have to marry him if father said so." Helena was unbearably smug. "And then you would have to leave the city! Forever!"

"If I married that old man," countered Theadora, "I should see that he brought his army to capture the city. Then *I* should be its empress instead of you!"

"Helena! Theadora!" scolded Zoe gently, but John Cantacuzene laughed heartily. "Ah, chick," he chuckled, ruffling Theadora's hair, "you really should have been a boy! What fire! What spirit! What a damned logical mind! I shall find you the most advantageous husband, I promise you."

Bending, he kissed his two daughters, then strode back out through the gate, mounting his horse, he waved and rode off, confident that his family was safe. Now he could begin his battle for the throne of Byzantium.

It was not an easy war, for the population of Byzantium was torn by loyalties. Both the Paleaologis and the Cantacuzenes were old, respected families.

Should the people support the young son of their late emperor or the man who had actually been running the empire for years? Too, there was the deep suspicion, kept alive by the Cantacuzene faction, that Empress Anna of Savoy intended to lead Byzantium back to hated Rome.

John Cantacuzene and his eldest son left the city to lead their forces against young John Paleaologi. Neither side would harm their beloved city of

Constantine. The war would be fought outside the capital.

Though Cantacuzene preferred diplomacy to warfare there was no choice. The two dowager empresses sought his death, and what should have been a quick victory turned into a war of several years' duration while the fickle Byzantines constantly switched sides. Finally, John Cantacuzene sought aid from the Ottoman Turks who ruled on the other side of the Sea of Marmara. Although the mercenary soldiers of Byzantium fought well, Cantacuzene could never be sure how many he might lose to a higher bidder. He needed an army he could depend on

Sultan Orkhan had already had a request for aid from the Paleaologi side. Unfortunately, they had offered only money, and the sultan knew their Imperial treasury was empty. John Cantacuzene offered gold, which he really had; the fortress of Tzympe in the Gallipoli peninsula; and his little daughter, Theadora. If Orkhan accepted the offer, Tzympe would give the Turks their first toehold in Europe—and without shedding a drop of blood. It was too tempting to refuse, and the sultan accepted. Six thousand of his best forces were dispatched to John Cantacuzene and, together with the Byzantine forces, they took the coastal cities of the Black Sea, ravaged Thrace, and seriously threatened Adrianople. In short order they were besieging Constantinople, to which the young emperor had fled.

Safe behind the walls of St. Barbara's Convent, little Theadora knew nothing of her impending marriage to a man fifty years her senior. But her mother knew, and Zoe wept that her exquisite child should be sacrificed. Such was the lot, however, of royal princesses, whose only value was in a marriage trade. Zoe actually believed that the sultan had helped John simply because he desired Theadora. Zoe was a devout woman—and the church kept alive the stories of the infidel's evil ways. It did not occur to the anxious mother that Tzympe was what the sultan was really after.

It was Helena who maliciously broke the news to her younger sister. Four years older than Theadora, she was as beautiful as an angel with her golden hair and lovely blue eyes. But she was not an angel. She was selfish, vain, and cruel The gentle Zoe had no influence over Helena.

One day when Mother Thamar had left the girls to practice a new embroidery stitch, Helena whispered, "They have chosen you a husband, sister." Then, without waiting for Theadora to ask who, Helena continued "You are to be the old infidel's third wife. You will spend the rest of your days locked up in a harem. . . while *I* rule in Byzantium!"

"You lie!" accused Theadora.

Helena giggled. "No, I don't. Ask mother. She weeps often enough about it these days. Father needed soldiers he could depend on, and he offered you in exchange for troops. I understand the Turks love little children in their beds. Even boys! They . . ." And Helena lowered her voice while she described a particularly nasty perversion

Theadora paled and slowly crumpled to the floor in a faint. Helena regarded her curiously for minute, then she called for help. When questioned by her mother she blandly disclaimed any understanding of why her sister had fainted—a lie that was quickly exposed as Theadora returned to consciousness.

Zoe rarely chastised her children physically, but this time she angrily slapped Helena's smug face several times. "Take her away," she told the servants. "Take her from me before I beat her to death!" Then Zoe gathered her youngest daughter into her soft arms. "There, my little one. There, love. It is not so bad."

Theadora sobbed. "Helena said the sultan likes little girls in his bed. She said he would hurt me! That when a man loves a woman it hurts her, and with little girls it is worse! I am not yet a woman, mother! I will surely die!"

"Your sister is deliberately cruel, and she is also badly informed, Theadora. Yes, you are to marry the sultan. Your father needed the aid Orkhan could give him, and you were not yet betrothed. It is the privileged duty of a princess to serve her family by an advantageous marriage. What other good is a woman?

"However, you will not live in the sultan's house until you have begun your womanly show of blood. Your father has arranged it that way. If you are lucky Orkhan will die before then, and you will come home to make a good Christian marriage. In the meantime, you will reside in your own house, safe within the walls of St. Catherine's Convent in Bursa. Your presence there will guarantee your father Ottoman aid."

The child sniffed and nestled close to her mother. "I

do not want to go. Please don't make me, mama. I would sooner take the veil and remain here at St. Barbara's."

"My child!" Startled, Theadora looked up into her mother's shocked face. "Have you heard nothing I have said?" exclaimed Zoe. "You are Theadora Cantacuzene, a princess of Byzantium. You have a duty. That duty is to aid your family as best you can, and you must *never* forget that, my daughter. It is not always pleasant to do one's duty, but our duty separates us from the rabble. They exist merely to satisfy their base desires. You must never shirk your duty, my dearest daughter."

"When must I go?' whispered the child.

"Your father now besieges the city. When it is taken, we will see."

But Constantinople was not easily taken, not even by one of its own. On the land side, the walls—twenty-five feet thick—rose in three levels behind a moat sixty feet wide and twenty-two feet deep. Normally dry, the moat was flooded during siege by a series of pipes. The first wall was a low one used to shield a line of archers. The next wall rose twenty-seven feet above the second level and sheltered more troops. Beyond lay the third, and strongest, bulwark. The towers—some seventy feet high—held archers, Greek fire machines, and missile throwers.

On the sea side, Constantinople was protected by a single wall with towers set at regular intervals which also enclosed each of its seven harbors. Across the Golden Horn was stretched a thick chain which prevented unwelcome ships from sailing up the horn.

And across the horn the two sub-cities of Galata and Pera were also well-walled.

The city was besieged for a year. And for a year its gates remained closed to John Cantacuzene. But the presence of his army on the landward side of the town and the sultan's fleet sitting off the harbors were beginning to take a toll. Food and other supplies began to dwindle. Cantacuzene's forces found the source of one of the city's main aqueducts and diverted it so that Constantinople's water supply was cut.

Then the plague broke out. The infant daughter whom Zoe Cantacuzene had borne in sanctuary died. Frantic that he might lose Theadora and, thus, lose the sultan's aid, John Cantacuzene arranged an escape from the city for his wife and two youngest daughters.

At the Convent of St. Barbara only two people knew of the departure—the Reverend Mother Thamar and the little nun who kept the gate. The night chosen was during the dark of the moon and, by a fortunate coincidence, there was a storm.

Dressed in the habit of the order that had sheltered them, Zoe and her daughters slipped out into the night and walked to the Fifth Military Gate. Zoe's heart was hammering wildly and her hand, holding the lantern that lit their way, shook uncontrollably. All her life she had been surrounded by slaves. She had never walked through the city at all, much less gone out unescorted. It was the greatest adventure of her life and, though frightened, she walked with determination, breathing deeply, mastering her fear.

The wind whipped their rough, dark skirts about them. Large fat raindrops were beginning to spatter them. Helena whined and was firmly told to be quiet. Theadora kept her head down, walking doggedly along. The months during which her father had besieged the city had been a blessed reprieve for her. At the final end of this journey waited her bridegroom, the sultan. Theadora dreaded it. Despite her mother's reassurances she could not rid herself of Helena's evil words, and she was frightened. She did not reveal it, however. She would neither give Helena the satisfaction nor grieve her mother further.

The tower of the Fifth Military Gate loomed above them, and Zoe fumbled in her robes for their pass. It had been signed by a Byzantine general within the city—a man friendly to John Cantacuzene. Zoe checked to be sure that the girls' faces were covered by their heavy black head veiling. "Remember," she warned them, "keep your eyes lowered at all times, your hands hidden in the sleeves of your robes, and speak not! Helena, I know that you have reached an age where young men fascinate you, but remember that nuns are not interested in men. If you flirt, if you attract attention, we will be captured. You will never get to be empress then, so mind my words."

A moment later came the challenge, "Halt! Who goes there?" A young soldier blocked their way.

They stopped. Zoe said, "Sister Irene of St. Barbara's Convent. My two assistants and I are bound outside the walls to help a woman in labor. Here is my pass."

The guard glanced briefly at the parchment, then said, "My captain will see you in the guardroom, good sister. You and your nuns may pass through my checkpoint," and he pointed the way up the steps of the tower to a landing with a door.

They climbed the unrailed stone steps slowly, clinging in the strong wind, to the side of the tower. Once Helena slipped, and she whimpered in fright. Theadora grasped her older sister and shoved her to her feet. Finally they reached their goal. Pushing the door open, they entered the guardroom.

The captain took the parchment from Zoe's slim white hand.

"Are you a doctor?" he asked. In Byzantium it was not unusual for women to be doctors.

"Yes, captain."

"Would you look at one of my men? I think he may have broken a bone in his wrist today in a fall."

"Of course, captain," said Zoe kindly, and with more assurance than she felt. "But might I do so on my return? Your man's case is not desperate, and the woman we go to attend is the young wife of a childless old merchant. The gentleman has always been *very* generous to St. Barbara's, and his anxiety is great."

Theadora listened in utter amazement. Zoe's voice was calm, and her story plausible. At that moment Theadora's respect for her mother increased a hundred fold.

"He is in pain, sister," said the captain.

Zoe drew a small box from her robes and shook out two small gilded pills. "Have your man take these," she said. "It will ease his pain, and he will sleep until I return."

"My thanks, good sister. Trooper Basil! Escort the

doctor and her nuns out the moat postern." Saluting neatly, the captain bade them a safe journey.

Silently they followed the soldier down several flights of stairs into a long stone corridor, the walls of which were wet and green with slime. It was damp and bone-chilling cold in the tunnel. The corridor was lit at intervals by smoking pitch torches stuck into rusting iron wall holders.

"Where are we?" asked Zoe of their guide.

"Beneath the walls, sister," came the reply. "I'll let you out a small postern gate on the other side of the moat."

"We pass beneath the moat?"

"Aye, sister," he grinned at her. "Just a couple of feet of dirt and a few tiles between us and nearly a sea of water!"

Plodding along behind her mother, Theadora felt a swelling of panic in her chest, but she bravely fought it down. Beside her, a white-faced Helena was barely breathing. That's all we need, thought Theadora: Helena fainting! She reached out and pinched her older sister hard. Helena gasped and shot her a venomous look, but the color began to creep back into her face.

Ahead of them was a small door set into the wall. The soldier stopped, relit Zoe's lantern, fit a large key into the lock, and slowly turned it. The door swung silently open, allowing the wind to rush into the tunnel, blowing their robes about them. The lantern flickered.

"Good luck, sisters," said the soldier as they stepped out into the night. The door closed quickly behind them.

For a moment they stood silent, then Zoe raised her lantern, and said, "Here is the path. Your father said we were to follow it until we were met by his men. Come, my daughters, it cannot be far."

They had walked a few minutes when Theadora begged, "Stop a moment, Mama. I would look a final time upon the city." Her young voice shook. "I may never see it again." She turned, but could see nothing more than the great walls and towers, dark against a darker sky. Sighing with disappointment, she said sadly, "Let us go on."

The windy rain was falling harder now. They walked and walked. Their heavy robes grew heavier with the rain and their shoes were soaking. Each step was torture. Then suddenly, ahead of them, they saw bobbing lights. And soon they were surrounded by soldiers and there was Leo's friendly face.

"Majesty! Praise God you are finally safe with us, and the princesses too! We were not sure you would come tonight because of the weather."

"The weather was God's blessing on the venture, Leo. There was no one on the streets to observe our passage. We have seen only three people since we left the convent. All soldiers."

"There was no difficulty, Majesty?"

"None, Leo. But I am eager to see my husband. Where is he?"

"He is waiting at his main camp a few miles from here. If Your Majesty will allow me, I will help you into the wagon. I regret the crude transport, but it is better than walking."

The next few days were a blur for Theadora. They

had arrived safely at her father's camp where warm, dry clothes and hot baths waited. She slept a few hours and then was awakened for the march to Selymbria, where her father had his temporary capital. The journey took two long days in the wagon, plowing through muddy paths beneath torrential rains.

It had been almost six years since she and her father had seen one another. John Cantacuzene embraced his daughter and then held her back so he could look at her. Satisfied with what he saw, he smiled and said, "Orkhan Gahzi will be very pleased with you, Thea. You are becoming a real beauty, my child. Have you yet begun your show of blood?"

"No, Papa," she said calmly. And may I not for many years, she thought!

"A pity," replied the emperor. "Perhaps I should send your sister instead. The Turks like blonds, and she is now a woman."

Yes! Yes! thought Theadora. Send Helena!

"No, John," said Zoe Cantacuzene, looking up from her embroidery. "Thea is content to do her duty by our family. Are you not, my love?"

"Yes, Mama," came the whispered reply.

Zoe smiled. "The young Paleaologi is seventeen—a man ready to bed his wife. Helena is fourteen and ready to receive a husband. Leave things as they are, my lord."

"You are right, my love," John said, nodding. And several days later Theadora's wedding took place.

The bridegroom was not present but was represented by a Christian proxy. Afterward, the bride was taken to the emperor's military encampment where she ascended a jeweled throne atop a carpeted pavilion sent by the sultan for the occasion. The throne was surrounded by curtains of red, blue, green, silver, purple, and gold silk. Below, the armies of Christian and Moslem soldiers stood proudly under arms. Only John, as the emperor, was on horseback. At his signal the curtains of the pavilion were opened to reveal the bride surrounded by kneeling eunuchs and hymeneal torches.

Flutes and trumpets proclaimed that Theadora Cantacuzene was now Sultan Orkhan's wife. While the assembled choir sang joyous songs of the bride's happiness, of her great charity, and of her devotion to her church, Theadora stood quietly, alone with her thoughts. In the church she had been sulky, but her mother warned her afterward that if she did not appear happy she would disappoint the troops. So she wore a fixed smile.

The following morning, as she was about to be taken away, she had a fit of weeping and was comforted by her mother one last time.

"All princesses feel this way when they leave their families for the first time," said Zoe. "I did. But you must not give in to self-pity, my child. You are Theadora Cantacuzene, a princess of Byzantium. Your birth sets you above all others, and you must never show weakness to your inferiors."

The child shuddered and drew a deep breath. "You will write to me, Mama?"

"Regularly, my dearest. Now, wipe your eyes. You would not insult your lord by weeping."

Theadora did as she was bid and was then led to a

purple and gold draped palanquin. This litter was to carry her to the ship, which would then take her to Sultan Orkhan who awaited her across the Sea of Marmara in Scutari. The sultan had sent a full troop of cavalry and thirty ships to escort his bride.

Theadora looked small and vulnerable in her pale blue tunic dress, despite the elegant gold floral embroidery adorning it at the cuffs, hem, and neck. Zoe nearly wept at the sight of her child. The girl seemed sophisticated and yet touchingly young!

Neither the emperor nor his wife accompanied their child to the ship. From the moment Theadora entered the royal palanquin, she was alone. It was to remain that way for many years.

One year later the gates of Constantinople opened to John Cantacuzene. Several weeks after that, his daughter Helena was married to John's young co-emperor, John Paleaologi. The wedding was celebrated with the full pomp offered by the Orthodox Church.

PART I

Theadora

1350 to 1351

Chapter 1

THE CONVENT OF ST. CATHERINE IN THE CITY OF BURSA
was a small one, but it was rich and distinguished. It
had not always been so, but the recent prosperity was
due to the presence of one of the sultan's wives.
Princess Theadora Cantacuzene of Byzantium lived
within the convent walls.

Theadora Cantacuzene was now thirteen, and quite
capable of childbearing. Sultan Orkhan, however, was
sixty-two and had a harem full of nubile females both
innocent and experienced. The little Christian virgin
in the convent had only been a political necessity after
all. And so she remained there, forgotten by her
Ottoman husband.

Had he seen her, however, even the jaded Orkhan
could not have ignored Theadora. She had grown tall
and had long, beautifully shaped arms and legs, a
slender torso, firm, high, cone-shaped breasts with
long pink nipples, and a beautiful heart-shaped face.
Her skin was like smooth cream, for although she
enjoyed the outdoors, she never tanned. Her dark
mahogany-colored hair with its golden lights hung
straight down her back to just above the soft swell of
her sweetly rounded buttocks. The violet eyes were
startlingly clear, and as candid as they had always

been. Her nose was small and straight, her mouth lush with a full lower lip.

Within the convent grounds, she had her own house consisting of an antechamber for receiving guests—though none came—a dining room, a kitchen, two bedchambers, a bath, and servants quarters. Here she lived in isolated semisplendor—lacking nothing. She was well-fed, well-guarded, and very bored. She was rarely allowed to leave the convent grounds and when she did she was heavily veiled and escorted by at least half a dozen sturdy nuns.

In the summer of Theadora's thirteenth year her life changed suddenly. It was a hot mid-afternoon, and all the servants lay dozing in the sticky heat. Theadora was alone, for even the nuns slept as she wandered the deserted, walled convent garden. Suddenly a small breeze brought to her the scent of peaches ripening in one of the convent orchards, but the door to the orchard garden was locked. Theadora was annoyed, and as her desire for a peach became overwhelming she looked for another means of entry into the orchard, and she found it.

Where the garden wall met the orchard wall along the street side of the convent property, there was a thick gnarled vine. Tucking up her simple lime green cotton tunic dress Theadora clambered up the vine to the top. Then, chuckling gleefully to herself, she walked carefully along the wall looking for a similar vine so she might get down into the orchard. Finding it, she descended, picked several of the plumpest fruits, and put them in her pockets. Then she climbed back up to the top of the wall.

The wall, however, was old, and worn away in several places. Its only traffic for many years had been the cats of the city who frequently courted the privacy of the convent gardens. Flushed with her success, Theadora did not watch her footing and suddenly she found herself falling. But, to her surprise, she did not hit the ground. Instead, she fell—shrieking—into the strong arms of a laughing young man.

The arms cradled her, gently but firmly, and seemed in no hurry to release her. Jet-black eyes looked her over thoroughly, admiringly. "Are you a thief? Or merely a naughty little nun?" he asked.

"Neither." She was amazed to find she still had a voice. "Please put me down, sir."

"Not until I learn your identity, violet eyes. You are not veiled, so you cannot be Turkish. Who are you?"

Theadora had never been this close to a man other than her father. It was not unpleasant. The man's chest was hard, somehow reassuring, and he smelled of sunshine.

"Have you lost your tongue, little one?" he queried softly.

She blushed and bit her lip in vexation. She had the uncomfortable feeling that he knew what she had been thinking. "I am a student at the convent," she said. "Please, sir, would you help me back up onto the wall? If they find me gone, I shall be scolded."

Setting her down, he quickly climbed onto the wall. Leaning over, he pulled her up onto the wall. Then, leaping lightly into the convent garden, he held out his arms to her. "Jump, violet eyes." He caught her easily and set her on her feet. "Now you won't be scolded," he chuckled. "What on earth made you climb the wall?"

Feeling more secure now, she looked up at him mischievously. Reaching into a pocket of her tunic dress, Theadora drew out a peach. "I wanted one," she said simply, biting into it. The juice ran down her chin. "The gate was locked, so I climbed the wall."

"Do you always get what you want?"

"Yes, but I do not usually want very much," she answered.

He laughed. "My name is Murad. What's yours?"

"Theadora."

"Too formal. I shall call you Adora, for you're a most adorable creature."

She blushed, then gasped in surprise as he bent and kissed her. "Oh! How dare you, sir? You must *not* do that again! I am a married woman."

The black eyes twinkled. "Yet, Adora, I will wager that was your first kiss." She flushed again and tried to turn away from him, but he gently caught her chin between his thumb and forefinger. "And," he continued, "I will also wager that you're wed to an old man. No young man with blood in his veins would leave you languishing in a convent. You are quite outrageously fair."

She raised her eyes to him, and he saw with amazement that in the sunlight they shone an amethyst color. "It is true that I have not seen my husband for several years, but you must not speak thusly to me. He is a good man. Please go now, sir. If you were caught here, it would not go well for you."

He made no move to leave. "Tomorrow night

28

begins the week of the full moon. I shall wait for you in the orchard."

"I will certainly not come!"

"Are you afraid of me, Adora?" he taunted.

"No!"

"Then prove it—and come." Reaching out he caught her to him, kissing her slowly with a gentle, controlled passion. For the briefest moment she yielded to him, and all the things she and her classmates had discussed with regard to kissing flashed through her mind, and she realized that they knew nothing of the truth. This was sweetness beyond belief, ecstasy beyond her wildest imaginings, and honeyed fire poured through her loins, making her weak.

Releasing her mouth, he held her gently to him Their eyes met for a moment in a strange understanding. Then, suddenly terrified by her response to him, Theadora tore herself free and fled down the neat gravel path. His mocking laughter followed her. She heard his voice. "Tomorrow, Adora."

Gaining the sanctuary first of her house, and then of her bedchamber, she collapsed on her bed, trembling violently, ignoring the peaches that spilled from her pockets and bumped across the floor.

She had not known that a kiss could be so—she sought for the right word—so powerful! So intimate! That was certainly what it had been. Intimate! An invasion of her person. And yet—a little smile played about her lips—and yet she had liked it.

Murad had been correct in assuming that she had never been kissed. In fact, Theadora knew nothing of what happened between a man and a woman for she had spent all but four years of her young life behind convent walls. When she had been married Zoe had wisely refrained from discussing the duties of the marriage bed with a child years away from puberty. Consequently, the sultan's youngest wife was a total innocent.

Now she wondered about the handsome young man whose strong arms had saved her from serious injury. Tall and tanned, she knew he was as fair as she, for where his black hair had been newly cropped, his skin was quite light. His jet dark eyes had been caressingly, even boldly, warm; his smile, which had revealed straight white teeth, very impudent.

Of course she would not see him again. It was simply unthinkable. Still, she wondered if he really would come tomorrow night. Would he actually be bold enough to climb the convent's orchard wall again?

There was only one way to find out. She must hide herself in the orchard before dark and watch. When he came—*if* he came—she would not, of course, reveal herself. She would remain hidden until he left. But at least her curiosity would be satisfied.

She giggled, imagining his chagrin. He obviously thought himself quite irresistible if he expected a respectable girl to sneak out and meet him. He would soon learn differently.

Chapter 2

Murad had been amused by his encounter with the girl, Theadora. He was a grown man, experienced in the amatory arts. Her sweetness, her unaffected innocence, enchanted him.

Legally, she was his father's third wife. But he felt there was virtually no chance that Sultan Orkhan would ever bring her into his palace, let alone his bed. The little princess was merely a political pawn. Murad felt no remorse over dallying with her. He was an honorable man and had no intention of seducing her.

Murad Beg was the youngest of the sultan's three sons. He had a full brother, Suleiman, and a half-brother, Ibrahim. Ibrahim's mother was the daughter of a Byzantine nobleman who was distantly related to Theadora. Her name was Anastatia, and she looked with haughty disdain upon Murad's mother, who was the daughter of a Georgian hetman. Anastatia was the sultan's first wife, but Murad's mother, who was called Nilufer, was the sultan's favorite. Her sons were the most beloved of their father.

Murad's half-brother, Ibrahim, was the eldest of the sultan's sons, but he had been dropped on his head as a baby and had not been right since. He lived in his own palace, lovingly tended to by his slaves and by his women, who were all sterile. Prince Ibrahim alternated between normality and periods of wild insanity. Still, his mother hoped he would follow his father as sultan, and she slyly worked toward this goal.

Prince Suleiman also kept his own palace, but he had sired two sons and several daughters. Murad had no children. His women were, by his choice, incapable of childbearing. The youngest son of Orkhan knew that his father's choice for successor was Suleiman.

Though Murad loved his older brother, he intended to fight him for the empire when their father died. But there was always the chance that he might lose—and that would mean not only his own death but the deaths of all his family. So Murad chose not to have children until he was sultan and his sons could be born into relative safety.

Mere chance had brought him past the Convent of St. Catherine that afternoon. He had been visiting a charming and delightful widow who lived in a nearby neighborhood. He had passed the convent just in time to catch Adora. He chuckled. What a minx! She had wanted peaches, and she had gone after what she wanted. What a worthy wife she would be for some man. He stopped, a smile lighting his face. Muslim law decreed that a man might take any of his dead father's wives for his own, provided there was no incest committed. How much longer could Orkhan live?

The girl was safe—and unlikely to be called upon to serve her royal lord. Theadora Cantacuzene had been forgotten. And it was better that way, thought Murad grimly, for rumors had been circulating in the last few years about the sexual depravities practiced by his father in efforts to retain his potency.

Murad wondered if she would come the following night. She had scolded him for kissing her that first time. But she had yielded the second time, and he had felt the turmoil that swept over her before she fled.

The next day seemed to drag for Theadora. As it was mid-summer the convent's school was closed, and the daughters of Bursa's wealthy Christians had repaired to their seaside villas with their families. No one thought to invite the emperor's daughter to spend her holidays with them. Those sympathetic to her hesitated because of her position. The others considered her déclassé because of her marriage, though they would never have dared to voice such thoughts publicly. So Theadora was forced by circumstances to be alone at the very time in her young life when she needed a friend.

Sharp of mind, she read and studied everything she could. Still Theadora grew restless with a longing she could neither name, nor understand. There was no one in whom she might confide. She was alone, as she had always been. Her classmates were polite, but she was never with them long enough to be able to form any real friendships. Her servants were palace slaves, and they were changed thrice yearly since serving the sultan's child wife in her convent was considered dull duty. Consequently the sultan's wife was more innocent of the world and of men than any other girl her age. She was eager for adventure.

As the hot afternoon drew to a close, Theadora

attended vespers in the convent church. Returning to her house she ate sparingly of capon, a salad of new lettuces from the convent's kitchen garden, and the last of her stolen peaches. She drank of a delicate white wine from Cyprus.

Aided by her slaves she bathed in lightly scented warm water which eased the heat. Then a short, white silk shift was slipped over her dark hair which was unbound and brushed.

She waited for those few moments between sunset and dusk when she might slip unobserved into the peach orchard. She now possessed a key, having boldly asked the reverend mother for one and, to her surprised delight, received it.

"I am restless with the heat," she told the nun. "If the orchards are open to me, I will have more space to roam in. May I eat the peaches?"

"Of course, child! What is ours is also Your Royal Highness's."

The convent was now quiet. The residential neighborhood about it was quiet too. Only the little twilight creatures, cheeping and chirping, broke the purple stillness. Theadora rose and drew a dark-colored, lightweight cloak about her nightshift. She left her ground floor bedroom by a window, then hurried along the gravel path toward the orchard. Her soft kid slippers made virtually no sound at all. The little key was clutched tightly in her damp palm.

To her relief, the small door into the orchard opened noiselessly. Closing it carefully behind her, she leaned against it, eyes closed, weak with relief. She had made it!

"You came!" The low, deep voice broke the stillness.

Her eyes flew open. "Wh—what are you doing here?" she demanded, outraged.

"Did we not agree yesterday to meet here tonight?" he asked. She could hear the laughter in his voice.

Oh, good St. Theodosia! What kind of a wanton must he think I am? she thought. Mustering all the dignity she could, she said severely, "I only came to tell you that you must not violate the sanctuary of this convent, of which the orchards are a part." Her heart was hammering wildly.

"I see," he said gravely. "I thought perhaps you had come early so you might hide yourself and wait to see if I came." The silence that followed seemed eternal. "You're blushing," he said mischievously.

"H—h—how can you tell?"

His hand gently touched her face, and she jumped back. "Your cheek is warm," he answered.

"The night is hot," she quickly replied.

Again he laughed that soft laugh. Taking her hand, he said imperiously, "Come! I have found us a perfect place—towards the middle of the orchard, beneath the trees. We cannot be seen there." She was pulled along until he ducked beneath the spreading branches of a large tree and drew her in after him. "Here we are," he said. "Safe . . . and very private." To his amazement, she suddenly burst into tears. Surprised, Murad put his arms about her. "Adora, my sweet, what is it?"

"I—I—I—I am afraid," she stuttered, sobbing.

"Of what, dove?"

"Of *you*!" she wailed.

And then he realized how very innocent she really

was. Gently he drew her down to sit on his cloak, spread on the grass. "Do not be frightened, Adora. I will not harm you."

He held her tenderly, close against his chest, and the front of his shirt was quickly soaked. "I—I have never been with a m-man before," she confided, her sobs lessening somewhat. "I do not know what I should do, and I would not have you think me ignorant."

He swallowed his laughter. "Adora," he said gravely, "I think it might help if you know who I am as I know who you are. Your Highness." He heard her soft gasp. "I am Prince Murad, the third son of Sultan Orkhan. The gossips would have you believe I am a profligate. But I obey the Koran, and I would certainly never seduce my father's wife—even if she is very tempting. And only a political pawn."

For a moment all was silent. Then she asked, "Have you known my identity from the beginning?"

"Almost. When we met, I was returning to the palace after visiting a friend who lives nearby. There is no other way to go except past St. Catherine's. When you told me your name it suddenly came to me that you were *the* Theadora."

"And knowing who I was, you still kissed me? And made an assignation with me? You are despicable, Prince Murad!"

"You came, Adora" he reminded her quietly.

"Only to tell you that you must not come here again!"

"No. Because you were curious, dove. Admit it."

"I admit nothing."

He took a gentler tone with her. "Curiosity is no crime, my sweet. It is natural for a young girl to be curious about men. Especially a girl as cloistered as you are. Tell me, when was the last time you saw a man?"

"Father Bessarion hears my confession weekly," she said primly.

He laughed low. "I said a *man*, not the dried up husk of an elderly priest."

"I have not seen a man since I entered St. Catherine's. The other students do not live here, and no one comes to visit me." It was stated simply, matter-of-factly.

He reached out and covered the slim little hand with his own large, square one. His touch was warm. He felt her relax. "Is it very lonely for you, Adora?"

"I have my studies, Prince Murad," she answered.

"No friends? Poor little princess."

She snatched her hand away. "I do not need anyone's pity. Least of all yours!"

The moon had risen. It was very round and very full; its bright light cast a silvery glow on the fat, golden peaches that hung like perfect globes from the heavy branches. It touched the fair-skinned face of Theodora Cantacuzene, and Murad saw that her look was proud, though she fought to keep tears from filling her amethyst eyes.

"I do not pity you, dove," he said. "I merely regret that someone as alive as you are should be wed to an old man and incarcerated in a convent. You were made for a young man's passionate caresses."

"I am a princess of Byzantium," she said coldly. "I

was born to the title, even before my father became emperor. It is the duty of a princess to wed where she may do her family the most good. It was my father the emperor's wish that I wed the sultan. As a good Christian daughter it was not my place to question his wish."

"Your filial devotion is to be commended, Adora, but you speak like the child you are. If you had ever known love you would not be so stiff and unyielding."

"My family loves me," she retorted, outraged.

"Do they? Your father bartered you into marriage with a man old enough to be your grandfather, simply so he can call upon the sultan's armies to help him keep his stolen throne," said Murad. "He gave your sister in marriage to his rival, the boy emperor. At least she has a husband only three years her senior. And should the young John overcome the old John eventually, your father's life would still be safe because his daughter would then be empress! But what of *you*? Do you know that your sister, Helena, recently gave birth to her first child, a son. She preaches a holy war against the 'infidel'! Helena obviously has *great* love for you. She is aided in her endeavors by your half-sister, Sophia, whose piety is second only to her sexual excesses, which are the scandal of Constantinople. When was the last time either of them communicated with you? And what of your brother, Matthew, who is now to become a monk? Has he written to you? These are the people who love you?"

"My father did what was best for the empire," she said angrily. "He is a great ruler! As to my sisters, Sophia was already a woman when I was yet a child.

I barely know her. Helena and I have always been rivals. She may talk of holy wars," and here Adora's voice became scornful, "but it will never be. The empire can barely defend itself, let alone do battle against the sultan." Her grasp of that particular political truth impressed him. "My mother," she continued, "keeps me fully informed. Though we have not seen each other since I left Constantinople, she writes to me each week. And my lord Orkhan has a special messenger, for me alone, who brings my letters directly from the coast and returns with my replies. My half-brother John was killed in battle a few months after I came here, and she sent me word of his death immediately, so that I could pray for his soul. My mother cannot visit me. You surely know that travel is dangerous. And the wife of the emperor of Byzantium would make a fine prize for pirates and robbers! But I am very much loved, Prince Murad! I am!"

"You know *nothing* of love," he said fiercely, pulling her into his lap, holding her firmly.

"You remember only the vague affection of a child for its family. No one has ever truly touched you, or stirred your proud, cold little heart. But I will, Adora! I will awaken you to life . . . to love . . . to yourself!"

"You have no right," she spat angrily at him, struggling to break his grip on her. "I am your father's wife! Is this how you honor the Koran? What of your promise not to seduce me?"

He smiled grimly. "I will keep that promise, my innocent little virgin. There are a hundred ways I can pleasure you without robbing you of your maidenhead. We will commence lessons now!"

But as he bent toward her, she put her hands against his chest to hold him off. "Your father . . . "

"My father," he said, loosening the ties of her cloak, "will never call you to him. When he dies, Adora, and I am sultan, I shall arrange with whoever is emperor of Byzantium for you to be my bride. In the meantime, I will school you in the arts of loving."

And before she could protest further he had found her mouth. She could not struggle, for he held her far too tightly. She could barely breathe. Her heart was thumping wildly and she could feel his, beneath the flattened palms of her bands, matching the rhythm of her own. She tried to turn her head away, but one hand wound itself within the scented, silken tangle of her hair. He held her fast.

The mouth on hers was warm and firm, but surprisingly tender. The kiss was more frighteningly wonderful than it had been the first time, and once again she felt her resistance wearing away. As she relaxed, his kiss deepened, and she felt herself growing weak. Her young breasts grew strangely tight and the nipples ached.

His grip on her eased, and he released her mouth from its sweet captivity. She was speechless and lay unresisting across his lap. Smiling down at her, he traced a gentle line down her cheek with his finger. Her mouth felt dry. Her pulse raced. Her head was giddy, yet somehow she managed to find her voice.

"Why are you doing this?"

"Because I want you," he said quietly, and she trembled at the intensity in his voice. Again his mouth found hers, but this time he kissed not only her lips, but her eyes, her nose, her cheeks, forehead, and chin. These gentle kisses sent small shivers of hot and cold through her all at once. Eyes closed, she sighed with unconcealed pleasure.

His black eyes twinkled. "You like it," he accused, laughing softly. "You *like* being kissed!"

"No!" Oh, lord! What was she thinking of to act this way! Again she tried to escape his grasp, but again he found her mouth, and now she felt his tongue running lightly over her tightly closed lips. Pushing insistently against her clenched teeth he murmured against her mouth, "Open to me, Adora. You cannot deny me, dove, or yourself."

Her lips parted, and his tongue thrust inside. He stroked and caressed until she was close to fainting with the intensity of it. The feeling grew, and she trembled.

Removing his mouth from hers he held her tenderly, looking down at her through half-closed eyes. Her young breasts rose and fell swiftly, the nipples showing clearly through the thin silk of her shift like little buds. His heart beat fiercely with an exultation such as he had never before experienced. He longed to touch those tempting little peaks, but he refrained. It was much too soon to subject her further to her own sensual nature.

He had not believed such innocence existed. In his world a woman came to a man fully trained to please him. She might be a virgin, but she had been carefully taught to give pleasure and to receive it. Yet this lovely creature was untouched by man or woman. She would be his! He would allow no one else to ever possess her. He would mold her, teach her to please him. No one would ever know of her sweetness but him.

She opened her eyes and looked up at him. Her face was very pale, and her beautiful eyes were like large violets in the snow.

"It's all right, my sweet," he said gently. "We have concluded the lesson for tonight." Then he teased, "It pleases me, however, that you like my kisses."

"I did not!" she hissed. "I hate you! You had no right to do *that* to me!"

He continued as if she had not spoken. "Tomorrow night we shall proceed further. Your education as a woman is just beginning."

She sat up. "Tomorrow night? Are you mad? There will be no tomorrow night! I will never see you again! *Never!*"

"You will meet me here in the orchard as long as it pleases me, Adora! If you do not, I will appear at the convent gate demanding to see you."

"You would not dare!" But her eyes were filled with doubt.

"I would dare almost anything to see you again, dove." He stood, drawing her up with him. Gently wrapping her cloak about her, he walked silently with her to the orchard door. "Until tomorrow night, Adora. Dream of me." And then, vaulting up, he disappeared over the top of the wall into the night.

With trembling fingers she unlocked the door, went through, relocked it, and then fled through the gardens to her own house. Within the comparative safety of her bedchamber she relived in her mind the scene in the orchard. She realized that, though he had kissed her most thoroughly, he had not touched her otherwise. And yet she ached! Her entire body ached with a longing she did not understand. Her breasts were swollen, the nipples sore. Her belly felt tight, and the secret woman's place between her legs was throbbing. If this was being a woman, she wasn't sure she liked it.

But the greater problem was Prince Murad's threat to appear at the convent gate. His rank would make the nuns obedient. Why should they refuse the sultan's son permission to visit his stepmother? They might even believe that the sultan himself had sent him. When the truth was learned, the innocent little religious community would be punished and disgraced.

If she refused to see the prince, and told Mother Marie Josepha the truth, then Murad might be punished—perhaps even killed for his boldness. Theadora did not believe she could live with a death on her conscience. She was trapped. She would meet him tomorrow night.

Yet, as she lay in her chaste bed she remembered his deep voice saying, "My father will never call you to him. When he dies and I am sultan, I shall arrange for you to be my bride." She trembled. Were men always so intense?

Was it possible that he might be her lord some day? It was a tantalizing thought. He was very handsome—with his jet black eyes, dark, wavy hair, tanned face, and the white teeth flashing that impudent smile.

She shivered again. The mere memory of his kisses made her giddy, and that was wrong! Very wrong! Even if Sultan Orkhan never called her to him, she was still his wife.

She could not sleep that night, and in the morning she was irritable. She could not concentrate on her book. She tangled her embroidery threads and angrily threw the linen to the floor. Her slaves were astonished, and when an older woman questioned her, fearing she was becoming ill, Adora boxed her ears and then burst into tears.

Iris, the slavewoman, was wise enough to pursue the matter. She was relieved when the princess sobbingly confided that she had not slept well. Immediately the woman prepared a warm bath for her young charge and, after Theadora had been bathed and massaged, Iris tucked her into bed. She was then fed a cup of warm spiced wine into which the slavewoman had put a mild sleeping potion.

When Theadora awoke, the last rays of the sun were staining the western sky, and the purple mountains about the city were already crowned with faint silver stars. Iris brought the princess a small, roasted pigeon, the skin crisp and golden. The tray also held new lettuce, a honeycomb, and a carafe of white wine. Theadora ate slowly, her thoughts sorting themselves.

The prince had given his word not to tamper with her virginity. And if he spoke the truth, she was not likely to ever see the sultan again. It was entirely possible that Prince Murad would one day be her true husband.

The night darkened. Finishing her meal, Theadora washed her hands in a silver basin filled with rose water. Her good humor had been restored by the sleep. She dismissed her slaves for the evening. Unlike the majority of women of her class, she was capable of dressing and undressing herself. She despised the awful ignorance and the idleness of most women of rank.

She slipped into a caftan of violet silk gauze with a row of little pearl buttons down the front. The color was meant to flatter her amethyst eyes, yet be dark enough that she would not require a cloak. Her feet were shod in matching kid slippers. Her dark hair hung freely down her back bound only by a silk ribbon.

She slipped silently into the orchard and found her way to the tree they had sheltered under the previous night. He was not there. But before she could decide whether to return to her house or wait, the heavily laden branches parted with a rustle, and he was with her.

"Adora!" He slid an arm about her tiny waist and kissed her, and she returned his kiss for the first time. Her soft lips parted willingly, her tongue darting like a little flame about his mouth. To her delighted amazement he shuddered, and she was filled with a triumphant awe that she, an inexperienced virgin, could rouse this sensual, experienced man! For the briefest moment it was she who held the upper hand.

But then, cradling her with one arm, his other hand parted the topmost buttons of her caftan and his warm hand slid in to caress a breast. She gasped, catching at his hand.

He laughed low. "Lesson two, my dove," and pushed her hand away. She was trembling with a mixture that was half fright, half pleasure, though at first she could not identify the second sensation. His hand was gentle, tenderly stroking the soft flesh. "Please, oh, please!" she whispered, pleading. "Please, stop it!" Instead he rubbed the sensitive nipple with his thumb, and Adora almost fainted with the pleasure that swept over her.

When his mouth covered hers once again, she thought she would surely die with the sweetness of it. He was looking down at her now, his jet black eyes tender. "Always remember, my little virgin, that I am the master."

"Why?" she managed, though her voice was ragged. "It is the woman to whom God gave the privilege of bearing new life. Why then, are we subservient to men?"

He was startled. She was not the soft, complacent female he had first thought her to be, but that most rare and intriguing of creatures—a woman with a mind. Murad was not sure he approved. But, he thought, at least she will not bore me. And what sons she might bear me!

"Did not Allah create woman second—and from a man's rib?" he said quickly. "First came man. He must therefore have meant for man to be the superior, the master of woman, else he would have, created woman first."

"That does not necessarily follow, my lord," she replied, unimpressed.

"Would you be my superior, Adora, and instruct me," he asked, amused.

"Do not dare to laugh at me," she stormed.

"I am not laughing at you, my dove, but neither do I wish to debate the logic of the superiority of men over women. I wish to make love to you." And he felt her tremble against him as, again, he began to caress her soft breasts.

The gentle hand undid the remaining buttons on her caftan, rendering her naked. The hand moved lower to touch her little mound of belly. Her skin was like the finest Bursa silk, cool and smooth, yet the muscles were tense beneath his skilled fingers. This further confirmation of her innocence pleased his vanity.

He moved lower yet, one long, slim finger poised to touch her more intimately. And then, for a moment, their eyes met, and he saw her open terror. He stopped, and his hand gently touched her cheek. "Do not be afraid of me."

"I do not mean to be afraid," she said in a shaking voice. "It is wrong, I know, but I want you to touch me. Yet, when you do l am afraid."

"Tell me," he asked gently.

"I feel I am losing control of myself. I do not want you to cease, though I know you must" Swallowing hard she said, "I want to know *everything* about being a woman, even the final act of love. I am married, but I am not your wife, and what we do is wrong!"

"No," he said fiercely "We do no wrong! You will never go to my father! You are nothing to him but a political necessity."

"But when I am widowed I may not come to you either. If I belong to anyone I belong to the empire of Byzantium. Once your father is gone, my next marriage will be arranged for me, as this one was."

"You belong to me," he said huskily, "now and always."

She knew that she was lost, whatever happened. She loved him. "Yes," she whispered, amazed at her own words. "Yes! I do belong to you, Murad!"

And as his mouth savagely moved against hers, she felt a wild joy flood her. She was no longer afraid. Hands passionately caressed her, and her young body rose eagerly to meet his touch. Only once did she cry out—when his fingers found their way to the sweet core of her. But he stilled her protests with his mouth. He felt her wildly beating pulse beneath his lips. "No, dove," he murmured hungrily, "let my fingers have their way. It will be sweetness, my love, only sweetness, I promise you."

And he could feel her slowly relaxing in his arms. Smiling he teased the sensitive flesh while the girl beneath him moaned softly, her lashes dark smudges against her white skin, her slim hips writhing. At last, satisfied that she was ready, he gently thrust a finger into her.

Adora gasped, but before she could protest she was lost to the sweet wave of delight that possessed her completely. She arched to meet his hand, floating weightless until the tightness building within her shattered like a mirror into a rainbow of flashing lights.

Her amethyst eyes finally opened, and she asked,

her voice soft with the wonder of it, "How can such sweetness be, my lord?"

He smiled down at her. "It is but a taste of delight, my dove. Just a taste of things to come."

Chapter 3

In Constantinople, the night was as dark as Emperor John Cantacuzene's mood. His beloved wife, Zoe, was dead in a last futile attempt to give him another son. The awful irony was that she had given her last bit of strength to push twin sons from her exhausted and weakened body. Misshapen scraps of deformed humanity, they were joined at the chest and shared, so the physician claimed, a single heart. These monstrosities had been, praise God, born dead. Their mother, curse God, had followed them.

If this tragedy were not terrible enough, his daughter, Helena, wife to the co-emperor John Paleaologi, was plotting with her husband to overthrow him, to take complete control of the empire. While her mother had lived Helena had been recognized only as wife to the young Paleaologi. Her mother had been recognized as the empress. Now Helena wished to be recognized as empress.

"And if I remarry?" asked her father.

"Why on earth would you remarry?" demanded his daughter.

"To give the empire more sons."

"My son, Andronicus, is the heir. Next comes the child I now carry."

"There is no decree to that effect, my daughter."

"Really father!"

Every day Helena sounded more and more like her mother-in-law, the wretched Anna of Savoy.

"My husband," continued Helena, "is the rightful emperor of Byzantium, and therefore our son is the true heir. Surely you must realize that by now. God has spoken quite plainly. Your eldest son is dead, and my brother, Matthew, has chosen to follow the monastic life. In the last six years mother miscarried five times of six sons. Now God has taken her from you—in obvious disapproval. What more do you want? Must the words of God's will be engraved in clouds of fire over the city for you to accept it?

"The seer, Belasarius, has predicted that from my loins and my seed would spring a new empire out of Constantinople. How can this be if I do not have sons to carry on my line?"

"Perhaps through me, father," said Helena smugly.

"Or your sister, Theadora," he snapped back.

Helena glared and, without another word, left the room. John Cantacuzene paced restlessly. He would have more sons, but before he could take another noble wife he must make his position more secure. John Paleaologi must be disposed of, along with his snotnosed offspring. Remarried elsewhere, Helena would forget. Perhaps he would offer her blond beauty to Sultan Orkhan's heir, Prince Suleiman.

This thought reminded him of his youngest daughter, Thea. How old was she now? Thirteen? He thought so. Certainly old enough to be bedded, and to bear a child. He was going to need fresh military aid from the sultan—aid that was more likely to be given if Orkhan were enamored of his young wife. Especially a young wife who proclaimed her elderly husband's, virility with a belly full of new life.

The girl was still within her convent, and the latest miniature he had of her showed a young creature beautiful enough to rouse a stone statue. Her only failing was that she had a mind. Mother Marie Josepha was forever writing him of the girl's intellectual accomplishments. A pity she had not been a son. Well, be would write and instruct her to behave meekly, modestly, and quietly with her husband.

He would also write to Orkhan tonight, reminding him that the marriage contract called for the consummation of the union when the girl was mature. She certainly was mature now. It meant, of course, that he would have to come up with the final third of Theadora's dowry, and relinquish the fortress of Tzympe—but no matter. Opening the door to his private suite he summoned the monk who was his secretary.

Several weeks later, in Bursa, Sultan Orkhan chuckled over the recently received correspondence from his fellow ruler and father-in-law. He was well aware of the reason behind the Byzantine's sudden desire for his marriage to Theadora Cantacuzene to be consummated. John Cantacuzene was expecting another fight for his shaky throne and needed the Ottoman's support. He offered his daughter's virginity plus the rest of the gold from her dowry. Most important, he would finally turn over Tyzmpe to the Turks.

Orkhan the Ottoman had grown sexually insatiable in his old age. Each night he was presented with a new and well-trained virgin. His appetite varied and it was rumored that he even occasionally amused himself with young boys. His young wife, Theadora, was a totally innocent girl. It would take months to train her so that she would be able to please her lord.

But there was no time. Her father wanted her with child as proof of the consummation, and Orkhan wanted Tyzmpe and the remainder of her dowry gold. When great rulers plan together, matters can be arranged.

The maiden's moon cycle would be determined, and he would mate with her during her most fertile four days. He hoped her link with the moon would then be broken. If not, the process would be repeated again, and again—until the girl proved fruitful.

He was not the least interested in Theadora. A political pawn, she had been forgotten and was now annoyingly thrust forward.

He had experienced the emotion called love in his youth, with Nilufer, his second wife and the mother of his two favorite sons. Now that was all behind him. All that was left was the physical pleasures given him by the skilled, young slave girls and boys of his harem.

He resented having to breed the maiden as a bull breeds a cow, and this resentment would probably communicate itself to Theadora. Perhaps the girl herself had encouraged her father to suggest this, in an effort to better her position. Well, he would see that she was treated with the respect due her rank. He would impregnate her as quickly as possible, and then he would have nothing further to do with her.

And at the very moment Theadora Cantacuzene lay within the strong arms of Prince Murad. Their eyes adored one another. "I love you!" she said in a tremulous voice. "I love you!"

"And I love you, my dove! Allah! How I love you!"

"How long, my lord? How long must we wait before we dare to be wed when *he* is gone? I want to walk in the sunlight beneath the olive trees with you. I want the world to know that I am yours!"

"I love my father," he said slowly. "I would wish him no less a portion than is his. In his old age he is content and seeks only more gold and the sensual pleasures offered him. He will no longer lead our armies."

"Would you expand your kingdom?" she asked.

"Yes! I would cross the Bosphorus, and rule from the city of Constantinople itself. Would you like to return home, my dove, as queen of the city of your birth?"

"Yes!" She said it so fiercely that he laughed.

"You do not mind that I would displace your sister and her husband? What a little savage you are, Theadora Cantacuzene."

"Before I became the sultan's wife, my sister loved to torture me with the fact that she would rule over Constantinople some day, while I would be sent into exile in the sultan's harem. How I would love to return to the city as the wife of its conqueror!"

"Even a Moslem conqueror?"

"Yes, my lord. Even a Moslem conqueror. We both

worship the same God, do we not? I am no fool, Murad, though I be a woman. Within the bounds of this kingdom a traveler may go safely at any hour of the day or night. Non-Moslems are permitted the freedom to worship as they choose. The law is administered fairly to all who ask judgement of the kadi, be they rich or poor. I am ashamed to say that I cannot claim these virtues for the empire and its rulers. I far prefer to live under Ottoman rule, as do many non-Moslems."

"What a marvelous creature," he said admiringly. "Though I find it strange to talk so openly with a woman, I find your logic without flaw."

"I am my father's daughter," she said proudly. "He has a great mind and is a fine scholar. He always said I should have been a son."

The prince smiled. "He is wrong, dove. There is no more exquisite female alive than you," and he drew her back into his arms, sighing deeply and burying his face in the cool, scented mass of her hair. "Ah, dove, how I love you!"

Above them, the stars traveled across the sky towards the morning. It was almost dawn when Theadora returned to her house and fell asleep. Too soon, Iris awoke her.

"Highness, forgive me, but the white chief eunuch is here from the palace to see you."

Theadora was instantly awake. Never, since she had arrived in Bursa as a child and been installed in this house, had anyone important come from the palace to see her. "Tell him I shall be with him presently, Iris."

The woman bowed out of her mistress's presence

and delivered the message to the chief eunuch. She was about to return when his voice stopped her.

"What is your name, woman?"

"Iris, master." Her head was bowed.

"Do you deal well with your mistress?"

"Yes, master."

"Does she confide in you?"

"Confide what, master?" Iris pretended stupidity.

"Anything. Little secrets? Girlish dreams and hopes?"

Iris raised her eyes and looked directly at the eunuch. "Master," she said quietly, "my little mistress has been cloistered here since her childhood. The only one she ever sees is the elderly priest who is her spiritual advisor. She leaves the convent but rarely. What possible secrets could she have? She confides in no one since she has no one. The palace slaves sent to serve the princess are rotated on a three-month basis, which hardly gives her time to make friends. Most serve her only once, but I have been asked to come back several times."

"Why?" He observed her from beneath his hooded eyelids.

"Because I would advance myself, master. I was not always a slave."

"I will appoint you chief waiting-woman to Princess Theadora. In return, you will keep me fully informed about her life. She will go to the sultan soon. Now tell me, when was her last show of blood?"

The woman thought, then said, "Almost two weeks ago, master."

"Exactly how many days from the first showing of

blood, Iris?"

"Twelve, master."

The eunuch frowned. "She must go today else we will be forced to wait another month," said the chief white eunuch almost to himself. "Pack nothing for your mistress. All will be provided."

"She is scholarly, master. She will want her books. She is not idle, like other women."

The eunuch looked surprised. But he was not an unkind man. "Very well, Iris, I will see that the princess's books are sent to the palace. But not today. We barely have time to do what must be done." He reached into his voluminous robes and, drawing out two packets, thrust them at her. "Give your mistress the powders in the blue packet before you leave here. She is to have the other one at sunset."

"Please, master," said Iris boldly, "what are they? I would not harm her."

"The powders are drugs to relax her and prepare her virgin body for her husband's attentions this night. But you are presumptuous, Iris! Do not ask questions of me or I will withdraw your appointment."

The door to the antechamber opened and Theadora entered. The eunuch quickly scrutinized her with a practiced eye. He was pleased. Her stature was regal. She was slimmer than his master liked, but the high, full, cone-shaped breasts more than made up for that. She had clear, fair skin and amethyst-colored eyes . . . or were they violet? The shining dark hair hung to her hips. She even had well-formed white teeth. These were all signs of excellent physical and mental health.

The eunuch bowed politely. "I am Ali Yahya, Your

Royal Highness. You are the most blessed of women my princess. Your lord husband—Sultan Orkhan, son of the sultan of the Ghazis; Ghazi, son of Ghazi; Marquis of the Hero of the World—has chosen this night to be your night of nights. Your marriage, celebrated when you were but a child, will be consummated this night. May Allah bless you, and may you be fruitful with my master's seed."

Theadora looked at him, blankly, for a moment Then she turned deathly pale and crumpled to the floor. The eunuch looked down on her still form. She was *very* lovely. The sultan would be quite pleased. "Virgin vapors," he pronounced to Iris who was kneeling by the girl, patting her wrists. "I will send a litter for you in one hour. Be ready."

When Theadora came to herself she found her shoulders supported by Iris's strong arm. A cup of wine was being forced between her lips. "Drink, my princess, and do not be afraid. Ali Yahya has appointed me your chief waiting woman. I will not leave you, and no matter what that fat slug may think, I will be loyal to you alone! Drink, my baby. It will help."

Theadora gulped at the wine, her mind whirling. What had suddenly possessed the sultan? Could he have found out about Prince Murad? No! It was not possible. Why then?

"When are we to go to the palace?" she asked.

"The litter comes in less than an hour."

Oh, sweet Jesu! There was no time to send for Murad and, once at the palace, she dare not communicate with him. Oh, God! This was to be her punishment. If she had not committed adultery in fact, she

58

had certainly committed it in her heart and now God was punishing her. To be wife to an old man while loving his son! They would live within the same palace, possibly even see each other, and never be able to speak! Theadora began to weep violently.

Not understanding the true nature of her mistress's grief, Iris tried to comfort her. "Do not weep, my baby. It was bound to come, and all women must accept their fate. I would, of course, wish that you had a younger husband, but they do say the sultan is still very potent—and a good lover." Seeing that Theadora's eyes were shut in her agony, Iris slipped the contents of the first packet into the wine. Then she watched as the girl drained it, unaware that it was drugged.

There was no time left. The nuns were in the courtyard, crowding about her to bid her Godspeed, farewell. "If you can help the Christian captives and slaves, Highness," said Mother Marie Josepha, "please do. Their lot is so bad, and it is your duty. We stand ready here to aid you in all your charitable endeavors."

Theadora nodded dumbly and allowed them to help her into the large litter. Iris climbed in after her, drawing the curtains shut, and they were away. The slavewoman looked at the pale girl opposite her. The princess said nothing, made no sound at all, yet the tears continued to pour down her cheeks. Iris was worried.

She had been a slave for only five years, but her knowledge of the world was greater than most. These were not the tears of a frightened bride. They were the tears of a broken hearted woman. But what had *she* to be broken hearted about? Iris knew that Theadora did not wish to become a nun, so that was not it. There was only one other possibility, and it was so far-fetched as to be absurd. Still . . . looking back over the princess's behavior during these last two months, Iris began to understand many things.

Iris took a deep breath. What she was about to do was very dangerous. She had no proof and, cornered, the princess could instantly order her death. Iris leaned forward and said, very quietly, "If we are to talk, Highness, it must be now. Once we are in the palace we will be constantly spied upon, not only by the chief eunuch's underlings, but by those in the pay of the sultan's other two wives—and God only knows how many of his favorites. They will all seek to discredit you in an effort to advance themselves. If you would unburden yourself and tell me what troubles you, it *must* be now. Please, Highness. I wish to remain your friend, and it is obvious to me that you weep for a man."

The violet eyes that raised themselves to hers were so filled with raw pain that Iris nearly wept herself. "I will tell you," said Theadora, "for I must tell some one, or I will go mad. If you betray me you would be doing me a kindness for I would as soon be dead now." And slowly the tender little story came out, haltingly, until there was nothing left to say.

Iris sighed. It would not be easy, but having allowed her mistress to shift some of the burden to her own shoulders, she could now concentrate on preparing the girl for what was to come.

"I will try to speak with the prince myself," she promised Theadora, and was rewarded by a smile that lit the girl's whole being. "But, my lady, you must accept the fact that you are the sultan's wife. Tonight he will consummate that marriage, and you must accept that as fact also."

"I thought he had forgotten me, Iris. Never since he brought me to St. Catherine's has he even acknowledged my existence. Why now?"

"I do not know, my princess, but I think the answers we seek are to be found at the sultan's palace. A word of warning, however, my princess. You are so innocent, and do not know the wicked ways of people. At the palace you must trust *no one* but me. When we wish to speak privately we must do so out of doors only. There are listeners everywhere."

"You have been in the palace, Iris. What is it like? Will I have privacy, or do all the women live together?"

"One section of the palace is set aside for the women, but the wives and the favorites have their own apartments and rooms within this section. The chief eunuch appointed me your waiting woman, but you will be assigned other slaves and eunuchs. Your rank demands it."

"Can we trust them, Iris?"

"No! They will all be spies for someone or other. But we will tolerate them for now, until we can choose our own people. Do not fear, my princess, I will protect you."

The litter stopped, the curtains were drawn back, and Ali Yahya was handing Theadora out into a tiled courtyard. "Please to follow me, Your Highness," he said. They followed him through a maze of corridors until he stopped before a single carved door and, opening it, led them into a small room. "Your bedroom is through there, princess."

Iris looked unbelievingly about her. These two small rooms for her mistress? She said a quick silent prayer that she would live to see the next day, and rounded on the chief eunuch. "Is my mistress some slavegirl that you insult her in this fashion? These rooms are not fit for a dog let alone an emperor's daughter! Two tiny rooms with two barred windows overlooking an inner courtyard? Where is her garden? Where are her servants?"

"Your mistress has not yet found favor with my master."

"My mistress does not have to find favor with your master," answered Iris boldly. "She is the emperor's daughter! Why, her servants at St. Catherine's were better housed than this! How the sultan will enjoy his wedding night when his bride complains of her apartments, I do not know."

Ali Yahya looked uncomfortable. He did not believe that there was any chance of this inexperienced girl pleasing his very experienced, jaded master. Still, it could happen. And if it did . . .

"You fill the position I assigned to you most admirable, Iris," he said sourly. "This is but a place for your mistress to rest. It was imperative that we bring her to the palace today, but her apartments could not be made ready in time. In another hour they will be fit to receive the princess. I will send a girl with something to eat, and by then all will be perfect," he concluded, and gathering the shreds of his dignity about him, he departed quickly.

"Humph," sniffed Iris. "The only snake wriggled out of that one fast enough."

"It does not matter," said Theadora softly.

"Yes it does! Whatever happens, my child, you must never forget that you are Theadora Cantacuzene, Emperor John's daughter. Hold your head up in this place, my lady, else you will be overcome by your inferiors."

Within the hour they were brought to a spacious suite containing six large, airy rooms and its own beautiful walled garden with several tiled fountains and a view of the mountains. "My lady is well pleased," said Iris loftily, noting the dozen slavegirls and two black eunuchs.

Ali Yahya nodded. "Take your lady to the mistress of baths immediately. It will take the rest of the afternoon to prepare her for tonight."

Usually the harem baths were noisy and full of chattering women. This afternoon, however, the women of the sultan's house were being entertained by an elderly Egyptian magician. The bath mistress greeted Theadora briskly and before the startled princess knew what was happening she found herself completely stripped and her nude body subjected to a most thorough inspection. Her most intimate parts were squeezed, pulled apart, prodded, even smelled for signs of disease. Theadora blushed to the roots of her hair and felt a helpless sense of outraged shame.

Finally satisfied, the bath mistress stepped back. "Your body is flawless and healthy, Highness. You are as fresh as a new rose. I am relieved, for the sultan dislikes blemish of any kind. We can proceed now."

Theadora had the urge to laugh. They were all so seriously concerned about her pleasing the sultan, yet she herself didn't care. All she wanted was to be back at St. Catherine's convent, preparing to meet Murad in the orchard. *Murad! Murad!* She silently intoned his name over and over as the women spread a pink paste smelling of almonds over the haired areas of her body.

Unknown to Theadora, the men's baths were on the other side of the harem baths. And while she stood, quietly submitting, Orkhan's favorite sons, Suleiman and Murad, sat companionably talking within the hot room.

"What is there to the rumor that John Cantacuzene seeks our aid against his son-in-law?" asked Murad.

"It's true," Suleiman assured him. "That's why the maidenhead of the Princess Theadora will be breached tonight."

Murad felt a wave of dizziness assail him. Unknowing, his brother continued. "The old man might have left the girl in her convent, but her father insisted that *all* the terms of the marriage contract be fulfilled. Our father couldn't resist the final third of the little Byzantine's dowry. That includes Tyzmpe, and I am going to be sent to command the fort. Want to come along?"

"Is the princess here yet?" Murad hoped he sounded casual.

"Yes. She's a pretty piece, though a bit too pale to suit my taste. I caught a glimpse of her when she arrived this afternoon. Probably scared, poor little girl. Well, by morning she'll be well-tamed. Our father may be old, but he can still leave a woman begging for more. May we be as potent as long, eh brother?"

"Yes, yes," said Murad absently, his whole heart going out to Theadora, his dove, his precious little love.

Suleiman chattered on. "The lady Anastatia says that the little princess probably put her father up to improving her position. She says all the Cantacuzenes are ambitious."

"I've had enough steam," said Murad, rising. Walking out into the tepidarium, he grabbed a basin and vomited into it. "Damned fish must have been tainted," he muttered, shoving the basin into a slave's hands. After rinsing his mouth with mint water, he donned his clothes and found his way to his mother's apartments.

To his immense surprise Anastatia was with Nilufer. "Is it true?" he demanded brusquely. "Is the old satyr taking the Byzantine girl to his bed tonight?"

"Yes," said Nilufer. She was a handsome woman in her mid-forties. Her wheat-colored hair still shone with golden lights, and her amber eyes were bright and wise. "Anastatia and I were just discussing this very unusual turn of events and how to meet them."

"The girl is ambitious," said Ibrahim's mother.

"She is just like all the Cantacuzenes—greedy and venal. I should know. Is not the emperor my cousin? The girl obviously became bored in her convent and complained to her father. But after Orkhan's had at her, she may wish she was back there." Anastatia laughed cruelly.

Murad stared hard at this woman who had always been their enemy. She was ten years his mother's senior, petite with steel grey hair, and the coldest blue eyes he'd ever seen. "What makes you two allies after all these years?"

"Your father's new wife," said Anastatia honestly.

"He married her years ago, and it didn't bother you then. Nor did you and my mother become bosom friends over the matter."

"But tonight he takes her to his bed. If she proves fertile and bears him a son—" She looked levelly at him.

"He would scarcely name an infant his heir over Suleiman or me, both grown men. Not at his age," snapped Murad. "I hope, mother, that you will have no part in a campaign of unkindness against this poor child. She will need friends here." He angrily left the room.

Allah! She was here! Within this very palace, and he could do nothing. Whatever his mother and Anastatia said about Theadora's ambition, he knew it was untrue. He knew her. They did not. How frightened she must be, poor child, and shortly she would be delivered up to that oversexed old man. He felt the nausea gripping his guts again. He had to get away from the palace. He could not remain here this night, knowing that her innocence was being violated on the altar of greed.

Suddenly, a heavily-veiled older woman glided out from the shadows. "The princess wants you to know that though this situation is not of her making, she will do her duty as she has been taught," said the woman. And then she was gone.

He almost cried aloud at the swiftly retreating fig-ure. Then Prince Murad made determinedly for the stables and called for his horse. He mounted, rode through the palace gates and headed the animal into the autumn mountains.

Chapter 4

THEADORA HAD NEVER BEEN SO CLEAN IN HER ENTIRE life. She had thought they would scrub her skin away. Except for her eyebrows, lashes, and long tresses, she was completely denuded of hair. Her fingernails and toenails had been pared to the quick. Allah forbid she offend her lord and master by scratching—even inadvertently—his royal person! Her long, straight, mahogany-colored hair shone with its lovely gold lights. Her skin glowed with good health. The soles of her feet and the palms of her hands were tinted pink with henna.

But the amethyst eyes were worried, frightened. She did not understand all this haste, and when she tried to question Ali Yahya, he looked troubled, then brushed her question aside. "Princess, you have been married several years. Now that you have reached physical maturity the sultan wishes you to grace his bed. There is nothing odd in that."

She was, he could tell, not satisfied by the answer. He felt more uncomfortable than ever, for he suddenly realized that she was innocent of deceit. She simply did not wish to bed with the sultan. He was sure that, had her father not insisted on this, the girl would have remained quietly at St. Catherine's. The realization made what he must do even harder for Ali Yahya.

Precisely four hours after sunset Ali Yahya, accompanied by the lady Anastatia and the lady Nilufer, arrived at Theadora's apartments to escort her to her destiny. The two older women, each dressed magnificently in silk garments heavy with gold embroidery and jeweled work, were a somewhat startling contrast to the young girl in her plain white silk robe.

Though tradition and good manners dictated that they speak politely to her, wishing her joy, neither said anything. Nilufer looked curiously at the girl. So, thought Iris, that is how it is to be! The mean old cats! The chief eunuch turned his head towards Iris and said quickly and softly, "Your mistress will be returned in an hour or two. Be ready! She will need you." My God! What were they going to do to the child?

The litter moved with stately measure through the silent halls of the harem, finally coming to rest before two enormous bronze doors. Ali Yahya helped the trembling Theadora from the litter and escorted her through the doors—which slammed behind them with frightening finality.

It was a most luxurious room. Marble floors were covered lavishly with thick wool carpets. The walls were hung with exquisite silk tapestries. In each of three corners of the room a tall, masterfully wrought gold censer burning with fragrant aloes. In the fourth corner was a large tiled stove burning applewood. Two silver and stained glass lamps hung from the dark beamed ceiling, casting soft light over a massive bed on a raised dais. The bed had rich, parti-colored silk hangings and carved posts. It was toward this bed that Theadora was led by Ali Yahya. From apparently nowhere, slavegirls appeared and removed her one garment.

"Please lie upon the bed, princess," said Ali Yahya. She obeyed. To her shock he leaned over her and bound one of her arms to the bedpost with a soft silken cord. Her other arm was tied by a slavegirl and her long legs were pulled apart and secured in the same manner.

A wave of panic gripped her and she cried out. The eunuch clapped his hand over her mouth. "Be silent, Highness! No one will hurt you. If I remove my hand, do you promise not to scream?" She nodded and he lifted his hand from her face.

"Why am I being bound?" she asked in a shaking voice.

"Because the sultan has ordered it, my lady. When you were wed the marriage contract called for the consummation of the marriage when you reached maturity. The sultan, quite frankly, would have left you at your convent. But your father insists that the marriage contract be fulfilled."

"My *father*?" she cried unbelievingly. "My father insisted? Oh, God! How could he?"

"He needs the sultan's aid again, Highness. Your sister and her husband are proving troublesome. The remaining third of your dowry, which includes a gold payment and the strategic fortress of Tzympe—which my master desires greatly—will remain outstanding until you are with child."

For a moment she was silent. Then she exclaimed bitterly, almost to herself, "For this I so carefully preserved my maidenhead! To be forcibly delivered up to an old man for a troop of soldiers, a handful of gold, and a fort!" She sighed, then turned her eyes to the eunuch again. "Why has my lord ordered me bound to the bed?"

"Because you are inexperienced in the ways of love. Lacking knowledge, you are apt to struggle and displease the sultan. There is a need for haste, and no time to teach you the things you must know. You were brought to the palace today because this is the first fertile day in your moon cycle. For the next four nights you will bed with the sultan. It is hoped that you will be proved with child within the next month. If not, you will be bred again until my master's labor bears fruit."

She was stunned by this terrible revelation. Perhaps if she had not known the sweetness of lovemaking with Prince Murad it would not hurt so much. How the sultan must hate her! And she silently cursed the father who had sacrificed her in this cruel manner.

And in that one moment of blinding understanding, Theadora Cantacuzene grew up.

Ali Yahya spoke again. He was obviously in sympathy with her. "You must be prepared for your master, my princess. Do not be afraid of what will transpire." And at her puzzled look he went on. "Your body is not yet ready to receive a man."

He clapped his hands and two pretty women appeared, each carrying a white ostrich plume. They settled themselves quietly on stools by either side of the bed and, at a nod from the chief eunuch, began to touch her breasts with the soft plumes.

Theadora regarded them with a frankness that soon turned to amazement as the gentle caresses began to rouse her body. Her young breasts began to swell and harden, the nipples grew pointed and tingling. She gasped softly, surprised at herself. The eunuch watched her for several minutes from beneath hooded lids, noting her every movement.

He clapped his hands once more and two young girls, children really, approached with a woman. Without a word the two girls positioned themselves on each side of her, bent over, and gently pulled her nether lips apart. The woman leaned forward and, drawing a long pointed feather from her sleeve, delicately applied it to the most sensitive spot. Theodora stiffened with shock at this frightening invasion but, when she opened her mouth to protest, it was quickly stuffed with a silk handkerchief.

The agony was exquisite, but Theadora was outraged. She was being treated like a mare led to stud.

She silently screamed as wave after wave of delicious feeling, similar to that which Murad's supple fingers had worked on her, washed over her. Christos! Why would her hips not lie still!

There was another movement in the shadows, and a tall man in a brocade robe appeared by the bedside. Her eyes were glazed with fear and reluctant sexual stimulation, but she recognized Sultan Orkhan. The hair she had remembered as dark was now mostly gray, but the eyes—dear lord—were *black like Murad's*. The sultan looked down on her dispassionately and remarked to Ali Yahya, "She is really quite lovely. What a pity there is no time to train her properly." He spoke as if she were not even there. "Is she still intact, Ali Yahya?"

"I did not think to check, Most High. She has, after all, been safe within her convent."

"Be sure! Girls are known to play lewd games."

The eunuch nodded curtly to the woman with the feather who ceased her ministrations. Bending, Ali Yahya gently inserted a finger into the helpless girl. She strained wildly against her bonds. Withdrawing from her, the eunuch straightened and said to his master, "She is intact, my lord sultan."

"I don't want to bother with the business of breaching her maidenhead. Mara will be waiting for me when this business is over with. See to it that she is deflowered. I will be ready shortly for the mounting."

Theadora could not believe her ears. If Orkhan did not deflower her, how was it to be done? But she had little time to wonder. The chief eunuch gave swift orders and, moments later, he bent over her holding a long, thick, smooth, highly polished piece of wood shaped like a phallus. "The pain will be but momentary, Your Highness," he said apologetically and then, in a lower voice which only she could hear, "Forgive me, princess."

She felt the cool, smooth wood against her shrinking flesh and silently wailed her shame. A swift thrust! A sharp and burning pain spread through her loins before gradually dying. Warm wetness trickled down the insides of her thighs. She wanted to faint, to escape all this, but she remained conscious. And now her attention was drawn away from herself to the sultan.

He had watched without emotion as she was deflowered. Now he spread his arms wide and instantly the slaves removed his loose brocade gown. She was surprised to see that his body was as firm as a young man's, if somewhat thinner.

Theadora watched, mesmerized, as a naked girl with long, golden hair stepped forward, bowed to her master, and knelt before him, her beautiful hair tumbling about her as her head touched her master's foot in the ago-old gesture of subjugation. Still on her knees, the girl raised her body and rubbed her cheek against the sultan's groin. Now she was taking his limp organ and caressing it with delicate, slender fingers, kissing it with quick, teasing little kisses. Theadora felt a wave of desire as the girl gently took the swelling organ into her rosebud mouth. Horrified at herself, Theadora turned her head away to meet the amused gaze of one of the girls who was stroking her hard, hurting breasts. Shamed color flooded her face, and she closed her eyes. The sensations were intensified now, but she made herself keep her lashes lowered.

The quick patter of running feet forced her eyes open. She was alone with the sultan. He moved across the room toward her, his manroot now enormous, its angry, red head glistening with moisture. He jammed a bolster beneath her hips to raise her, to make her body more easily available to him.

She was mounted like a mare and she felt his penetration—hard and brutal—as he thrust into her. He rode her smoothly, his hands crushing her breasts, pinching at the nipples. Cruelly, he forced her head forward so he might look into her face. Afraid to close her eyes now, she met his impersonal gaze steadily, silently screaming Murad's name over and over again. Suddenly the man above her shuddered and collapsed on top of her. They lay quietly for a few minutes, then he climbed off of her. Loosening the bonds on her spread legs, he shut them and pushed them up. Then he said the only words he had spoken to her during the entire nightmare. "Keep your legs up and closed, Theodora, lest you lose my seed." Turning, he disappeared back into the darkness and she heard the door close.

She was alone. Her whole body began to shake, and the pent-up tears poured down her cheeks. A few minutes later Ali Yahya emerged from the shadows and removed the silk from her mouth. Quietly he unbound her arms and gently rubbed her wrists. He brought forth a handkerchief from his robe and silently wiped her tears away. Then, helping her up, he wrapped her silk robe about her icy body and led her back into the corridor and to the litter. Soon Iris's loving arms were about her and the slavewoman led her to her bed.

Ali Yahya waited in the antechamber of Theodora's apartment, warming himself by the tile stove. Finally Iris emerged and stood before him questioningly. In his high soft voice he told her all of it. "It is up to you to see that the princess does not become melancholy," he finished.

Iris laughed harshly. "And how am I to do that,

master? The girl is young and has been gently reared. A wedding night is frightening to any young virgin, but," she, lowered her voice, "the sultan has brutalized my little mistress. And what is worse, she must endure the same treatment for the next three nights! Why? What has this child done that he would hurt her so?"

"It is not your place to question, woman."

"If I am to keep the girl alive I must know *all*, Ali Yahya."

"The sultan was angry at the princess. He thought she had induced her father to force compliance of the marriage contract and, thus, better her position. I believed that possible until I met the princess. There is no guile in her. And the two wives, Anastatia and Nilufer, have encouraged the sultan's anger toward the princess. They are fearful of a third wife."

"My princess is like a delicate flower, eunuch. You must convince the sultan to treat her gently these next few nights. If she goes mad and dies, to what purpose is this cruelty? Do you think the emperor will award your lord the remainder of my lady's dowry when he learns what has happened to his favorite daughter? The Byzantine may have used the girl to his political advantage, but she is still his child, and he does love her."

Ali Yahya nodded. "You are right, woman. I will see that the sultan's heart is softened toward the princess. But you *must* see that the girl lives." Without another word he turned on his heel and left.

Iris waited until the doors had closed behind him. Then she ran across the room into Theadora's bedchamber. The girl lay on her back, barely breathing. She made no sound, but her beautiful face was wet with tears. Iris drew a stool up to the bedside and sat down. "Tell me what you are thinking," she asked.

"I think that the humblest beast in the field is more fortunate than I," came the soft reply.

"Do you wish to die, my princess?"

"*Die?*" The girl sat up. "*Die?*" She laughed bitterly. "No, Iris. I do not want to die. I would live to avenge this insult! How *dare* the sultan take me as he would some savage barbarian? I am Theodora Cantacuzene, a princess of Byzantium!" Her voice was bordering on hysteria.

"Hush, my princess. Remember?" And Iris pointed to her ears.

Theodora instantly grew silent. The slavewoman rose and poured out a goblet of rich red Cyprus wine. She added a pinch of herbs to it and handed it to her mistress. "I have put a sleeping draught in the wine, my princess. You must get a good night's rest if you are to face tomorrow with wisdom and courage."

The girl drained the goblet. "See that I am awakened by mid-day, Iris," she said, and lay back down to sleep. The slave crept from the room. But Theodora's amethyst eyes remained open and focused on the ceiling. She was calmer now, the worst of the shock having worn off. But she would never forget the insult.

Her innocent dalliance with Prince Murad had led her to believe that what happened between a man and a woman was always sweet. Her husband had robbed her of a perfect wedding night, but never again would she allow herself to be treated as she had been treated tonight. If her father—curse him!—wanted her to bear Orkhan a son, then she would do so. But she would make her husband regret this night.

He would desire her above all women, and when she had obtained his desire . . . she would refuse him.

When her jaded husband finally groveled at her feet for her favors—and he would—she would dole them out sparingly or refuse them, as her whim dictated.

Theadora now began to relax and allowed the sleeping potion to take hold of her. When Iris looked in later, the princess was asleep.

Chapter 5

ALI YAHYA WAS IN SERIOUS DANGER OF LOSING HIS dignity. He gaped at the child before him, and she repeated in her piping voice,

"My mistress, Princess Theadora, commands your immediate presence, sir. You are to come with me." Tugging on the fat hand, the little girl led the amazed chief eunuch down the hall to Theadora's apartments.

When Ali Yahya had seen Theadora last he had not been sure she would survive the night. But the ravaged creature of the night before bore no resemblance whatever to the young woman he now faced. And for the first time in his life, Ali Yahya understood the true meaning of the word "royal."

Theadora had caused a small throne to be set upon a raised dais, and she received Ali Yahya there. Her long dark hair had been plaited into two braids, and looped on either side of her head. Her clothing was all silk, in shades of Persian blues and sea green. She wore no jewelry, for she had none.

The amethyst eyes looked gravely at the eunuch. Abashed, he bowed low, and was rewarded by a faint smile. She raised her hand in a regal gesture of dismissal to her slaves.

Alone with Ali Yahya she said quietly, "Tell, my husband that if there should ever be a repeat of last night, I will inform my father, Emperor John. I am aware of my duties, and will produce a child as quickly as nature will allow. But the sultan must come to me alone in future, and accept my lack of experience as any Christian husband would do—with delight at that proof of my innocence.

"If he wanted me experienced in the arts of love, he should have had me tutored. I was available. I am not newly arrived in this land.

"I request of you teachers who can help me overcome my ignorance. For now, perhaps, the sultan will find it amusing to tutor me himself. It should be quite a novelty for him."

The chief eunuch swallowed his surprise. "I will do what I can to plead your case, Highness," he said gravely.

"I know you will, Ali Yahya. You alone of those I have met since entering here yesterday have remembered my position. I will certainly not forget your kindness. Thank you for coming."

He turned to go, but she spoke again. "I had almost forgotten. Please arrange for Iris and me to visit the slave markets of the city tomorrow."

"If you need more servants I shall be, glad to supply them, Highness."

"I need my own servants, Ali Yahya. Not spies. I will people my household with my own slaves, not those in the pay of the lady Anastatia or the lady Nilufer, or whoever is my husband's latest favorite. Or you, for that matter. Do I make myself clear, Ali Yahya?"

He nodded. "It will be as you wish, Highness," be said, and hurried off to seek his master.

He found the sultan in the company of one of his new favorites, a blond Circassian named Mihrimah. The girl was a credit to her harem schooling, a veritable model of good manners, total obedience, and advanced sexual training. Ali Yahya watched impassively as Mihrimah took a sweetmeat delicately between her lips and offered it to her eager master. The eunuch marveled that a man of the sultan's years could still be so quickly aroused and perform so well. Disregarding his servant's presence, Orkhan mounted the slavegirl, driving her to a sobbing surrender.

His hot lust sated, he looked to the eunuch. By a flick of an eyelid, Ali Yahya asked dismissal of the girl. Orkhan shoved Mihrimah with his foot. "Go!" She obeyed instantly, getting to her feet and running from the room. "Speak, Ali Yahya. What is it?"

The eunuch fell to the floor and, taking the sultan's foot, placed it on his bowed head. "I have erred, my lord. I have erred in judgement, and I beg that you forgive me."

Orkhan was intrigued. Ali Yahya had been his slave for some twenty-five years. He had held his office as chief of the white eunuchs for the last fifteen. His judgements had always been cool, impersonal, and correct. Never before had he asked forgiveness. "What is it, my old friend?" asked Orkhan kindly.

"It is the princess Theadora, sire. I have been wrong about the girl, and so have your wives. She is innocent of any intrigue to better herself. I knew it last night, but it was too late to stop—" He hesitated, allowing the sultan time to reconstruct the events of the previous evening. "This morning," continued the eunuch, "she begged my ear, and pleaded with me to ask your forgiveness for her ignorance in the arts of pleasing you. She has also asked that I find her tutors to teach her so she may remedy this lack."

"Has she?" Orkhan was interested. He would not have been surprised if the girl had tried to take her own life after last night. Then, he would not have cared. But now he was fascinated.

"Perhaps it would be a titillating novelty, sire, if it were you who acted as her first teacher. Who knows your desires better? She appears eager to learn, and she really is quite lovely, my lord."

The sultan's black eyes narrowed with remembrance and he chuckled. "So she is eager to learn, eh? Even after last night? And you think I should school the little wench?"

"It would be something different, my lord. I would not know, of course, but is it not dull, being continually catered to by the women of your house? As her tutor you could teach her what pleases you best. When she succeeds you will reward her. And if she is slow in her lessons, you will chastise her."

The sultan's eyes gleamed. He was known to occasionally enjoy whipping a slavegirl. "You are sure, Ali Yahya? You are sure she did not nag her father and force herself on me?"

"I am quite sure, sire. She would have sooner remained at St. Catherine's. This was her father's doing entirely."

Orkhan smiled slowly. "She will soon change her

mind, my old friend. I will teach her to crave my touch. Tell her she is forgiven her ignorance, Ali Yahya, and that tonight I will begin her lessons in love."

The eunuch bowed himself out, barely able to contain his mirth.

With the princess, however, he would have to be completely truthful. Yesterday he had thought of her as only another girl, like thousands of others. Today, however, seeing her rise so strongly from her despair, he had—with a sure instinct for his own survival—revised his opinion. Ali Yahya was not sure what Theadora Cantacuzene was, but he knew she would be a power to be reckoned with.

Theadora was again bathed, creamed, and perfumed. But this time Ali Yahya brought her silk gauze night garments and simple jewelry. The pantaloons and open bolero were rose-pink, which heightened the creamy fairness of her skin. The anklebands were done simply in gold-thread embroidered flowers. The bolero was edged along the sides and bottom in tiny crystal beads. The chief eunuch had brought her several very delicate little gold chains of different lengths to wear about her neck. He himself put upon her slender finger a rough-cut deep-blue Persian turquoise set in heavy red gold.

"*My* gift to you, Highness."

"Thank you, Ali Yahya. I shall treasure it." Then she looked at him questioningly.

"It will be all right, Highness, I promise you," he said as he helped her into the litter. He bent over her and fastened gold and crystal ornaments to each of her little earlobes.

She reached up and touched them, delighted. He smiled back at her. Though he sensed greatness in her, she was still a child. The earlobes sparkled prettily, fully visible as her dark hair was drawn back. It had been braided with pale pink ribbons and seed pearls. The sultan would be foolish to mistreat so delightful a morsel, thought the eunuch.

And that was most unlikely. Sultan Orkhan had thought most of the day of the novelty of teaching his young wife the amatory arts: he could barely wait for evening. He hoped she was passionate by nature. But even so, she was likely to resist him at first, her shyness overcoming her. Resistance! The thought excited him. He could not remember the last time a woman had resisted him.

The great double doors to his rooms were flung open, and he could see his new wife in the corridor beyond, being assisted from her litter. He watched with open approval as she moved gracefully toward him, her lovely head bowed modestly. She stopped—and knelt to prostrate herself before him in the gesture of humble submission,

"No!" he was amazed to hear himself say. "You are a princess born, my Theadora."

"But you, my lord husband, are my master," her low, melodious voice replied as she touched her forehead to his slippered foot. He raised her up and pulled her veil away from her face, tossing it to the floor. "Look at me," he commanded. And she raised her head to him.

The clear amethyst eyes did not waver under his dark glance. "Your manners are flawless, my young wife, but your beautiful eyes speak differently from your posture!"

For a moment her white teeth caught at her lower lip. She flushed becomingly, but her gaze did not falter. "I am," she replied, "as Your Majesty has said, a princess born."

The sultan laughed heartily. The girl had spirit. Surprisingly, he did not mind. She was a breath of cold, crisp air after an overheated, overscented room. "Leave us," he commanded the waiting Ali Yahya and the other slaves. When they had gone, he turned to her. "Are you afraid, my Theadora?"

She nodded. "A little, my lord. After last night."

He cut her short with a wave of his hand, saying fiercely, "Last night did not happen! We begin tonight!"

Remembering the rape by a wooden phallus she seethed but quickly said sweetly, "Yes, my lord!"

He drew her down to the pillows on the large divan.

"You are an unexplored garden of delights, my bride. For the present, *I* shall seek to please *you*." He pushed the little bolero off her, and, cupping her breasts in his hands, kissed first one and then the other. "Your breasts are like unopened roses," he murmured deeply against her silken, perfumed skin.

A streak of lightning ripped through her at his gentle touch, and she gasped with shock, instinctively raising her hands to fend him off. But he was too quick for her. Pushing her back amid the pillows he covered her bare breasts with hot kisses. His tongue lapped at her large nipples, sending wave after wave of shivers over her trembling body. Then his mouth closed over one hard peak, and sucked hungrily. "My lord," she moaned! "Oh, my lord!" She was close to fainting by the time he finally stopped.

"Did you like it?" he asked. "Did you like what I just did to you?"

She could not answer, and he took her silence for maidenly modesty, which delighted him. What she could not tell him was that she *had* liked what he had done. She liked it as much as she had liked it when Prince Murad did it to her. This confused her terribly. Did she not then love the prince? Was love a different thing from the delicious feelings that rippled through her body when she was touched in this way? She did not understand.

What she did know was that she liked a man's hands on her, and she was, after all, this man's wife. So where was the harm? But as his arm encircled her and his free hand stroked her again, she remembered last night—when he had coldly ordered her precious virginity wasted upon a lifeless piece of polished wood so that he might not waste his time. He only wooed her now because of Ali Yahya's intervention. Without that intervention, she would again have been bound to the bed and mated like an animal.

Her beloved Murad had never hurt her. He had touched her gently, with tenderness. He had wanted her for his wife, and she in turn had wanted him for her husband. She had wanted to please him. *That* had been love! Fragile, barely born—but *love!*

She did not love the sultan, but she did enjoy his attentions and, God have mercy on her, it was all she was going to get in this life. Princesses were not expected to enjoy their marriages.

Sighing, she gave herself over to his ministrations, delighting him by drawing his head back down to her breasts, and begging prettily that he do again what he had just done. He could feel his own desire rising fast, for she excited him greatly. It took all his strength to remember how very unskilled she really was. Like a green youth, he fumblingly drew her pantaloons down over her hips to where she might easily kick them off. His fingers eagerly sought for her mound of Venus, and found it already moist. Panting, he tore open his robe and flung himself on her, feeling with ecstatic pleasure her youthful warmth.

His fingernails scratched the insides of her thighs as he pulled her legs apart. To her amazement he was nearly sobbing his hunger for her. His eagerness astounded her. She had no fear of him. She wondered if she closed her eyes, and pretended he were Murad . . .

Moving provocatively, she whispered huskily, "Kiss me, my lord. Kiss me, my husband." He quickly obliged her, and to her delight his mouth was firm, and strangely familiar. It was—oh, dear God!—like Murad's. He kissed her deeply, passionately. First he was the aggressor and then, to their mutual surprise, she was. She allowed his mouth to sweep her into a purely physical world of sensual pleasures.

She was again in the orchard of St. Catherine's. Again in the strong arms of the prince. It was his dear, familiar mouth that now possessed hers, his hands that swept over her smooth skin. With a will of its own, her young body moved voluptuously, instinct rather than experience guiding her.

Maddened with desire, Orkhan drove himself deep into the eager, willing body. He needed all of his self-control not to take his release immediately. Instead he guided her gently through a maze of passion, helping her to find her way until she thought she could bear no more.

At first Theadora fought against the force that took her higher, higher, and higher before sweeping her away with an overpowering sweetness that drove her to the teetering brink of unconsciousness. Then she stopped fighting. At last, bathed in a golden light, she felt herself shattering into a thousand little pieces. She cried out with a terrible sense of loss, and heard him cry out as well.

In the absolute quiet that followed she hesitantly opened her eyes. He lay on his side, propped up on one elbow, gazing down at her. His dark eyes were filled with admiration, and he smiled tenderly. For a moment she was puzzled. Where was Murad? Who was this old man? Then, as reality returned, she almost wailed aloud.

"You are magnificent!" the sultan cried. "That an innocent girl should feel so deeply! Be so passionate! Allah! How I adore you, my little bride. Thee-adora! Thee-adora! I believe I am falling in love with you!" He took her in his arms and kissed her hungrily. His hands could not stop fondling her breasts, her buttocks . . . and he was quickly roused. Again he sought her warmth, and she could not deny him. Nor could she deny her own physical desire. She hated herself.

Afterwards he called for refreshments. "I will see to it that you have the finest teachers, my little one. You were made for love, and for loving." He sipped a fruit sherbet. "Ah, my sweet wife, how you delight me! I must admit that. I did not expect to find such fire in you. You are mine, my adorable Theadora! Mine alone!"

In his voice she heard the echo of Murad's voice, speaking nearly the same words. She shivered. He put an arm about her. "I am at your feet, my lovely Adora." The name seemed to have slipped out, and when, shocked, she stared up at him his face was a mask of delight. "*Adora*!" he exclaimed. "Yes! You are my own Adora!"

"Why do you call me that?" she whispered.

"Because," he said as he bent and kissed a plump breast, "because you are an adorable creature."

She felt tears prick at the back of her eyelids, and quickly she blinked them back. How ironic that the father should be so like the son, even in the language of his love-making. She sighed. She was caught like a bird in a snare, and there was no help for it.

She was the sultan's wife. She must put Prince Murad out of her thoughts. Her energies must be devoted to giving her husband a son and her father a grandson who would link John Cantacuzene by blood to Sultan Orkhan. She was Theadora Cantacuzene, a princess of Byzantium, and she knew her duty. She was Theadora Cantacuzene, the sultan's wife, and she knew her fate.

Chapter 6

THEADORA SAT QUIETLY SEWING BY THE BUBBLING, TILED fountain. The fantailed goldfish chased each other amid the sparkling, splashing water. About her the almond and cherry trees blossomed, and the flower beds, bordered with blue hyacinths, were filled with white and yellow tulips.

Next to her sat Iris, who now hissed, "Here comes the old crow and the dove on their daily visit."

"Hush," Theadora gently chided her. But she had to bite her lip to keep from laughing.

"Good afternoon, Theadora."

"Good afternoon, Theadora."

"And good afternoon to you both lady Anastatia and lady Nilufer. Pray be seated. Iris, see to the refreshments."

The two older women settled themselves, and Martina drew from her flowing sleeves a piece of embroidery. Anastatia, having peered at Theadora's large belly, commented, "Such a big child! And you with two more months to go. T'will be a wonder if you're not torn asunder at the birthing."

"Nonsense!" replied Nilufer as she saw Theadora grow pale. "I was enormous with Murad, Suleiman, and Fatima. And it was mostly the waters, for none of them was unusually large." She patted the young girl's hand. "You are doing just fine, child. Your baby is sure to be a lovely, healthy one."

Theodora sent Murad's mother a grateful look, then turned icy eyes on Anastatia. "I have no fears for either myself or my *son*," she said evenly.

Iris, returning with a tray, heard enough to be angry She stumbled and the pitcher she carried tipped, spilling its contents into Anastatia's lap. The sultan's first wife leapt up as the cold, sticky liquid poured over her, seeping through her rich clothing to her skin.

"Clumsy fool!" she shrieked. "I'll have you beaten black and blue for this deliberate insolence!"

"You will do no such thing," said Theodora coldly. "Iris is my slave, and this was an accident. Iris, humbly beg the lady Anastatia's pardon."

Iris knelt, bowing her head. "Oh, I do, my lady Theodora. I do!"

"There," said Theodora calmly as if that settled everything. Then she called to her other slaves, "Hurry, girls, or Lady Anastatia's gown will be ruined." And she looked up to find Lady Nilufer's eyes brimming with laughing admiration.

If Theodora could claim to have a friend other than Iris, it was the sultan's second wife. Once Nilufer had met the Byzantine princess she immediately revised her opinions of the girl. She saw in Theodora a substitute for her own beloved daughter who was married to a prince of Samarkand and lived so far away that it was unlikely mother and daughter would ever meet again in this lifetime. Had it not been for Nilufer's kindness, Theadora might have miscarried her child, for Anastatia took great delight in provoking her.

The slavegirls had managed to sop up the sherbet from lady Anastatia's gown. Cleansing it with cool water, they spread it across her wide lap to dry. It was at this moment that the sultan and his two favorite sons chose to visit Theadora. Her feelings for Orkhan were friendly now that she did not have to endure his insatiable sexual appetite. For four months after her bridal night he had visited her five nights out of every seven; the other two nights were reserved by Koran law for his other two wives.

During these months Theadora's education had been considerably broadened. True to his word Orkhan had sent her the best tutors available in the harem. These redoubtable ladies had lectured on and demonstrated the arts of love until Theadora thought she could no longer be shocked or even surprised. But her husband, praising her new skills, had taught her things not even hinted at by her teachers, and Theadora had found that she could still blush.

As he strode across her garden towards her she felt her heart lurch painfully. Murad walked on his left. She had not seen him since their last night together in St. Catherine's orchard. He was not looking at her, but towards his mother. It seemed to her that he was making a great effort *not* to look at her. Seeing both her sons, Nilufer rose with a glad cry, her arms outstretched.

On the sultan's right was his heir, Prince Suleiman. Theadora had met this young man on many occasions since her entry into Orkhan's house. He was a tall, handsome man with his father's olive skin and dark hair, and eyes like his brother's. Unlike the rest of his family, he was open, charming, and merry. He treated his father's youngest wife as he might treat a favorite little sister.

The trio had reached the women now and, as Suleiman and Murad bent to kiss their mother, Orkhan embraced Theadora. He then turned to Murad and said, "Come, my son, and meet my precious Adora. Is this not a sweet armful for an old man on a cold winter's night?" He chuckled and gently patted her swollen belly. "Not so old, however, that I cannot still plant a good crop in fertile ground."

"You are very fortunate, my father," said Murad stiffly, bowing slightly to Theadora. As he rose and raised his eyes to her she saw that they were cold and scornful. "Are you so sure it is a son my *father* has given you, princess?" His voice was mocking, and for a moment she thought she would faint.

She drew a deep breath to steady herself and said proudly, "The women of the Cantacuzene always breed strong sons for their *husbands*, Prince Murad."

A scornful little smile touched the corners of his mouth. "I shall eagerly await the birth of my half-brother, princess."

Nilufer looked at her younger son, puzzled. Why on earth had he taken such a dislike to Theadora? She was such a sweet girl.

Later, as Theadora relived the incident, she grew angry and furiously threw several pieces of crockery to vent her temper. Her slaves, all carefully chosen by her in the open markets of Bursa, and trained in loyalty and obedience by Iris, were quite surprised. How could he be so cruel, wondered Theadora. Did he expect her to commit suicide because his father was suddenly reminded of her existence? Did he think she enjoyed the lust-filled hours she spent at Orkhan's mercy? She sighed deeply. Men, she concluded, were but fools.

When her son was born she would devote her energies to him alone. She hoped her husband would leave her alone. She had recently taken to shopping the better slave marts with Iris for the most beautiful virgins available. She had trained the girls to perfection and then presented them to her husband. If she could keep his interests directed toward others, she might escape him. The thought of his hands on her again sent a shudder through her.

She had endured the hours with Orkhan only by pretending that he was Murad. Now she could no longer do that. It was obvious that Murad despised her. Alone in her bed, the slaves dismissed, she allowed herself the luxury of tears, but they were silent tears, for not even dear Iris must suspect her sadness.

The child in her womb kicked vigorously, and Adora placed protective hands over her belly. "You are awake much too late, Halil," she scolded lovingly. "I suppose you'll be a rowdy, noisy thing like my brother, Matthew, refusing to go to bed until you drop where you stand." She smiled at her memory of Matthew. He was the only little boy she had ever known, and they had been together for only a few years. Her position had robbed her even of a childhood.

She gave a watery chuckle. Her baby was not yet born, but she knew for certain that it was a son. How she knew she did not understand, but she was as certain as if she held the child now.

The sultan had said that his son would be called Halil after the great Turkish general who had defeated the Byzantines. Adora had already accustomed herself to the name, and was amused by her husband's clever slap at her father.

Halil, unlike many royal children, was going to have a childhood. She was determined on that score. He would play with other boys his age, ride, learn archery, and how to use a scimitar. Most important of all, he would have his mother. For she did not intend that he be taken from her to be raised by slaves. He might be an Ottoman prince, but with two much older brothers there was very little chance of his ever ruling, and she would not allow him to be taken away to his own court where he would be debauched by the eunuchs.

It was comforting to think of her baby, but it still did not erase from her mind the look in Murad's eyes. How he hated her! The silent tears began to flow again. He would never, never know how often she had relived the precious moments they had spent together. He would never know that each time Orkhan kissed her she pretended it was Murad. Her memories had kept her alive, and kept her sane. In one cruel look he had torn those memories from her, and she did not know if she could ever forgive him. What right had he to judge her so harshly?

Two months later, on a hot June morning, the sultan's youngest wife, Theadora, gave easy birth to a healthy son. One month later the gold balance of the princess's dowry was paid, and the strategic fortress of Tzympe was deeded to Orkhan.

The sultan was delighted by his little Halil and visited him often. His desire for Theadora, however, had waned during the months of her pregnancy. There were so many beautiful women in the palace, all willing to be his bed partner. Theadora was safe from him now and, once again, she was alone.

PART II

Bursa

1357 to 1359

Chapter 7

THEADORA WAS IN A RAGE. "I HAVE ALWAYS encouraged Halil to pursue manly sports," she exclaimed furiously, "but I warned him, Ali Yahya. And I warned that useless body slave of his—who will now receive ten lashes for disobeying me! I told them both that Halil was not yet to ride the stallion Prince Suleiman sent him. Halil is only six! He could have been killed!"

"He is Osman's grandson, my lady Theadora, and Orkhan's son. It is a wonder he was not born with spurs already attached to his little heels," replied the eunuch.

Theadora laughed in spite of herself. Then, sobering, she said, "This is very serious, Ali Yahya. The doctor says Halil may always limp because of the fall. The leg is not healing properly, and it now appears to be a bit shorter than the other leg."

"Perhaps it is better that way, my princess," sighed Ali Yahya. "Now that your son is physically imperfect, he will be considered unfit to rule."

She looked stunned and he was amazed. "How can it be that you have lived among us, my princess, in this palace, and you do not realize that the first thing any new sultan does is to order the execution of his rivals? In most cases, these are his brothers. But our laws do not permit the imperfect to inherit, so be grateful, my princess. Your son will now live a long life. Why do you think Prince Murad has had no children? He knows that his life, and that of any of his sons, are forfeit when Prince Suleiman inherits."

Suleiman kill her little Halil? Impossible! He adored his little half-brother. Spoiled him continually. But she remembered that Suleiman's eyes could grow cold. She remembered the command in his voice and that he was always obeyed instantly. She also recalled something her father had said long ago, before she had become the sultan's wife. He had said that the Turks made good mercenaries because they delighted in killing. He said they had no mercy and no pity.

She shuddered. God was, after all, looking after her. When Orkhan died she would be a dead sultan's wife—a most unenviable position. Halil was all the family she had. And now he was no threat to anyone.

Her father had been deposed three years past, but unlike so many Byzantine emperors who had lost their lives along with their thrones, John Cantacuzene had retired to the monastery of Mistra, near Sparta. With him was her brother, Matthew, who had taken holy orders earlier.

Theadora's older half-sister, Sophia, had come to a violent end when her third husband had caught her with a lover and stabbed them both to death. Helena, now the undisputed empress of Byzantium, behaved as if Theadora barely existed. They might be sisters, but the sultan's third wife was hardly on a social par with the holy Christian empress of Byzantium!

Theadora smarted under her sister's contempt. Because Orkhan was almost seventy, Theadora had recently broached the subject with Helena of her possibly retiring to Constantinople when the sultan went to his reward. She had been cruelly rebuffed. Helena claimed that the daughter of the usurper, John Cantacuzene, would hardly be welcome in the city. The same, Helena added, might be said of Orkhan's widow. The infidels were the greatest enemies of the Byzantines.

Helena conveniently forgot that she too was John Cantacuzene's daughter. And she overlooked the fact that, had her little sister not been wed to the Ottoman, their father might not have been able to hold onto his throne long enough for Helena to become John Paleaologi's wife, and empress. Helena was not particularly intelligent. She did not comprehend that what had once been the vast empire of Byzantium had now dwindled to a few sections of the Greek mainland, some cities along the Black Sea, and Constantinople.

Helena did not see that the royal jewels that adorned her state robes and crown were merely glass. The robes themselves were no longer real cloth of gold, but tinsel. The state dishes were copper. And everything that appeared to be rich brocade was only painted leather. It never occurred to Helena that being empress of Byzantium was very much like being empress of an empty eggshell. Theadora saw all of this, and though she did not think the Turks' capture of Constantinople was likely to happen in her lifetime, she knew that they would eventually prevail over Byzantium.

Still, Theadora longed for the city of her birth. And she felt sure that when Orkhan was gone, there would be no place for her in Bursa, at Suleiman's court.

For a moment she thought of Murad. He was still without a wife or favorites. She wondered if he ever thought of her. He was rarely in Bursa, but spent most of his time in Gallipoli.

Theadora chuckled as she remembered how Orkhan had cleverly tricked her father over Gallipoli. With the birth of Halil, her remaining dowry had been paid to Orkhan. Prince Suleiman and Prince Murad had been sent to occupy Tyzmpe for the sultan. The fortress was located on the European side of the Dardanelles, on the Gallipoli peninsula. When the ancient walls of the nearby town of Gallipoli had collapsed during a mild earth tremor, the Ottoman Turks had quickly occupied it. Their next task was to fortify and rebuild the town's walls, which they did. Once this was done, the Ottoman princes brought over from Asia the first colony of Turkish settlers. Other colonies followed in quick succession, comprised of Orkhan's former warriors and their women, who all settled on the lands of the fugitive Christian nobles, under their own Moslem beys. The peasants of the region remained, preferring life under the Ottoman rule to the Byzantine. Occupation by the Turks meant freedom from Christian feudal power with all its abuses and its heavy taxation. It also meant equal law for all, regardless of race, religion, or class.

As the Turkish occupation spread, even the

Christian lords whose lands bordered on newly acquired Ottoman territory began to accept Orkhan's sovereignty. As his vassals, they paid him a small annual tribute in token of their submission to Islam. And from the beginning, the Ottoman state adopted a conciliatory attitude towards their Christian subjects.

In Constantinople, Emperor John Cantacuzene suddenly realized what was happening and complained bitterly to his son-in-law, the sultan. Orkhan offered to sell Tzympe back to the Byzantines for ten thousand gold ducats, knowing full well that he could retake it any time he chose to retake it. Gallipoli, however, he would not return, claiming that he had not taken it by force. It had fallen to him by the will of God, in the earthquake. Theadora could not help laughing at the thought of her clever father finally outwitted, even though it meant his downfall.

With her father and brother exiled, Theadora had no one to whom she could turn. She was fearful of what would happen to her and to her son. Then suddenly Prince Suleiman solved her problem.

Halil's injury had been brought to his attention, and he called on Theadora in order to apologize for the horse he had given to his younger sibling, and which had proved dangerous. Theadora accepted his apology, saying, "Ali Yahya tells me it is a blessing in disguise, for now Halil will be no threat to you."

The prince replied candidly, "That is true, princess. But since the boy is no longer a danger, let us concentrate on planning his future. He is a highly intelligent lad and could be of great use to me."

"I had thought to return to Constantinople with

Halil some day," she answered him. He need not know that that road was probably closed to her.

"But you must not do that! If you are truly unhappy I would not keep you here, but you are an Ottoman now, Adora, and we are proud of you."

"There could be no place for me at your court, Suleiman."

"I will make a place for you," he said huskily. She looked up just in time to catch him mask the flicker of desire in his eyes. She was startled and quickly lowered her eyes so he might not see how upset she was. It seemed, she thought with wry amusement, that she held a fascination for the men of the Ottoman family "You are most kind, Prince Suleiman, to offer us a home. I will rest more easily now, knowing that Halil's future is secure."

The prince bowed suavely and left her. Well, she chuckled to herself, Halil was safe, but was she? It disturbed her that Prince Suleiman should desire her. He had always treated her like a sister. And she had never encouraged his desire. She frowned. The voice of her servant, Iris, cut through the silence.

"Look in your mirror, my lady. The answer to your unspoken question is there."

"You were eavesdropping!" Theadora accused.

"If I did not eavesdrop I should learn nothing, and then how could I protect you? You are as deep as a well, my princess."

Adora laughed, "Give me a mirror, you incorrigible old snoop!"

Iris handed it to her, and Theadora looked at her image with careful scrutiny for the first time in many years. She was somewhat startled to find an incredibly beautiful young woman staring back at her. She had, it seemed, a heart-shaped face, a long straight nose, well-spaced amethyst eyes fringed heavily in goldtipped black lashes, and a wide generous mouth with a full, almost pouting, lower lip. Her creamy skin was flawless.

She placed the mirror on the divan and walked over to its tall standing counterpart of clear Venetian glass which was set in a heavily carved gold frame. Eyeing herself critically, she noted that she was taller than most women, yet willow slim, with high breasts. A good figure. She peered hard at herself. *Is it really me?* she asked silently. She was not vain by nature, and since the one thing she did not want to do was attract Orkhan's attention, she had never really taken much care with her appearance.

"I am beautiful," she said softly, her hand absently patting her dark hair.

"Yes, my princess, you are. *And* you are not even in your prime yet," cackled Iris. "If Prince Suleiman desires you," she continued in a low voice, "perhaps he will make you his wife when you are a widow. Then will your fortune and your future be made!"

"I have no desire to be his wife," snapped Theadora in an equally low voice. "Besides he already has four wives, and he can have no more. I will be no man's concubine!"

"Pah! It is easy enough for him to divorce one of his wives. They are only slaves. You are a princess." She looked slyly at her mistress, her eyes bright. "Do not tell me you do not long for a young man's love, a young man's caress. You move about your room half the night. A few good tumbles with a lusty man would cure you of your restlessness."

"You are impertinent, Iris! Beware, or I will have you whipped!" Damn the woman! Iris was far too observant.

Halil chose that moment to burst in upon his mother. "Look! I can walk again, mother, without the crutches!" He ran into her arms and she almost wept at the sight of his very pronounced limp. His right foot was twisted inward.

"I am so proud of you," she said kissing him soundly as he squirmed away, making a face. "Rude boy!" she scolded teasingly, drawing him down by her side. "Tell me, Halil, does it still hurt?"

"Only a little." But he said it so quickly that she knew it probably hurt him a great deal.

Impulsively she asked, "How would you like to take a sea voyage, my son?"

"To where, mother?"

"Thessaly, my love. There are ancient hot springs there whose waters would aid the soreness in your foot."

"Will you come with me?"

"If your father will allow it," she answered him, surprised that she hadn't considered it before.

He struggled up, tugging at her hand. "Let us go now,"

Theadora laughed at his impatience but then thought, why not? She quickly followed her small son through the winding corridors that led from the haremlik to the selamlik, which were in turn followed by several panting eunuchs. They arrived quickly at the doors to the sultan's apartments.

"Tell my father, the sultan, that Prince Halil and his mother, Princess Theadora, seek audience with him immediately."

A few moments later the janissary returned. "The sultan will see you both now, Your Highness." And he flung open one of the great oak doors.

They walked through into the lush chamber where Orkhan sat cross-legged upon a pile of cushions. Several young girls sat to his left playing softly upon stringed instruments. The most current of Orkhan's favorites, a sulky mouthed, dark-haired Italian beauty, reclined next to him. Theadora and her son moved to the foot of the dais, but when Theadora moved to kneel, her son restrained her, glowering at his father's concubine. "On your face, woman! My mother kneels only to my father and to her God!" And when the girl had the temerity to look to the sultan for confirmation, the child was on her with a roar of outrage. Pulling her from the cushions onto the floor, he cried, "Insolent one! You beg for a beating!"

Orkhan's laughter rumbled through the room. "You have given me a true Ottoman, my Adora. Halil, my son, go gently with the girl. A slave such as this one is valuable merchandise." He turned his gaze on the woman at his feet. "Leave me, Pakize. You will receive ten lashes for your lapse in manners. My wives are to be treated with the respect they deserve."

The girl scrambled up and, body bent, backed her way out of the room.

Theadora now knelt and made a respectful obeisance to her husband while her son, Halil, bowed beautifully to his father.

"Sit next to me," Orkhan commanded them, "and tell me why I have been honored by this visit today."

Theadora settled herself by her husband and then said, "I wish to take Halil to Thessaly to the Springs of Apollo near Mount Ossa. The waters there are famous for healing, and though Halil will not admit it to me, I know he is in great pain. His foot and leg will never really mend properly, but at least the waters might help with his pain."

"And you want to go with him?" asked the sultan.

"Yes, my lord, I do. He is still a little boy, and needs his mother. I know that you honor me, my lord, but you do not really need me. Halil does. Also, I would not trust our son to slaves on such a long journey."

The sultan nodded. "You would not take him to Constantinople?"

"Never!"

Orkhan raised an amused eyebrow. "You are very vehement, my dear. Why is that?"

She hesitated, then said, "I had discussed with my sister the possibility of someday retiring to Constantinople with Halil. She made it quite clear that neither of us would be welcomed. She is an arrogant, stupid woman."

He had known all of this, of course, for none of her private correspondence left or entered his palace that he did not read it first. Theadora was not aware of this, and she would have beth very angry if she had known. He knew her far better than she realized, and though he would never have admitted it to her—for to do so would have been a sign of weakness—he admired her strength of character. And he was genuinely fond of her. She was a proud little creature. He realized how deeply her sister had hurt her.

"Take Halil to the Springs of Apollo, my dear. You have my permission to do so. Ali Yahya will see to your travel arrangements." He turned to the boy. "You will look after your mother, Halil, and protect her from the infidel?"

"Yes, father! I have a new scimitar with a blade of real Toledo steel that my brother, Murad, sent to me from Gallipoli."

Orkhan smiled at the child and patted his dark bead. "I will trust you to guard her well, Halil. She is most precious to me, my son." The sultan clapped his hands for refreshments.

And while the little boy happily munched honey-and-sesame cakes, Orkhan and Theadora talked. To her surprise, he no longer treated her as an object existing solely for his sensual pleasure, but rather like a favorite daughter. She, in turn, was more relaxed with him than she had ever been.

He spoke of eventually moving his capital to Adrianople, a city on the European side of the Sea of Marmara that he now had under siege. Theadora's dowry gift had given him the toehold he had needed in Europe.

"When Adrianople is secure," she asked, "will you take the city?"

"I will try," he answered her. "Perhaps you will retire to Constantinople after all, my dear."

She laughed. "Live a thousand years, my lord

Orkhan! I am as yet too young to retire anywhere."

He chuckled. "Too young, indeed, and far too love-ly. You are easily the most beautiful woman in my house." Then, seeing the wary look spring into her eyes, he gently dismissed her and the boy.

Alone, he wondered, as he had wondered a thousand times since she had first come to him, why she did not like love-making. She had never known any man but him, of that he was certain. She had been a virgin. She was wildly passionate when roused, but he had always felt that she was not with him—but with some ghostly lover. He might have suspected another man, but cloistered as she had been within her convent, she could not have had another man.

It was a mystery that still intrigued him after all these years. He knew she did not dislike him. The sultan shrugged. His harem was filled with young beauties only too willing to please him. Why one young Byzantine princess should intrigue him so, he did not understand.

Chapter 8

THE SKY HAD BEEN A CLOUDLESS BRIGHT BLUE ALL DAY. Too cloudless. Too bright blue. Now the captain watched the sunset in his vessel's wake and frowned. The colors were too bright again—and too clear. As the orange sun sank behind the purple Pindus mountains, a tiny flash of emerald green was followed by a muted lavender streak. The captain nodded, and gave curt orders. He had seen a sky like this one before. Before a great storm.

He prayed to Allah that he was wrong. He was too far out to go back, and had it been only himself, his crew, and a cargo to worry about he would not have considered it; but he carried on board the sultan's youngest wife, Princess Theadora, and her son, Prince Halil. He had brought them to Thessaly several months earlier, and now he was taking them home.

Ahead the darkness was starless; behind him the sunset had become a wash of flame-tinged gray. The winds, which had been fresh and light all day, now blew in strong gusts from the north and the west. Captain Hassan called to his first officer, "See that all the galley slaves are fed a good hot meal, and tell the overseer that when the storm hits he is to unlock their

111

chains. If we go down I'll not have their souls on my conscience."

The officer nodded his agreement. "Is the danger that great, sir?"

"Perhaps having the sultan's wife and son aboard makes me nervous, but the last time I saw a sky like that it was followed by a great storm."

"Aye, sir." The mate moved off the bridge to do his captain's bidding, while Hassan turned and made his way down the steps into the passageway leading to his royal passengers' quarters. He knocked and was admitted by Iris. The princess sat at a small table opposite her son. They were playing jackals-and-hares. He waited for her to grant him permission to speak.

She looked up almost at once, smiling. "Yes, captain?"

"I am expecting a severe storm tonight, Your Highness. I would prefer that you and your household remain within the safety of your quarters. If you wish hot food, please have it soon. Once the sea becomes rough, the cook has orders to close his galley and put out his fires."

"You will keep me informed, captain?"

"Assuredly, Highness! Your safety and Prince Halil's is of the greatest importance."

She dismissed him with a nod and returned to her game. Captain Hassan bowed himself out and walked swiftly through his ship, checking ropes and hatches as he went. He stopped in the galley and sat down. Without ceremony the cook set before him a steaming bowl of spicy fish stew and a hunk of bread. The captain ate quickly, sopping up the gravy with the bread. Finished, he turned to the cook. "Have you all you need to feed the men, Yussef?"

"Aye, sir. I baked this morning. There's plenty of bread. I've dried fish, beef, and fruit. And I can make coffee on the spirit lamp."

Suddenly the ship lurched violently and began to pitch. Yussef began to damp down his cookfires and the captain rose to his feet, saying grimly, "Here we go, my friend. From the feel of that, we're in for quite a ride."

Theadora and her party had been eating when the storm began. Walking across the spacious stern cabin she gazed through the small bowed window out into the half dark. Behind them, through the sheets of rain, the sky still glowed faintly with a red sunset. The sea was now black, relieved only by the white foam of its peaks. Theadora shivered with a premonition of danger. Then, holding down her emotions, she said, "I think we would do well to retire early." She ruffled her small son's hair. "This is not the time for setting up the telescope your father sent you, Halil. There'll be no stars tonight."

"Oh, mother! May I not stay up and watch the storm?"

"Would you like to?" She was surprised, but pleased that he was not afraid.

"Yes! I only wish the captain would allow me on deck now."

"Even if he would, I would not!"

"Oh, mother!"

She laughed. "But you may stay up, my son."

He curled contentedly into the window seat, face pressed against the small panes of glass. She sat quietly at her embroidery frame, stitching a pastoral scene. The slaves cleared the meal away and then disappeared into their own small quarters. Iris trimmed the lamps which were swaying precariously from their chains. Glancing over at Halil, Theadora saw that the boy had fallen asleep. She nodded to Iris who gathered the child up and tucked him into his bed.

"Only an innocent could sleep in this storm," the older woman noted. "Me? I am terrified, but I suppose if it's my fate to feed the fishes, I won't escape it." She plumped herself down on her mistress's bed and began calmly to mend one of the little prince's silk shirts.

Theadora silently continued with her embroidery. It was not particularly comforting to know that Iris was as frightened as she was—but, remembering her late mother's words about the difference between the ruling class and the rest of the world, she again called on the deep reserve of discipline that was her heritage. She was Theadora Cantacuzene, a princess of Byzantium. She was Theadora Cantacuzene, the sultan's wife. She must be strong for the sake of her little son and for her slaves who were, after all, not just her property, but her responsibility as well.

She glanced instinctively towards the small bowed window as the ship gave a particularly violent lurch, and, for one terrifying moment, she felt as if her heart had stopped. There was so much water she was not sure that the ship had not sunk. Then, like a bobbing cork, the ship rose again on the angry white crest of the waves. As she regained her breath, she realized her finger was throbbing. Looking down, she saw that she had pricked it with her needle. A bright red drop of blood lay for a moment upon the white linen before soaking into the embroidery. She made an irritated sound and, picking up the carafe of fresh water near her, dribbled some of it on the stain. By rubbing vigorously she managed to remove the blood. She then put her injured finger into her mouth and sucked on it.

She discovered that she was shaking, and it suddenly occurred to Theadora that she did not want to die. She was just twenty, which was really not all that old—and, except for those few brief hours in the convent garden with Prince Murad, she had never really known any happiness. And what of her son? He had known only seven years.

The ship was pitching wildly now, and Iris moaned. Her face had taken on a sickly green tinge, and Theadora shoved a basin at the woman just in time.

When Iris had finished, Theadora took the basin and hurried out of the cabin with it in deliberate defiance of the captain's orders. She was not, she thought grimly, going to spend the rest of the storm locked in a cabin that reeked of vomit. That would be sure to prolong Iris's illness and possibly weaken her own fluttering stomach.

By hugging the passageway she was able to reach the exit. Standing in the hatchway, she flung the entire basin out into the storm, watching with amazement as the wild wind caught the brass vessel and held it aloft as though deciding whether it wanted it or not. After a moment, it plunged into the boiling sea. There was something so wonderfully alive about the storm that for a moment Theadora paused where she was, and her fear temporarily gone, she laughed aloud at the fierceness and the beauty of it.

Making her way back to her cabin, she found that poor Iris had fallen asleep on her narrow couch. Theadora sat again at her embroidery. She had worked for several hours when she suddenly became aware that the sea was once again calm. She rose and stretched her cramped limbs. A knock sent her quickly to the door where the captain waited, looking very tired.

"Are you all right, Highness?"

"Yes, Captain Hassan. We are all fine."

"I came to warn you that the storm is not yet over."

"But the sea is as calm as a fishpond."

"Yes, my lady, it is. We call it the 'eye' of the storm. A center of calm in the midst of turbulence; When we reach the other side of that calm, may Allah preserve us. Please continue to remain in your cabin."

"How long will the calm last?"

"Perhaps half an hour, my lady."

"Then I will, with your permission, come up on deck for a few minutes, captain. My son and my servants are sleeping, but I confess that I am restless."

"Of course, Highness. I will escort you myself."

She closed the door quietly and, taking his arm, walked out onto the wet deck. The heavy air was still, and it appeared as if they sailed into an ink pot. Above and around them, the sky and the sea were a flat black. But then the captain pointed ahead, and in the strange half-light Theadora could see the water some distance ahead of them, roiling a foaming white

"The other side of the storm, Highness. There is no escaping it."

"It is magnificent, Captain Hassan! Will we survive its savagery?"

"As Allah wills it, my lady," replied the captain fatalistically, shrugging his shoulders.

They stood at the rail for some minutes. Then, sensing the captain's impatience, Theadora said, "I will return to my quarters." Inside again she bent over her son and kissed him gently. So deep was his slumber that he did not even stir. Iris lay on her back, snoring gently. It is better this way, thought Theadora. I can maintain my own calm more easily if no one else frightens me.

She could feel the ship beginning to pitch again as they approached the other side of the storm. Theadora sat quietly with her hands folded tightly and prayed silently for the safety of the vessel and all who sailed on it. Never, since leaving St. Catherine's, had she immersed herself so deeply in prayer.

Suddenly, as the ship lurched sickeningly, there came a tremendous crash that rocked the ship to its foundations, and above the roar Theadora heard shouting. Then the little bowed window of the cabin blew in, spraying glass and water across the floor.

She leapt to her feet and stood helplessly for a moment as the rain and sea spray soaked her. Iris tumbled from her couch, half awake and screaming. "Allah preserve us! We're sinking! We're sinking!"

Theadora whirled about and yanked the slave

woman to her feet, slapping her as hard as she could. "Be quiet, you foolish woman! We are not sinking! The storm has blown the window in and that is all."

Over the roar of the wind and the rain and the sea they heard a frantic knocking at the cabin door. The princess yanked the door open and a sailor fell into the room. "Captain's compliments, Your Highness," he panted. "I'm to check for any damage. I'll see that window is boarded over at once."

"What was that tremendous crash?" demanded Theadora.

The sailor was back on his feet now, and he hesitated before answering. Then, shrugging, he said, "We lost the main mast, my lady, but the storm is almost done with us now, and we're near dawn." Then he hurried out.

"Wake the slaves, Iris, and have them clean up this mess so the sailors can make their repairs quickly." She turned to see Halil sitting straight up in his bed, his eyes wide. "Are we sinking, mother?"

"No, my lamb," she forced a laugh. "The last of the storm blew out the window, and gave us all a good fright. That is all."

Within minutes the repairs had been made to the window. The remaining pieces of glass were carefully removed from the frame and replaced with boards and a curtain. The storm had subsided.

Venturing out onto the deck, Theadora was shocked at the damage. The main mast was indeed gone and so was most of another of the three masts. The sails, or what remained of them, were mere shreds fluttering in the breeze. It was obvious that they would have to rely on the galley slaves for movement. She wondered how those poor souls had survived the night and made a mental note to check for Christians among the rowers so she might buy their freedom. It had been her policy since becoming a mother to buy the freedom of whatever enslaved Christians she came upon. She sent them to freedom in Constantinople.

She turned when she heard the captain's voice at her side. "Your people are all right, Highness?"

"Yes, thank you. We were warm and dry most of the night. How did the ship's crew fare?"

"We lost four rowers, and two of my sailors were washed overboard. That damned overseer! Your pardon, Highness. The overseer was told to unchain the galley slaves when the storm hit. He disobeyed orders, and the four we lost were drowned at their benches. As soon as we clean up this mess, the overseer will be brought up for punishment. It will not be a pretty sight, my lady. I advise you to go below."

"I will, captain, but I am so delighted to be alive to see this dawn that I would stay on deck a while longer."

The captain grinned with delight. "Your highness will forgive me if I say you are a very brave young woman. I am very proud to sail with you." Then, flushing at his own boldness, he turned and hurried away.

Theadora chuckled softly to herself. It had been wonderful being away from Bursa these last few months. She had enjoyed herself very much. The world was an absolutely wonderful place! It was not going to be pleasant returning to the harem and the constant company of the other two wives. It would not be easy returning to the endless boredom.

She gazed at the rainbow dawn that colored the soft grey-blue skies, and suddenly it occurred to her that the east was not where it ought to be! Stopping a sailor, she asked, "Have we been blown far off course?"

"Yes, Highness. We are way south of where we should be, but the captain will right it soon enough."

She thanked him and returned to her cabin. Iris was making coffee on their spirit lamp, and the cook had sent a small basket of dried fruit, some warmed-over day-old bread, and a small hard cheese. Halil, up and dressed, grabbed a handful of dried fruit as he passed her on his way out. "The captain has offered to let me steer while they are cleaning up," he said excitedly Theadora let him go, and signaled to the boy's body slave to follow him.

"I am too tired to eat," she told Iris. "I spent most of the night praying. I am going to try to sleep now. Wake me in mid-afternoon." She was half asleep before her head touched the pillow.

The sun woke her before Iris had the chance. Theadora lay on her back in the delicious world of half-sleep, lulled by the gentle rocking motion of the ship. She was alone, and a ray of sunlight came in through the hastily placed boards. As she became more aware of her surroundings, she heard a strange sound above her. "Whistle. Slap! Groan. Whistle. Slap! Groan." Suddenly, wide awake, Theadora realized that the punishment of the overseer must be taking place on deck, and her little son was there!

Theadora flew to the door and wrenched it open. She reached the deck and stopped, frozen, in the doorway. The unfortunate overseer had been bound to the one remaining mast. At this point, he was mercifully unconscious, his back a raw and bloody mass of welts. The whip still rose and fell, and to Theadora's horror her son stood next to the captain, straight and proud, his young voice counting the strokes. "Thirty-seven, thirty-eight, thirty-nine . . ."

The sultan's youngest wife grew faint. She clutched at the doorframe, and drew several deep breaths. She had not wanted Halil to see this kind of thing. He was still a child. And yet, he did not seem at all distressed.

"Forty-three, forty-four, forty-five."

Theadora found she could not move her legs. She gazed around the deck. The entire ship's company was present, including a delegation from the galley slaves. Everyone stood silently watching.

"Forty-nine, fifty."

The rhinoceros-hide whip was dropped to the deck, the overseer cut down, and salt rubbed into his wounds. This elicited a faint groan, and Theadora was amazed that the man was alive—let alone that he had the strength to groan. The onlookers began to return to their tasks, and Theadora managed to find her voice.

"Captain, please attend me at once!" She turned and walked into her cabin for she would not embarrass him before his men.

"Madame?"

She rounded angrily on him. "How could you

allow a child to observe such brutality, let alone participate in it? The prince is only seven years old!"

"Please, Highness, hear me out. Perhaps you did not know, but this ship, which is named *The Prince Halil, belongs* to your son. A gift from his father. We on board all serve the child. I wanted to send him below before the punishment began, but Prince Halil said that as owner of the vessel it was his duty to mete out justice. The overseer served him, and the slaves who were drowned were his. That dragon who guards you approved, and would not wake you. Highness, though the prince is only seven, your son is all Ottoman. By law he is my lord. I could not refuse him."

"Why did you not inform me that the ship was my son's?"

"Madame," exclaimed the astounded captain, "as the child knew, I assumed you also knew. I only just realized you did not."

Theadora shook her head helplessly, but before she could say anything further there came a cry from the deck: "Pirates!"

Captain Hassan went white and threw himself through the cabin door, almost knocking down Iris who was just returning. The slavewoman was wide-eyed. "Mistress! Pirates! We cannot escape them! Allah have mercy!"

"Quick!" commanded Theadora. "Fetch my richest robes! The gold brocade will do. My finest jewels! Baba!" She called to a black slave entering the cabin. "Hurry! Get the prince, and garb him likewise!"

Several minutes later Theadora came on deck just in

time to see the pirate ship draw alongside the disabled royal Ottoman vessel. From its rigging hung some of the most evil-looking men Theadora had ever seen. God help us, she thought. But she stood still, proudly.

The sultan's young wife was a regal sight with the heavy gold brocade caftan, a magnificent necklace of rough-cut rubies, and matching dangle earrings of red gold and rubies. She wore several rings: a ruby, a turquoise, and a pink diamond on her left hand; a blue diamond and a sapphire on her right hand. Over her dark hair was a long sheer silver-and-gold-striped gauze veil. A smaller veil was drawn across her face.

Prince Halil was equally magnificent in striped pants of white silk and silver brocade, a long, open matching coat with a white silk shirt. He wore a little cloth-of-silver turban with a peacock feather sprouting from a large tiger's eye. He stood next to his mother, his hand upon the gold scimitar given him by his brother, Murad. The royal Ottoman couple were protectively surrounded by their slaves, the woman Iris, and a half a dozen prime, young black fighting eunuchs.

Because of his two royal passengers and also because of the pitiful state of the ship, Captain Hassan surrendered immediately to the obvious disappointment of the pirate crew who were spoiling for a fight. The pirate captain stood out easily among his men. He was a tall blond giant with a short, dark gold beard. He wore white pantaloons sashed in black silk. His bare chest was covered with a mat of tight gold curls. He was sun-bronzed, very muscular, and carried a beautiful gold scimitar in his hand. His feet were shod in knee length boots of softest leather, with gold designs stamped on them.

At his order, Captain Hassan and his three officers were lined up and forced to their knees. At a nod from their captain, four pirates stepped forward, quickly strangled their unfortunate prisoners, and then threw the bodies overboard.

The ship was now deathly quiet. The blond giant turned slowly and looked over the assembled crew of *The Prince Halil*. "I am Alexander the Great," his deep voice boomed. "I sail out of Phocaea. I offer you a fair choice. Join me, or die as your captain and his officers died."

"We join you!" the Ottoman sailors shouted with one voice.

Alexander the Great now turned to Theadora and her son. Instantly the black eunuchs closed ranks and assumed a defensive position about the prince and his mother. "No!" she commanded them. They stepped aside, allowing the pirate captain a clear passage to her. He approached her and, for a moment he and Theadora stood silently, gauging one another. He had, she noted, eyes the color of a fine aquamarine—a clear blue-green.

Reaching out, he fingered the ruby necklace. Then he ripped it from her neck. All the while his blue eyes never left her violet eyes. Swiftly he tore the veil from her face, but she did not flinch. He sighed. Flinging the ruby necklace to the deck, he said, "One look at your beautiful face, my exquisite one, has rendered the jewels worthless. Is the rest of you as incomparably fair?" His hand went to the high neck of her brocade robe, and then it was she who spoke.

"I am Princess Theadora of Bursa, wife to Sultan Orkhan, sister to the emperor and empress of Byzantium. The child is the sultan's and my son, Prince Halil. Unharmed, we should bring you a great fortune. But if you continue to make extravagant gestures—" She glanced first towards the necklace on the deck, and then down to his hand which still held her gown, "you could easily end your days a poor man."

His eyes swept admiringly over her and it seemed he was weighing her words. Then he laughed. "What a pity I value gold so highly, beauty. I should have enjoyed teaching you how to be a real woman." He laughed again as the color flooded her face. "I must transfer you to my ship," he continued, "but you and your party will be safe, my lady. We will be in Phocaea by nightfall, and then I will house you in my palace until your ransom is paid." His big hand then moved from her neckline to cup her chin. Shaking his head, he sighed. "Keep yourself veiled, madame, or I may regret my practical nature. I already feel myself growing reckless."

He turned abruptly away from her and began calling out orders. *The Prince Halil* was to be sailed into Phocaea by a skeleton crew where it would be repaired and join the pirate navy. Its crew and galley slaves would be dispersed among other ships once they arrived in Phocaea. Theadora and her party were helped aboard the pirate vessel and taken to the captain's cabin, where they would remain until they reached their destination that night. Still exhausted from the previous night, Theadora made herself comfortable on the captain's bed with Halil for company. Iris guarded the door while the princess and her son slept.

In the very late afternoon they reached the pirate city of Phocaea, and Alexander sent for a barge to transport his captives to his palace. It was located on the sea some two miles from the city. Sitting amid the velvet and silk cushions of the luxurious vessel with her captor Theadora learned that he was the younger son of a Greek nobleman and therefore forced to make his own way in life. Since his youth he had loved the sea and had turned to it for what was proving a most rewarding living.

His wife, a childhood sweetheart, was dead now. He had not remarried, but rather kept a harem of women in the Eastern way. He assured Theadora that she would not be cloistered. She would be free to roam the grounds of his estate, providing she gave him her word that she would not try to escape. Theadora gave it. Had she been alone she would not have acquiesced so easily, but she had Halil and Iris to consider.

As if he read her thoughts he inclined his head towards her son. "I am glad they are with you, beauty. You are too lovely to have to be caged."

"Do you read minds also, pirate?"

"Sometimes." Then in a lower voice. "You are too lovely to belong to an old man, beauty. If you had a lusty young man between your legs it might take the sadness from your eyes."

She flushed crimson and said, in a soft, angry voice, "You forget yourself, *pirate!*"

The aquamarine eyes laughed at her outrage, and the man's mouth mocked her. "My lineage is almost as good as yours, *princess*. Certainly the younger son of a Greek noble is equal to the younger daughter of a Greek usurper."

Her hand flashed out, leaving its imprint on his cheek. But before she could hit him again he caught her by the wrist and held the hand in a firm grasp. Fortunately, Iris and Halil were too interested in the sights of the busy pirate harbor to witness the exchange between Theadora and Alexander. Slowly, the pirate captain turned Theadora's hand palm upwards and, holding her startled glance with his, placed a burning kiss in the center of the soft flesh.

"Madame," his voice was dangerously low, "you have not yet been ransomed. Another man might fear to take what is the sultan's, but I do not. And who would know if I did?"

The kiss had sent an almost painful ache through her. Now, white with shock, she whispered shakily, "You would not dare!"

He smiled his slow, mocking smile. "The idea is beginning to tempt me, beauty."

The barge bumped against the side of the marble quay, and Alexander leapt out to help tie it to his pier. Well-trained slaves appeared to help Theadora and her party from the boat and led her to her quarters. The royal party had three spacious rooms with a private bath and a terraced garden which faced west over the blue sea. A sweet-faced slavegirl showed Theadora a wardrobe filled with her clothes, brought from the ship. Halil and Iris found that their possessions had been brought as well.

"The master does not steal from his guests," said the slavegirl primly, and Theadora bit back an urge to laugh.

They did not see Alexander again that day. A well-cooked meal accompanied by an excellent wine was served to them. After the ordeal of the storm they all sought their beds early.

Theadora awoke in the night to find Alexander standing over her bed. In the moonlight that poured through the windows she could see the desire on his face. She moved to turn her naked body from his sight and trembled when he said, "I know you are awake, beauty."

"Go away," she whispered fiercely, not daring to turn back to face him. "If anyone knew you were here, do you think the sultan would pay to get me back?"

"You forget that this is my house, beauty."

"Even your house has its quota of spies," she answered. "Go away!"

"If it will reassure you, I entered the room through a little-used interior passage—the existence of which is known by no one other than myself. Besides, your son sleeps the sleep of the innocent and your slave drank a cup of wine tonight that had a sleeping draught in it. Even now she is snoring like a pig."

"You dared?" She was incredulous.

"My very existence is a dare," he replied. "Come, beauty, do not turn from me." Reaching out, he turned her to face him. "Christos!" His voice was awed. "The body more than rivals the face!"

She shrank from him. "You can rape me," she said

quietly, "and though I cannot hope to overcome you I will later find a way to kill myself. I swear it, Alexander!"

"No, beauty, no," he protested, drawing her into the circle of his arm. "Do not speak such foolishness to me." His hand moved boldly, with assurance, making her tremble with a terrible mixture of fear and open desire. "I will not force you, for you are a guest in my house. But, ah, these sweet breasts will be very sad to go unloved this night." Ever so gently he fondled the soft swell of flesh. The coral nipples sprang erect, and a little moan escaped her throat

"Ah, beauty, you want it as much as I do! Why do you fight me?"

"Please!" She pushed his hands away. "You say you will not force me because I am a guest in your home. Your honor forbids it, does it not? Think then of *my* honor, Alexander. For though I am but a woman, I too have my honor. I am Orkhan's wife, the mother of his son. I do not love my husband, and I will not deny that my body hungers for a young man's touch. But as long as my lord lives, it will not be! You see, captain pirate, I too, have my honor to consider. Even if no one but us knew, I should feel that my honor was compromised. Can you understand that?"

He smiled ruefully. "I had heard that John Cantacuzene had an overeducated daughter. You reason like a Greek, beauty! Very well. I am bested for now, and I will leave you in peace this night. But I cannot promise to stay away forever. My baser instincts may overcome me.

"I will, however, exact a small vengeance before I

go, for I do not think I shall quench the fire you have raised in me."

And before she understood his intent he had clasped her tightly in his arms, their bodies touching from breast to thigh. They sprawled across the length of the bed, and she felt the softness of his chest hair tickling her bare breasts, the hardness of his manroot butting against her shaking thighs. His lips captured hers in a searing kiss, his tongue raping her mouth with a naked passion that left her nearly fainting. She wanted to yield to him. She wanted his hardness deep inside her!

Releasing her, he smiled and stood up. "May you and your honor enjoy your stay in my house, Theadora, wife of Orkhan," he said mockingly.

Frozen with shock, she watched as he disappeared behind a wall-hanging. Only when she was sure he had left the room did she weep. He had reminded her of something she had managed to hide from herself for all these years. He had reminded her that she was a woman. A young woman. With the same hot desire running through her as any young woman had.

She had no outlet for her hunger. Her husband's touch disgusted her, and the memory of Murad burned deep within her secret heart. She almost regretted sending Alexander away. His body had felt wonderful against hers, and she sensed that he would be a magnificent lover. Was he right? Indeed, who *would* know? Could she live with her guilt if she allowed the liaison? Theadora wept bitter tears, for she could see nothing but a long and loveless future stretching endlessly ahead of her.

Chapter 9

THE MAN WHO CALLED HIMSELF ALEXANDER THE GREAT was not a reckless gallant, but a shrewd businessman. His main base, the city of Phocaea was located between the emirates of Karasi and Sarakhan, opposite the island of Lesbos. Though Phocaea had a ruler, it was Alexander and his pirates who brought prosperity to the city and who really controlled it. Alexander also had bases on the islands of Chios, Lemnos, and Imbros. He had spies and coast-watchers on the smaller islands as well, thereby effectively controlling the shipping lanes in the Aegean and the areas leading to the Straits of the Dardanelles, into the Bosporus, and beyond into the Black Sea.

Merchants whose vessels regularly traveled these waters paid him an annual tribute plus a percentage of the proceeds of each voyage. There was no chance of cheating Alexander—for they were required to stand for inspection prior to each voyage. Without the inspection there was no pendant issued for their top masts. And ships without Alexander's color-coded pendants were considered fair game and usually had their entire cargos confiscated.

Alexander preferred to receive his tribute in gold,

but he would accept merchandise. Twice yearly, several of his ships sailed west into northern Europe where their cargos of silk, perfumes, and spices brought the highest possible prices. They returned bringing their master gold and fair-haired, fair-skinned, light-eyed young slaves of both sexes. There were many large landholders who were willing—for a length of silk or a packet of precious spices or a silver coin—to send attractive, healthy, young serfs from their holdings into slavery. These young people were then sold to the highest bidder in private auction, attended only by wealthy connoisseurs. Alexander thus realized a double profit on his investments.

It was the Byzantine military intelligence service, known as the Office of Barbarians, that brought Alexander the Great to the Empress Helena's attention. Her current lover was the officer who ran the service. Knowing that her sister would be returning by sea from the Springs of Apollo, Helena sent word to Alexander that she would like Theadora and her son killed. For this service she agreed to pay a large sum of gold. Alexander was many things, but he was not a paid assassin. And he knew more about the Byzantines than they knew about him. Helena could not afford the money she offered.

But he was greatly in her debt for the information she had unwittingly tendered him. The sultan's wife and son would fetch a very high ransom. He had therefore arranged to know when and by what route their ship was sailing. He would have lost them but for the storm which so kindly deposited them off his city's coast.

One glimpse of Theadora had cost Alexander his heart. She was lovelier than any woman he had ever known. It did not bother him a bit that she was the sultan's wife. He was a ruler in his own right and what he wanted, he took. But he had miscalculated when he assumed that she would be eager enough for love to forget all else. He had pushed her too far and too quickly. To win her he would have to out-think her. Alexander was a hunter by nature, and the thought of the chase was quite stimulating. It would be weeks before his council could agree on a ransom price for the princess and her son. After that further time would be spent in negotiations. Several months would go by before the ransom was settled and paid. He had time.

For the next few days Theadora saw little of her captor, and she was quite relieved. It had not been easy to withstand his assault. She remained in her apartments, and for exercise she walked out several times daily, in the garden, with Iris for company. She rarely saw Halil. He was busy with his new friends, Alexander's several sons by his concubines, even eating and sleeping with them.

"It is better this way," she told Iris. "To him it is simply an adventure. He will bear no scars from the experience."

After several weeks Alexander appeared in her apartment one evening, carrying a chess set. "I thought we might enjoy a game together," he said pleasantly.

She smiled. "How do you know I play?"

"Because you are your father's daughter and flawless in the art of logic. The game of chess is an exercise in logic. However, if you don't play then I shall teach you, beauty."

"Set up the board, Alexander, and prepare to be beaten. Iris, fetch some chilled wine and some cakes for us."

The chessboard was a work of art. Its inlaid squares were of ebony and mother-of-pearl, its pieces carved from black onyx and pure white coral. They played two games that evening. He won the first easily, for she played cautiously. Then she took the second from him, playing with an almost reckless abandon.

He laughed as she checked his queen. "You were only gauging my measure in the first game," he accused.

"I was. I could hardly beat you if I did not study your method of playing."

"I have never been beaten by a woman."

"If you continue to play with me, my lord Alexander, you will have to take that chance. I play to win, and I will not contrive to lose simply because I am a woman."

"Spoken like a true Greek!" he approved teasingly.

Now it was her turn to laugh. "I am not sure whether you approve or disapprove, Alexander."

"I am Greek born, beauty, and therefore am used to women of great intellect. But I have lived here in Asia long enough to understand the Eastern treatment of women. It has its good points also. But it's been a long time since I've really *talked* to a woman."

"It has been a long time since I've really talked to a man," she rejoined.

For a moment he was startled. Then he chuckled heartily. "I forgot that you live in a harem, beauty, with only eunuchs and other women for company. Are you not often bored?"

"Sometimes, but not these last few years. My son is bright, and I have spent my time in teaching him. Then, too, I work to return Christian captives to Byzantium. When we return to Bursa, however, Halil will leave me for his own court at Nicea. I have had my son longer than most sultan's wives are allowed their sons."

"What will you do when he is gone, beauty?"

She shook her head. "I do not know. I begged my lord Orkhan to allow me to go with Halil to Nicea—but he will not."

"He is right," replied Alexander. "The boy needs to be on his own, else he will never be free of your protective skirts. Remember that in ancient Sparta boys were taken from their mothers at age seven."

She made a face at him and he chuckled. "Besides, beauty, if I were your husband, I should not want you leaving me."

"Nonsense. Orkhan has a harem of women, many of whom are far lovelier than I am. He does not need me."

"Then why return to him? Stay with me, and be my love. I will make it so sweet for you, beauty, that you will never want to leave me."

She laughed shakily. "I thought you were a man of business, my lord Alexander. If I seriously considered your flattering offer, you would lose a great deal of money. Therefore, I know you cannot possibly be serious.

He regarded her with his jewellike eyes and then said quietly, "May I come and play with you again, beauty?" She nodded. "Then I will leave the board and pieces," he said. And he departed.

She sat, heart pounding, hands tightly clutching each other within the cradle of her lap. He *had* meant it! *He had really meant it!* She was the sultan's wife, and yet he boldly paid her court. What would happen if she accepted him? Would Orkhan really care, surrounded as he was by all those lush young beauties? She shook her head. This was madness! Of course Orkhan would care! Were she the humblest slavegirl he would care, for she was his property. What was the matter with her, to even consider such a thing? She was Theadora Cantacuzene, a princess of Byzantium. She was a wife! A mother! Not some silly girl!

He did not come the next night, but on the following evening they played two games—Theadora winning the first and Alexander winning the second.

"This time," he teased, "I have studied your method of play."

"We appear to be well-matched," she answered him. Then, realizing that he might misunderstand her words, she blushed and hastily added, "in chess."

"Indeed," he replied calmly. "If you should find the need for company, please feel free to visit the women of my house. They are all very curious about the sultan's wife."

"Perhaps some day," she answered absently. But as the weeks dragged on she began to feel the need for company. She would go to the harem only once, she decided, for undoubtedly the women of Alexander's harem would prove as silly and as vicious as those in her husband's harem.

To her surprise she was greeted cordially by all of the pirate's women, including his three favorites—all of whom had children by him. They were pretty women with docile dispositions, whose only apparent goals in life were to make their lord and master happy. She found herself wondering if they satisfied the raging passion she had seen lurking behind the well-mannered man. Quickly she brushed the thought away, flushing guiltily.

Alexander's harem was a place of peaceful pleasures. Everything was a delight to the touch. The air was sweetly scented with exotic flowers. Soft music was played by the skilled fingers of pretty young girls. The food was delicious, and it was served beautifully. What Adora did not know was that the harem's menu was comprised mainly of foods thought to be aphrodisiacs—and therefore conducive to the subtle arousal of the females.

Theadora did not usually seek the company of other women. But Alexander's concubines were most kind to her, quite unlike the women of Orkhan's house. They were overwhelmingly curious about her life in Bursa and in Constantinople as well. It was hard to resist their flattering pleas for stories about her life.

They were also curious about the sexual practices of Ottoman women. Perhaps they hoped to learn something new, something to please their lord. With a dignified skill she had not had occasion to use before, she enlightened them in several areas. They were delighted. Often Theadora found herself breaking into gig-gles. For the first time in her life, she had friends of her own age. And though they were not her intellectual equals, she enjoyed them. She was having almost as much fun in captivity as her little son was having. Her particular favorite was Cerika, an adorable Circassian girl with a delightful sense of humor and the sweetest nature Theadora had ever encountered in a woman.

Soon she found herself spending her time with them, not only in the harem, but in the baths and at meals as well. It was as if she had joined Alexander's harem . . . but for one aspect. As Alexander was a vir-ile man there was not a night that he did not call for one of his women. In the morning there would be much good-natured teasing of the fortunate one, and recently there had been questions regarding whether their new skills were pleasing the master. Caught in this sensual, silken atmosphere, Theadora began to grow edgy. It was easy to deny her own sensuality when she could live a sensible, orderly life, but her life in Alexander's house was neither.

The weeks went by. The pirate captain knew that his beautiful captive was weakening, but the progress to her capitulation was far slower than he had hoped. She was a very stubborn woman, and though she had relaxed a great deal, she had yet to forget who she was.

The price for her ransom had been agreed upon, and word came from the sultan that he was preparing to send the gold. Now Alexander debated with his conscience—a thing he rarely did. As usual, however, his own desires won out. For, charming as he was,

Alexander was a hedonist. He *wanted* the beautiful Theadora, and he fully intended to have her.

Given more time, she might have allowed her own desires to rule her head—but there was no more time. The sultan's emissary was less than two weeks away. Alexander knew he must act now or lose his chance. If he did not taste of her charms, and if she returned to Bursa, he would make himself sick with longing. Alexander was a man used to getting his way.

Theadora's seduction was carefully planned. One evening, Alexander sent his regrets that he would be unable to join her for their chess game. She was disappointed, for the games had become an almost daily pleasure, and she enjoyed them. He sent, by way of apology, a round crystal bowl filled with Gold of Ophir roses, a small flacon of golden Cyprus wine, and a silver dish of green grapes. Theadora, feeling sorry for herself, sent Iris to bed and drank all the wine herself. Then she fell into a deep sleep.

She dreamed a strange dream. Sightless, for she could not seem to see, she was led from her bed. Then, suddenly, she could see again. A silk had been bound about her eyes. Looking about she saw that she was in a windowless square room. The walls and ceiling of the room were black. One quarter of the way up the wall was a gold border in the ancient Greek key-and-scroll design. Above it were beautiful paintings of men with women, women with women, men with men, and men and women with animals—in various attitudes of sexual play. Above the drawings was another gold border.

The room was lit by flickering hanging lamps,

burning a musk-scented oil. As Theadora stood there two young women appeared at her side and began to massage her body with a scented cream that left her skin tingling, both hot and cold. Slowly, sensuously, they caressed her until the exquisite sensations assailing her flesh threatened to cause her to faint.

Before her, on a raised and carpeted dais, amid multi-colored silk and velvet pillows, reclined the three favorite ladies of Alexander. They were, as was she, completely nude. Smiling, they beckoned her to join them. Moving slowly forward, she allowed them to draw her down among them. They were so kind to her, and it didn't seem at all strange when they began to caress her body. It was the loveliest dream! Their hands were so soft. They fondled her breasts, kissing and nuzzling at the nipples, then sending a painful ache through her as they sucked hard on the coral points.

Cerika's hands strayed downward and stroked the insides of Theadora's thighs, playfully touching at her womanhood. Theadora sighed deeply, trembling when her friend lowered her blond head and kissed her within the soft, sensitive cleft of her sex. Now the three women held a cup of wine to Adora's lips, urging her to drink. When she did so her feeling of well-being increased.

Then, from the darkness, Alexander appeared. Naked, he looked like the marble statue of the ancient God, Apollo. Tall, with well-muscled legs and a flat torso, he was deeply bronzed by the sun. Between his powerful thighs was a triangle of gold hair, and springing forth from the tight gold curls was a long, swollen manroot.

Theadora felt no fear, for she wanted him. And as this was but a delightful dream, she felt free to indulge. Two of the other women spread her legs wide. Smiling, Theadora opened her arms to him. For a moment he stood spread-legged above her, a smile of triumph on his handsome face. Then, kneeling, he straddled her so that he might enjoy the full breasts, and she felt his maleness against her belly. Gently he played with her, pulling the long nipples out, rolling them between his thumb and forefinger. She tingled all over with the full pleasure of it, and rubbed her navel against the pulsing muscle that throbbed against her.

He nibbled on her lips, placing little kisses at their corners and on her closed eyelids. For the first time, she heard his voice, and for a moment she was frightened. She did not recall ever hearing a voice in her dreams. But the sensations assailing her were so intense they banished fear. "What do you want me to do, beauty?" he said.

Slowly, she opened her heavy-lidded eyes and said in a sweetly serious voice, "You must make love to me, Alexander. You must make love to me," and then her eyes slowly closed again.

She could feel his hands grasping her buttocks, and she smiled with delight as she felt him drive deep into her willing body, raising her to the pinnacle of passion. He was enormous. He filled her to overflowing, and she thought she would surely die, for in truth she had never been so satisfied.

But soon the sunlight was in her eyes, and the sound of Iris's voice woke her from her deep sleep.

Her mouth was sour, and her head ached horribly. She had had such a strange dream . . . but she could not quite remember it. When she tried to concentrate, her head ached.

"Draw the drapes," she ordered her servant. "The wine that Alexander sent me last night has come close to assassinating me. God! My head hurts unbearably"

"You should not have drunk it all, my lady," scolded Iris. "You are not used to strong wines."

Theadora nodded regretfully. "I will stay in bed today," she said, "for to tell the truth I do not think I can get up." She lay back amid her pillows to doze in the cool, darkened room.

But sleep was restless, with wild and obscene images floating through her troubled mind. A dark room with flickering golden lights. Alexander's three favorites—nude, caressing her naked body. Cerika kissing her on the mouth and on the—oh, Christos! No!

Now she lay back, her clear camellia skin a startling white against the rainbow pillows. Above her, the ceiling was of Venetian glass, and she could see Alexander between her spread legs. She moaned desperately, trying to escape the dream, but she could not. In the dream he took her once, then took each of his favorites in turn, dismissing them afterward. She watched with amazement as he performed with his women. The man was a stallion and did not seem to tire. Alone now, he took her a second time, and turning her onto her stomach took her again in *that* manner.

She struggled to escape these images and woke to

find that it was already late afternoon. Her headache had gone but she felt confused and tense. Although her skin was now cool, the sheets were soaked with perspiration and were badly tangled. Again, she knew she had dreamed but she could only remember that it had had something to do with Alexander. They had made love together. She blushed with shame. How absurd!

Shrugging, she called to Iris to bring her a carafe of pomegranate juice and some food. After she had eaten she entered her bath, and the skillful fingers of her slave soothed away the last of her tensions. When Alexander arrived for their chess game she greeted him warmly.

"I missed you last night," she said. "I enjoy our games. Instead I drank that vicious wine you sent me, and I spent a restless, impossible night. When I awoke today I had a monstrous headache. I have been in bed all day."

He chuckled. "I should have warned you. The golden wines of Cyprus are deceptive, beauty. They appear to be sweet and mild but in actuality are wicked and potent."

"Could you not have warned me?" she said somewhat sharply. He chuckled again.

While they played she stole little looks at him from beneath her lowered lashes. He behaved no differently towards her. Surely if what she had imagined had really happened, they would not be carrying on in the usual manner! No! It had been a wild dream, brought on by the strong wine. What was the matter with her, to make her imagine such things? But she knew the answer to that: she longed for a man's love, and as long as her elderly husband lived, she was not apt to get it. Sighing, she made a careless move and heard her captor say, "Check and mate, beauty!"

She looked down at the board and made a little moue with her mouth. "Oh, Alexander, how stupid of me!"

He laughed at her distress. "It is not like you to give me a game, beauty." Then in a more serious tone, "What is it that troubles you?"

She shook her head. "Bad dreams, Alexander. Such very frightening bad dreams."

"Can you tell me? Talking often puts such dreams in their true perspective."

"No, my friend. It is far too personal. I behaved in a way most unlike myself, and it troubles me. I hope never to have such dreams again!"

He looked at her gravely, and his conscience nagged him painfully. He had drugged her and then seduced her in order to satisfy his own craving for her. She had been absolutely magnificent, for although she did not know it, she was made for a man's love. She had pleasured and had been pleasured.

His problem now would be to let her go, for he had fallen deeply in love with Theadora during the period of her captivity. One thought consoled him. When the old sultan died, she would be returned to her family in Constantinople. When that happened, he intended to have his father, who was a vassal of the emperor, ask for Theadora for him. His father would be delighted that he finally wished to remarry and give the family legitimate heirs.

"I do not think that you will be troubled further by such dreams, beauty," he said quietly. "And I have good news for you. Your ransom should be here shortly. Your captivity is almost over."

Smiling, she leaned across the chessboard and touched his hand. "I have been neither uncomfortable nor sad, my friend. Captivity in your house is very pleasant, and your kindness to my son and me will not be forgotten."

He rose. "I am sorry, Theodora of Byzantium, that your sense of duty is so strong. Else you might have remained here with me."

"Had I been childless, Alexander, perhaps I might have been tempted. But though my son can never be sultan, he is an Ottoman. I will not deny him his heritage."

He nodded with understanding. "You are an admirable woman, beauty. What a pity the men in your world will never really understand or appreciate you."

She smiled ruefully "Nevertheless, my friend, I shall survive, and perhaps in the end I shall even triumph."

He laughed. The big, even teeth seemed a white flash against his bronzed face.

"Yes," he said. "If any woman was meant to triumph, beauty, I believe it is you." Still chuckling, he left her.

Chapter 10

MURAD, THIRD SON OF ORKHAN, HAD RIDDEN HARD FROM the coast. He had left behind his escort several hours earlier, allowing his big black stallion to move as fast as it wished. The horse, barely winded, clattered into the tiled courtyard of Bursa Palace. Sliding from the saddle, the prince flung the reins to a slave and walked quickly into his father's house.

He was shocked by the old man's appearance. Orkhan looked his full seventy years. His hair and beard were snow white. His dark eyes were faded. His hand quavered slightly. He seemed to have shrunk, and his body even smelled of age. Yet, Orkhan's voice was strong.

"Sit down," he commanded his son. The prince obeyed silently. "Coffee?"

"Thank you, father." Murad waited, as good manners dictated, for the boiling hot coffee to be poured into the eggshell-thin cups. A slave handed him the coffee which he politely sipped before setting it upon the round brass tray table. "How may I serve you, my father?"

"Theadora and her son have been kidnapped," said Orkhan. "She took the boy to the Springs of Apollo in

Thessaly. Returning home, the ship got caught in a severe storm. Praise Allah that they were saved! But the ship was badly damaged and virtually helpless when it was attacked by pirates. They are being held for ransom in Phocaea by the pirate lord who calls himself Alexander the Great. I want you to take the ransom there and bring my wife and son back safely."

"I hear and obey, sire," replied the prince with a calm he did not feel. Orkhan went on to explain the financial arrangements, but Murad heard only a few words.

He had seen Theadora only once since her marriage to his father, and then they had sniped at each other. He had been hurt and had wanted to hurt in return. He grimaced. It was just like her to have gotten herself into this situation. She could not, of course, accept the fact that her son was a cripple. No! She must take the child across wild seas to a supposed healing place.

Murad listened with hidden, impotent rage as his father babbled on about his precious Adora and the importance of her safety. Orkhan spoiled her! She had always been cosseted and spoiled. But if she had been *his* woman he would have taught her obedience! Suddenly the memory of her swept over him with a force that stunned him. He remembered a lithe young body with soft breasts; a heart-shaped face with amethyst eyes that looked so trustingly up into his; a sweet, kissable mouth that quivered beneath his. Allah! She was a temptress, he thought bitterly. Given the chance, she would probably be a whore like her two scandalous sisters in Constantinople. Sophia had been killed recently with her latest paramour, and the empress Helena openly took lovers. He gritted his teeth and forced his mind back to what his father was saying. "... And you will personally escort them back to Bursa, my son. My poor Adora will undoubtedly have suffered greatly. And little Halil, too."

Pah! thought Murad, sourly. The witch will undoubtedly have been made quite comfortable. All she need do is dazzle the pirate chief with those fabulous eyes. As for my little half-brother, he is probably treating this whole thing as great adventure.

It did not help Prince Murad's temper to find, on his arrival in Phocaea, that his predictions were apparently correct. The sultan's third wife was quite elegantly housed, and Prince Halil was obviously doted on by his captor. In fact, the pirate seemed on excellent terms with both of his royal captives.

Murad arrived in Phocaea in late afternoon. It would have been impossible to complete the business of ransoming before nightfall. It would have also been an appalling breach of manners not to accept the pirate chief's hospitality. To Murad's surprise, this hospitality was not only lavish but in excellent taste.

First, however, he was taken to see that Theadora and Halil were safe, and were being honorably treated. Murad had been troubled all the way from Bursa. He had not seen her in nearly eight years. Had she changed? Probably. Byzantine women could run to fat, and his father liked women with meat on their bones.

It didn't help Murad's troubled mind that she was still willow slim, or that when she looked up her eyes were filled with an emotion he did not comprehend.

Then she stood and came towards him, her slim hands outstretched in welcome, her face a polite mask.

"Prince Murad. How very kind of you to come to our rescue. How is my lord Orkhan? I pray we have not distressed him greatly by our unfortunate situation."

He bowed curtly. "My father is fine. You have been well treated, Your Highness?"

"Lord Alexander has been the soul of courtesy from almost the first moment of our capture," she replied.

Was there a hint of laughter in her voice? Why did that big blond buffoon who called himself Alexander the Great look so uncomfortable? "I will complete the ransom negotiations tomorrow and come for you and Halil then," Murad said gruffly. "Be ready."

It was not, however, as easy as Prince Murad had anticipated. After a marvelous feast, excellent entertainment, and an exquisite blond Circassian virgin to warm his bed, he awoke to a rainy morning and the realization that his host was adamant in his demands.

"I told your father one hundred thousand gold Venetian ducats, Prince Murad. I am not a merchant to be haggled with. Nor are the princess and her son to be bargained over like yesterday's melons in the marketplace. I will accept the fifty thousand that you have brought me in exchange for the princess. But the boy must stay here in Phocaea until I receive the other fifty thousand ducats."

"Why not let the boy go, and hold his mother?"

Alexander laughed. "Because I am not a fool, Prince Murad. Your father has many women to amuse himself with, but few sons. If I let the boy go I might never hear from your father, but Princess Theadora is not going to allow your father to leave her only child in captivity. No, Highness, you may return to Bursa with the princess, but Prince Halil remains until I am paid in full."

"You do not know her, Alexander. She is stubborn. She will not leave the boy behind."

"That, Prince Murad, is your problem. But I think it is you who do not know her. She is a highly logical woman, and we Greeks have always valued women of intelligence. She will see the sense in this."

Murad gritted his teeth and went to tell Theadora that her son was to be left behind because Orkhan had not sent the full ransom. To his surprise she fell into neither hysterics nor a rage. She said quietly, "Your father is a great warrior and ruler, but he is a poor diplomat. Very well. Halil must remain for the present. I will have Iris stay with him, and I will go with you."

"Allah! What kind of mother are you? Will you not even *offer* to remain in the child's place?"

She looked surprised. "Would lord Alexander permit it? I think not, for he is no fool. Your father would surely haggle over my ransom for my only importance to him was Tyzmpe, which is now his. But he will not haggle over money for Halil, for my little son is his pride. In his old age, the boy is proof of Orkhan's continuing virility. That seems to be important to him."

Murad was infuriated by her calm, and even angrier that Alexander, on such short aquaintance, seemed to know her better than he did himself. "You hold yourself in low esteem, madame," he said coldly.

"Your husband wept and babbled over your safety."

"Did he really?" she asked, mildly interested. "How strange. I have not seen him in several years now, except on state occasions." She shrugged, then said, "I must tell my son of this turn of events. When do you wish to depart?"

"Within the hour."

"I shall be ready."

He sat quietly for a few minutes after she left him. She had changed from the innocent, willful girl she had been. She was serene now, but one thing had not changed. She was unable to hide her intelligence and in fact did not even try. He had grown older in the years since their first meeting, and he flattered himself that he had also grown wiser. Yet he still found it hard to accept the fact that Theadora had a mind. It was unnatural in a woman, especially a woman of such beauty. Women, beautiful ones in particular, were meant only for a man's pleasure, and a man did not want to discuss matters of importance with them. Allah! No!

He laughed aloud and went out into the rainy courtyard to make the final preparations for their departure. He had been forced to leave his escort outside the walls of Phocaea and had arrived alone. Alexander the Great made arrangements for Theadora to travel across the city in a closed litter. Once met by her escort, she would be transferred into a royal Ottoman vehicle, and the pirate's litter would be returned to him.

Theadora came into the courtyard dressed for travel, accompanied by Iris and Halil. The boy ran eagerly to his elder half-brother, and Murad lifted the child up. "So, Halil! You are finally to escape your mother, and be a man!"

"Yes, my brother!" The boy's eyes were shining with excitement. Then he lowered his voice and whispered confidentially, "I have learned many things of value to you, Murad. Because I am a boy they do not pay much attention to me, and they do not think I understand." He grinned impishly "But I do! When you are the sultan I shall be a great help to you, for I have a quick mind."

"Our brother, Suleiman, is our father's chosen heir, Halil."

The boy looked at his older brother with his mother's violet eyes and said, "That is true, Murad, but will you let him reign?"

"Wise monkeys often get their noses pinched, little brother," chuckled Prince Murad. As he put the boy down the child again flashed his impudent grin, then ran back to his mother.

Theadora held her son close. "I do not like to leave you, Halil, but if I do not deal with your father personally—" she hesitated. The boy laughed. "I should end up being a grown man with children of my own before you saw me again, mother," he finished for her.

Now it was her turn to laugh, and Murad was pained by the sight of their heads, so alike, close together. There was an intimacy between them that he could not penetrate, and he felt almost jealous. "We must go," he said gruffly. "I want to reach the outside walls before dark."

She looked across at him, and her gaze was so

understanding that he felt himself flushing. Bending, she hugged the boy tightly. "Obey Iris and do not annoy Alexander too greatly, my Halil. I love you, my little darling, and I will eagerly await the day we are reunited." She kissed him, and then climbed into the waiting litter.

Alexander came into the courtyard and, leaning over, said quietly for her ears alone, "Do not fear, beauty. Your son will be as safe with me as my own sons are."

She smiled up and pressed his arm with her fingers. "I know you will care for him well, Alexander. But do not spoil him too greatly, I beg of you. You know what a clever little monkey he is—so keep him occupied."

"I will, beauty, but who will keep *me* occupied now? I shall regret the loss of our chess games."

"So shall I. In my world the men do not treat their women with such respect. I shall miss you, Alexander. God keep you. Farewell."

"Farewell, beauty." The pirate chief straightened to find Prince Murad's eyes on him, blazing and angry. Holy Christos! thought Alexander. I wonder if she knows. So I have a rival for her! But I am aware of you, my fine prince, while you cannot really know *my* intentions. He walked over to where the prince sat mounted on his stallion. "Tell your father, my lord prince, that Prince Halil will remain safe and honored in my house until his ransom is paid." And without giving Murad a chance to reply, he turned and walked back into his house.

Furiously, the prince pulled at his horse and signaled the others forward. The slaves picked up the litter and moved out of the courtyard into the city. Alexander had provided them with a small but very impressive escort which accompanied them to the north gates of the city where the sultan's soldiers were waiting.

It had begun to rain again, and Prince Murad dismounted to carry Theadora from one litter to the other. She looked him full in the face for a moment before, modestly lowering her marvelous amethyst eyes. She was soft, and sweet, and her perfume intoxicated him. He stumbled, and she laughed low. He could feel a pounding in his temples. He wanted her! Dear Allah, how he wanted her!

Depositing her roughly within her litter he remounted his stallion. There were still some hours of daylight left, enough to put more miles between them and the city of Phocaea. He rode silently at the head of the cavalcade, and the soldiers accompanying him thought his grim look resulted from his having to leave Halil behind. Murad, Beg of the Ottoman, always prided himself on doing a job well.

But the truth was that the prince was thinking of the woman in the litter. He had never lacked for women, but Theadora Cantacuzene had been the only woman who had ever engaged his heart.

He remembered once telling her that when his father died he would make her his wife. It surprised him to admit to himself that he still wanted her. But not for his wife! No! He shook his head angrily. She was a Byzantine whore like her sisters and wasn't to be trusted. Look how she had tempted him just a while back and then laughed at his discomfort.

When it was nearly dark Murad gave the order to

make camp. The men were used to sleeping in the open, but a tent was set up for Theadora. To her delight it was quite luxurious. As she had left Iris behind to care for her son, she was waited upon by an elderly soldier. He brought her water warmed by the fire for washing, and he flushed and grinned foolishly when she thanked him sweetly.

Her tent had been set upon a wooden platform whose rough boards were covered with colorful, thick wool rugs and sheepskins to keep out the cold and damp. It was not a big tent. There was a large brass tray table set on folding ebony legs, a charcoal brazier for heat, and a bed made of sheepskins covered with a velvet mattress and some silk pillows. Two small glass lamps hung on brass chains from the tent poles.

The old soldier returned bringing her food—small pieces of barbecued lamb with pepper and onions, seasoned with rosemary and a touch of olive oil, and served over a bed of saffroned rice. Accompanying it was a small, flat loaf of bread, just baked in the coals of the fire, a skin of icy water from a nearby stream which had been flavored with orange essence and cinnamon, and two crisp apples. She thanked the soldier. Asking after the prince, she was told that he was eating with his men.

Feeling a little sorry for herself Theodora prepared to eat alone. She had long since gotten over her anger towards Prince Murad. Today, when he had stumbled carrying her, she had felt his heart pounding and had laughed with joy to think he still cared for her. Suddenly all the old feelings rushed to the surface, surprising her with their intensity.

She had not shared Orkhan's bed for several years, and though her husband had once roused her physically, only her fantasies had kept her from going mad. In his old age, in the desperate attempt to preserve his potency, Orkhan had turned to perversion. The last time she had shared his bed he had included a ten-year-old virgin from the Nile River basin, a gold-skinned child with lovely onyx eyes. Orkhan had forced Theadora to sexually stimulate the girl while he watched and became aroused. He had then brutally deflowered his screaming victim while Theadora vomited the contents of her stomach over the side of the bed. Never again, to her vast relief, was she ever commanded to share her lord's bed. Had she been asked again, she would have suffered death rather than face another such experience.

Remembering back to the precious hours she had spent with Murad in the orchard, it seemed that was the only time in her life she had ever known any tenderness from a man. Would he be as tender if he were her husband? Would she ever know? Theadora licked her fingers thoughtfully. Then, after rinsing them in a small copper ewer, she picked up an apple and bit into it.

"Did you enjoy your supper?"

Startled, she looked up to find that Murad had entered the tent.

"Yes," she answered, "but I have been lonely. Why did you not eat with me?"

"A woman? Eat with a woman? Has my father taken to eating with his women?"

"Of course not! But this is different. I am the only

156

woman here, and I have not even a slave to keep me company. You are the only person of rank available to me."

He chuckled, his good humor restored. "I see. You only want my company because you are a princess and I am a prince. I did not think you were a snob, Adora."

"No! No! You misunderstand me," she protested, blushing.

"Then explain it to me," he teased, kneeling down before her amid the cushions. She raised her lovely face to him. "What I meant was that since our situation is an informal one, I thought you might keep me company while I ate my meal."

He looked back at her with jet black eyes, and then before she realized what was happening he had caught her to him and was kissing her. The world about her exploded into a million glittering pieces. Oh, God! Oh, God! His mouth was so sweet! The kiss was tender, yet at the same time passionate. For a minute she gave herself up to it completely, savoring the warmth and sweetness of him. It had been so long, so terribly long!

Then as her senses cleared she pulled her head free and whispered frantically, "No, Murad! Please, no! This is wrong!"

His hand moved up her back, tangling itself in her dark hair. "Be silent, my sweet Adora," he commanded, and his mouth took possession of hers again. This time, however, he kissed her hungrily, his lips searing hers, savagely demanding her complete surrender. Helpless to control the desire welling within her, she slipped her arms up and around his neck, and drew him down among the pillows.

Time lost all meaning for her. She knew that what they did was morally wrong within the precepts of both their religions, yet so great was their need of each other that the raging hunger wiped everything else out of their minds. She knew that he had completely unbuttoned her blouse for his lips now ran riot over her throat, moving downward to her breasts, hungrily sucking on the nipples until they were sore with longing.

He found his way beneath the silk of her full pantaloons, and stroked her between her quavering thighs, finding her already wet with fierce desire. His hand teased deliciously at her, and she squirmed under his touch, a low sob escaping her as he gently thrust two fingers into her body. She arched and strained, desperately seeking a fulfillment that would not, could not, seem to come.

"Easy, my sweet Adora," he soothed, "do not strive so hard, my love. It will happen." He was kissing her again, but this time his lips moved to her ear, and he whispered softly, "I want you, Adora, but as a man wants a woman. I don't want to play lover's games any longer. I want to be deep within your sweetness, crying for joy of the beautiful thing we will do together."

She shivered, weakening, and he nibbled at her little earlobe. "Open your legs to me, Adora. I am hot to fuck you, my lovely Byzantine whore. Let me taste the delights you have so willingly given to my besotted father and your Greek pirate lover."

She froze, unable to believe what she had just heard.

"I shall be a better lover to you, my dove, than either of them," he went on, heedless.

Then suddenly he howled with pain as her knee caught him in the groin. She scrambled up, eyes shooting amethyst fire, frantically buttoning her blouse, desperately striving to hold back the tears that were already pouring down her cheeks.

"Though Halil's the joy of my life, I *never* went willingly to your father's bed," she raged at him. "And though it is none of your business, Alexander was certainly not my lover! Unlike you damned Ottomans who consider a woman's use to be limited to a man's bed, the Greeks admire women of intelligence. They are not afraid, as you seem to be, that a woman of learning may render them impotent. And as to my own intelligence, I am beginning to doubt its very existence. Else how could I have believed you still cared for me as you once did?" She was crying hard now, not caring how she looked. "I hate you! Get out of my tent or I shall scream. Your father's soldiers will not hesitate to kill the rapist of the sultan's wife!" She turned her back on him.

Slowly, he pulled himself up, using the brass tray table to brace himself. For a moment a wave of dizziness assailed him in echo of the pain, but he breathed slowly, deeply, and his head cleared. "Theadora. I am sorry, my dove."

"Get out!"

"I have ached for you since the first moment I saw you falling from your convent wall. I was physically ill when you were made my father's wife. And yesterday I arrived in Phocaea to find that peacock of a pirate openly solicitous of you."

"So you assumed I had played the whore. I shall never forgive you! Never! Get out!"

"I thought you were like your sisters."

"Get out!"

"My father is old, Adora. Soon he will join his ancestors, and I will claim you as I promised so long ago."

"I would die before I ever yielded to you!"

He laughed harshly. "No, you won't, my dove. You were like a bitch in heat but a few moments back. You will come when I command it." And turning on his heel, he walked from the tent.

Theadora clenched her fists tightly. He was right! God curse him, he was right! She wanted him as much as he wanted her. And sinking to the pillows, she wept all her bitter tears.

Chapter 11

ORKHAN THE SULTAN GAZED AT HIS THIRD WIFE. IN anger she was especially beautiful. It made him almost sorry he could no longer function with her as a man. He kept his face impassive, though he was mightily amused. There was not another woman in his harem who would dare to shout at him, and though he would punish her for it, he admired her courage.

His hand flashed out, slapping her cheek hard enough to leave an imprint. "Be silent, Adora! Halil is my son also, but now that I have found out that your sister, Helena, is behind this kidnapping, I will not pay that Greek pirate another dinar!"

"Do you mean to abandon *my son*?"

"No, my dear, I do not mean to abandon Halil. And again I remind you that he is my son also. Since your sister was imprudent enough to attempt to get at me by using my wife and son, I feel that Byzantium must pay the remainder of the ransom. I should also tell you that, were Alexander the Great not so greedy, you and Halil would now be dead. Your sister wanted him to murder you, but he knew she could not pay him, and he decided that you two were more valuable to him alive than dead. A wise fellow, that pirate."

Theadora's eyes were wide with shock. "But why, my lord? Why does my sister wish me and her innocent nephew dead? I have never harmed her."

Orkhan put a kindly arm about his wife and shook his head wearily. Poor Adora. She had been much too sheltered. It was past time she grew up. If she did not, he feared for her safety after his death. "Your sister," he said, "hoped that your death and Halil's would cause my death. Then she intended to foster dissension between Suleiman and Murad. When they had destroyed each other, only my poor, mad son, Ibrahim, would remain. Though our laws forbid a mentally or physically impaired heir, there are those who would crown Ibrahim and use him. Your sister knows this. Trouble within our Ottoman realm would suit Byzantium."

"So you will force John Paleaologi to pay the rest of Halil's ransom. He will have to do it, of course, as we are much stronger than he is."

The sultan smiled, noting her use of the word "we." Theadora continued, "But I would punish my sister for what she has attempted to do."

"And what would you do, my dear?"

"Helena has two sons, my lord, but only one daughter—upon whom she dotes. My niece, Alexis, is the same age as our son, Halil. In her correspondence with me, Helena has often bragged of the girl's blond beauty. My sister hopes to marry her daughter into the House of Savoy or the royal House of Muscovy. She has also, as you know, delighted in making a mockery of our marriage because I am a Christian, and you, my lord, are a Moslem. What if we demand Princess Alexis as a bride for our son, Prince Halil? Helena dare not refuse us lest we destroy her."

The sultan chuckled. Perhaps he would not have to worry about his little Theadora after all! Her looks were most deceptive. "You are diabolical, my dear," he said, pleased.

She looked directly at him, her eyes hard. "We revere the same holy book, my lord. Does not the Bible say 'an eye for an eye' "?

He nodded slowly. "It will be as you suggest, Adora, and I will even ask for your advice in this delicate negotiation since you obviously know the empress and her spouse better than I had suspected."

So the citizens of the fast-shrinking empire of Byzantium found that their new emperor, John Paleaologi, was as much at the mercy of the sultan as the old emperor, John Cantacuzene, had been. Orkhan was quite adamant. Not only was the young emperor to pay the remaining fifty thousand gold ducats of Prince Halil's ransom, but he was also to go to Phocaea himself to escort the boy back to Bursa.

The empress Helena shrieked her frustration and outrage. There was barely half that amount in the whole royal treasury, and then only because the taxes had just been extorted from the already overtaxed population. The jewelry that the empress had carefully been collecting from her lovers would have to be sold. The royal jewels had been mere paste imitations for many years.

Helena inveigled her put-upon spouse to besiege Phocaea instead of paying the ransom. Both Orkhan and Theadora were amused by the emperor's action and Helena's desperate attempt to hold on to her jewelry. They knew Halil would be safe with Alexander, and Orkhan assured Alexander that he would be paid.

The sultan used the absence of the Byzantine forces from Thrace as an invitation to invade it further. This invasion was met with virtually no resistance. Indeed, the local populace rather welcomed the Turks as liberators, having had enough of serfdom under their greedy local lords.

Alerted to this attitude by his wife, the emperor hurried back to Constantinople—only to be commanded back to Phocaea by the sultan. Weary, feeling more like a shuttlecock than a man, John Paleaologi set out for Phocaea *again* . . . only to encounter his returning fleet which had abandoned the siege and could not be persuaded to continue with it.

Desperate, the emperor begged Orkhan for mercy. The Ottoman sultan was now the recognized overlord of the hapless emperor, and he remained firm: the ransom must be paid. The year was now 1359, and John went humbly to his overlord at Scutari, a vassal asking pardon of his suzerain. He was told again that he must pay the ransom, now increased by a five-thousand-ducat fine. He had to accept the status quo in Thrace as well, and give his only daughter, Alexis, as bride to Prince Halil. Weeping bitterly, the emperor agreed. He had no choice.

But the empress was another matter. Helena screamed her palace down, tearing at her long blond hair. She threw whatever came to hand, and beat the slaves unfortunate enough to approach her. The wits of the court said one could not be sure what the empress regretted more, the loss of her jewels or the loss of Muscovy—for the negotiations betrothing Alexis to the Tzar's heir had almost been completed.

Those closest to the empress, however, realized that she doted upon her only daughter. Knowing this, the emperor quickly removed Alexis from her mother's care. Helena protested. "Do not let her go to the infidel," she begged her husband. "Oh, God! This is my bitch sister's doing! The Ottoman's whore has finally revenged herself on me by making my beloved child as low as she is!"

John Paleaologi's usual good nature evaporated, and he hit his wife so hard that she fell to the floor, bleeding from the mouth. "Your sister, Theadora," he said in low, even tones, "is a good and decent woman. She was wed according to the rites of our Church, which hardly makes her a whore. *And* were it not for her great sacrifice, your father would not have been able to hold out against my mother's forces as long as he did. And you, my dear wife, would not be the empress. Theadora practices her faith daily. She redeems Christian captives and sends them to safety. She is loyal and faithful to her husband. Frankly, Alexis will be safer at Orkhan's court than in this one."

"But she will have to share Prince Halil with others when they are grown enough to know what marriage is about!" wailed Helena.

A sarcastic smile lit the emperor John's lips. "I share you with many others, my dear, and I have survived," he said quietly.

Shocked into silence, the empress could do nothing but continue to prepare for her daughter's wedding. The emperor returned to Phocaea and paid the fifty-five thousand gold Venetian ducats to Alexander the Great. John was further humiliated by having to stand and wait while the gold was weighed out before his nephew was turned over to him. At last he proceeded by sea and then overland to Nicea where the betrothal was to be celebrated.

The empress had attempted to avoid her daughter's wedding, but the emperor made it quite plain that only Helena's death would be considered a valid excuse for her absence. After all the years of mocking her sister, Helena was finally going to have to face Theadora-and on her sister's own territory. She shivered. She didn't expect Thea to be merciful: if their positions were reversed, she would not be.

Strangely, the little princess Alexis was, delighted to be marrying her cousin, a boy her own age.

"I could have made you queen of Muscovy, or duchess of Savoy," sighed Helena.

"But Savoy and Muscovy are so far away, Mama," replied the child. "They say the sun rarely shines in the cold north. I should far rather wed my cousin, Halil, and be near you and father."

Helena hid her tears from her daughter. The little one was so sweet. Surely Thea would see that, and not wreak her vengeance upon an innocent child. Helena wondered if she would be that kindly if she were in her sister's shoes. Knowing the answer, she shivered again.

The few remaining weeks sped quickly by, and it

was time for Alexis of Byzantium to be delivered to Nicea. Accompanied by her mother, her two brothers, Andronicus and Manuel, and members of the royal court, she was rowed across the Sea of Marmara to Asia.

The galley that carried her was gilded completely with gold leaf. Its oarstems were gilded with silver and had scarlet lacquer paddles. The deck of the bridal galley was of highly-polished ebony. The rowers were perfectly matched young blacks and fair skinned northerners. The blacks wore gold satin ankle length pants, while the light-skinned, blond, blue-eyed northerners wore purple satin pantaloons. These young men had been picked by the empress herself. If she must be humiliated and abused by her younger sister, reasoned Helena, she would have need of comforting.

She let her eyes wander over the broad young backs, the muscles rippling smoothly—and considered the aesthetic effect of smooth black skin against her own fairness and of muscular golden thighs against her own long, white legs. A recent lover had compared her legs to perfectly matched marble columns, a description she found both original and highly pleasing.

She stretched languidly and sank deeper into the silken pillows. Alexis, resplendent in her nuptial finery, had dozed off. The empress let her sleep. The day was hot, especially out here on the water, and Helena was grateful for the awning that sheltered them. It was held up by four posts carved round with mythological creatures—dragons, unicorns, griffins, phoenix—all painted most realistically. The awning itself was striped in silver and blue. The draperies, now held back with braided-gold tasseled cords, were azure-blue and sea-green silk.

Helena had nodded sleepily for what seemed only a minute before the voice of the helmsman behind her was saying, "We approach the opposite shore, Hallowed Majesty."

Her eyes flew open. Reaching out, she shook her daughter. The child opened her blue eyes. "Are we here?"

"Almost, my love. I must stand outside now, and the drapes will be drawn. You will remember your part?"

"Yes, mama."

Helena looked over her daughter once more. The child's undergown was scarlet silk, the long tight sleeves buttoned in pearls from the wrist to the elbow. Her surcoat was cloth of gold with the two-headed eagle of Byzantium woven into it with scarlet threads. Her pale blond hair was loose about her shoulders and she was crowned with a small pearl-and-gold fillet. The empress gave her daughter a kiss on the cheek and rose, stepping out from beneath the awning. She drew the curtains closed behind her.

She, herself, was a stunning vision. Her own longsleeved undergown was of white silk, shot through with silver. The buttons, which appeared to be round diamonds, were actually clever paste imitations. The empress's surcoat, like her daughter's, was cloth of gold, but the two-headed eagle on Helena's garment was embroidered in silver threads and tiny brilliants. Her beautiful blond hair was parted in the middle and plaited into four braids, two on each side of her head, wound about her ears and tucked into silver wire cauls. Upon her head was a small gold coronet from which floated a sheer, silvery gauze veil. The empress of Byzantium was an impressive sight standing regally in the bow of the royal galley as it glided smoothly to dock.

She was greeted effusively by officials of the sultan's court and escorted to a waiting litter. Seating herself within, Helena peered through the curtains to see some dozen eunuchs boarding the royal gallery. They drew its draperies aside and the sultan's chief white eunuch, Ali Yahya, handed Alexis out. The little princess was instantly surrounded by the eunuchs, quickly veiled, and led to a second, waiting litter whose curtains were tightly drawn. The litter was surrounded by soldiers, eunuchs, and a host of naked, dancing, skipping children who sang songs of welcome and threw gold pieces and confections into the crowds who were lining the road. The procession made its way into Nicea.

The Christian wedding ceremony had been celebrated quietly, by proxy, prior to their departure from Constantinople. Now, as they traveled the small distance into the city, the moslem ceremony was being performed. The attendance of the bride was unnecessary. Therefore, when the eight-year-old princess, reached the palace in Nicea, she was already a married woman.

Two separate wedding feasts were being held. Sultan Orkhan and his sons Murad and Halil hosted the men. Princess Theadora would host the women.

Of the sultan's other wives, only Anastatia would be present, for Nilufer was in deep mourning. Her eldest son, Suleiman, had been killed several months before in a fall from his horse while hawking. The ridiculous accident had catapulted Murad into the undisputed position of heir to the Ottoman throne.

As the litters reached the courtyard of the haremlik, Theadora appeared at the top of a small flight of steps. And as the child was handed out of her litter, the sultan's youngest wife flew down the steps and, kneeling, folded the little girl into her soft arms. "Welcome, Alexis, my dear. I am your Aunt Theadora." She loosed the child and, holding her lightly by the shoulders, set her back a bit and removed her veil. Theadora smiled. "Ah, little one, how much like my mother, your Grandmother Zoe, you look. But then you have been told that many times before, I'll vow."

"Never, my lady aunt," came the reply.

"Never?"

"No, madame. They say I look like mama."

"A bit. But your mama's expression was never sweet like yours, Alexis. Our mother's, however, was always sweet. Therefore, I think you look more like my mother."

"Well, sister, I see you still speak bluntly. Have you no welcome for me?"

The sultan's youngest wife rose and looked at her sister after these many years of separation. Helena was four years older than Theadora, and her self-indulgent nature was beginning to show on her beautiful face. She looked closer to ten years older. She was petite, plumply voluptuous, and blond, whereas Theadora was tall, slender, and dark-haired. Also, while Theadora still had an innocence about her that was touchingly young, Helena's look was knowledge-able and as old as Eve.

For a brief, uncomfortable moment Helena felt the younger again, as she had so often felt with Theadora when they were children. She saw the gleefully malicious sparkle in those amethyst eyes as the low, cultured voice said to her, "Welcome to the *new empire*, my sister. I am truly happy to see you, especially on such a joyful occasion." She linked her arm in Helena's and led her into the haremlik where the other wedding guests awaited them. The little bride was taken off by the eunuchs to be presented to her husband and the sultan before being allowed to join them.

Her daughter gone, Helena spoke urgently to her sister. "Thea, I would talk privately with you before Alexis returns!"

"Come with me," came the reply.

And the empress of Byzantium followed the sultan's wife to a private chamber where they both sat down at a low table, facing one another.

"Bring fruit sherbet and honey cakes," commanded Theadora. No sooner had the slaves done her bidding than she dismissed them and, gazing at her sister, asked, "Well, Helena?"

The empress hesitated. Swallowing hard, she said, "We have not been close since childhood, my sister."

"*We were never close, my sister*," came the quick reply. "You were always too busy taunting me with the fact that you should be empress of Byzantium one day, and that I should merely be the 'infidel's' concubine."

"So now you take your revenge on me by forcing my beloved daughter into this matrimonial mockery!" burst Helena.

"*You* brought this on yourself, my sister!" snapped Theadora, her patience gone. "Had you not attempted to have Halil and me murdered, your daughter might well have been queen of Moscovy. My God, Helena! How could you!? Did you really think you could destroy the Ottoman by such perfidy? The empire of Constantine and Justinian is a dying old man, sister, but the empire of Osman the Turk is a young and vigorous boy. We are the future—whether you like it or not, Helena. You cannot destroy us by killing one woman and a small boy. Orkhan is nearing the end of his life, I fear, but Prince Murad will prove a strong sultan, I assure you."

"Why should Murad be sultan, Thea? If Orkhan chose in favor of Halil—" The empress paused a moment. Then she continued. "With a Christian mother and a Christian wife, Halil could easily be converted to Christ—and with him, his entire empire! My God, Thea! We would be sainted for fostering this marriage."

Theadora burst into laughter and laughed until she was weak and her eyes were filled with tears. Finally she said, "Helena, you have not changed. You are still a great fool! To begin with, Halil is a cripple—for which I thank the lord. Were he not, the first act his half-brother would perform upon becoming sultan would be to command Halil's death. If Halil were whole he might rule, but a physically or mentally impaired sultan is against the law. My son is a cripple, and the lady Anastatia's is a madman. My lord Orkhan has only Murad."

"And Murad's son," said Helena.

Theadora thanked God that she was sitting for she might have fainted otherwise. "Murad has no son," she said quietly in an amazingly steady voice.

"But he does, my dear," Helena whispered fiercely. "He got the boy on a Greek priest's daughter in Gallipoli several years ago. The prince will not officially recognize him because the girl's reputation is not as pure as one might expect of a holy man's daughter. She has nerve, however. She has named the boy Cuntuz, and refuses to allow him to be baptized, saying he is a Moslem as is his father."

Theadora was silent a moment, calming herself. Finally she asked, "Is this what you wished to speak privately to me about, Helena?"

"No! No! Who cares with whom the prince lies? It is my daughter. Please, Thea, be kind to her! I will do anything to insure your kindness towards Alexis. Do not take our quarrels out on my innocent child, I beg of you!"

"As I have often said, Helena, you are still a fool, and how little you know me. I have no intention of mistreating Alexis. She will be as my own daughter would be. I was never vindictive toward others, if you will remember." Theadora rose. "Come, my sister, the others await our arrival to begin the feasting." And she led Helena to the banquet hall within the harem, where Anastatia and the other women of the house waited.

There were the sultan's daughters and their daughters. There were the sultan's elderly sisters and cousins and their female offspring. There were his favorites and those who still hoped to catch his eye. There were the women of the Byzantine court who had accompanied the empress and her daughter. All in all, there were over a hundred females at the bride's feast. Theadora presented her sister to those few important enough to merit an introduction to the empress of Byzantium. By the time she had finished, Alexis was being ushered into the room.

The little bride was led to her mother-in-law who kissed her on both cheeks before signaling the eunuchs to lift the child onto a table where all might see her. There, in the presence of the other women, the bride was stripped of her Byzantine clothes and dressed in Turkish fashion. Only then did the feast begin.

When it was over, several hours later, Prince Halil arrived with his father. Together with Theadora, they escorted Princess Alexis to the Convent of St. Anna where she would live for the next few years.

The following day Emperor John and his two sons Prince Andronicus and Prince Manuel knelt before Sultan Orkhan and renewed their vows of vassalage to their overlord. The Byzantines then returned to Constantinople and the Ottoman royal family went home to Bursa.

Chapter 12

THEADORA LAY IN THE SHADOW WORLD BETWEEN SLEEP and waking. She could hear the distant sound of running feet and a pounding on her apartment doors that grew louder and louder. Then Iris was shaking her shoulder. Theadora shrugged her off, grumbling sleepily, but Iris persisted.

"My lady, wake up! You must!"

Slowly the mists cleared, and she half-woke. "What is it, Iris?"

"Ali Yahya sends word, my princess. The sultan is very ill. Ali Yahya believes, though the doctors have not said this, that Sultan Orkhan is dying."

Theadora was fully awake now. Sitting up, she asked, "Has he sent for me?"

"No, my lady, but it would be best if you were ready should the summons come."

With Iris's help Theadora dressed quickly. It was still dark as she paced restlessly about her antechamber. After the slaves laid a good fire in the tiled corner fireplace, she sent them back to their beds. Theadora preferred to keep her vigil alone. At last, Ali Yahya came for her and, catching up a sable-lined red-silk cloak, she followed him silently to the sultan's chambers.

The deathchamber was filled with doctors, the mullahs, and government and military officials. She stood quietly, holding the hand of Nilufer, Murad's mother, in an effort to comfort her. Nilufer, the sultan's wife all these years, truly loved Orkhan.

Anastatia, bent and broken since her son Ibrahim's suicide of only weeks past, stood by herself, her gaze vacant. The two princes stood together by their father's bedside, Murad's arm flung about young Halil's shoulders.

The women were brought to the bedside. The sultan lay quietly, obviously drugged and free of pain. The once mighty Orkhan, son of Osman, had shrunk to a frail scrap of his former self. Only his black eyes were lively as they moved from one to another of his family. He looked at Anastatia and whispered, "There's one who'll soon be joining me in death." The gaze moved on to the other two women. "You were the joy of my youth, Nilufer. And you, Adora, the joy of my old age." His eyes flicked to Murad "Guard the boy! He's no danger to you, and he'll soon be valuable to you."

"I swear it, my father," said Murad.

Orkhan struggled to sit up. Slaves propped pillows behind him. He was racked by a fit of coughing, and his voice was noticeably weaker when he said, "Do not stop until you have Constantinople! It is the key to all! And you cannot successfully hold the rest without it. Halil's supple mind will help you. Won't you, my boy?"

"Yes, father! I will be Murad's most loyal right arm . . . and his eyes and ears as well," the boy declared.

The ghost of a smile flickered on Orkhan's lips. Then his eyes moved past his family to a place across the room. "Not yet, my friend," he said so softly that Theadora was not sure she had heard him. The lamps flickered eerily, and the smell of musk, Orkhan's favorite perfume, was overpowering.

The chief mullah made his way to the sultan's bedside. "You have not yet confirmed your heir, Most High. It is not right that you leave us before doing so."

"Murad! Murad is my successor," gasped Orkhan, and another fit of coughing racked his fragile body.

The chief mullah turned to face the assemblage and raised his hands, palms up and outward. "Sultan Orkhan, son of Osman, Sultan of the Ghazis; Ghazi, son of Ghazi, has proclaimed his son Murad as his heir."

"Murad!" The assembled called in return. And then, as if with one mind, they all filed silently out of the room leaving the dying man with his wives and sons. The quiet was frightening. To calm her nerves, Theadora, lashes lowered, glanced about her. Poor Anastatia stood staring vacantly. Nilufer, Christian-born, prayed quietly for the man she had loved. Halil shuffled his feet with nervous boredom.

Her glance moved on to Murad, and she swayed with shock to find that he was staring straight at her. Color flooded her face, her heart pounded noisily in her ears, yet she could not tear her eyes away from his face with its faintly mocking smile.

The sudden movement of the sultan broke the electricity between them. Orkhan sat straight up in his bed and said "Azrael, I come!" and fell back, the life gone from his dark eyes.

Murad reached over and gently closed his father's eyes. Nilufer, putting an arm about Anastatia, led her from the death chamber.

Young Halil knelt before his brother, placing his small hands in Murad's large ones and saying, "I, Halil Beg, son of Orkhan and Theadora, am your liegeman, Sultan Murad. I pledge you my total fealty."

The new sultan raised his sibling up and, placing the kiss of peace upon the boy's forehead, sent him from the room. Then he turned to Theadora and she trembled beneath his burning gaze. "You have a month to mourn your husband, madame. At the end of that time you will join my harem."

She was astounded by his boldness. His father lay just dead, and the son lusted after her already. "I am a freeborn woman! I am a princess of Byzantium! You cannot compel me to be your wife, and I most certainly will not be!"

"I do not need your consent as you well know And I have not asked you to be my wife. I have only said you will join my harem. The emperor would not dare oppose me in this. You know that, too."

"I am not some slavegirl to be fawningly grateful for your favor," she spat.

"No. You are not. A slavegirl has had a value put on her. So far, you have not proved your worth to me."

For a moment she was speechless with shock. He had loved her once. She was sure of it. Yet now he seemed to want only to hurt her. His brutal barbs were aimed at her heart and her pride.

Sadly she realized that, against all sense, he held

her responsible for what had been between her and Orkhan! He wanted her to be a soft and compliant female—yet he had expected her to defy his father! Did he truly not understand that she had been given no choice?

She did not intend to be torn apart. She intended to marry again and to marry a man who would love her and give her more children. Theadora would not spend the rest of *her* life fighting *Murad's* ghosts. She fixed her amethyst eyes on him and said quietly, with great dignity, "Once you called me a Byzantine whore, but I am not—as you well know. You would treat me as one, but I will not let you, Sultan Murad. You insult me by telling me I must join your harem. I will not join it, even as your wife. You direct your anger at me over something I could not prevent, frail woman that I am." She added this maliciously. "You will be happier if you put me from your thoughts and populate your harem with only untouched virgins."

"Do you think I can ever forget you, you violet-eyed witch!" he hissed, stepping forward and grasping her tightly. His fingers dug into the soft flesh of her upper arms.

She winced, almost crying out, but—refusing to give him that satisfaction. "I have lain naked in your father's arms," she taunted him cruelly. "He has known my body completely, in a variety of ways, as no other man ever has! It was his right as *my husband*!"

Suddenly he reached out and quickly wrapped a thick strand of her dark hair about his hand. Imprisoning her thus, he kissed her savagely, his mouth pressing brutally on her soft lips until he bruised them. Furiously, she brought her hands up from her sides and raked his face with her nails. Too late, she realized her mistake. The rage in his eyes was terrible to behold. She turned to flee him, but the hand holding her hair yanked her back. Their eyes locked in a wordless battle. He seemed nearly mad with his rage. He forced her back across the room until she felt the divan against the backs of her legs. With a horrified gasp she realized his intent. "My God, Murad! Not here! For pity's sake, no!"

"He took you from me in his lifetime! Now let him know that I take you in his deathchamber, while his body is not even cold," came the hoarse reply

She fought him as one possessed, but her struggles were useless. She felt her robes pushed up about her waist—and then a brutal thrust into her dry, unready body that sent a shaft of pain racing through her. "No! No! No!" she sobbed over and over again, but he did not hear. Then she felt a familiar tension building within her and, with horror, renewed her struggles against him.

She could not be! Not under such a violent assault! But helpless against her own body, she yielded finally to the ecstasy sweeping over her and cried out at the moment of their mutual release. Releasing her, a cruel smile of satisfaction on his face, he pulled her up, led her to the door, and pushing her through it, said, "One month, Adora."

The door to Orkhan's deathchamber closed behind her, leaving her alone and trembling in the cold corridor. Slowly, dry-eyed, she stumbled back to her own apartment and sank wearily into a chair before the dying fire.

She had one month. One month in which to escape him. She didn't know how she was going to do it, but she would find a way. She would have to leave her son behind. But this thought did not disturb her. Halil spent most of his time now at his own court in Nicea, and he was safe from harm because Murad loved him.

She must get back to Constantinople. John Paleaologi would grant her asylum even though Helena would rage. Though her brother-in-law was vassal to the Ottoman ruler, he would protect her.

Murad would do nothing about that, at least not openly. His Turkish pride would not allow him to go to war over a woman, and if he pressed the matter too hard, it could become public knowledge. Sultan Murad would be a laughing stock for pursuing his father's reluctant widow when he might have *any* other woman.

The idea of outwitting him was irresistible, and she chuckled low in her throat. He would not expect it of her, of course. He had always underestimated her intelligence. She knew very well that he expected her, now properly cowed, to wait helplessly until he sent for her to come to his bed. For a moment, she sobered. Even now, after tonight, she loved him. She had always loved him. Widowed, she was finally free to be with him, to belong to him, to give him children. Why should she run from him? She loved him!

She sighed deeply. He was arrogant, stubborn . . . and he could not forgive her for not being a virgin. So she could not remain with him, for he would only hurt her. She would resent every budding houri who glanced at Murad. No, far better for her to return to Constantinople.

She went back to her bed and slept, awakening with a plan of action so simple that she wondered why she had not thought of it immediately. On the following day, after Orkhan had been borne to his tomb to the accompaniment of the mourners, his youngest widow visited the Convent of St. Catherine to pray for him.

Her litter moved easily through the streets of Bursa—quite unnoticed and free of guards. Each day that followed she spent part of her time at the convent church. Twice she sent the litter back to the palace, walking home alone, heavily veiled like other respectable women of the town. She let herself in through a little-used garden gate.

She had been correct in believing that the sultan assumed she would accept his decree. And he was far too busy now taking charge of his government to be bothered with her.

Theadora sent Iris off to Nicea to check on little Princess Alexis's welfare. She was now safe from busybodies, and knew that she could be gone at least overnight before anyone thought to look for her.

Arriving at the convent one day, almost a month after Orkhan's death, she sent her litter back to the palace, telling her headman, "I intend to spend the night here. Return for me late tomorrow afternoon. I have already informed Ali Yahya of my plans." The litter moved off down the narrow street as Theadora rang for the gate-keeper and was admitted. But instead of going to the convent church, the princess headed for her little house which was always kept in readiness for her.

Alone, she moved silently to her old bedroom and, opening the little trunk at the foot of her bed, drew out the garments of a peasant woman. On the two occasions that she had sent the litter back to the palace, she had gone to a nearby market and bought the clothing and a few other items she would need in order to make her escape. Returning to this house, she had secreted them in the old trunk. Now she quickly drew off her own rich clothes and, folding them carefully, lay them in the trunk and covered them with a blanket.

She opened a small pot on a table and rubbed a light walnut stain over her entire naked body, being careful that even her ears and toes were well-covered. She was able to reach her shoulders and back by means of a long-handled brush wrapped with a soft piece of chamois. For a few minutes she stood shivering in the cool air, allowing the stain time to dry.

Finally satisfied, she pulled on her new garments and braided her hair into two long plaits. Wrapping the other things she needed into a kerchief, she placed them into a woven, covered basket.

Theadora slipped from the house. The convent grounds were deserted as the nuns were now praying in the church. Even the entry was deserted but for a horse and cart. The elderly driver was unlatching the gate. "Here, let me help," she said, running up to him. Grasping the horse's bridle she led it into the street while the old man closed the gate behind them.

"Thank you, little girl," he said coming around to her. "And where did you come from?"

"In there," she replied, pointing at the convent. "I've been visiting my sister, Sister Lucia. She's a nun here."

"Well, thank ye again. My name is Basil, and I am the convent's fishmonger. If I can ever serve you—"

"But you can," she said. "My sister said I was to ask if you would take me with you to the coast. I can pay you a bit for your trouble."

The old man eyed her suspiciously. "Why do you go to the coast?"

"I come from *the city*. My name is Zoe, and I am the daughter of Constans the blacksmith whose forge is just outside the Gate of St. Romanus. I am newly widowed, and I came to visit my sister and make a religious retreat. Now I have received word that my twin sons are ill, and I cannot wait for a proper caravan. If I may travel to the coast with you I can take the ferry and get home to my boys quickly." Her upturned face was the correct mixture of concern and sincerity.

"Come along then, Zoe, daughter of Constans," growled the old man. "Never let it be said that Basil the fisherman would not help a mother in distress."

It was so easy. So incredibly easy! Old Basil and his wife insisted she stay the night with them in their cottage, for it was well past dark when they finally arrived at the coastal village. The following morning they took her to the ferry which quickly made its way across the Sea of Marmara into the harbor of Eleutherius. She felt a shiver of delight as she glimpsed again the city of her birth—the city she had not seen since she left it as the bride of Sultan

Orkhan. Constantinople! The name itself evoked a thrill! She was safely home!

She didn't even know she was smiling until a voice said, "A sane man would kill for you if you smiled at him like that, pretty girl. I don't suppose you've time for a bit of wine with a sailor?"

Theadora laughed aloud, and it was a joyous sound. "Why sir," she said in the common dialect of the city, "you turn a poor widow's head. But alas I must hurry to my father's house where my little sons lie ill."

The sailor grinned back ruefully. "Another time," he said, helping her down the gangplank and handing her her basket.

"Perhaps," she said smiling at him again, and turned away into the crowd. While she walked she searched for something, and suddenly she found it. Placing herself in front of an imperial soldier, she said, "I am the empress's sister, Princess Theadora, just escaped from Bursa. Arrange an escort for me and take me to the emperor—at once!"

The soldier looked down at the dark-faced peasant woman and raised his hand to shove her away.

"Touch me and you die! Fool! How many peasants speak the tongue of the city's upper class? Take me to the emperor or I'll have the skin stripped from your body and fed to the dogs!"

The soldier shrugged. Let his superior handle the madwoman, he thought. He gestured for Theadora to follow him, and led her to a nearby guardhouse. As he entered, he called to his captain, "Here's a crazy woman for you. She claims to be the Empress

Helena's sister, Captain Demetrius."

"I am Princess Theadora, Captain Demetrius. If you will have someone bring me a basin of warm water, please, I will prove it to you."

The captain, an older man, was intrigued by the sunburned peasant who spoke the elegant Greek of the city's upper class and who carried herself so proudly. "Get water," he commanded, and when it was brought Theadora washed the stain from her face and hands. "As you can now see, captain, I am not a peasant," she said holding out her smooth, white hands to him. She next reached into the bundle she carried and drew out a beautifully jeweled crucifix. "It is engraved on the back. Can you read?"

"Yes," the captain said taking the pendant from her.

"My father gave it to me an the occasion of my marriage to Sultan Orkhan."

"To my daughter, Theadora, from her father," read the captain, "It's interesting, but it doesn't prove you are the princess, lady."

"Nevertheless," replied Theadora, "it should be enough for you to take me to the emperor. Or perhaps peasant women come to you every day, wash stain from their bodies, hand you valuable jewels, and demand to see the emperor."

The captain laughed. "You certainly reason like old John Cantacuzene," he said. "Very well, I'll take you to the palace, but I will have to have you searched before we leave. What if you were an assassin?" Catching Theadora's look of outrage, he quickly added, "My woman will do it, lady."

She was taken into a small room and joined by a pretty girl who said, "Demetrius says you must strip completely so that I can be sure you conceal no weapons." Theadora obeyed, and when the girl had satisfied herself, she returned the garments to the princess. While Theadora dressed, the girl poked through the few items in her basket. They then rejoined the captain.

"No weapons, Demetrius," said the girl, "and do you know what? She has no hair on her body! Isn't that funny?"

The captain looked at Theadora and said quietly, "Welcome home, Your Highness."

"Thank you, captain," Theadora replied as quietly. "May we go now?"

"Of course, Highness. I regret, however, that I shall have to take you up before me on my saddle. There is no litter available."

"I have not been on a horse since I was a child," said Theadora as they left the guardhouse.

The soldier who had brought Theadora to the captain looked at the captain's woman and said, "He called her 'Your Highness.' What convinced him that she speaks the truth?"

The girl laughed. "Only highborn women pluck the mound of Venus free of hair, silly, and only the Turk's women are completely free of body hair. It was that plus her language and the pendant that probably convinced him."

Captain Demetrius lifted Theadora up in front of him on his saddle, and they rode across the city to the Blanchernae Palace where the imperial family now resided. Theadora noted that though the city was filled with people, many of them seemed to have nothing better to do than wander about the streets. She also noted that more shops were shuttered than were open. She sighed. What she had told Helena but a few weeks back was true. Constantinople was a dying old man.

They rode unchallenged into the court of the Blanchernae. The captain dismounted, politely lifting his passenger down. She followed him to the captain of the watch. The two men greeted each other cordially.

"Captain Belasarius," said Captain Demetrius, "I have the honor to present to you Princess Theadora Cantacuzene. She arrived in this extraordinary disguise just this morning."

Captain Belasarius bowed. "You wish to be taken to your sister, Highness?"

"No. To the emperor."

"Immediately, Highness. Please follow me."

Theadora turned to Captain Demetrius. "Thank you," she said simply, touching his arm. Then she followed the palace soldier. When they reached the antechamber they were told that the emperor was with the chief prelate of Constantinople, the prelate's staff of lesser bishops, and other churchmen.

"I must see the emperor at once," said Theadora, knowing that even now her sister would be receiving word of her arrival in the palace. "Announce me without delay!"

The majordomo shrugged. With royalty everything was imperative. He flung open the doors to the audience chamber and said in his best stentorian tone, "The princess Theadora Cantacuzene!"

Theadora hurried to the foot of her brother-in-law's throne and, kneeling, held out her hands in a gesture of supplication. "Sanctuary, Majesty! I beg the sanctuary of your throne and that of the holy Church!"

John Paleaologi leapt to his feet. "Good God, Thea! What are you doing here?"

"Grant me sanctuary, John!"

"Yes! Yes! Of course! It is granted." He helped her up and signaled for a chair for her. "How did you get here?"

Theadora looked about her. "Could we speak privately, John?"

The young emperor looked to the chief prelate. "Bishop Athanasius, this seems to be a rather delicate and pressing family problem. Would you and your people excuse us?"

The old bishop nodded sympathetically and retired from the room, taking his people with him.

"No one," said the emperor firmly to the majordomo, "no one, not even the empress—*especially the empress*—is to enter my presence until I give you leave. If you fail me in this your own life is forfeit. Use whatever means you must, even physical means, to guard my privacy."

The door shut behind the majordomo. Sitting back down on his throne, John Paleaologi looked down on his sister-in-law and said, "Now, Thea, tell me why you are here."

"Orkhan is dead," she began.

"We had heard rumors, of course," replied the

emperor, "but as yet we have no official word."

"He died nearly a month ago. Murad was declared his heir, and is now sultan. I was forced to flee Bursa because Sultan Murad wishes me to join his household."

"As his wife?"

"No," she whispered, and two fat tears spilled down her cheeks. "Just as a member of his harem. John, I must be honest with you since by asking you to grant me asylum I ask you to defy your overlord.

"Before I was brought to the palace in Bursa to be Orkhan's wife, I met Murad by accident. We met secretly in the convent orchard for many weeks. We fell in love and were confident that I should never be called to my husband's bed. We actually planned to wed when Orkhan died.

"But then father wanted military aid from the sultan in order to keep you and Helena at bay, and Orkhan wanted Tyzmpe as a toehold here in Europe. So the marriage contract had to be fullfilled . . . which meant that I had to bear my husband a child. I was removed from St. Catherine's without any warning and brought immediately to Orkhan's bed.

"Ever since then Murad and I have been at swords-points. He believes that I might have avoided my fate somehow and remained true to him. Of course that is not true. I was helpless. He is a fool!"

She gave a sob, and the emperor rose from his throne and put an arm about her. How she had suffered! And she had been all alone in her suffering. To him the miracle was that she had survived all this.

"Oh, John! I maintained my sanity only by keeping

the love between us alive in my mind and heart. Have you any idea what hell it was for me to be a dutiful wife to Orkhan while loving his son?"

"Then why have you run from him, Thea? I am sure you must have misunderstood him. He must want you for a wife."

"No, John, he was hurt, and he wants to hurt me now in return. I love him. I have always loved him. Why must I be forced to accept this hurt? I will not! Let me stay here for the present while I decide what to do. Even Murad will have a bit of a time tracing me as long as we are discreet."

"It matters not if he knows you are here," said the emperor. "I will protect you. Our walls will. Tell me, however, for I burn with curiosity . . . how did you get here?"

Theadora gave a watery chuckle and then told him.

The emperor laughed heartily. "What an ingenious little witch you are, little sister! A mind such as yours belongs either back in the Golden Age of Athens or somewhere in the future."

"Perhaps I was there, and perhaps I shall incarnate again in a more enlightened age. But for now I am here, and as I must make my peace with this time, it must make its peace with me."

John Paleaologi smiled. "I will provide you with everything you need, Thea. I am happy you came to me. First, I expect you will want to bathe. I will have the servants arrange for more suitable clothing for you, my dear."

"Lord, yes! Bless your thoughtfulness, John."

The emperor stood and, taking Theadora's hand,

smiled. "Let's see if we can avoid Helena completely You look too exhausted to cope with her now. *I* will handle Her Majesty, the empress."

PART III

Alexander and Theadora

1359 to 1361

Chapter 13

THEADORA SETTLED QUIETLY INTO A LARGE APARTMENT in the palace. True to his word, the emperor kept his wife from her younger sister for more than a week while Theadora ate and slept, regaining her strength and her peace of mind.

Ten days after her return to the city the emperor held a banquet and she was invited. She entered the great dining hall of the Blanchernae Palace to the warm welcome of people she had not seen since her childhood and, in most cases, barely remembered. It seemed that everyone was happy to see her. She was led to the main table where the emperor and empress awaited her. Smiling, Helena kissed her younger sister on both cheeks, murmuring in her ear, "Bitch! If you have put us in danger I will kill you!" Then the empress proclaimed loudly, "Thanks be to God, dear sister, for your safe return from the infidel!"

"Thanks be to God" came the echoing reply from all those in the hall.

Theadora was seated on her brother-in-law's left. The Byzantine nobles in the hall were forced to agree that they had never seen such beauty as the two sisters possessed between them. This was grudgingly conceded by their wives.

The empress was gowned in white silk heavily embroidered with gold and silver thread, turquoises, pearls, and pink diamonds sewn into exquisite floral designs upon the material. With her rose and white complexion, sky-blue eyes, and shining golden hair topped by a gilt crown, Helena was at the height of her beauty.

In striking contrast, but no less lovely, Theadora wore a simple pale-green silk gown that molded her high breasts and then fell away. The flowing sleeves of the gown were embroidered slightly at the edges in gold thread. There was a faint, very becoming flush to her creamy gardenia skin, and her amethyst eyes sparkled beneath their dark, gold-tipped lashes. Her shining dark hair was braided and looped about the sides of her face and held by golden cauls.

John Paleaologi leaned over and said quietly to Theadora, "I have never seen you look lovelier, my dear sister. You will simply captivate our guest of honor when he sets eyes on you. I have arranged that he sit next to you."

"Are you trying to marry me off so soon?" she teased him.

"Would you not like to remarry, my dear?"

She was silent, and he saw the sadness in her lovely eyes.

"You love Murad, don't you, Theadora? No, no, you need say nothing. Your eyes tell me all. Perhaps marriage to a good man and having several children would ease your pain."

"Who is this man you would have me meet, John?"

"The new lord of Mesembria."

"And he has no wife?"

"He had one in his youth, but she died and he never married again. He was not Mesembria's lord then. In fact, that he is its lord today is a bitter twist of fate for him. He was a third son and when his father died his eldest brother inherited. He ruled well for us. Unfortunately, the elder brother had no sons. So his heir was the next brother. That man had two boys. Several months ago the palace in Mesembria caught fire and burned to the ground. The entire ruling family perished. Only this third brother, who lived in another city, was left alive. He was recalled, confirmed, and crowned despot of Mesembria. Though he has several illegitimate sons, he has no legal heir. So he must marry."

"And you think to match me with him?"

"If it pleases you. Understand, my dear, that I will not force you to *any* marriage. I am not your father seeking aid or alliances. Perhaps you would remain single, or take the veil, or," and his eyes twinkled, "perhaps you would choose your own husband. You may, however, like the lord Alexander. He has charm, and there is not a woman at my court who hasn't thrown herself at him. But all to no avail."

"He sounds unbearable and quite the peacock. If he avoids women, perhaps they are not to his taste. Are you sure he is a real man?"

John chuckled. "I am sure he is a real man, Thea, but I will allow you to judge for yourself. Here he is now."

"Alexander, lord of Mesembria," intoned the majordomo.

Theadora looked to the end of the hall and gasped, feeling as if she had been struck. The man striding toward them was the pirate she had known as Alexander the Great. Her mind frantically sought to assemble the few facts she recalled about him. He had told her he was the youngest son of a Greek noble, and his speech, taste and manners had certainly attested to that. But he had never named his father, and it had never occurred to her to ask him.

He bowed, flourishing his long cape elegantly as he reached the high table. He was tanned, his hair bleached to its usual golden color. His eyes were still pure aquamarine. She could hear the audible sighs from the other women and saw her own sister quickly assess the newcomer with speculative, lust-filled eyes.

"Come, Alexander," welcomed the emperor, "join us. We have seated you next to our beloved sister, Theadora."

A beaming John made the introductions and then left them to become acquainted. She was silent, and Alexander said softly, "Are you not glad to see me, beauty?"

"Does Helena know who you are—were?"

"No, beauty. No one does, not even your revered brother-in-law. I must rely on you to keep my secret. Will you—for old times sake?"

A smile played at the corners of her mouth. "I never thought I would see you again," she said.

He chuckled. "Yet here I am, turning up like a bad copperpiece. And what is worse, *they* are proposing a match between us."

She blushed. "You know about that?"

He did not tell her that it had been his idea, and that he had approached the emperor about it first. "The emperor and I have discussed it, but he tells me it must be your decision." He took her hand beneath the table, and his was warm and strong. "Do you think you could be my wife, beauty?"

Her heart quickened. "Do not hurry me, my lord Alexander. I know nothing really of you."

"What would you know? My father was Theodore, despot of Mesembria. My mother was Sara Comnenus, a princess of Trebizond. I had two older brothers, Basil and Constantine. My mother has been dead for several years, my father nearly two years, and a fire in Mesembria's palace several months ago left me bereft of family—and an unwilling ruler. The rest you know, beauty"

"I am truly sorry for your great loss," she said softly.

"As am I, beauty, for my brothers were good men. Yet, as in all situations, there is a good side. As the lord of Mesembria I am able to ask the emperor for his widowed sister-in-law's hand in marriage. Look at me, Theadora!"

It was the first time he had ever called her by her name. Surprised, she raised her eyes to his.

"I am an impatient man, beauty. You cannot deny the attraction we felt for each other when I held you and your son captive in my city. I believe you could learn to love me. You know more of me than most women know of their bridegrooms. Say you will wed me."

"My lord, you hurry me too quickly. I am confused. My husband is only recently dead, and I was forced to flee the unwelcome attentions of the new sultan. I do not even know if I wish to remarry."

The hand holding hers beneath the table loosed it and moved to gently caress her thigh. She quivered. "Ah, beauty, you were not meant to live a celibate life. And you are not a wanton woman to take lovers like your sister. You are meant to be married, and to have children about you. I would have you, and I would have our children."

"Give me but a little time, my lord Alexander," she pleaded.

He did not press her further during the feast, turning instead to talk with the emperor. Yet he watched over her, seeing that she had the choicest viands and that her cup was kept filled with sweet wine. Towards midnight the emperor gave the signal that those who wished to leave might, and Theadora took the opportunity to flee the hall.

There was no doubt in her mind that Alexander attracted her, and he had been correct about one thing. She was meant to marry. Long ago her mother had promised her that when Orkhan died she would be brought home to Byzantium to make a good Christian marriage.

As a princess of Byzantium, however, she could not marry just anyone. There was no one within the emperor's court who was of sufficient rank to be her husband. Among the city-states belonging to the empire, there was no prince other than Alexander who was not married, too old, or too young.

Practical considerations aside, Alexander was handsome, educated, and sensitive to her as a woman with a mind of her own. She did not think she loved him—but she thought she could. She was strongly attracted to him. He would not be a hard man to live with. And she did want more children.

Absently, she let her women disrobe her, sponge her with warm perfumed water, and slide a blossom-pink caftan over her. Dismissing them, she lay upon her bed.

If Murad had really loved her he would have offered marriage, not the shameful bondage he had suggested. Alexander offered her his heart and his throne.

She smiled to herself in the darkness. Alexander was a very stubborn man, and she did not think he would accept a refusal from her. A giggle of amusement escaped her. A determined Murad to her right, an equally determined Alexander to her left. The truth was that she had no other choice than to accept one of them.

It did not surprise her to see a shadow suddenly loom on the balcony behind the gently billowing sheer silk curtains. She had thought he might come to press his suit more forcefully. There were times when even the most enlightened of men fell back on sex as a persuader. She knew it would disappoint him to learn that she had already reached a decision in his favor, using logic to do so.

Entering the room he walked quickly to her bedside. "Are you really asleep, beauty?"

"No, Alexander. I am thinking."

"Of what we spoke about this evening?"

"Yes."

Without being asked he sat down on her bed. 'I have not kissed you in so long," he said. Reaching out, he drew her into his arms and kissed her gently.

He loosed her, and she said softly, "Is that how you would make love to me, Alexander? I remember my first night in Phocaea when you were far more articulate on much shorter acquaintance. Come, my lord, I am no easily broken toy. If your love is that tame then perhaps I should not marry you. I am no wanton, but even my elderly husband was more vigorous a lover."

A deep rumble of delighted laughter echoed in the darkness. "So, beauty, you will not be put upon a pedestal and worshiped like some ancient goddess?"

"No, I will not, my lord, for I am a flesh-and-blood woman."

She heard him moving about and soon one of the lamps by her bed was lit, and then another, and another. "I would see you when I make love to you," he said, drawing her up from the bed. His fingers swiftly undid the pearl buttons on her caftan, sliding it from her shoulders and letting it fall to the floor. His own robe quickly followed hers, sliding to the soft rugs.

Falling back on the bed, he held her above him, rubbing his smooth face against her breasts. Then he slowly lowered her, folding her into his strong arms. She sighed deeply. Expertly he reversed their positions, and she suddenly found herself lying beneath him. He gazed down at her and she blushed under his inspection.

"Christos, how beautiful you are," he muttered

hoarsely, and his hands stroked her breasts. His soft fingertips brushed against her skin again and again, and she could feel the familiar tension beginning. He sat up, pulling her back between his legs. He cupped the cones of her breasts, gently pulling and pinching the large coral nipples, and she could feel his maleness butting against her lower back. Now she lay across his lap, and the big hands caressed her belly with a strength of touch that made her shrink slightly.

He laughed softly. "So, beauty, you recognize your master. Did your greybeard husband ever make you feel this way? I'll wager not! Marry me, my darling, and I will teach you to crave my touch. I can pleasure you as no man can, and no woman will ever please me as you do, beauty."

"You talk a good deal, my lord," she mocked him, and his mouth crushed against her lips, bruising them, his white teeth drawing salty blood, his tongue subduing hers. He trailed a path of fiery kisses across her breasts and belly, finding the softness of her inner thighs with his mouth.

Theadora stiffened with shock as his soft, insistent tongue reached where no one had ever ventured. Her body shrank from him, her voice shook with protest. "N—No!"

He raised his head and stared at her, his eyes glazed with passion. "Has no one ever tasted of you, beauty?"

"No!"

"But you are like honey. A woman is sweetest there, beauty."

"I—it is w—wrong" she managed to gasp. "You must not!"

"Who tells you it is wrong? Does it not give you pleasure, my love? Whom do we hurt? I will soon teach you how to pleasure me in the same sweet way." Then he lowered his head again and, pushing her legs up and apart, sought again the sweetness he craved.

At first she was tense beneath the velvety, probing tongue, but suddenly a wave of pure pleasure washed through her defenses and she groaned. Deep, deep within her she could feel the tenseness mounting until it was almost unbearable. She was desperate for release, but he withheld it. Instead, he carefully eased off so that the tension receded like a wave. It began to return as he pulled himself up and threw a leg over her.

With the instinct of Eve that is born into every woman she sought for his manhood with her hands and, capturing it, eagerly guided him to her. She wrapped her arms about him. At first he would not enter her but, instead, rubbed the tip of the turgid root against the soft, throbbing flesh until she thought she would scream with the intensity of the pleasure.

"Look at me," he commanded. "I want to see you when we mate."

Hesitantly, she raised her eyes to his, and he slowly entered her, gaining almost as much pleasure from watching the ecstasy that transformed her face, as from the act of possession itself.

To her shame she climaxed almost immediately, and he laughed gently. Tenderly, he said, "Ah, beauty, has it been that long for you? I will teach you how to prolong the pleasure, my darling. No, don't turn away from me. Don't you know how much I love you, beauty? Please don't ever shut yourself away from me."

From that moment on her eyes never left his as he moved within her, the tempo of his passion increasing as the minutes passed. Then she surprised him by speaking, and so sensual did he find the sound of her voice that his hot seed thundered into the hidden valley of her womb.

"I will marry with you, my lord Alexander," she said. "I will marry you, my darling, as soon as it can be arranged."

Spent, he murmured, "Ah, beauty, how I love you!" and she held him close against her, smiling in the near darkness. He could not know it, for no man ever did— but in the end it was always the woman who was the victor.

In the early dawn he left her, and she slept peacefully and soundly for the first time in months. She had enjoyed his lovemaking very much. It was masterful and experienced, though he never gloated over his masculinity. In bed they were equals, each giving, and each taking.

On the following day they went to the emperor and asked his permission to marry. If John Paleaologi was surprised by this sudden turn of events, one look at Theadora's face swept away his doubts. All the tension had gone from her. She was radiant.

"I gladly give you permission to wed with my dear sister," the emperor told the lord of Mesembria. "But you must grant me a boon in return. You must remain in Constantinople while your palace in Mesembria is being rebuilt."

"Agreed," grinned Alexander. "There is a lovely villa down on the Bosphorus, at the narrow place between us and Asia. I have long admired it. Its owner recently died. I will arrange to buy it, and we may live there until we return to Mesembria." He turned to Theadora, "Would that please you, beauty?"

She nodded, smiling. "If you buy me this villa I shall spend a great deal of money furnishing it."

He chuckled and remarked mischievously, "It will be all right, Theadora. I once had some dealings with your late husband, Sultan Orkhan, and I made a great deal of money in the transaction."

Theadora burst out laughing. The emperor looked puzzled but Alexander stopped his question by asking, "May we wed tomorrow, Majesty?"

"So soon, my impatient friend? What of the banns? You give us no time for preparations. Thea is, after all, a princess born."

"I want no festivities, John. When I was wed to my lord Orkhan I was decked out like a heathen idol. There was a two-day festival. I hated it all! I would be married quietly with only you, the priest, and my dear Alexander present. Have the bishop waive the banns. Grant me this, my brother."

So John Paleaologi acquiesced, and the following day at mid-morning Theadora Cantacuzene and Alexander, despot of Mesembria, were wed before the high altar in the Church of St. Mary in Blanchernae. Their only witnesses were the emperor, the bishop who married them, the priest who assisted him, and two altar boys.

At the noonday meal, the emperor brought forth a

roar of delight from the diners in the hall when he announced the surprise marriage. Though the noble-women of the court were disappointed to see Alexander wed so quickly, their men were greatly pleased. Everyone crowded about the newlyweds, congratulating the lord of Mesembria, and claiming kisses from his blushing, rosy bride.

Only the empress looked sour. Even now Helena did not wish her sister well. Helena could not bear to see Theadora happy and now her sister was radiant. When the uproar had died down Helena said softly to her sister, "You have surprised me this time, Thea, but beware. Next time it will be I who will surprise you."

Chapter 14

THE EMPRESS OF BYZANTIUM WAS IN A COLD RAGE. "Have you lost what little brains you possess?" she demanded of her husband. "God have mercy on us! You are just like your father—with one difference. He, at least, had my father to run the empire."

The emperor was barely perturbed. "As I recall, you did not like it when we had your father running our empire. You could barely wait to get him out."

She ignored his remark. "You have opened the city to attack, you fool! If Sultan Murad wants Theadora, he'll have her, though why he would be interested in that skinny, purple-eyed bitch is beyond me! And you, you fool, have dared to marry her to the lord of Mesembria!"

"Murad is not going to war over a woman, Helena. This is Constantinople, not Troy. Your sister has been incredibly brave and damned clever in escaping the sultan. He has no legal right to her, and I did not force her to this new marriage. She and Alexander came to me. Yes, I gave them my blessing! Thea is entitled to some happiness. God only knows she got none with Orkhan. Your father sacrificed her to that old man in order to usurp my throne. I hope she is always happy. She deserves it."

"She endangers us by her very presence here. And what of our daughter, alone in a hostile land and at the mercy of the Turks? Have you thought of Alexis, fool?"

"Your sister will be returning with her husband to Mesembria in a few months time. I hardly think she constitutes a danger. As to Alexis, Sultan Murad is an honorable man, and he assures me that she is safe and well at St. Anna's."

Helena threw up her hands in disgust. He refused to understand. Or else, the thought lingered in her mind, he was deliberately being obtuse, wanting to annoy her. John Paleaologi was a fool and always had been. He could not see that by annoying his overlord, the sultan, he practically invited Murad to attack the city. She would lose her throne because of this stupidity.

Byzantium stood alone, a faint, continuously threatened Christian light on the edge of the dark, infidel world. The rulers of Europe gave lip service to protecting Byzantium. This was due to squabbling over religion.

In fact, in the year 1203, the Fourth Crusade, originally dispatched to retake Jerusalem from the Saracen Moslems, diverted instead to Constantinople. This diversion was engineered by the Venetians and by their vengeful doge, Enrico Dandolo, who had been blinded thirty years earlier while being held hostage in Constantinople by the Greeks.

He had been allowed the freedom of the city, having given his word that he would not try to escape.

Escape was the furthest thing from Dandolo's mind. The son of a noble merchant family, he was far more interested in wooing to Venice the foreign trading houses that were the strength of the Byzantine Empire.

Too, Dandolo had developed an unhealthy interest in Constantinople's defenses. When his two breaches of conduct were discovered, he was punished by having his too-inquisitive eyes exposed to a concave mirror reflecting the sun. Blind, he was returned to Venice, where he spent years overcoming his handicap and dreaming of revenge. He was ultimately elected to the highest office in Venice, a position which offered him his opportunity for vengeance.

Besides his personal motives, the elderly doge wanted the destruction of Constantinople for the economic advantages that destruction would afford his own city.

The excuse for this betrayal of a Christian city by fellow Christians was the restoration of a deposed emperor. He was Alexius IV, though the Crusader lords knew he was already dead. He had been strangled by Alexius V, who then fled the city in the face of the oncoming European army, leaving his people to their terrible fate. Constantinople found itself taken in 1204 and mercilessly pillaged by soldiers, clerics, and nobles. No infidel city ever suffered at the hands of Christian invaders as did Constantinople, the capital city of Eastern Christianity.

What was not destroyed by fire or vandalism was carted off. Gold, silver, jewels, plate, silks, furs, statuary, and people—whatever held value, and could move or be moved. The city had never recovered, and Helena was terrified lest the next invasion be the last.

Her fears were increased considerably when Sultan Murad and a small but formidable army appeared outside the city's walls.

"In God's name give Thea back to the sultan," Helena begged her husband.

"Do you think Murad will go away if I do?" mocked John Paleaologi. "Christos, Helena, do not be a bigger fool than you already are! Orkhan's last words to his sons were to take Constantinople. He has not come for Theadora, my dear, but for my city. I shall not, however, let him have it."

Helena did not know what to do, or even where she might turn. Her sister and her new bridegroom were the darlings of the city. The story of Thea's escape was even being sung by the street minstrels.

Suddenly, it appeared that her prayers would be answered.

Into Helena's presence came a tall, soft-looking man who quietly introduced himself. "I am Ali Yahya, Majesty, chief of the sultan's household. I wish to see Princess Theadora and hope that you may arrange it."

"My sister will not see you, Ali Yahya. She has recently been remarried to the lord of Mesembria. She honeymoons even now in a dear little villa on the sea."

"What a pity, madame."

Helena could not resist. "Does the sultan really want my sister in his harem?"

"He wishes the princess back with her family, and those who love her," came the evasive reply.

Helena's blue eyes narrowed. "Possibly," she said, "it could be arranged. *But* it would have to be done my way."

"And what way is that, Majesty?"

"With my father and brother no longer concerned with a secular life, I am head of the Cantacuzene family. In this capacity I am responsible for the fate of the members of this family. I will sell my sister to Sultan Murad for ten thousand gold Venetian ducats and one hundred of the finest Eastern pearls. The pearls, must be between one and two centimeters in size. My price is firm. I will not haggle."

"And what of Her Highness's new husband, Majesty? Our laws forbid taking the wife of a living man."

"For that price, Ali Yahya, I will see that my sister is quickly widowed. Her new husband has offended me. He is an insolent man who lacks respect for the empire."

What Helena did not say was that Alexander of Mesembria had insulted her unforgiveably by refusing to lie with her when she had offered herself to him. No man had ever refused Helena. Usually they were greatly overcome by the honor. Alexander, however, had gazed down on Helena from his great height and said coldly, "I choose my own whores, madame. They do not choose me." Then he had walked away.

The eunuch suspected something of this sort and pitied both Theadora and her husband. Then he shrugged. It was not his place to feel anything. His first obligation was to his master, Sultan Murad, and his master had sent him for Theadora. Under these new circumstances, however, Ali Yahya was not sure if Murad would want her back. He would have to play for time until he could ascertain the sultan's will.

"You will, of course, provide us with proper legal papers to verify such a sale," he said smoothly.

"Naturally," replied Helena calmly, "and I will make it possible for you to transport her quickly from the city before my husband discovers her gone."

"Although I am empowered by the sultan to make whatever arrangements are necessary to assure the princess's return, this is an unusual situation, majesty. I must speak with my master."

Helena nodded. "I will give you two days, Ali Yahya. Come to me at this same hour. Remind your master that the longer he delays his decision, the longer the object of his lust lies in the arms of another man." She laughed cruelly. "My sister's new husband is quite handsome. The silly women of my court compare him to a Greek god."

The eunuch withdrew from the empress's private chamber. Two days later he returned and was again received.

"Well?" she demanded impatiently.

He reached into his robes and drew out two velvet bags. He opened the first and spilled some of its contents into a flat dish. Helena's blue eyes widened with greedy delight at the perfectly sized and matched pearls. The other bag was opened to reveal a bar of gold.

"Have it weighed, Majesty. You will find it ten thousand ducats worth." To his vast amusement, she went directly to a cabinet and drew out a scale. She weighed the gold.

"A trifle over," she remarked knowledgeably. "The sultan is more than fair." Returning the scale to the cabinet she drew out an unrolled parchment and handed it to Ali Yahya. "These papers give your master, the sultan, complete custody and legal ownership of a female slave known as Theadora of Mesembria. She and her bridegroom are still at their villa near the city. However, you cannot get her there without placing open, public suspicion on your master which I am sure he does not wish. The execution of my plan will take time. To act hastily would mean to risk questions, which your master certainly does not want. No, it is better if my sister is widowed in Mesembria. You see, no one there would think to harm Alexander. They all love him. For that very reason his death will look perfectly natural.

"When he does die, in a few months, I will beg my poor sister to come home. I will house her royally at the Boucolean Palace, which happens to be directly adjacent to the imperial yacht basin. You and I will arrange a time, and I will see that her wine is drugged on the appointed day. You and your men will then remove her through a secret passage which opens out by the harbor. The guards will be bribed. They will let you through without question."

Ali Yahya bowed, filled with a grudging admiration for the empress. She was a wicked woman, but this knowledge allowed him to complete his mission. There would be no blood on *his* hands. "What drug will you use to put her to sleep?" he asked.

She reached once more into the cabinet and, drawing out a small vial, handed it to him. Uncorking it, he sniffed. Satisfied, he handed it back to her. "I do not have to tell you what will happen to you if you attempt to trick me, or if you harm the princess," he said quietly.

She smiled nastily "I will not harm her. Why? I will gain far more pleasure in the weeks ahead by knowing that she is a slave. She must obey her lord and master, or be punished. If she obeys, she suffers—for I believe she is a cold woman. But if she refuses her lord and master she will be beaten. I do not know which gives me more pleasure, the thought of Thea naked and enduring the sultan's vigorous attentions, or Thea being whipped."

"Why do you hate her so?" Ali Yahya was unable to contain his curiosity any longer.

For a moment Helena was silent. Then she said, "I am the elder, but my parents always preferred Thea. They never said so but I knew. When my mother died I nursed her, and what do you think her last words were? I will tell you, Ali Yahya! Her very last words to me were, 'Theadora, my best loved! Now I will never see you again.' No word for me! I loved her too! It was always Thea!

"Then there was my father, always talking about her intelligence, and how she should have been his heir. Such drivel! What has she won with her wonderful brain? Nothing! Nothing! Now she endangers *my* city, and my husband defends her every move, and grows soft-eyed at the mere mention of her name. I want her out of my life. Now! Forever!"

"You have gained your heart's desire, Majesty. Within a few short months your sister will be back across the Marmara and well on her way to Bursa." The eunuch rose and bowed. "How will I know the correct dock in the imperial yacht basin?"

"There is a wharf decorated with statues of lions and other animals in the Boucoleon Harbor. Have your galley wait there on the date we agree upon. The passageway exits just a few feet from that wharf." She reached into her robes and drew out a red silk pendant with a two-headed imperial eagle embroidered on it. "Have your galley fly this from its mast and no one will challenge you coming or going."

For the rest of the day Helena could barely contain her excitement. At last she would be rid of Thea. Never again would she have to fear her sister's threat of so long ago . . . the threat of her returning to the sultan's side, to snatch the city from Helena! Thea would finally be powerless! A slave! Why, when Sultan Murad tired of her, as he inevitably would, he might even sell her farther east! Helena laughed with joy. Her vengeance would be complete.

That night the empress sent for a man who was one of Byzantium's most respected physicians. Julian Tzimisces occasionally enjoyed Helena's favors. Tonight she awaited him in a loose robe of palest turquoise-blue gauze through which her lush body gleamed like mother-of-pearl. Her nipples were painted vermillion, and they were provocatively visible through the silk. By her side was a beautiful little girl who, like Helena, was a blue-eyed-blond. The child was garbed as the empress was, even to having the tiny buds of her unformed breasts painted vermillion. Tzimisces' particular perversion was children.

Helena smiled a feline smile and said bluntly, "I need a very special poison, dear friend. It must kill quickly, harm only its intended victim, and leave no trace."

"You ask a lot, Majesty."

Again Helena smiled. "Do you like my little Julia?" she asked him. "She is a Georgian, and just ten. Such a sweet little girl," and the empress kissed the child on her rosebud mouth.

Julian Tzimisces shifted nervously, his eyes moving rapidly from the child's unformed body to the empress's large, gleaming red nipples. Helena lay back, drawing the child with her, and slowly caressed the little slave's body.

"I have something new from Italy," said Julian Tzimisces a trifle breathlessly. "Is the victim male or female?" He was beginning to perspire beneath his robes, and he felt himself growing harder with each minute.

"Male."

"It can be put in his bath water."

"No! He may bathe with his wife, and I do not wish her harmed. In fact, it is vital that she *not* be harmed."

"Then it can be put in his shaving water. It will take several days for the poison to be absorbed through the skin. There will be no signs of illness, nothing to raise suspicion. When the poison has been absorbed, the man will simply drop dead. Will that be satisfactory?"

"Yes, Julian, that will be very satisfactory."

The physician could not take his eyes from the two females on the couch. He was in a terrible quandary for he wanted them both—the child first, then the woman. The empress laughed. She knew his tastes.

"You have been very cooperative, old friend, and you shall be rewarded. You may have my sweet Julia. But you must not spend, Julian! That joy you must save for me."

The physician tore his robe open and flung himself on the child who, although she knew what to expect, nevertheless screamed in agony as the man drove himself into her. The screams continued for several moments, finally fading into pitiful little moans.

Beside them Helena crouched on her heels, her eyes shining, her lips wet and slack. "Yes, Julian! Yes! Yes! Hurt her! Hurt her!"

The child had fainted now, and Tzimisces's passion was reaching its peak. Panting, Helena ripped her own robe off and, lying back, spread her legs wide. Shoving the child away, the man covered the eager woman's body with his own. Together they writhed in an almost violent mortal combat until suddenly, with a shriek, the empress was spent. Her partner quickly followed.

A few minutes later, after the sounds of their rasping, panting breath had died away, Helena said, "You will bring me the poison tomorrow night, Julian. Without fail."

"Yes, Majesty," said the man by her side. "I will bring it. I swear!"

"Good," purred the empress, "and when my enemy is dead I will have another sweet little present for you, dear Julian. Little Julia has a twin brother. I am saving him for you."

Shortly thereafter the physician left the palace

through a discreet side gate, and was carried in a litter through the silent night streets to his own residence. Once home, he entered his laboratory and searched in the cabinet. He drew forth the vial and held it up to the light. It glittered an evil yellow-green color. Placing the vial carefully on the table, he poured water from a pitcher into a small basin. Then, opening the vial, he allowed several drops of it into the water. The color disappeared as soon as it touched the clear water. The water remained colorless and odorless.

Julian Tzimisces recorked the vial and carefully disposed of the basin's contents. Walking to the window of his laboratory he looked out. The sky was gray and the dawn was beginning to break. He wondered who the poor soul was who had so deeply offended Helena. It was not likely he'd ever know, and it was better that way. He could feel no guilt about aiding in the murder of a faceless, nameless person. Sighing, Julian left his laboratory and went to bed.

While the physician fell asleep, Theadora and Alexander were awakening in the bedchamber of their honeymoon villa, blissfully unaware of the destiny the empress had in store for them. Adora had never been happier in her whole life. In the few days of her marriage she had found an extraordinary peace of mind. There was no longer any conflict in her life. Alexander loved Theadora for herself alone. And she realized very quickly that she loved him. It was not at all as it had been with Murad. Murad had, after all, been her first love.

No, life with Alexander was filled with a calm sweet love, one of pleasure, without conflict. It would always be good with him. He was gentle with her, though masterful. He encouraged her wit and intellect, even suggesting that she might enjoy establishing a school of higher learning for females. How well Alexander understood his wife! Yes, what had begun as a marriage of convenience had indeed become a love affair!

Now, in the early morning, the lord of Mesembria turned in their bed to face his wife. For a moment he watched her sleeping face. Then he leaned over and kissed her gently. Slowly her violet eyes opened, and she smiled at him.

"Let us go to the sea and greet the dawn," he said, rising up from their bed and drawing her after him. She reached for a pink gauze gown to cover her nakedness. "No, beauty. We will go as we are."

"Someone will see us," she protested shyly.

"No one will see us," he answered firmly. Taking her hand, he led her out onto the terrace, through their small garden, and down a gently sloping incline to a little strip of sand that served them as a beach. They looked east across the Bosporus to the green hills of Asia tumbling down into the still, dark sea. Beyond, the pearl-gray sky was beginning to lighten and fill with color. Pinks and mauves mixed with the swirling oranges, lavenders, and golds.

The couple stood quietly in their nude perfection, like exquisite statues. A light wind played gently over their bodies. All was quiet about them. Only an occasional bird song broke the silence.

Slowly, Alexander turned his wife so that she faced him and, looking down at her, he said, "I have never known such happiness as I have these last few days with you. You are perfection, beauty, and I love you very much."

Wordlessly her arms slipped about his neck, and she drew his head down so they might kiss. What began in tenderness quickly flared into passion as their desire for each other grew. Soon it could no longer be contained. She could feel his hardness pushing against her thigh, and she moaned against his mouth.

Their intertwined bodies fell slowly to the sand, and her legs opened eagerly. Slowly he entered into her. Her face was radiant with love. Their jewellike eyes locked onto one another, and Theadora felt her very soul being drawn from her body to meet with his in some star-filled place far beyond the mortal world. Together they floated until suddenly it was too sweet, too intense. Their passion crested, then broke over them like one of the waves that lapped at the sand just a few feet away.

When they had regained their senses, she spoke in a half-amused, half-shocked voice. "What if someone saw us, Alexander?'

He chuckled. "Then they will say that the lord of Mesembria serves his beautiful bride quite well." He scrambled up, pulling her with him. "Let us bathe in the sea now, beauty. The beach is a very romantic place, but I have sand in the strangest places."

Laughing, they plunged into the water. And later, if the servants saw them coming naked through the gardens, they said nothing, for they were enchanted by the love between their master and mistress.

Alexander was ambitious for his city and had plans to rebuild it. Mesembria had originally been colonized many centuries before by Ionian Greeks from Corinth and Sparta, and later it was conquered by Roman legions. The new lord of Mesembria spoke with his new wife of his plans to repave the broad avenues, restore the public buildings, and, after destroying the city's slums, to build decent housing for the poor.

"The avenues must be lined with poplars," said Theadora. "And the lady of Mesembria will plant flowers about the fountains for her people to enjoy."

He smiled, pleased by her enthusiasm. "I want to make Mesembria so lovely that you will never miss Constantinople. I want it to be a happy city for you and for our people."

"But, my love, this will cost a great deal of money."

"I could not spend all the money I have if I lived to be a hundred, beauty. Before we return to Constantinople I must tell you where my funds are hidden so that, if anything should ever happen to me, you would not be dependent on anyone."

"My lord, you are young. We are but newly married. Nothing will happen to you."

"No," he answered, "I don't expect it will. Nevertheless what is mine, beauty, is yours as well."

In Mesembria the city rejoiced in Alexander's marriage to Theadora Cantacuzene. His family had ruled the city in an unbroken line for over five hundred years, and was loved by its citizens. Through good and bad times, through war and peace, Alexander's family had always put the welfare of its people before their own. Their reward had been a fierce loyalty unequaled by any other city for its rulers.

Mesembria was set upon the shores of the Black Sea on a small peninsula at the northern end of the Gulf of Burgos. It was jointed to the mainland by a narrow isthmus which was fortified with guardtowers set into the walls every 25 feet. At the mainland end of the isthmus was a stone archway set with enormous bronze doors. These doors shut every day at sunset and opened at dawn. In time of war the doors remained closed. A matching gateway at the city end of the isthmus made the city a natural fortress.

Originally settled by the Thracians, the city had been colonized in the sixth century before Christ by a group of Ionian Greeks from the cities of Sparta and Corinth. Under their guidance, the little market town had become a cultured, elegant city which later became a jewel in the crown of the Byzantine Empire. In 812 A.D. the Bulgarians had managed to capture Mesembria briefly, looting it of its vast treasury of gold and silver and, more important, of its supply of Greek fire. The ruling family of the time had been entirely wiped out, and when the Mesembrians had finally rid themselves of the barbarian invaders they had elected as their ruler their most popular general, Constantine Heracles. He was Alexander's ancestor. The Heracles family had ruled Mesembria ever since.

Now, with Alexander's marriage, the populace became eager for their prince's return. They set to work immediately to build a new palace worthy of Alexander and Theadora. The old royal residence had been located on a hill above the city. Knowing their lord's love of the sea, and believing that rebuilding on the site of the old palace would be bad luck, the populace placed the palace in a newly created park on the water's edge. The building was done similar to the classical Greek style. It was pale golden marble with porch pillars of an orange-red veined marble. It was not a large palace, for the Heracles had never been formal people. There was to be only one large reception hall where the lord of Mesembria might hold court, or render public judgements. The rest of the palace was to be private and was separated from this reception hall by a long open porchway.

Before the palace in the center of an oval of green lawn was a large oval pool tiled in turquoise blue. In the center of the pool was a solid gold dolphin, its mouth wide in laughter. The ancient seagod, Triton, cavorted on its back. From the sides of the oval, small whorled shells of gold sprayed toward the center, just missing the fish.

Behind the palace a beautiful garden stretched down to a finely graveled terrace which hung over a beach. In high tide, waves splashed the coral-colored marble balustrade.

Everyone in Mesembria from the greatest artisans to the simple folk worked steadily, completing the new palace in the astonishingly short time of three months. Even the children helped, carrying small things, bringing food and drink to the workers, running errands. The women, too, were a vital part of the city's effort to bring their rulers home quickly. They worked side by side, maid and matron, the fishmonger's wife and the noblewoman. With delicate strokes they painted frescos on the walls, wove coverlets and draperies of fine Bursa silk and sheer wools, and beautiful tapestries to grace the walls.

Alexander and Adora set sail for Mesembria a scant three months after the day of their wedding. The little villa on the Bosporus was closed, the servants sent overland to Mesembria. Only the couple who served the newlyweds as tiring woman and valet would accompany the prince and his bride aboard ship. Although she missed Iris, Adora felt fortunate in having Anna to serve her. A large, motherly woman who stood close to six feet tall, she treated her mistress lovingly, but with great respect. No one, Anna soon made plain to the other servants, could care for the mistress as she could. Her husband, Zeno, a thin man barely five-and-a-half feet tall, adored her unquestioningly. Anna ruled him with a benevolent iron hand.

Helena knew all this as she knew everything that might be of eventual use to her. As the despot and queen of Mesembria were not returning to Constantinople but sailing directly from their villa on the Bosphorus, the emperor and his wife paid them the compliment of coming to bid them a personal farewell. Seeing her younger sister's happiness made Helena alternate between frustrated rage and secret delight. She took great pleasure in knowing that she would, within a few months, destroy her sister's happiness.

Reclining on a couch in the lovely rooms assigned to her at the villa, Helena instructed her personal eunuch. "Fetch the lord Alexander's man, Zeno, and bring him to me. Be sure that neither of you is seen. I want no questions."

Her eyes glittered and the eunuch shivered inwardly. He had served the empress for five years and be knew her moods. She frightened him, especially when her eyes glowed with malicious glee. He had stood silently by her side on more than one occasion and watched while some unfortunate soul was tortured, often to death, simply to amuse Helena. The eunuch had survived by instant obedience, by doing his job very well, and by never voicing an opinion. Now he brought Zeno to his mistress and quickly left the room, grateful to escape.

Zeno knelt, terrified, before the empress, glad he did not have to stand. He did not believe his legs could have held him. His head was bowed, his eyes lowered. His heart hammered with sickening thuds against his narrow ribcage. The room was deathly silent as Helena rose languidly from her couch and walked slowly around the prostrate man. Had he dared to raise his eyes he would have beheld an incredible vision of beauty for the empress was gowned in soft tones of turquoise-colored Bursa silk, her well-fleshed arms gleaming like creamy polished marble through the sheer gauze sleeves of the gown. About her neck she wore a long double rope of pearls interspersed with round gold beads. But all Zeno could see was the silken hem of her gown and glimpse of gold- and silver-striped clog shoes.

She stood behind him and spoke softly, sweetly, in contrast to the meaning of her words. "Do you know, my friend Zeno, what the penalty for murder is in our realm?"

"M—Majesty?" His throat was constricted with

fear, and he could barely force the word out.

"The penalty for murder," Helena continued softly.

"Like the murder your good wife, Anna, committed. How old was your daughter, Zeno? Ten? Eleven?"

What composure had remained in the servant now vanished. No one had ever suspected that Anna had smothered Marie. The child had been dying of a wasting sickness of the blood. The doctors had been quite frank. There was no hope. Day after day she had faded before their anguished eyes. Finally one night when Marie had lain half in sleep, half in delirium, Anna had silently placed a pillow over the child's face. When she finally lifted it, Marie was dead, a sweet smile on her little face. Man and wife had looked at each other with complete understanding and never spoken of it again. How this devil-woman had discovered their secret he knew not.

"The penalty for murder, Zeno, is death by public execution. It is not a pretty way to die, particularly for a woman. Let me tell you so you will understand what is facing Anna.

"The night before she is to die, the jailor and his men, as well as the most favored of their prisoners, will take turns using your wife. I have watched such sport occasionally, though I doubt you would find it very diverting. Come morning, her head will be shaved. She will be bound to the back of the wagon carrying her torturers and the executioner—and forced to walk behind it, to the place of her execution, barefoot and naked while being whipped. The crowds love a good show, and she will be pelted with all matter of debris and spit upon—"

"Mercy, Majesty!"

Moving around to stand before him Helena purred on with her recital. "Anna will, of course, be denied the last rites of our church for murder is forbidden by God's commandments. The murder of a child in particular is a heinous enough crime to ensure eternal damnation."

A sob escaped Zeno, and the empress smiled scornfully to herself. The plebes were all such weaklings! She continued.

"Anna will be bound, spread-eagled upon a rack. Her breasts will be torn off, her womb ripped out, her hands and feet cut off. She will be blinded with red-hot coals. Lastly, she will be hung by the neck, and she will be left hanging until the birds have picked her bones clean. Then the bones will be ground into powder and thrown to the four winds!"

Zeno finally dared raise his eyes to the queen.

"Why? Why do you tell me this, Majesty? If you wish my dear Anna's death why do you torture me?"

Helena smiled her sweet smile, and Zeno was amazed. How could a woman who smiled so sweetly be so cruel? And then he saw her eyes. There was no smile in them. They were like polished blue stones. "What I have told you need not be, and your wife may yet live with you to a peaceful old age . . . if you but render me one small service."

"Anything!"

Helena smiled again, this time showing her perfect little white teeth. "I am going to give you a box containing a small vial of liquid. In a few months time— and you will pick the time carefully—you will open the vial and begin to put a few drops each day into Alexander's shaving water. *Only his shaving water.* Coat your own hands with scented oil so that, if the water should touch your own skin, there will be no harm to you. Wash them thoroughly immediately afterwards. When the vial is empty, throw it into the sea. That is all I require of you, Zeno. It is so little. Do it, and your wife's, ah, indiscretion will be forgotten."

"Is it poison, Majesty?"

She looked coldly at him. "Will you obey me?" Numbly, he nodded. "Very well then, Zeno, you are dismissed. Be sure that no one sees you leaving my suite." He stumbled to his feet and fled towards the door. "Remember, Zeno" she warned, "that Mesembria is yet a part of the empire, and my reach is a long one. My spies are everywhere." The door closed.

Alone again, Helena laughed to herself. She had won. The serving man was terrified and would obey. She would dispose of him later.

On the following day Helena stood next to her husband and bade Theadora and Alexander farewell. She was calm and appeared most loving. Afterward Adora voiced her ever-present suspicion of her older sister, but Alexander laughed. "You will be far away from Constantinople to allay the royal virago's fears. Soon something else will catch her eye—a fancied slight, or a young man with beautiful thighs."

Now she laughed! His easy assessment of Helena's character made Helena seem so unimportant that her fears slid entirely away. He slipped an arm about her waist, and they stood quietly watching their little villa recede until it seemed no larger than a toy. Ahead of them the Bosporus widened somewhat as it opened into the Black Sea. Adora felt her heart quicken at the great expanse of rolling dark-blue water. Sensing this, Alexander turned her to face him.

"Don't be frightened, beauty. It is majestic and awesome and there are no tiny islands to give the comfort of constant land in sight. It is not like our turquoise Aegean. This great sea can be the most treacherous and wicked of bitches, but she can also be a good friend. The trick is not to take her for granted like a woman of the streets. But we will not venture out into her this time, my love. We follow the coastline to our own city."

"This time, Alexander? Then you do not mean to give up the sea?"

"The sea is Mesembria's lifeline, beauty. We cannot live on the profits of Phocaea forever. There are three trade routes across the Black Sea, the most important from my mother's city of Trebizond. If I offer the merchant traders a better price for their goods than Constantinople and a shorter voyage to boot, they will come to me instead. We will then take these goods into Constantinople and they will have to pay our prices, for there will be no other choice."

Adora's eyes widened with surprise and admiration. "Is this the sort of thing a loyal subject of the emperor should do?"

"My first loyalty must be to Mesembria, beauty. For too long has Constantinople sucked her vassal cities dry and given very little in return. Young Emperor John has enough on his hands contending with the

Turks. By the time Constantinople realizes what I have done, it will be too late for them to do anything."

"You are ruthless, Alexander," she smiled. "I had not realized it before."

"I did not become the pirate king of Phocaea by chance, beauty. To survive in this world one must understand that it is populated for the most part by ruthless people. And one must think like them or else be eaten alive." He fingered the silk of her gown, and his voice softened. "Enough of this debate, Adora. We are still on our honeymoon, and the ship is well captained. Let us amuse ourselves in our cabin for we are only in the way here."

"Ship's cabins are small, my lord, and bunks are hardly conducive to the sort of entertainment you propose," she teased. "After all, Alexander, you have not the privilege of the captain's cabin this time."

"No, beauty, I don't. I have instead the privilege of the prince's cabin!" And he pulled her along up several steps to the deck above. The deck had only about six feet of open deck because a cabin took up the rest of the space. Two small arched doors of carved and gilded oak served as an entry. He turned the gold handles and ushered her into a room of unbelievable luxury.

Above the room was a cloth of aquamarine silk, woven with pale gold and silver stars. It gave the ceiling the appearance of a tent. The lamps that hung by thin gold chains from this silken ceiling were of light amber-colored Venetian glass. A bay window with leaded-crystal diamond panes, also of hand-blown Venetian glass, graced the wall opposite the door and offered them a private view of the sea. Built into the window alcove was a great bed covered in a deep blue coverlet embroidered with gold and silver scenes of Neptune and all his court. There were nymphs riding seahorses, mermaids combing their long hair while their mermen lovers watched, leaping dolphins, and flying fish all merrily cavorting across the rich dark-blue velvet. The deck beneath their feet had been covered entirely in the soft white fleece of unborn lambs. It seemed to Adora that she stood in a swirl of seafoam.

At the foot of the bed were two small flat-topped twin trunks lined in fragrant cedar, bound in polished brass. Atop each in goldleaf was the royal insignia of the House of Mesembria. Beneath were the words "Alexander, Despot" on one and "Theadora, Despoena" on the other. On the wall opposite the bed was a long rectangular table that jutted out into the room. It was made of highly-polished ebony, and its legs were heavily carved. A great silver bowl with a raised relief design of Paris, the three goddesses, and the golden apple sat in the center and was filled with large round oranges, fat purple figs, and bunches of plump pale green grapes. On either side of the table were matching arm chairs with gold-colored velvet cushions.

It was an exquisite room and as her eyes swept over it they widened again and she cried out with delight, for on the wall to the left of the door was the most beautiful dressing table she had ever seen. Attached to the wall, it was an open, golden scallop shell. Its mirror, set into the upper half of the shell, was of highly-polished silver. Its base in the shell's lower half was carefully inlaid squares of pale pink mother-of-pearl. A smaller half-shell with a coral silk cushion filled with sweet lavender made the seat.

"From your people, beauty. I understand they made two. One for the ship and another with a glass mirror for your rooms in our palace. They already love you for you are going to be the mother of their ruling house." His deep voice vibrated with passion, and she felt herself growing faint with the longing she had begun to know so well.

His aquamarine eyes held her spellbound, and she never even heard the doors to their little world close or the bolt click home. He reached out and drew her into the circle of his arms. She lay her dark head against the hollow of his shoulder—her breathing slow, but increasing in tempo as he began to undress her gently. When she finally stood naked before him he stepped back to view her, delighting in her rosy blushes. There were no worlds between them. The only sounds came from the distant voices and movement of those who ran the ship and from the slap of the waves and the gentle whoosh of the wake behind them.

She stepped forward now and began to remove his clothes. He stood quietly, a tender smile on his, lips, his eyes alight. But when he stood stripped and she slid to her knees and bent down to kiss his feet, her long dark hair swirling about his legs, he broke the silence.

"No, beauty!" He drew her to her feet. "You are not my slave or my chattel. You are my beloved wife, my queen, and my equal. We are two halves of a whole."

"I love you, Alexander, yet words are simply not enough to express how I feel!"

"My foolish Adora," he said tenderly. "What makes you think I do not know how you feel? When our bodies are one and I look into your beautiful eyes, I see all the love and hear with my heart all the words for which there are no words. I know these things because it is the same for me."

Then their mouths met, and they soared together into that tumultuous world where only lovers are allowed. Their lips still joined, he picked her up and carried her to their bed. Cradling her with one arm, he drew the velvet coverlet back with the other and then placed her between the cream silk sheets.

She held her slender arms up to him, and he felt his desire quicken at the sight of her lovely body against the luxurious sheets. Her mahogany colored hair spread across the plump pillows like a floodtide upon the beach. Then he was astride her, his long legs with their soft golden down on either side of her. His hands played with her lovely breasts, touching with just the very sensitive tips of his fingers the smooth warm skin that seemed to vibrate beneath him. She placed her hands flat against his chest, rubbing lightly with little circular motions.

His eyes narrowed and he chided her laughingly, "Adora! Adora! You are such an impatient little vixen!"

She blushed furiously, but when she tried to turn her head away he caught it between his hands. With one smooth motion he thrust into her. "Oh,

Alexander!" she breathed. "I am so shameless with you!" And he laughed happily. "True, beauty, but I am ever eager to oblige you in your naughtiness."

Slowly her violet eyes closed, and she let her passions rule her, sweeping her away into a world of hungry sounds, sighs, and pleasures almost too sweet to bear.

Deep within her there lay the frightening sensation that none of this was real—that it was only a fantastic dream from which she would soon awake. She cried out his name and clung tightly to him, fiercely demanding reassurance. He gave it.

"Beauty, my beloved beauty," he murmured against her ear, and she sighed contentedly. When she finally slept, he walked across the cabin and, opening a cabinet near the table, drew out a decanter of red wine and a stemmed silver goblet. He sipped reflectively as he watched Theadora sleep.

His first wife had been dead so long he could barely remember her. It had, at any rate, been a childhood romance.

His harem, left far behind in Phocaea, were of another world. He had married all his women to the most deserving of his lieutenants before turning the city over to his two eldest, nearly grown sons. From the night he had seduced Adora, he had never really been content with the gentle girls of his harem. He had determined to make Adora his wife one day, and Alexander would never tell her that the strange dream she believed she had had in Phocaea had been real.

The winds held fair and brisk and several days later the royal ship sailed into the walled harbor of

Mesembria to be greeted by the cheering populace. The people stood on the shore waving colored silks and a small fleet of fishing boats clustered about the great vessel. From the rail, Adora had her first good glimpse of the city . . . her new home.

Strangely, it reminded her of Constantinople although it had been in existence longer. It was a walled city, a city of marble and stone amid which she could identify several churches, some pillared public buildings, and an ancient hippodrome. "Alexander!" she pointed.

He smiled down at her and then looked to where she pointed. Alexander swallowed hard, fighting back the tears. When he had left Mesembria the blackened ruins of the old palace had haunted him, sitting malevolently upon the crest of the city's highest hill. Now the hill was crowned by a beautiful, tall marble cross, heavily gilded. It stood as a shining tribute to the memory of the Heracles family.

The ship's captain spoke. "The city wanted to surprise you, my lord despot. The cross sits in a new park which, with your permission, will be opened to the people so they may pray there for the souls of your family."

Alexander nodded, overcome. It was in that moment that Adora performed her first act as queen of Mesembria. "The people will have our permission, captain. We will so inform them, and we will publicly express our gratitude."

The captain bowed. His fears for both his city and his lord vanished. Theadora was a gracious and gentle lady. She would rule well.

The barge arrived and bumped gently against the ship. Catching a rope, Alexander swung himself from the deck to the barge below. For Adora, however, a chair was rigged, and the new despoena of Mesembria was gently lowered from her ship into her husband's waiting arms. Though his face was grave, his eyes brimmed with amusement, and she was hard-pressed not to laugh. Everyone about them was so serious, so carefully courteous.

The royal barge was elegant yet simple in its design. Two small gilt thrones had been placed beneath an azure-blue-and-silver-striped awning. Only one other person was aboard the barge, and Alexander introduced him as Basil, the royal chamberlain of Mesembria. Basil was a courtly older man whose white hair gave him a patriarchal air.

The rulers of the city seated themselves. Their chamberlain, standing, gave the command, and the barge moved toward shore.

"Is it always going to be this formal?" Adora asked desperately.

Alexander chuckled. "You have to understand, beauty, that receiving the new queen of the city, a princess of Byzantium, the daughter of an emperor, the sister of an empress—it is very heady for our people. They are, I am quite sure, terrified lest they displease you and make a bad first impression. Am I not right, Basil?"

"It is so, Highness. They want very much for the princess Theadora to like them and to like her new home."

Silence descended again and Alexander noted with

amusement that Adora's brow was furrowed in concentration. He wondered what it was she was thinking about, but before he could ask, the barge arrived at the quay. He leaped to the steps and helped his lovely wife up. A beautifully-caparisoned white stallion awaited him, pawing impatiently, and he saw a flower-decked, silk-draped cart for Adora. Beyond the end of the quay the first of the hushed crowds awaited them.

He turned to hand her up into the cart, but she shook her head. "No, my lord, let us walk among our people."

His smile of approval warmed her. "You are the cleverest woman I have ever known, Adora. The people will take you to their hearts instantly." He grasped her hand and they moved forward.

An expectant hum was beginning to race through the crowds that lined Mesembria's main avenue, The Conqueror's Path. Led by a troop of the royal guard, Alexander and Theadora walked to their palace—to the stunned delight of their people. A pretty young woman held a plump, rosy-cheeked baby, and waved its tiny hand at the couple. Adora took the baby from its surprised mother.

"What is her name?" she asked.

"Z—Zoe, H—Highness."

"It was my mother's name! May your Zoe grow up to be as good and loving as my mother was." Adora kissed the baby's downy head. "God's blessings on you, little Zoe." She handed the child back to its overcome mother.

The people of Mesembria roared their approval as

their rulers continued to make their way around the city to their seaside palace. They stopped many times to speak with the citizens. Alexander was amazed to see Adora reach deep into her cloak pocket and offer the little ones sugared almonds. There were toothless elders smiling broadly, wishing them long life and many children. Adora blushed prettily to the glee of the old ones. The callused hands of workmen and the smooth hands of young matrons reached out to touch them.

After an hour they were prevailed upon by the captain of their guard to enter the cart. The procession was almost at a halt. Now more people could see them, and the cheers became louder. They were an outrageously handsome couple: the blond, blue-eyed Alexander dressed in the silver and blue colors of his House with the great sapphire seal of Mesembria upon his chest; Adora in creamy white velvet and gold, her violet eyes shining, wearing a small gold circlet on her dark head, her long hair loose.

At last they reached the gates of the new palace where they were greeted by Basil, representatives of Mesembria's noble families, and officers of the city's guilds. The royal couple descended from the cart and the chamberlain gravely handed them golden keys to the gates.

"The Palace of the Laughing Dolphin, my lord despot. From the loyal and loving people of your city. We wish you and our lady queen long life, good health, many strong sons and fair daughters. May the heirs of Alexander and Theadora rule over us for a thousand years!" he shouted, and the people roared their approval.

Alexander inclined his head to the representatives. "Our thanks to you all," he said. "Let word go out through the city that we are pleased and will be ever grateful for the generosity of those we rule.

"We will show our gratitude by restoring the city to its former glory. No one in Mesembria will go hungry or homeless ever again. Taxes will be suspended for one year. Schools will be opened to all the children— even the maidens! This city will again flourish. On this you have our royal word!"

The gates to the palace swung open behind him, and Adora called in a ringing voice, "Come! Come and share a cup of wine with my lord and me. Celebrate with us a new golden age for the city of Mesembria!"

Again she felt his approval wash over her. Hand in hand, they led their guests through the palace grounds to the garden terrace. Tables had been set up and servants waited with food and drink. Toast after toast was drunk throughout the afternoon until the last guest finally departed.

Unable to believe they were really alone, the two stood gazing happily at one another.

"Will you be happy here?" he asked her.

"Yes," she answered softly. "I am happy wherever we are together."

"I want to make love to you," he said evenly and then, looking helplessly about, complained, "But I do not even know where our bedchamber is!"

She began to laugh, and he joined her, the deep peals of his mirth booming over her bell-like amusement. "Anna!" she gasped out. "Anna!" and when her servant appeared Adora managed to say, "Our bed-chamber? Where is it?"

The servant woman's black eyes flashed delighted comprehension. "Come," she said. "I was just coming to get you both. I have your bath ready, my princess, and Zeno waits to attend you, sire."

They followed her into the palace through a corridor painted with frescos of the ancient Greek games. The ceiling beams were carved and gilded, the marble floors covered with thick blue and red rugs from Persia. At the end of the corridor was a double door marked with the Mesembrian coat of arms. Crowned Neptune, triton in hand, rose from the waves against a scallopshell background. Anna did not slacken her pace, and the soldiers standing guard on either side of the doors flung them wide.

Anna gestured. "My lord's apartment is to the right. I am sure he will wish to bathe the salt and wind of the sea voyage from his skin. My lady's apartment is here, and an oil bath awaits her."

Biting her lip to keep from laughing Adora looked helplessly to her husband. He shrugged and, catching her hand, kissed it. "Until later, beauty," he murmured. She nodded and followed Anna.

Theadora's rooms included a sunny dayroom with a large marble fireplace, the side pillars of which were carvings of naked young goddesses. The leaping flames cast red and gold shadows over them, giving them a seductive appearance. The walls of the dayroom were hung with the most beautiful silk tapestries Adora had ever seen. There were twelve, each one depicting an event in the life of Venus. The marble floors were covered by thick rugs. The windows were hung with silken draperies and the furnishings were a mixture of Byzantine and Eastern styles. The colors of this day room were predominantly azure-blue and gold.

Adora's bedroom was done in shades of coral-pink and a pale cream color with the barest touch of gold. The matching dressing table from the ship was there, as Alexander had promised. But to her delight the big bed was also shaped like a huge scalloped shell. Its feet were made of gold dolphins who rested on their curved tails balancing the shell on their noses. The bed was topped by a golden coronet and hung with sheer silk gauze draperies of coral pink. This fairy-tale room looked out onto the sea. She felt a flush creep up her neck as she imagined Alexander and herself making love in that marvelous bed in this wonderful room.

"Your bath is through here, my princess." She jumped at Anna's voice.

They entered a blue-tiled room with a sunken bathing pool where several young maidservants waited. Within the hour she was bathed, her skin and hair free of salt. After donning a loose caftan of pale apricot-colored silk, she entered her day room again and found a supper table set up by the windows. The sky had begun to darken and the moon was rising, reflected in the calm sea.

Awaiting her, in a white silk caftan, was Alexander. The servants had magically disappeared. "Do you mind playing the maid-servant, my love?"

"No, I want to be alone with you. It has been hours since we were able to be together without a crowd."

She poured him a goblet of golden Cyprus wine and then, giggling, filled his plate with raw oysters, breast of capon, and black olives. "Our cook lacks subtlety. Even the dessert is made of eggs!"

He laughed, then sobered and reminded her, Mesembria does need an heir, Adora. I am the last of my line. There is no one left after me, no one who might rule if I died. The fire that killed my brothers and their families also took many of my uncles and cousins, all my father's relatives. They were all there that night celebrating my eldest brother's birthday. Until we have a son, I am the last of the Heracles."

Standing beside him she drew his head against the scented softness of her breasts. "We will have a son, my lord. This I promise you!"

Looking up he let his aquamarine eyes lock onto her amethyst ones and saw mirrored there far greater promises: the promise of many happy years, of a large family to replace the one he had lost, of a thousand nights of delight followed by ten times a thousand. Standing up, he held her lightly by the shoulders and looked into her upturned face.

"The food will wait, my love" said Alexander. And sweeping his wife into his arms, he carried her off to the great shell bed.

Chapter 15

THEADORA HAD FALLEN IN LOVE WITH MESEMBRIA QUITE easily. But it did, as Alexander had said, need rebuilding. It was nineteen hundred years old. Its rulers studied an accurate scale model of the city and decided that, before the public buildings could be renovated, housing for the poor must be improved. There were at least three sections of wooden tenements that were always subject to fire, and a bad conflagration could do serious damage to the entire city.

Alexander arranged to have the owners of these buildings brought before him. Adora at his side, he quietly explained what he was going to do. The existing wooden buildings would be torn down and new brick buildings would be erected. The owners had a choice. They could sell to him if they wished, but he would set the price. Or they could bear half the expense of the new buildings. Those men who kept their buildings and worked with Alexander would be exempt from taxes for five years.

Only three old men chose to sell. Their buildings were quickly bought, not by Alexander, but by their fellows.

Only one section at a time would be done, and the residents of the section being worked on would be housed in a tent city.

Afterwards, the public buildings would be redone. And the parks would be done as well.

While this was going on, Alexander's plans for turning Mesembria into a great commercial center would also be progressing. Already he was planning a trip to Trebizond to negotiate an agreement. Trebizond, one end of an overland route from the rich Far East, was a desirable location.

There was an already established trade route from the North: from Scandinavia across the Baltic into the Gulf of Finland, then overland to Lake Ladoga, Novgorod, and down to Smolensk, where it met with another route from across the Baltic into the Gulf of Riga, and then overland. Carefully hugging the shoreline, the trading fleets stopped at Tyras and Mesembria to take on water before going on to Constantinople.

This year, when the trading fleets put into Mesembria, their owners found themselves invited to dine with the new ruler. As Alexander was no polished Byzantine courtier who played at word games he always came right to the point. "Tell me," he asked quietly, "what you'll get for your cargos in Constantinople?"

One merchant, cannier than the rest, named a figure that the prince knew was double the actual figure. Alexander laughed. "Half your price, my greedy friend, and then add twenty-five percent to it. That is my offer to you. Take it either in gold or in trade goods, or in some of each. I can offer you the same fine quality merchandise that Constantinople does, and at less cost to you."

For a moment the merchants were silent. Then one asked, "Why do you offer to buy our cargos at a price you know we would be foolish to refuse? Not only can we return home with fine merchandise to sell, but for the first time in years we will have gold in our pockets as well."

"I wish to rebuild my city, friends," replied Alexander. "For too long Constantinople has taken from us, yet we have received nothing in return. With your cooperation I shall make a great commercial center of Mesembria. Soon I go to Trebizond, the state from which my mother came. I shall speak with my uncle, its emperor. Already his emissaries have assured me of the emperor's interest in my plan. When you come again next year the riches of the Far East—the silks, the jewels, the spices—will be here for you, for Trebizond will do business with me first. The Commenii family have little love for the Paleaologi family."

"Let us see the quality of your goods, my lord," said the merchants' spokesman, and Alexander knew he had won this first round. Clapping his hands, he sent a servant to fetch Basil. "My chamberlain will take you," he said. "I realize that my presence might intimidate you. Talk freely among yourselves. When you have seen my goods we will speak again."

The merchants trooped out and Alexander sat back in his chair reflectively sipping wine from a Venetian crystal goblet set with silver and turquoise. The merchants would be foolish to refuse Alexander's offer.

And when they saw his trade goods they would be more than anxious to come to Mesembria rather than go to Constantinople. Mesembria was a shorter trip, but the real savings in time was the fact that their entire cargos would be bought by Alexander. There would be no more haggling with Constantinople's merchants for bits and pieces of cargos. There would be no port taxes, landing fees, or trading permits. There would also be no officials seeking bribes. And Mesembria offered sailors amusements just as varied as Constantinople's.

Upon returning the merchants could not hide their enthusiasm. The bargain was quickly struck. The prince would personally inspect their cargos and then payment would be made. Alexander was jubilant. His dreams were beginning to come true.

Adora had been working hard to give substance to her dream of education for all the city's youth. Schools were opened offering both classical and practical education. The new queen decreed that all the children of her city must learn to read and to write. From the age of six to the age of twelve they were expected to attend school six months of the year. People of any age, however, were welcome to attend.

Even little girls were expected to go to school. When at first a grumbling arose about the foolishness of educating women, Adora reminded the parents of Mesembria of their proud Greek heritage. The maidens of ancient Greece had been taught along with their brothers. She then offered to dower the ten best female students each year, thereby greatly enhancing the value of an educated wife!

The days moved swiftly in a haze of hard work, for neither Alexander nor Theadora was an idle ruler. The nights were slow passages of sensual delights. The lovers strove to found a new dynasty for Mesembria, but Adora did not conceive.

Two nights before he was to leave for Trebizond, Alexander surprised his wife by designating her his regent in his absence. Adora was furious. "But I want to go with you," she protested. "I cannot bear to be separated from you! I will not be!"

He laughed and, pulling her down into his lap, kissed her angry mouth. "I cannot bear being separated from you either, beauty. But I must go, and we should not both be gone from our city at the same time."

Her violet eyes were mutinous. "Why not?"

"What if you are with child? What if you came with me and the ship sank? Mesembria would be without a Heracles for the first time in five centuries."

"Mesembria," she answered with logic, "would be the poorer without the Heracles family. I will admit that. But it would survive. And besides, I have just finished my show of blood and so am not with child as you well know!"

"Ah, beauty, but we have tonight and tomorrow before us," and indeed his hands were wandering provocatively.

"No!" She leapt from his lap. "I am not a brood mare! A wife's place is by her husband's side. I would go with you, and I will!"

He sighed. "You are behaving like a child, Adora."

"And you, my lord husband, with all your talk of

dynasties are sounding more like a pompous ass every minute. I am not with child, and the likelihood of my becoming so in these next two days is zero! However, if you will let me go with you we may return from Trebizond with not only a trade agreement but the hope of an heir as well. Or is it that you have some agreeable little creature who eagerly awaits your arrival in Trebizond?"

"Theadora!"

"Alexander!"

Her outrage and determination heightened her beauty, and he nearly succumbed. But a man must still be master in his own house. With a swiftness that quite surprised her, he caught her and, turning her over his knee, pulled up her gown and paddled her bare bottom. She shrieked, more with outrage than with pain.

"If you behave like a child you must be treated like one," he said sternly, giving her a final swat. He turned her back over.

"I will never forgive you for this," she sobbed.

"Yes, you will," he answered with infuriating calm, and his mouth turned up in a mischievous smile as he bent to kiss her. She compressed her lips tightly together. Chuckling, he persisted, nibbling at her mouth while her eyes flashed outrage at him. Then he stopped and said quietly, "Theadora, my sweet Adora! I love you!"

"Damn you, Alexander," she responded huskily, and her arms encircled his neck. "First you beat me, and then you want to make love to me. I have heard about men like you, and I do not know if I approve!"

He began to laugh. "Where on earth did you ever learn of such things, Adora?"

"The women in Orkhan's harem may be cloistered, but they are quite knowledgeable, and there is little to do there but talk."

"It is a husband's duty to correct and chastise his wife," he teased her.

"Not just before he wants to make love to her," she teased him back.

That night he made love to her slowly and with such controlled passion that several times she screamed at him to take her *now*! She had never known him to be so deliberate. He used her body as he might have used a fine instrument—with great delicacy and with a skill that left her breathless and pleading for more.

His head moved slowly down her body, kissing softly, until he reached her secret place. He tasted her, and she moaned, her head thrashing wildly. He raised his golden head. "Do you remember the first time, beauty? The first time I loved you like this?"

"Y—Yes!"

He smiled tenderly down at her. "You've learned to like it, haven't you?"

"Yes!"

"You're like a fine sweet wine," he said thickly, and then swung over her. She writhed beneath him, her amethyst eyes pleading, and he gently thrust into her.

"Oh, Alexander," she breathed, eagerly receiving him. For the first time she used an ancient sexual art taught to her in the harem of her first husband. Her vaginal muscles tightened around him, gently at first, then with increasing pressure as the rhythm quickened. He groaned with surprised pleasure, murmuring against her ear, "Christos! You witch! Ah, stop—or there will be no time for you to reach the top of your own mountain!"

She was in control now, and the feeling of power was delicious. "Will you love me only once this night, my lord?" And she squeezed him tightly, almost hurting him. He cried out and, sobbing with relief, released his tortured seed. "Beloved," she whispered, tenderly cradling his head against her breasts.

They lay quietly for some time, and then she felt him suddenly hard again against her leg. "Now, beauty," he said, his voice strong again, "I shall have my sweet revenge!" And he was in her moving so rapidly that she could not grip him. Pleasure began to wash over her in wave after wave. Then she began to climb with him to the top of that mountain they both knew so well. Nothing mattered but the sweet, burning intensity between them. She could go no further, but he forced her onward until suddenly she was tumbling through a golden spiral, into a soft, perfect peace.

When she finally regained her senses she found herself in the warm, safe circle of his, arms. Raising her head, she gazed into his beautiful aquamarine eyes. He smiled. "We have loved each other well beauty, haven't we?"

"Yes," she answered, "It is always good with us."

"As I promised you," he teased.

"Peacock," she countered weakly. Then, in a more serious tone, she said simply, "I have never known such happiness, Alexander. I love you so very much!"

"And I love you, beauty! Without you there would be no place for me on this earth. You are my heartbeat, the very air I breathe." Sighing happily, he nestled in the curve of his arm and fell asleep.

Alexander smiled down at her. She was so very lovely that his heart contracted painfully with the knowledge of what he must do. Slowly, his own eyes closed and he slept.

When Adora awoke several hours later the dawn was flooding her bedchamber. Alexander was gone. But he frequently rose before she did. Calling to Anna, she ordered her bath and spent a leisurely hour bathing. Afterwards, as Anna helped her into her gown, Adora asked, "Will my lord break his fast with me, Anna?"

"No, my lady." The servant quickly turned away.

"Anna? What is it?"

"What is what, my lady?" The woman was being deliberately evasive.

"Where is my lord Alexander?" she asked evenly.

Anna sighed. Taking her mistress by the hand, she led her out onto the terrace and pointed seaward. "That dot out there, my princess, is the lord Alexander's ship. He sailed before dawn."

"*Christos!*" swore Adora angrily. "How could he? He promised I could go too!"

"He did?" Anna was amazed.

"Well," hedged Adora, "I believed it was understood."

"He left this for you, my princess."

Adora snatched at the rolled parchment. Breaking

the seal, she read, "*Beauty, forgive me, but one more night such as the last and I could never have left you. What then would have become of our fair city? I shall return within two months. Each minute away from you will be like a full day, and each day will be an eternity. It is a far worse punishment I inflict upon myself than you could possibly inflict on me for this deception. Rule well in my absence. And never forget, my Adora, that I love you. Alexander.*"

The parchment hung from her hand. Suddenly she laughed. Then, just as suddenly, she cried and cursed him. Catching the look of fright on Anna's face, she explained. "Do not fear for my mind, my good Anna. I am all right. My lord has simply outmaneuvered me in this chess game we are constantly playing. I must take it with good grace, though I would sooner take a ship and go after him."

A month passed, two months, and Alexander was due home. Then, one afternoon, there came word that the prince's galley had been sighted a few miles off the coast. Adora ordered her barge readied. Gowned in pale-blue silk, her dark hair braided with gold ribbons and looped about her ears, she set out to meet her husband.

Seeing the little barge coming towards them over the deep-blue waves, Alexander's men cheered their queen. When the two vessels met, Mesembria's ruler swung himself down from the deck of his great ship to the highly-polished deck of the smaller boat. In one fluid movement he swept his beautiful wife into his arms. Their mouths met fiercely. Adora was faint with happiness. Finally he let her go. "It was not the minutes, but the seconds away from you that were like days. The minutes were like months."

"For me also," she answered softly, "but you were right."

"Right? About what?"

"About the possibility of my conceiving a child."

His marvelous eyes widened, and she laughed at his look of delight. "Had a great storm taken you, my lord Alexander, Mesembria would still have had a Heracles to reign over it!"

"You are with child?"

"I am with child!" she answered proudly.

The barge lurched on the waves and Alexander quickly drew her down to the cushions. "Sit, beauty! I want neither you nor our son harmed."

"You are very sure it is a son?"

"I have never had a daughter," he said thoughtfully, "but if she were your daughter I could easily love her." He put an arm about her. "A daughter with your violet eyes, beauty."

"And your golden hair," she answered.

'She will be like an ancient sea nymph," be said, "and we will call her Ariadne."

"Or," replied Adora, "we will call him Alexander."

They laughed happily. Suddenly she exclaimed, "I have been so full of my own news that I forgot to ask of yours. Was your trip to Trebizond successful? Will the Comenii send their trading vessels to us?"

"Yes, beauty, they will! My uncle Xenos is happy to have the opportunity to work with Mesembria. He is, as you will remember, in complete charge of Trebizond's trading concessions. His brother, the emperor, accepts his word on everything. I have brought back with me a signed agreement between Trebizond and Mesembria that will guarantee our superiority over Constantinople within the next two years. Our city will soon become a power to be reckoned with, beauty. Our children will not inherit only an empty eggshell."

"Children, is it?" she teased him. "Am I to understand that one son is not enough for you, oh great and greedy despot of Mesembria?"

He chuckled. "Children seem to be a natural result of lovemaking, beauty. And since I will always want to love you, I assume our family will be a large one."

Adora sighed. She was completely happy. So unbelievably happy. She loved and was loved in return. And now she was to have another child. She had been hesitant, but now that this new life nested within her, she realized how much she really wanted it. Smiling to herself, she wondered why the tangible proof of love, a child, was so important to a woman.

The autumn came. And as the fruits in the orchards ripened so did the queen of Mesembria ripen with her child. The people of the small city-state were overjoyed.

But in Constantinople the empress fretted angrily. Why had that frightened fool, Zeno, not destroyed Alexander? Now Thea was pregnant, and if Murad lost his passion for her then Helena's revenge would be lost. She sent a spy to inquire and to further terrorize the prince's servant. Her spy reported that Zeno felt the time was not right. Let the prince and princess feel totally secure in their lives lest the plot be discovered and Helena's name revealed. The empress was forced to bide her time. She sent secret word to Ali Yahya, promising that soon her sister would be delivered into the sultan's power.

In Bursa, Ali Yahya received the message and was very skeptical. His own spies told him that Theadora was happy, and soon to bear her husband a child. Still, he hoped for her return to Bursa for Murad longed desperately for her, so desperately that he would take no other women. This left the Ottoman Empire without heirs until Prince Halil and his wife were grown and had consummated their marriage.

In January of the new year—two months early— Theadora went into labor. She was quickly delivered of twins, a son and a daughter. The little boy Alexander Constantine died within the week

The little girl survived. Both had been the image of their father, but as the little Ariadne grew her eyes became the wonderful amethyst color of her mother's. Adored by both her parents, she was nursed only by her jealous mother who could hardly bear to have the child out of her sight. As the months passed, however, and Ariadne thrived, Theadora became less fiercely protective.

One early autumn afternoon when the baby princess was eight months old, the family sat upon the soft green lawn of the palace gardens and watched their daughter crawling about the grass. She sat on a pink silk square, clapping her hands and crowing delightedly at the darting butterflies. Finally she fell asleep, thumb in mouth, one finger hooked over her button nose, her dark gold lashes fanlike on her rosy cheeks.

"If only the boy had lived too," said Adora sadly. She always called him the "boy," unable to think of him as Alexander.

"It was God's will, beauty. I do not understand it, but I must accept it."

Why? she wanted to shout at him. But she only said, "Your faith is greater than mine."

"You grieve for him yet, beauty?"

"I grieve for what he might have been. But I never knew him. Perhaps that is the reason for my sadness. Ariadne is already a complete person, but our poor little son will forever remain in my memory as an infant who had barely the strength to cry."

"We will have other sons, beauty."

Catching his hand, she held it to her heart. "I am selfish, my darling, for he was your son too. Yes! We will have other sons! Strong sons! And we are blessed in having an outrageously beautiful daughter."

"If we are to have sons," he said seriously, "you must stop nursing our daughter, beauty."

Adora looked rueful. "She is too young to be weaned, Alexander."

"Then get her a wetnurse. If you look carefully you can find a healthy young woman whose milk is fresh and wholesome. You spoil Ariadne. And," he added plaintively, "I should like to be spoiled too."

Adora laughed. But realizing his sincerity, she promised, "When you return from Trebizond Ariadne will have a wetnurse, my lord, and you will have your wife back again." Then she asked, "Why must you go *again*, Alexander?"

"Because, beauty," he explained patiently, "my

uncle's last message says that the last of the caravans from the East have arrived and are being transferred to the waiting ships. I must go to Trebizond as a matter of courtesy, and personally escort these ships back to Mesembria. Think of it, Adora! Those rich cargos are ours! Silks! Spices! Jewels! Slaves! Rare and exotic animals! Constaninople will pay dearly for these things. But this one time I must go or else those merchants may think I do not value them."

"Go then," she sighed, resigned. "But hurry back."

"It will not be as long as the last time, beauty. Just long enough to sail to Trebizond, fête the merchants, and return to Mesembria. A month at the most, with favorable winds."

"Take Zeno with you, Alexander. Ever since that poor servant girl was found at the back gate of the palace so hideously murdered he has been very nervous. Perhaps the sea voyage will soothe him."

Alexander nodded. "I cannot understand why anyone would do something so horrible to a person of such little importance. Murder is one thing, but the terrible way in which the girl was mutilated and blinded—I was sickened by it. I think what frightened Zeno so badly was the fact that the girl was called Anna, like his wife. Yes. I will take him with me. Perhaps by the time we return his nerves will be sound again."

That night they made love tenderly and slowly. When morning came Adora went with her husband to their daughter's nursery and watched fondly as he bid the baby good-bye. He playfully nibbled at the little girl's toes, eliciting delighted giggles. Picking her up, he inquired, "And what shall the mighty despot of Mesembria bring to the fairest of creatures, his princess Ariadne? Perhaps a porcelain bowl from Cathay filled with rare Persian tulips the color of your eyes? Or a carved golden goblet brimming over with Indian pearls that match your skin?"

"Da!" chortled the baby triumphantly. Then she cooed softly at her father. Adora's heart contracted at the sight of the two identical golden heads pressed together. The only part of her in Ariadne was the color of the little girl's eyes. Everything else, including the expression in those eyes, was Alexander.

Alexander kissed his daughter tenderly and then they left her to her nurse. Husband and wife went out to where the barge awaited them.

"Say good-bye to me here, beauty. If you come to the ship with me I shall not want to let you go."

"Let me come this time!" she suddenly begged impulsively. "Should we not return, Mesembria has another Heracles to rule it."

"But an heiress, beauty, not an heir. You must stay and protect our daughter. Should I not return, would you trust her fate to strangers?"

"No," she replied sadly, "but promise me that after this voyage you will *never* leave me again."

"I promise, beauty," he answered her. Bending, he found her lips. Her arms slipped around his neck and she molded her body to his. As they kissed she felt tears rise unbidden to dampen and prick her closed eyes. Sensing her tears, he kissed her eyelids. "No, beauty, don't weep. I will be home before you know it." Then, tearing himself from her grasp, he leapt to the barge. It pulled away from the palace quay and towards the waiting galley in the harbor.

That afternoon Ariadne became feverish and fretful. Adora, Anna, and the baby's nurse took turns sitting, by the child's cradle all night. The following morning the little princess's face and body were covered in a mass of red spots, and she wailed plaintively. Her tiny fists covered her eyes to shield them from the sunlight. The doctors came in their long black robes to poke at the child and examine her urine.

"Smallpox?" whispered Adora fearfully.

"No, my lady. You may rest assured it is not the pox, but merely a childish complaint from which the lady Ariadne will undoubtedly recover."

"Undoubtedly? You are not *sure*?"

"Highness, occasionally children expire from this spotted fever, but they are children of the poor, not well-cared-for babies like this one. It is very rare for a child of the privileged to die from this malady. Keep the room dark, for light bothers the eyes in this illness. See that the princess takes plenty of liquids. In a few days time all will be well."

But all was not well, and Ariadne did not seem to respond to the prescribed treatment. She grew too weak to nurse and Adora, forcing the milk from her breasts, spoonfed it into her child's mouth. Some of it got down Ariadne's throat, but most of it drizzled out the side of her mouth. Adora never left her daughter's side.

Then, finally, Ariadne showed some improvement, and Anna was able to get Adora to rest. Exhausted, she slept around the clock.

Adora threw herself into a frenzy of work. But despite the strenuous schedule she set for herself she still had trouble sleeping at night. It was lonely in the great bed without Alexander.

A week passed. And then on the eighth day after Alexander's departure for Trebizond, the dawn rose to reveal the royal ship sailing back into the palace harbor.

Anna frantically shook her mistress awake. "My princess! My princess! The prince's ship has returned!"

Adora was instantly awake and off the bed, barely waiting for the green silk robe Anna helped her into. Barefoot, her long dark hair streaming behind her, she ran through the gardens and down to the beach below just in time to meet the ship's little boat. There were three people in it; a sailor who rowed, the ship's captain, and Zeno. The boat slid up onto the beach.

"What is the matter?" demanded Adora. "Where is my lord Alexander? Why have you returned?"

The captain and Zeno climbed from the boat. Zeno was pale, stooped. He looked yellow and very ill. The captain was somber.

Adora was becoming frightened. "Where is my lord Alexander?" she repeated.

Zeno began to weep and fell to his knees at her feet. Adora felt a wave of dizziness sweep over her. She looked to the captain. His eyes were filled with tears.

"My lord Alexander . . . ?" she whispered.

"Dead." The word came out cold and hard. "Ah, God, my princess! I should sooner be dead myself than bring you this news!"

Theadora looked at him hard and slowly the terrible comprehension filled her eyes. Zeno whimpered at her feet. "Dead?" she said. Slowly turning away, she crumpled to the beach. "No! Not dead! Not dead!"

Feeling a great deal older than his years the captain lifted the woman. She was now unconscious. He carried her into the palace to her frantic servants, then delivered the tragic news to the chamberlain.

Basil immediately called a meeting of the royal council. The stunned councilors decided to ask their queen, when she had recovered, if she would remain as their ruler. Theadora Cantacuzene had shown the Mesembrians that she was truly one of them, and they far preferred a known ruler, even a female, to a strange, foreign prince.

In the great bed the queen of Mesembria lay unconscious, watched over by her women. Assured that Adora would not yet waken, Anna slipped from the room to confront her husband. There was more to this than met the eye. She knew Zeno well. His grief was more than simple grief. He lay upon the bed in their room, staring at the ceiling with sightless eyes. Firmly she closed the door, sat next to him, and spoke. "What have you done, my husband?" she asked him quietly.

"I had to, Anna! She knew about our Marie. She said she would have you executed, and she described. how they would do it! I couldn't let that happen. I had to kill him for her!"

"Who, my husband? For whom did you do this terrible thing?"

"The empress Helena."

"Tell me everything, Zeno, my love. Tell me now."

She listened as her husband poured out his story When he had finished, she shook her head sadly. "Oh, Zeno, we are little people. Unimportant in the eyes of God and our fellow man. Prince Alexander was a great man. Better we had died instead of the prince. And all because of a wicked woman's envy. May God forgive you, Zeno, for I never shall."

"I did it to save you, Anna!"

"Save me? From what? Death? We must all die eventually, Zeno. I do not fear death. Far more do I fear having to live side by side with the princess, knowing what I do. Oh, my husband! Had you only had the wit to tell the prince when that evil creature approached you! He would have protected us, and been on his guard against her. Now he is needlessly dead, and who will protect you from the empress's assassin? She must dispose of you, for only you can connect her with this terrible deed." Anna stood up. "I must return to my princess. She is still unconscious." And without even a backward glance at her husband, Anna left the room.

Several hours later the prince's man servant, Zeno, was found in the gardens, hanging from a tree.

"He loved his lord deeply," declared the widow. "He has chosen to follow him in death rather than remain without him. I would do the same for the princess."

For two days Theadora lay unconscious on her bed while the royal council planned the state funeral. They feared they might have to bury Alexander without her presence, but on the afternoon of the second day she awoke, stared at the exhausted Anna, and whispered,

"Is it true?"

"Aye, my princess."

"How long have I been like this?"

"Two days."

"What has been done in my illness?"

"The council has prepared for a state funeral. It is tomorrow. They have also appointed you their ruler." Anna paused. There was no gentle way to tell her mistress the terrible thing she did not yet know, and so Anna simply gazed into the eyes of the princess and said, "I wish I had anything but this to tell you, my princess. Anything but this."

"Not Ariadne?" murmured Adora, beginning to feel strangely numb. Anna nodded.

"It happened suddenly, at the moment the ship was spotted on the horizon."

Adora nodded, now entirely devoid of feeling.

"I see. Thank you, Anna." A moment later she asked, "Where is my lord?"

"His bier is in the palace audience chamber. The people have been passing through since yesterday."

"Clear the hall. I would have a few minutes alone with my husband."

Anna nodded and went silently out. She was worried by Theadora's strange calm. The princess had yet to shed a tear. It was not natural.

Quickly she found Basil. "The princess has awakened from her swoon, my lord. She desires that the audience chamber be emptied so she may be alone with the prince."

The chamberlain nodded. "It will be done immediately."

264

Shortly after that Theadora walked alone to where her husband's bier rested. She saw no one. In deference to her feelings even the guards had withdrawn. Pushing open the doors to the hail she entered the room. Alexander's bier had been placed in the center. The hall was filled with tall, beeswax candles that flickered in an oddly cheerful fashion. The room was cold.

Slowly Adora walked to the bier and gazed down at the body. They had dressed him in an azure-blue velvet robe, the Mesembrian arms embroidered in gold thread on the front of the robe. The robe cuffs, hem, and neckline were edged in ermine. Upon his softly curling blond hair they had placed the crown of Mesembria's despot. On his chest was a gold chain and the city's sapphire seal. His wedding ring was on his hand. On his feet were fine soft leather boots.

Adora viewed the body from all angles, walking slowly around the bier. What she saw convinced her firmly of the existence of a soul: for though the body was his, this was not truly Alexander. Without the spark of life this was only an empty shell, a cocoon without its butterfly.

She knelt at the prie-dieu set before the bier, but she did not pray. She spoke silently to him. *I want to be with you. It is too great a burden to bear alone. I have not even the comfort of our child.*

It is not meant to be, beauty, came his reply. *Your fate is to follow a different path. I know that now.*

"No!" she shouted aloud. "I will not accept that fate."

Ah, beauty, he chided her, *why do you always struggle*

so hard against your fate? What is meant will be. The logic of our Greek ancestors should tell you that.

Suddenly she began to weep. "Do not leave me, Alexander! *Please* do not leave me!"

Ah beauty, would you keep me a prisoner between the two worlds? I cannot go unless you let me. Release me from this earth of which I am no longer a part.

"No! No!"

I love you, beauty, and if you love me you must let me go. What has been between us can never be taken away. Our story is firmly engraved in the pages of the world's history. You will always have your memories.

"Alexander!" It was an anguished cry.

Adora, please! She understood the plea. Tears poured down her face, but she did not feel them. Her heart ached so painfully that she thought it would burst. Her voice caught in her throat, but she managed to force the words out.

"Farewell, Alexander. Farewell, my beloved husband!"

"Farewell, Beauty!" She heard his voice!

"Alexander!" she screamed then, but the room was silent. "Alexander!" came back the frantic, mocking echo. Slowly, she rose from her knees.

Tomorrow they would commend to God the soul of the last Heracles to rule in Mesembria, and then she would found a new dynasty whose first son, she vowed, would be called Alexander.

It rained heavily the next day, yet the streets of Mesembria were filled with silent mourners. They took strength from their queen. She sat straight on the white palfrey led by Basil. Her gown was black velvet

—long sleeved, plain, completely unadorned. She wore no jewelry but her wedding band and, upon her unbound dark hair, the small gold consort's crown. The patriarch of Mesembria conducted the funeral mass in St. John the Baptist's Cathedral, which had been built some four hundred years prior by Alexander's ancestors.

Afterward the mourners made their way to the memorial park above the city where Alexander's family had been buried. Here his coffin was placed in a marble tomb facing the sea. Ariadne's little coffin was placed beside her father's.

Adora performed her widow's duties in stony silence. At the palace, she snapped when Anna questioned her. "Mourn for your husband in your way, old woman! I will mourn for mine in my way. And for my child, too, as I choose. Alexander has left me a great trust, and if I spend my time in idle weeping I shall fail him. I will never fail him!" But in the silent cold hours before dawn she wept secretly. Her grief was a private thing, not to be shared with anyone. From that moment on, Theodora refused to release herself from her feelings about either Alexander or Ariadne. What she felt about the loss of the two people closest to her heart was a matter she shared with nobody at all, from then until the day she died.

Each day she presided over her council, following the progress being made on the city's renovations, meting out justice, working with the city's merchants.

Then, one day, a delegation arrived from Constantinople led by a nobleman Lord Titus Timonides. Adora knew him to be an occasional lover of Helena's. He brought two messages. The first, from Helena to her sister, was filled with a false sympathy Adora recognized immediately. She tossed the offending parchment aside and opened the second message. It was an imperial edict signed by the empress, appointing Lord Timonides governor of Mesembria. Wordlessly, Adora handed it to Basil. He quickly scanned it, then spoke aloud to the assembled council. "The empress wishes to appoint this man our governor."

"No!" came the collective shout of outrage.

Basil turned to Timonides. "You see how it is, my lord. They do not want you. But far more important, the empress has no legal right to make such an appointment. Our charter, which is as old as this city and older than Constantinople itself, gives us the right to choose our own leaders. We have chosen the princess Theadora to rule over us."

"But she is a woman," came the condescending reply.

"Aye, my lord," replied the old man. "How clever of you to notice that. She is a woman! A beautiful woman! Nonetheless a capable leader. She is Mesembria's choice. It is not up to your empress to appoint us a ruler."

"But the empress wants her sister to return home. In her great grief she surely needs the comfort of her family."

Adora choked with outrage. "Helena has never had any but the most hostile feelings towards me, Titus Timonides. You know that. My beloved Alexander left me his city as a trust, and these good men of my royal council have confirmed that trust. I have not lived in Constantinople since was a child. With both my parents gone from there, the city holds no fascination for me. Mesembria is my true home, and here I will remain. Return to my sister, and tell her that. Also tell her that if she again attempts to interfere with our government, we will take the appropriate action."

"You will regret this, princess," snarled Timonides

"Do you dare to threaten the queen of Mesembria?" thundered Basil. Timonides saw that about the council hands had gone to sword hilts. Their grim looks made it clear that he had gone too far. These men would not hesitate to kill him. "Get you back to your mistress, Byzantine, and give her our message. Mesembria will not be interfered with!"

Titus Timonides did not hesitate. Gathering up his party of idle courtiers and hangers-on, he returned to his ship. They sailed back to Constantinople where he sought immediate audience with the empress.

Helena received in her bedchamber. She was looking particularly stunning in a chamber robe of sheer black silk with a painted gold design. Her long blond hair was loose about her shoulders. Reclining on one elbow on her side, she allowed the seductive outline of hip, thigh, leg and breast to be visible. Timonides felt a sense of frustrated lust, for, reclining next to Helena was the smiling current captain of her guard. While Timonides offered his report the handsome young soldier, naked save for a breechcloth, fondled the empress's ripe breasts. At one point he even pushed his hand between Helena's soft thighs, and dallied there.

"Why are you back here instead of in Mesembria? And where is my sister?" demanded Helena.

"Their charter allows them to choose their own ruler. They have chosen your sister. They expect her to eventually remarry, and found them a new dynasty."

"In other words, Titus, they sent you packing. That is very unfortunate, Titus. You know how I dislike failure. Paulus, that is too delicious." Helena stroked the soldier's cheek. "However, Titus, I will give you a chance to redeem yourself," she continued. "You will take a message from me to the Bulgarian general, Symeon Asen. He will take care of this troublesome matter, and my sister will return home to Constantinople. Go now and rest. You must go alone on this new journey."

Titus Timonides bowed himself from the empress's presence, thankful to still be alive. Helena did indeed dislike failure. It was reassuring to know that the bitch had some feeling for him.

In the royal bedchamber Paulus moved to mount his mistress but she pushed him aside. Rising from the bed, she began to pace. "You will have to go to Mesembria by sea, and rescue Theadora."

"Rescue her?" He looked puzzled.

"Yes, rescue her. The message Titus carries offers our friend General Asen the city of Mesembria if he will but take it. The Bulgarians captured Mesembria over five hundred years ago but held it only for a short period. They have always coveted it. My note will explain to the general that he may have the city and its people. I only want my sister returned safely to me. Of course, if he should choose to amuse himself with her for a short bit before be returns her, I cannot prevent it. Your job, my brave Paulus, will be to bring your ship into the imperial boat basin and remove Thea from the mouth of danger. Do not fail me, Paulus!"

"It shall be done, my empress," smiled the handsome soldier. He drew Helena back onto the bed and, opening her gown, rubbed his face against her breasts. "What of Timonides? He is no fool, and will quickly make the connection between his message and Mesembria's downfall."

The empress's red nipples hardened. "Poor Titus will not be returning to us. My message also asks that the messenger be executed. There must be no connection between General Asen and me. Paulus, darling! Ohhh, yes!"

The empress lay on her back now, murmuring with pleasure as her lover's lips moved over her body. "Such a clever girl, my beautiful Helena," whispered Paulus. And then they lost themselves in carnal pleasures.

Adora, her council, and the laborers all worked hard. The weeks sped by, and Alexander's plans for the city began to take shape. Three districts which had contained wooden tenements were now completely rebuilt. The public buildings were now under renovations, with the city's ancient Hippodrome to be the first completed. There were plans to celebrate the reconstruction with a series of games, as had been held in earlier times.

But suddenly one night the countryside about Mesembria erupted into flames. From the city walls the burning villages and fields could be seen for miles. The following day Mesembria's gates remained closed, and Adora stood with her soldiers on the city walls staring out into the silent land. Nothing moved, not man nor beast. Even the birds had stopped singing. Within the city the people moved quietly, nervously, about their tasks. Their queen refused to leave the walls—but stood watching. Then, on the winds came the frightening booms of the war drums, the steady tramp of marching. Boom! The drums resounded through the city.

"Bulgars! Christos! Bulgars!" swore Basil.

"War?" asked Adora.

"I do not know, Highness, but do not fear. They have not taken the city since the year eight hundred and twelve, and we were not fortified then as we are now. And we have the sea. The Bulgars are not sailors."

"What must we do, Basil?"

"Wait. We will wait to see what it is they want. I think, however, that you would be safer in your palace. Now, Highness, do not argue with this old man. You are Mesembria's hope, and you must be protected at all costs."

Theadora patted the old man's cheek. "Basil, were you young enough to give me sons, I should name you my consort."

He chuckled. "Nay, Highness, I should make a poor one. You need a strong hand, and I have not one where you are concerned."

She laughed. Blowing him a kiss, she climbed into her litter and returned to the palace. Several hours later an explosion shattered the city. At almost the same time a white-faced Basil arrived in Theadora's private chamber.

"What has happened?"

"I cannot explain it, Highness. The Bulgars arrived at our outer gates. They sent no heralds with messages, they did not even fire upon us. Of course our archers held their fire.

"A strange looking little man—his skin yellow!—was escorted to our gates. We could not see what he was doing but he stepped back, dragging what looked like a soft rope with him. A torch was set to the rope, and there was this terrible explosion. When the smoke cleared our great bronze gates were open. Fortunately, I was on the upper walls, and leapt upon my horse to hurry here. There is little time. Whatever magic they used to get through the outer gate they will use to get through the inner gate. You must flee now, my princess! The sea is your best escape!"

At that moment another explosion rocked the city, and they could hear the triumphant shouts of the invading army, the screams and shrieks of the frightened people. Fires began to spring up, the flames pointing toward the palace.

Adora shook her head. "I will not leave my people, Basil. The Bulgars will not harm me. I am the ruler of this city and the emperor's sister. They seek only to pillage and loot. We will pay whatever ransom they demand, and then they will go."

"Nay, my princess. They want the city, and with Alexander gone they feel you are easy prey. I know, not by what magic they gained entry through our bronze gates, but it is a stronger magic than we possess. You must leave!"

They argued, not even hearing the approaching Bulgars until the screams of the women in the outer chamber alerted them. Anna burst through the door and shielded Theadora with her big body. Between Anna's tall body and Basil's, Adora could see nothing, but she could hear the shrieks and moans of her abused women, and the cruel shouts of laughter from the Bulgars who attacked them. Then, as if they had been struck by the hand of God himself, both Anna and Basil crumbled to the floor leaving Adora visible.

She stared, horrified, at her two friends. Their murderers were casually wiping their bloodied swords on Anna's skirts. Adora's senses returned at the appearance of a huge bearlike man. He stood close to seven feet tall with arms and legs like tree trunks. He had a huge head and dark red hair, with a full red beard.

"Princess Theadora?" said a harsh voice. "I am General Symeon Asen."

She did not know where her own voice came from. "Why have you attacked my city?"

"Your city? No, princess, *my* city! However, I fancy it will be a lot easier to subdue the people with you at my side, so let us say I have come courting." He nodded almost imperceptibly at his two men. Before she realized what they were doing, her gown was being torn off. In seconds she was naked, and when she sought to cover herself her arms were brutally pinioned back. The look in General Asen's eyes terrified her, and she struggled not to faint. "By God!" swore the Bulgarian, "Even naked you can tell she's a princess. What skin!" He reached out and squeezed one of her breasts. She struggled, which only seemed to amuse the men. Asen licked his lips. "See if you can find a priest left alive in this city. He'll marry us in the morning. And get those bodies out of here. They disturb my bride-to-be."

The two men released her arms and dragged the lifeless Anna and Basil from the room. Adora was left alone with her captor.

She backed away from him, and he laughed. "There's no place to run, Theodora. But you are right to fear me. I am not an easy man to please. But somehow," his voice became soft, "I think you'll please me well. Come and give me a kiss now. I must see to my men before we can take our ease. Who is to criticize if we celebrate the wedding night before the wedding? Rulers, after all, set the fashions."

Wordlessly she shook her head, but the general simply laughed. "A shy widow? It speaks well of your virtue, Theodora, and that, too, pleases me." He reached out and drew her struggling body to him. His chain mail cut her breasts, and she cried out. Ignoring her, he pressed his open mouth on her lips and thrust his tongue into her mouth. She gagged at the taste of sour wine and garlic. His mouth was wet and slimy, and his lips moved swiftly to race over her shrinking breasts. One arm about her waist, he bent her body this way and that as suited him, his other huge paw clasping one of her buttocks, kneading it more frantically as his excitement grew. She fought harder and, to her growing horror, felt his engorged maleness butting against her thigh. He laughed huskily. "Would that I could bury my giant's spear in you right now, Theadora. But alas, duty first. That is why I am a good general." He released her so suddenly that she fell to the rug. "Yes," he murmured, "that is a woman's place—at a man's feet. I will be back shortly, my bride. Do not grow overeager," he laughed uproariously as he left the room.

She did not know how long she lay there, but suddenly she felt a gentle touch on her shoulder. Raising her head, she stared into the blue eyes of a Byzantine captain of the Imperial Guard. He put a finger to his lips to indicate silence, then helped her up. He wrapped a dark cloak about her swiftly and led her through the terrace doors. They ran through the gardens, down the terrace steps, and onto the beach where the silent captain lifted her into a waiting boat.

In total silence he rowed out into the dark of the imperial yacht basin. Theadora saw a ship looming in the blackness. It showed no lights. The small boat bumped the sides of the ship softly, and the captain noiselessly shipped the oars. He pointed to a rope ladder hanging from the ship. Silently Theadora climbed up into the dark and was lifted over the ship's rail. Her rescuer came up behind her. Taking her hand, he led her to a large cabin. Inside, he checked to be sure the porthole was covered, then lit a small lamp.

"Welcome aboard, Princess Theadora. Captain Paulus Simonides of the Imperial Guard, at your service."

The cold night air had cleared her head and she had lost her fear. "How came you here, captain, in time to rescue me? I cannot believe in that kind a fate."

The captain laughed. God, she was beautiful. Even

more so than Helena. And intelligent, too. "The empress was informed by an old friend in the Office of Barbarians of General Asen's impending attack on your city. She was also informed that he had with him a great magician from Cathay, one who could open even great doors of bronze—doors like your city gates. She dispatched me at once to aid you, should you need it. I regret I was not sooner, Highness. When I arrived the general was already in your room, and I had to wait until I was sure he was gone."

Theadora nodded. "I have no clothes, not even shoes."

"In the trunk, Highness. The empress has been quite thorough."

"Helena is always quite thorough, captain," replied Theadora dryly.

The captain bowed. "By your leave, Highness," he said, backing out the cabin door. Once outside, he chuckled. The princess had wit as well as intelligence and beauty. Perhaps he would attempt to become her lover. If she were also as passionate, uninhibited, and inventive as Helena, then God had truly created the perfect woman.

Mesembria was in flames. Watching by the rail, Paulus marveled. The empress's hatred of one woman had destroyed a whole city, and the princess wasn't even aware of it. He wondered what fate Helena had in store for her sister, but then he shrugged. That was not his business. He had done his job and the empress would be pleased. Especially when he told her of the general's intention to marry the princess. He had rescued her just in time.

When the vessel docked in the yacht basin of the Boucoleon Palace several days later, Helena was waiting eagerly. Unknowing onlookers attributed her excitement to relief and joy at her sister's successful escape from the fallen city The truth was far different. Soon . . . soon . . . thought Helena exultantly. Soon I shall be free of her forever!

Enfolding Theadora to her ample bosom, the empress said, "Thank God and the blessed Maria that you're safe!"

Theadora pulled away from her sister. One perfect eyebrow arched, she said calmly, "Come now, Helena, I think I fear your concern more than truthful wrath."

Helena laughed in spite of herself. Sometimes Thea's quick tongue was amusing. "We may not always like each other, Thea," she replied, "but you are my sister."

"And now that you have me safe, Helena, what comes next?"

"That is up to you, sister. Your husbands all seem to have such brief lives. Perhaps it would be better if you rested for a time before you chose another mate."

"I shall never marry again, Helena."

"Then you will take lovers."

"No, sister, I shall not take lovers. No man will ever have me again. After I have rested I shall consider entering the Convent of St. Barbara. There is no life for me without Alexander."

It was all Helena could do to conceal her joy. It was going to be better even than she had hoped. In Murad's harem Theadora would suffer the tortures of the damned. It was simply *too* delicious. Helena nodded soberly. "I thought you might still feel bereaved, Thea, and so I have arranged for you to stay here in the Boucolean Palace rather than come home with me to the Blanchernae, to our noisy court. Will that be satisfactory, or do you prefer the Blanchernae?"

Adora was surprised by Helena's thoughtfulness. "No, I am content to remain here, Helena. It is not simply Alexander's death that torments me but the capture of Mesembria by the Bulgars. It was so quick! So devastating! They destroyed in a few hours all the work we had done to restore the city. Work of months!"

"Sister, I would not pain you . . . but how exactly did Alexander die? The only word we received from your council was of his death."

Even now Adora knew she dare not tell Helena of Alexander's trip to Trebizond. "The doctors," she replied with perfect honesty, "believed that he had a weakness of the heart. His man went to awaken him; and he was dead. Poor Zeno. He was so heartbroken he hanged himself."

Good! thought Helena. "Did his wife not serve you?"

"Anna? Yes. The Bulgars killed her."

Excellent! the empress thought to herself. No loose ends. "Ah, sister, surely you have seen enough tragedy to last a lifetime. Rest here. I will come in a few days time to see how you are."

Once again the sisters publicly embraced, then parted. Helena climbed into her barge to be rowed up the Golden Horn to her palace, and Theadora was escorted to her apartments.

For several days Adora abandoned herself to total rest. She slept. She bathed. She ate. She saw only the servants. She spoke to no one except to ask for something. Slowly her mind began to clear.

Several months ago Theadora had been an ecstatic bride, queen of a beautiful and ancient city. She had been a mother again after all these years. Then suddenly she had lost her child and her husband. But at least she had then looked forward to a future as the ruler of Mesembria.

Then suddenly everything in her life was gone. Everything.

The empress allowed her younger sister a week to rest. Twice she sent Adora small gifts: once a silver dish of honeyed dates and figs; then a crystal flacon of perfume. Adora took one sniff and laughingly disposed of that.

Like a spider, Helena spun her wicked web about her unsuspecting sister. Ali Yahya was secretly sent for and a time was arranged for the abduction. The eunuch asked, "She is not with child, is she? If this prince was the stallion you claim, she could well be."

"No, thank God, else I should have had to arrange an abortion too. No, eunuch, set your mind at ease. She has just finished her show of blood," replied the empress.

Two hours after midday on the appointed day, Helena, Ali Yahya, and two other eunuchs entered the royal bedchamber in the Boucoleon Palace. They found Theadora sleeping peacefully on the bed. Gently they tied her ankles and wrists together with silken cords and bound a soft gauze handkerchief about her mouth. She was next wrapped in a large, dark, hooded cloak.

The empress opened the secret passageway. Preceded by one eunuch and followed by the other, Ali Yahya picked up Theadora and traveled the length of the passage. They emerged within a few yards of his galley. They boarded the ship quickly, the oars-master began the measured beat that set the pace for the rowers, and they were swiftly out of the little walled harbor and into the Sea of Marmara. A brisk breeze filled their sails and they were soon safely on the other side, back in Turkish territory.

The still unconscious princess was then placed carefully in an awning-covered wagon to begin her journey back to Bursa. There was some daylight left in which to travel, and Ali Yahya was not very surprised to see a troop of imperial Janissaries ride up to escort them. Their captain sought him out and said, "The sultan is encamped but a short distance from here, sir. We are to lead you there."

The chief white eunuch was most distressed. Damn Murad's lust! He was so overeager for the princess that he would spoil everything. Ali Yahya had not even been aware that the sultan had crossed back over the Sea of Marmara from his minor siege of Constantinople. He had hoped to get Theadora safely back to Bursa where he could calm her fears, deal with her anger, and reason with her. With time, he could convince her of the great opportunities opening to her. Why, if she bore Murad a son, the boy might well be the next sultan!

But the grieving princess would awaken to find

herself in the presence of the very man she had fled. Allah! There were times when Ali Yahya blessed the stroke of fate that had rendered him free of a man's passion. He knew he would not be able to keep Murad from the princess long. But if he could tell the sultan— even briefly—of the princess's unhappy sexual experiences with Orkhan, then perhaps Murad would be compassionate and alleviate Theadora's fears. Ali Yahya had not been able to explain things properly to Murad since Theadora had fled.

Too soon they were entering the sultan's campsite, and Ali Yahya looked down at his helpless captive. Though she still slept it was no longer a deep sleep. She would soon awaken. He had little time. The wagon stopped, and before he could move, the curtains were impatiently flung back and the sultan climbed inside.

"Is she all right? Why is she so still? Does she understand her position?"

"Please, my lord, let us go into your tent. The princess is fine, but she is still under the influence of the sleeping draught the empress gave her. I do not want her to awaken prematurely. She knows nothing of what has happened. It will all be a terrible shock to her, especially the knowledge that her sister has sold her into slavery." He turned to the two eunuchs who had accompanied him. "Take Princess Theadora to her tent," he commanded them. "And have someone keep watch. Send for me when she appears to be ready to awake."

The sultan leapt from the wagon and helped Ali Yahya down. Together they entered his large, luxurious tent and settled themselves about the coffee burner. The chief eunuch reached into his voluminous robes and drew out a rolled parchment which he handed to the sultan.

Breaking the red-wax seal the sultan unrolled it and read. A slow smile lit his face. "She is mine now!" he exulted. "She belongs to me alone! No man will ever have her again but me!"

Ali Yahya looked puzzled and the sultan's dark eyes fastened directly on his servant. "You wonder if I am mad, do you not, oh keeper of imperial secrets? Well, I shall give you another secret to hoard to yourself. One day many years ago, as I walked past the Convent of St. Catherine, I heard a cry. I looked up to see a girl falling from the wall. It was the princess, and she had been in the orchard stealing peaches. I caught her and returned her safely over the wall.

"She was alone in those days, without friends. We struck up a friendship and, may Allah have mercy, we fell in love. We dared to hope that my father with his vast harem had forgotten her and would die leaving her a virgin widow. Then I intended to make her mine. But Orkhan had not forgotten her, and she quickly yielded to his wishes, giving him a son. When my father died I told her she would have a month to mourn him, and then she would join my harem. Instead she fled me and rashly married with a Greek lord. How can I forgive her, though I still love her and desire her? I cannot! But I will have her, Ali Yahya! She'll belong to me, and pleasure me, and by Allah she'll give me sons. She is mine, and always will be."

For the first time in his forty years Ali Yahya was

truly surprised. This new knowledge made clear so many things that had previously puzzled him. Now he must tell the sultan of the princess's wedding night with Orkhan so Murad would not rape the girl in his angry passion. Murad must understand how the innocent girl had been treated by her jaded husband. What had happened had not been her fault. She could not be blamed for hating the Ottomans and fleeing them. Obviously, Theadora had been too proud to tell Murad the truth about her marriage to Orkhan. Even the most intelligent woman occasionally betrayed a streak of stupidity

"My padishah," he began, "There is something that you should be aware of—" but he was interrupted by one of the lesser eunuchs who arrived to announce that the princess was awakening.

Sultan Murad sprang to his feet and Ali Yahya, forgetting his dignity and court protocol, cried out, "Master! Let me go to her first, I beg you! The shock will be terrible. Forgive me for saying it, but if she sees you first—" He let the unspoken words hang between them.

Murad stopped. "How long?" he demanded.

"Just a little while longer, my lord," said Ali Yahya, and he quickly hurried from the sultan's tent to Theadora's quarters.

They had placed her on a wide divan within the luxurious tent. Now she was stirring restlessly. Ali Yahya drew up a chair and sat by the princess's side. Slowly her violet eyes opened. Heavy-lidded, she looked about her. That she was at first confused was obvious, then suddenly fear began to creep into her face.

"Ali Yahya?"

"Yes, Highness. It is I."

"Wh—where am I, Ali Yahya? I last remember visiting with my sister, Helena. I grew sleepy."

"That was several hours ago, Highness. We are encamped on the Bursa road now. The sultan is here, and he wishes to see you."

"No!"

"You cannot refuse him, Highness."

"I can! I do not wish to see him ever again!" She rose from her couch and began pacing back and forth. "Oh, Ali Yahya! Why have you brought me back? I wanted to remain in Constantinople! What is there for me here?"

"The sultan loves you, Highness."

"The sultan merely desires me," she moaned hopelessly. "Why cannot he let another woman satisfy his lust?"

"The sultan *loves* you, my princess, and has from the very beginning." She looked sharply at him, wondering how he knew. He continued. "He loves you enough that he threatened Constantinople to gain your return."

"Had my beloved Alexander not died I should be safe in Mesembria." She sighed, then a strange gleam came into her eyes. "Just how did Murad gain my return, Ali Yahya? It was not my dear brother-in-law, John, who betrayed me, was it?"

"No, madame."

"My loving sister, Helena," said Theodora quietly. The eunuch nodded. "And what concession did she wring from the sultan? What was so important to her that she betrayed me in such a fashion? Did she convince him to lift his siege? The return of her daughter? What, Ali Yahya? What has my sister gained for this?"

This was the moment he had dreaded, the moment in which he must tell her. There was no way to soften the blow he must inflict on her proud spirit. "Highness," he began, "do you acknowledge that your sister is the current head of the Cantacuzene family, now that your father and brother have left the public life?" She nodded, puzzled. "Then I must tell you," he hesitated a moment, drawing a deep breath, "I must tell you that in her capacity as head of your family the empress has sold you into bondage for ten thousand gold Venetian ducats and one hundred perfectly matched Indian pearls. You are now, legally, Sultan Murad's slave," he finished.

She could only gape at him. Fearful for her sanity, he reached out and touched her gently. She started, then turned her beautiful eyes on him. "My sister has sold me into slavery?"

"Yes, Highness. It is all . . . quite legal."

"I never realized that she hated me so much. I thought—she is my sister, flesh of my flesh, we have the same mother and father. To sell me into slavery—" A violent spasm shook her and she turned a frightened face on the eunuch. "Give me a dagger, old friend! A bit too much of the poppy!" She was begging, desperate. "Don't make me live in shame. I loved my lord Alexander. I can never love Sultan Murad like that. He *hates* me, hates me for something I could not prevent. Help me, Ali Yahya! *Please.*"

BERTRICE SMALL

But he was firm. She was in shock. When she regained her composure she would accept the situation and avail herself of the opportunity offered her. She might have loved the Greek lord to whom she had been married, but he also knew that, despite her denials to the contrary, she loved the young sultan. If Murad would but reassure her—and Ali Yahya would try and see to that—all would be well between them.

"There is no shame," he said, "in being the sultan's favorite."

"Are you mad?" She began to sob. "I was *wife* to a sultan. I was *wife* to the despot of Mesembria. I will not be Sultan Murad's whore!"

"You will be whatever I desire and command," came Murad's voice from the entry. "Leave us, Ali Yahya!" He strode forward.

"No!"

He laughed at her cruelly. "You may have been born a princess, Adora, but you are now my slave. It is time you began to behave like one. It will give me great pleasure to school you properly. Neither of your husbands did. They indulged you, but I will not."

He turned again to the eunuch. Ali Yahya bowed and departed.

For a moment they stood surveying each other. Her heart was pounding wildly. She looked hard at him, desperately trying to find any sign of the tender young man who had once loved her. He was handsomer than he had ever been. The years he had spent as a soldier had hardened his body. His dark hair showed no sign of gray.

His jet eyes frightened her. There was no warmth in

them. They surveyed her coolly, as they would any possession. And suddenly it hit her that that was exactly what she was—his property. She shuddered.

He laughed. It was a mirthless sound. "I will come to you tonight," he said quietly.

"No," she could barely speak, and her voice was a whisper.

"Come here to me," he commanded coldly.

"No!" She defied him.

Suddenly he laughed gently "In the end," he said softly, "you will have to obey me, my dove. I can make you, you know."

Her violet eyes were dark with fright, yet she wordlessly fought with him. Murad was both pleased and amused. Whatever happened between them, he did not want to break her spirit. But she would obey him. Her reluctance surprised him. She was no virgin. And he was not aware that she had loved either of her husbands. Why must she play the reticent widow?

Holding her gaze in his like a wolf with a lamb, he slowly narrowed the space between them. She could not move. Her legs had become paralyzed. His arm reached out and tightened about her. A strong, square hand imperiously lifted her chin up. His mouth swooped down and closed over her lips.

Deep within her he touched a familiar chord. Unable or perhaps unwilling to struggle, she let him claim momentary possession of her very soul. At first his mouth was warm and surprisingly gentle but then his kiss deepened, becoming demanding, almost brutal. With a sudden cry she struggled to escape him, and when she scratched him he swore angrily, "Little bitch! You belong to me now. You'll soon learn that, Adora! You are mine! *Mine!*" And he turned furiously and left the tent.

She sank to her knees, shaking uncontrollably. How long she huddled there, clutching herself and sobbing pitifully for Alexander, she did not know. Then strong arms raised her. She saw that a large oaken tub had been brought into her quarters and filled with steaming water and fragrant oils. Her clothes were stripped away and she was lifted into the tub. The slavewomen who served her were all older than she. They treated her gently as they scrubbed the dust of her journey from her body and hair. She was then seated and a pink paste, smelling of roses, was rubbed over the haired areas of her body. Her long, dark hair was rubbed with a linen towel and then brushed and rubbed with silk until it was dry, soft, and shone with reddish-blond lights.

The depilatory paste was rinsed from her body, her hair was pinned atop her head with jeweled pins, and she was stood in the tub while cool, scented water was sluiced over her. A warm towel was wrapped about her. She was carefully dried, then led to a bench where she was stretched prone and massaged with a pale green cream smelling of nightblooming lilies.

Theadora was weak with shock and the kindly attentions of the bath attendants when Ali Yahya entered the tent carrying a garment. She flushed under his careful scrutiny. Although she should have long been used to these maleless men viewing her nudity, she was not. At a glance from the eunuch, the slavewomen quickly departed.

Ali Yahya shook his head in disbelief as he ran a soft hand over her body. "You are perfection, Highness. Your body is without flaw. Magnificent! The sultan will be very pleased." He bent and fastened a thin gold chain about her just above the curve of her hips. From this he hung two ankle-length pink gauze veils shot through with silver threads. One covered her buttocks, its mate covered her lower belly and thighs. Kneeling, the eunuch slipped several gold bangles about her ankles. Then he stood and nodded, satisfied.

"The sultan will join you momentarily, Highness," he said formally. Then, lowering his voice, he said urgently, "If this were not your fate, princess, it would not be happening! Accept it, and climb to greatness."

"In the sultan's bed?" she asked scornfully.

"It has been the way of women since the world began. Are you any more or less than other females?"

"I have a mind, Ali Yahya. In my Greek heritage, women of intelligence were sought after, appreciated. Here a woman is a body upon which a man may sate his lust and nothing more. I will not be just a body"

"You are still very young, my princess," smiled the eunuch. "What does it matter the road one takes as long as one arrives safely at one's destination?

"You say you do not wish to be just a body, but what is it you do wish to be? Win the sultan first with your beautiful body, my princess. Then use your intelligence to gain whatever goal it is you seek—if you even know what it is you seek." He then turned abruptly and left her alone to contemplate his words.

"You look ready to do battle, Adora."

She whirled about, forgetful of the fact that her breasts were naked. Briefly his eyes caressed the proud high, coral-tipped cones, bringing an unwilling flush to her cheeks. He laughed. "How will you fight me, Adora?" he asked mockingly.

"What kind of a *man* are you?" she hissed at him. "Knowing that I hate you, you would still take me?"

"Yes, my dove, I would!" His even white teeth flashed in his wind-bronzed face, and he stripped off the red-and-gold-striped robe he wore, baring an equally bronzed chest with its tangled mat of dark hair. Beneath the robe he wore soft white wool pantaloons and dark leather boots. Seating himself on a chair he commanded her, "Take off my boots."

She looked shocked. "Call a slave to do it. I do not know how."

"*You are my slave*," he said deliberately, his voice even. "I will show you how." He stuck out his foot. "Turn your back to me, and take my leg between your legs. Then simply pull the boot off."

Hesitantly she obeyed him, and to her secret delight the boot easily slid off. Confidently, she grasped the other boot and pulled, but this time the sultan mischievously placed the sole of his boot on her pretty bottom and pushed, sending her sprawling into a pile of cushions. She had no time to voice her outrage for, laughing, he was atop her. Quickly turning her over, he kissed her slowly and deliberately until she scrambled to her feet, her eyes large with a mixture of outrage and fear.

She backed away from him. His black eyes narrowed dangerously. Standing up, he stalked her slowly across the tent. The situation was ridiculous. She had no place to run. Sobbing involuntarily, she stood waiting for him to reach her. He towered over her, looking sternly down at her. His hand reached out to snap the thin gold chain above her hips, allowing the gauze to slide to the floor. She was completely naked. The big hand moved up to pluck the jeweled pins from her head, and dark hair swirled about her down to her waist.

Sweeping her up in his arms, he strode across the tent through silken hangings and deposited her on the bed. "If you make any further move to escape me, Adora, I'll beat you myself." He began to slip his pantaloons off.

"You'd like that, wouldn't you," she snarled at him. "You'd like an excuse to beat me!"

He bent and thoughtfully stroked her round bottom. "It's tempting, I will admit, my dove. But there are other things I would far rather do. Things I've waited ten years to do."

"You'll have no joy of me, infidel!" she spat.

"I think I will," he countered. Naked now, he stood over her, a mocking smile on his handsome face.

She looked him over as boldly as he did her. Dear heaven, he was magnificent! There wasn't an ounce of fat on the tall, well-formed body. His legs were firm, rising up into shapely thighs, slim hips, a flat belly, and the broad hairy chest. Between those beautiful thighs, within a dark triangle, nestled his manhood and, as she had suspected, he was large even at rest. When excited he would be enormous, like a damned stallion. She flushed with her thoughts and the sultan laughed as if reading her mind.

He lay down next to her and drew her into his arms. She stiffened, but he did nothing further. This only increased her suspicions. Then suddenly one hand began a gentle stroking motion, soothing the tenseness from her back and buttocks. She was confused. He should be ravaging her now. Her eyes sought his, silently questioning.

"Once long ago," he said quietly, "in a moonlit orchard I loved an innocent maiden. She was taken from me once, and then I lost her another time. But now she is once more in my arms. This time no one will take her from me!"

She swallowed the lump that was rising in her throat. "I am no longer an innocent maiden, my lord," she whispered. Why was he doing this to her?

"No, Adora, you are not innocent in the true sense of the word. You were brutally robbed of your maidenhead. You lived as my father's wife and bore him a son. As to the Greek lord, he could not love you as I do. I believe that in your heart you are yet a virgin."

"How can you know of these things?" she asked him tremulously. *Tell him nought of Alexander*, an inner voice warned her.

"Am I not correct, my dove?" And when she did not answer him he continued, "I am a fool, Adora! Knowing you, how could I believe you had betrayed our love? Yet I did. I believed you ambitious, and when I thought of you coupling with that obscene old man I nearly went mad! There was nothing l could do."

"There was nothing I could do either, my lord," she

answered.

They lay quietly for a few more minutes, and her heart sang with joy It was going to be all right. She knew the reason for his change of attitude. Ali Yahya had obviously told him what she had been too proud to tell him. Knowing the truth of her marriage to Orkhan, Murad's anger had dissolved. She would be his wife now. She glanced at him shyly. "Will we be wed as soon as we return to Bursa, or have you already wed me?" she asked him.

She felt him start against her. "I will take no wife in either the Christian or Moslem sense and neither will my descendants. The Ottomans grow more powerful each day, and no longer need make political alliances through marriage. I will take kadins as did my ancestors."

Angry, disappointed, and hurt, she pulled away from him. "Two men have wanted me enough to wed with me, my lord Murad! I will not be your whore!"

"You will be what I want you to be! Adora, Adora, my sweet, little love! Why do you deny the truth of your feelings for me? Will some words mumbled over us by a holy man make those feelings any different?"

"I am not some ignorant peasant girl to be honored by the sultan's attentions," she raged. "I am Theadora Cantacuzene, a princess of Byzantium!"

He laughed. "You are first a woman, Adora. And second, my dove, though you are not used to it yet, you are legally my slave. It is," he teased her, "your duty to please me." Pulling her back into his arms he kissed her. But it was like kissing a doll for she stiffened her body and compressed her lips tightly together.

Tenderly he rained kisses on her face, hoping to weaken her. It took every ounce of will power she had to remain impassive to the soft lips that gently touched her closed eyelids, her forehead, the tip of her nose, the corners of her mouth, her stubborn chin. Angrily she turned her head away from him, foolishly exposing her slim, white neck to his mouth, and he quickly availed himself of the opportunity she presented. Deep within herself she felt the beginnings of a tremor as his lips moved swiftly down to nibble on her earlobe, then further down to her breasts. She managed to fight down the trembling, but panic was fast setting in, and her hands tried to push him away.

"No! No!" Her voice shook. "No! I won't let you do this to me!"

He raised his head, and his black eyes looked deep into her amethyst ones. "You belong to me," he said quietly in his deep voice. "I do not need papers of ownership to know that. You long to yield to me as much as I long to possess you. Why are you fighting me, my foolish love? Already you tremble with desire, and soon you will cry out your pleasure at the sweetness we will make between us."

His dark head lowered again, and his mouth fastened over a taut nipple, sucking at it gently, tearing a sob from her unwilling throat. Her walls breached, he now increased his attentions, spreading her thighs so quickly that she had no time to fight him. Kneeling between them, he gained greater access to her lovely body.

Leaning forward, he found her lips once more. This

time her sweet mouth was soft beneath his, the lips parting easily. Their tongues stroked each other until she tore her head away with a moan that he recognized as pure passion, and his desire for her flamed higher.

While his lips once more teased at her breasts she felt his great manhood growing hard against her and, unable to restrain herself, she reached down and grasped him in her hands. A groan of agonized pleasure escaped him as she caressed him. She felt his fingers seeking her, sighing with impatient pleasure to find her ready to receive him.

He could wait no longer. Slipping his hands beneath her buttocks he drove fiercely into her—again and again—until finally she cried out, "I yield, my lord!" Only then was he purged of the cruelty that had built up in him. Now she felt his hardness tenderly caressing her, moving with a voluptuous abandon that brought complete pleasure.

"Don't stop! Oh, please don't stop!" she was horrified to hear herself beg him. Her own body would not lie still. It moved frantically, seeking to absorb him. It was too intense, too sweet. "God! God!" she cried out, "you will kill me with it, Murad!"

"No, my insatiable little sweet," she heard him mutter huskily, "I will only love you with it."

She knew she should fight him, for he was using her shamelessly. Yet she could not fight him. She wanted his bigness, his hardness within her. She could deny no longer the desire racing through her veins and, with a sob of despair, she surrendered herself to him completely.

Through a half-conscious mist she heard him saying

her name. Slowly she opened her eyes to find him looking passionately down at her. Color flooded her face.

"I will never, forgive you for this, nor myself," she whispered fiercely, the tears filling her eyes.

"For what?" he demanded. "For making you admit the truth to yourself? That you are a beautiful, desirable woman and that, though you deny it, you love me."

"For making me your whore!"

"Allah, Adora! Why do you refuse to understand? You are my favorite. Bear me a son, and I will make you my kadin. I will set you above all other women in my kingdom."

"No!" She scrambled off the bed.

"*Stop!*" Strangely, she obeyed the angry voice. "Now, slave, come to your master." For a moment she remained frozen, and his voice cracked sharply again, "To your master, *slave!*" Reluctantly she turned back to him. "Now, *slave*, kneel and beg my pardon."

"Never! Never!"

He quickly pulled her back into his strong arms and began kissing her passionately. She struggled fiercely and he laughed. "I'll keep kissing you as a punishment until you obey me, Adora."

"I apologize!"

"I said kneel and beg my pardon."

She shot him a furious look. "I would rather kneel to you, you lecher, than endure your kisses." She struggled from his grasp and, falling to her knees, burlesqued the humblest slave. "Forgive me, my lord."

"My lord, *and* master, Adora."

She grit her teeth in rage. "My lord *and* master," she finally managed to say.

He pulled her up and kissed her again.

"You promised!" she shrieked, outraged that he would break his promise so quickly "You promised not to kiss me again!"

"I did not," he chuckled, pleased at having made her obey him. "I said I would not kiss you as punishment. Now I kiss you to reward your improving behavior."

"I hate you!" she wailed.

"Do you?" His black eyes sparkled maliciously. "Then perhaps that explains why you begged me not to stop making love to you just a while ago. Little fool! Tonight is just the beginning for us, Adora."

Then his mouth closed savagely over hers again, And looking deep into his dark, passionate eyes she knew that she was lost. The miracle of her shortlived marriage to Alexander was gone forever. This was a new life, and she had no choice but to face it.

PART IV

Murad and Theadora

1361 to 1390

Chapter 16

FOR THE NEXT FEW DAYS THEY REMAINED CAMPED IN THE hills. Murad would allow no one but Adora to wait on him. Though the other servants might serve her and do her bidding, the sultan insisted that his beautiful royal slave do everything for him from bathing him to cooking their meals. This latter was proving a disaster, and Murad finally relieved her of that particular task after several badly cooked and burned meals.

"I cannot believe that anyone with your intelligence could be so clumsy, so inept at the cookfire," he chuckled as he rubbed lamb fat on her latest burn.

Furiously she yanked her hand away. "I have been trained to use my mind, not my hands! Inept at the cookfire! I should hope so! I am a princess of Byzantium, not a servant!"

A slow, lazy smile lit his features. "You are my slave, Adora, and while you may not be skilled at cooking, you are becoming skilled enough in other matters to make me forget your lack of culinary ability."

With a cry of outrage she hurled a silken pillow at him, snatching up a cloak she ran from the tent. But his deep mocking laughter followed her. She fled to a small, rocky glade set above the camp, a place she had discovered just the day before. It was lushly carpeted in thick, deep green moss, and hidden by beech and pine trees. She sat by a small natural basin hollowed out of the rock by dripping water.

She wept. She was not a slave! She was not! She was a princess born. She would not, could not, be his whore. She twisted the sodden linen handkerchief. The problem was that men treated her as a pretty plaything, a soft body upon which they could satisfy their lusts. An empty vessel, like a chamberpot, into which they could empty themselves. God! Had it always been like that? Must it continue to be?

The courtesans of ancient Greece were respected for their intellects as well as their bodies. So were the queens of ancient Egypt, who had ruled with their men as equals. But she could hardly expect that kind of thinking from a race just a generation off the steppes, who still preferred tents to palaces. These men expected their women to cook over fires and care for animals. She laughed aloud. At least she hadn't been subjected to the indignity of pitting her wits against a herd of goats! She had an uncomfortable feeling that the goats might outwit her. She could almost hear Murad's laughter.

On a branch beside her a wild canary sang his exquisite song, and she looked ruefully up at him. "Ah, little one," she sighed. "At least you are free to lead your life as you choose." A bird had more control over its life than a woman! She rose to return to the encampment, and was startled to find the sultan standing in the shadows of a large rock, watching her.

Irrational anger flooded her. She had thought of this

glade as a personal retreat. "Am I allowed *no* privacy?" she snarled at him.

"I feared for your safety."

"Why? What you want of me can easily be given by a thousand women far more eager to please you than I am." She attempted to push past him, but he gripped her cruelly about the soft upper arm. "You will bruise me!" she cried at him.

"And if I do? You are mine, Adora! Mine to use as I so choose!"

"The body, yes!" she flung at him. "But unless you have all of me, you have none of me. And you will never possess my soul!" Her voice was triumphant.

A black fury engulfed him. For four days she had been spitting at him like a hellcat. He could render her helpless to desire, but when he was finished with her, her amethyst eyes mocked him, telling him that he did not really own her. His anger had become uncontrollable. Kicking her legs out from beneath her, he sent her falling to the ground.

The wind was knocked out of her, seeing the vicious look in his eyes, she was truly frightened. Slowly, deliberately, he straddled her, pulling her cloak apart, methodically ripping her garments open. She fought him, terrified. "Please, my lord, please! No! I beg of you, my lord! Not this way!"

Brutally he drove into her resisting body. She moaned with pain. He increased his tempo and suddenly his seed was spilling into her. Then he lay still. When his breathing had returned to its normal pace he stood up, pulling her roughly after him.

"Return to the camp. You are not to leave it again

without my permission."

Gathering the cloak about her, she stumbled down the path. Safely within her own tent she gave orders for a bath. When it arrived she dismissed the slaves. Carefully she gathered the shreds of her clothing and, tying them in a bundle, stuffed them into the bottom of a trunk. She could dispose of them later, and no one would know what had happened.

He had raped her! Just as brutally as any soldier would rape a battle captive! He was a brute! If she had needed further proof of how he really felt about women, this was certainly it.

Then suddenly silent tears slid down her cheeks to mingle with the bath water. She hated him, yet she loved him. She disliked admitting this to herself. But it was possible that Ali Yahya was right. If she were to conquer Murad, she might have to use her body. She would, after all, be a fool to allow some brainless girl to gain control of the sultan. She had to face the fact that at twenty-three, the mother of a half-grown youth, she was no longer in the first flush of youth.

A sob escaped her, and she looked guiltily around. It would not do for the slaves to hear her weeping. She put her face in her hands to muffle her weeping and allowed her sorrow to pour forth. Then, as she began to grow calm, she faced the realization that she had driven him to it. It was as though she had wanted to force him into acts of bestiality so that the comparison with her beloved Alexander would be greater. She must face facts. Alexander was dead. He would never return again. She would never bear his voice calling her "beauty" in that tender, half-amused way. Her fate was with the man who had first touched her heart and soul. Her fate was with Murad.

Having him to herself was an incredible opportunity. If she had not been so busy feeling sorry for herself, she would have realized this. She swore softly. After today she would not be surprised to see him order their return to Bursa—and that must not happen! She must work quickly.

Shouting for a slave, she sent for Ali Yahya. By the time the eunuch arrived she was wrapped in a mauve silk robe. Dismissing the slaves, she swiftly told the eunuch what had happened, finishing with, "I am a fool, Ali Yahya! A fool! You were right, but if the sultan orders our return to Bursa now, I may have lost my best opportunity. Will you still help me?"

The eunuch smiled broadly. "Now, Highness, you speak as a wise woman!" he enthused. "I had begun to fear that perhaps I was mistaken in my judgement of you."

"What do *you* gain in all of this?" she suddenly asked.

"Power and riches," was the equally frank reply. "What else is there for me? I will guide you, and protect you against all enemies, including your own self. When your son is safely born I will help you to plan his future so that he will one day take up the sword of Osman as did his grandfather and father."

"And if Murad's seed is potent?" said Theodora quietly, "Then what of his other sons by other mothers? He has told me, Ali Yahya, that he will take no wives in either the Moslem or the Christian sense, but

305

rather he will choose favorites from a harem he intends to keep."

"And it is I who will choose that harem, my princess. I shall choose the youngest, the loveliest, the most exquisite of creatures for the pleasure of my lord and master. Each maiden entering his bed will surpass her predecessor in beauty." He stopped, and chuckled wickedly "And each maiden will surpass her predecessor in stupidity. Murad may rail at you for your intelligence, Highness, but it is your mind that fascinates him, far more than he knows or is willing to admit. You will shine like the full mid-summer moon amid a group of minor, insignificant stars. Fear not the children of these other women, for there will be none. There are ancient ways of preventing conception, ways known to me."

"And are these girls to be so free of brains that they will willingly permit you to render them sterile? Come, Ali Yahya! That is too much to believe."

"They will never know, Highness. Eunuchs are not born, my princess, they are made. I was born free, far to the east of this land, in a place where the religion of ancient Chaldea was still practiced. And still is worshiped, even now. I was neutered by my own parents and pledged to those ancient gods. I served in our temple as apprentice to the high priest. Together we served Ishtar of Erech, the Goddess of Love and Fertility. The temple's priestesses were trained to-service the lusty male worshippers of the deity, for each maiden was Ishtar incarnated, and to couple with a priestess of Ishtar of Erech was to lie with the goddess herself. Fathers brought their sons to experience their first carnal act in the arms of Ishtar. Men with problems of impotence paid great sums to be cured by these skilled women. Bridegrooms spent the night before their wedding with priestesses in order to insure their own fertility and that of their brides.

"If precautions had not been taken, few women would have remained priestesses long. Those girls consecrated to Ishtar of Erech enter the temple school at age six for at least six years of training. Once they reach puberty they must serve the goddess for five years. Therefore, before they sacrifice their virginity to Ishtar, they are placed in a light trance by the surgeon high priest, and a pessary device is inserted within their wombs. That device is removed and replaced regularly, always when the girl is in the trance state.

"None of the girls is permitted to perform their duties without the protection of this implant, not until they have served their five years. At the end of that time the pessary is removed for the Spring Festival of Ishtar, and enough of the maidens become pregnant at that time to satisfy the worshippers of Ishtar as to her influence on fertility.

"I served ten years in the temple, beginning when I was seven. I learned the arts of putting another person into a trance, and of making and implanting these pessary devices.

"When I was seventeen a troop of Moslems rode into my remote village and destroyed our temple. The priest and high priestess were killed. The rest of us were carried off into slavery. I have used the skills taught me many times. I will use them for you, if you will agree to bear the sultan his sons.'"

Theadora looked the eunuch over gravely. "You are indeed a powerful friend, Ali Yahya. But satisfy my curiosity in one thing. Why me? Why not some nubile, pretty, witless little thing?"

"It is your very intelligence that makes me choose you, Highness. You understand and quickly grasp situations. You will be loyal to the sultan—and to me. You are above the petty squabblings of the harem maidens and will be a stabilizing influence upon your lord. You will rear your children wisely to serve this empire well.

"A younger, stupid girl would inevitably turn out to be greedy for riches, greedy for power. She would try to play politics. We will have a certain amount of that as it is, Highness, but as long as you remain supreme in the sultan's heart, the small influence of these girls will be like an insect bites—occasionally irritating, but totally unimportant."

She nodded. "Now," she said worriedly, "I must consider best how to get back into Murad's good graces."

The eunuch's eyes twinkled. "Why, you will weep, my princess, and you will fling yourself into his arms, sobbing your apology," he said.

"Ali Yahya!" She was laughing. "He will never believe such softness from me. Rather, it will arouse his suspicions."

"He will believe if you are clever, Highness. He is angry and beginning to lose patience with this battle between you. I will gently stoke the fires of his anger, telling him he did right this afternoon in asserting his mastery over you. Encouraging him to continue the lesson this evening."

"And thus encouraged," Adora took up the thread of the eunuch's thought, "he will come roaring into my tent like an outraged bull. I will exhibit a momentary, small, defiant attitude before going to pieces."

"Excellent, Highness! As I have said, you are quick to grasp the point."

Again she laughed. "Go, then, old schemer, and rouse my lord and master to proper fury. But remember, to give me time to dress and anoint myself properly."

"I will send two serving women immediately," he said. Then he left her. The eunuch walked across the compound to find the sultan bathing in his tent.

"Ah, Ali Yahya," said Murad, "there you are. Make arrangements for us to leave for Bursa by noon tomorrow. I will ride back this night."

"I am sorry you choose to run, my lord, when victory is so near at hand. With your actions of this afternoon, I had thought you finally understood the situation and were prepared to handle Princess Theadora with firmness."

"Understood what, Ali Yahya?" He turned to the slave. "Be careful with that hot water, fool! Do you wish to scald me?"

"I thought," said the eunuch, "you realized that, to win the princess back, you must force her to admit your superiority. You have almost succeeded in taming her. I have just come from her, tent, where I left her in tears. She loves you! She hates you!" He chuckled broadly. "One more such lesson as this afternoon, and you will break her to your will, my lord."

"Do you really think so, Ali Yahya? I will admit that I love her, but I can take no more of her constant defiance and wicked temper. I would have you stock me a harem of quiet, gentle girls. One spitfire in my house is more than enough!"

"That is true, my lord, but a meal without a little pepper is a bland one. Go to her again tonight. I know she will be contrite. If you do not weaken, she will admit her faults. If she does, then you must remain here several more days to reinforce your position with her. What a sweet victory, eh, my lord?" finished the eunuch, pleased with the look of longing he detected in the sultan's dark eyes.

Murad rose up from his tub and slaves dried his big, well-muscled body. Finally Murad spoke.

"Very well," he said. "You may delay giving the orders to return to Bursa. We will see just how obedient my lovely Adora is willing to become." He stood, holding his arms out, allowing his slaves to clothe him in a black silk robe. It was embroidered with branches of golden mimosa and closed with delicately sewn gold frogs. Soft black kid slippers lined in the tender fleece of unborn lamb were slipped on his feet. Then, without another word, Murad left the tent and strode across the camp towards Theadora's tent.

Ali Yahya cast his eyes skyward and muttered under his breath, "Whoever . . . Let my plans succeed!"

"He comes, mistress!" whispered the slavewoman excitedly, peering from between the tent flaps.

"Get you gone! All of you! Quickly! Quickly!" commanded Adora. The women fled as Murad entered.

Allah, but she was lovely. Quickly he caught himself before he showed any sign of weakness. She wore a loose robe of pale lilac silk, similar to his but much simpler. It closed with a row of little gold knots beginning at the valley of her breasts. He noted with satisfaction that her eyes were slightly red-rimmed.

He said nothing, and she stood defiantly looking at him for a moment. Then her lower lip trembled. She caught at it with her little white teeth, hastily wiping away two large tears that slid quickly down her pale cheeks.

"My lord," her voice was a whisper. "Oh, my lord, I do not know how—I—I ask your—" Without warning she flung herself at him, and he found his arms automatically tightening about her. She wept softly against him, wetting his robe through to his chest.

He was delighted but dared not show it, He had expected fury at his treatment of her this afternoon, yet here she was, all soft and feminine, seeking to apologize to *him*. "Look at me, Adora." Without hesitation she raised her face to him. Her lovely amethyst eyes were bright with tears, the black lashes matted. Unable to restrain himself, he bent to kiss the soft, inviting red mouth. To his surprise, her arms twined about his neck and her lips opened willingly—Allah!—eagerly, beneath his. She was kissing him back, and then she was murmuring, "Oh, Murad! I have been such a fool! Please, please forgive me!"

He was at a loss for words.

"It was my pride, my lord," she said, drawing him down onto a pile of soft cushions, "surely you understand that, for yours is as great as mine, and I have a wicked temper. And both our fathers spoiled me terribly." Kneeling, she drew off his slippers. Then she cuddled next to him.

"Your behavior has been *almost* unforgivable," he said gruffly.

She raised herself up on one elbow and leaned forward just enough that he was treated to a generous view of her breasts. "But you will forgive this humble slave," she begged prettily. When he looked sharply at her he saw her mouth trembling with suppressed mirth.

Relieved that her spirit wasn't completely broken, he laughed and pulled her into his arms. "I do not believe you are *really* repentant at all," he teased.

Her eyes grew serious. "But I do apologize, my lord. I do! I would not blame you if you sent me away." She held her breath.

"Do you want to go?" he asked.

There was only the briefest pause. "No. Do not send me from you, Murad. Those years I lived as your father's wife were a living hell for me. I maintained my sanity only by believing in the promise you once made to me in a moonlit garden: that one day I should be your wife. When you told me the other night that you would take no wife, but only keep a harem . . ." She paused, then said, "I am only a woman, my lord, and easily hurt. You know how hard it will be for me to accept your decision. My religion views an unmarried concubine as lower than a creature of the streets."

"But *my* religion puts you above all women, Adora. I did not mean to hurt you, beloved. Understand me, my dove, I did not tell you I would not take a wife to sadden or shame you. For the last several generations the Ottomans have been forced to contract political marriages to aid them with their conquests. I do not believe we need do this any longer. We are at the very gates of Constantinople. When we conquer it, we will make it our own capital before moving out into Europe itself. The virgin daughters, sisters, nieces, and wards of those in our path will not be enough to bribe us—for we are stronger.

"Perhaps we Turks do treat our woman differently from the way the Greeks treat theirs, but we revere them for the one thing that only they can do. Only the female can accept and nurture the seed of life within her body. Only the female can bear that life safely, give it nourishment and care. It is his woman who provides a man's immortality by giving him sons.

"You have a fine son, Adora. Can you honestly tell me that you have made any greater accomplishment in your lifetime than to give Halil life?"

She was amazed at the depth of his thoughts. And then she realized how little she actually knew the man. They had never really talked as they were doing now. She wondered whether he was aware of the sweet victory this was for her. It mattered not! For now, it was enough for her.

She smiled up at him and said quietly, "I suppose Halil has been my greatest accomplishment, and my life would have been very empty without him."

"*Give me a son!*", he said fiercely. Her heart quickened at the passion in his gaze.

She could not tear her eyes from his. She felt strangely weak, held a half-willing captive of those dark eyes that burned with little red and gold flames deep within. His fingers slipped the row of little gold knots that held her robe together and she felt the big hands gently stroking the swell of her breasts. For the first time she did not resist him, and a delicious, languorous feeling began to creep over her. His hands were those of a warrior, large and square, the fingernails cut short. The skin of his palms and fingers were neither rough nor smooth, but rather a combination of both, and the touch of it on her silken flesh made her shiver. He caught a hard little nipple between his finger and thumb and rubbed, delighting in her gasp of pleasure.

To his surprise, she opened his robe and placed her warm palms against him. Her slim fingers began to tease the hair on his chest, twining amid the soft, tight curls, pulling gently. Her eyes were soft with a growing desire.

He stood up and let his robe drop to the floor, pulling her after him. He drew the lilac-colored silk from her. Standing for a moment, they openly admired each other's bodies. His hand reached out and gently caressed her. She returned the caress. Stepping forward, he gathered her up into his arms, her head nestled against his shoulder, and carried her slowly to their couch. Tenderly he placed her on the silken sheets, standing above her a moment. Then he eagerly joined her as she opened her arms to him.

His fingers removed the tortoise shell pins from her hair. Then he pulled the thick, lily-scented cloud down about the two of them. Only then did he seek her mouth, and she shivered for his kisses were sweet with remembrance, and spiced with expectation.

"You are perfection, my Adora," he murmured soft-ly. "And so there will never again be a misunder-standing between us, let me tell you plainly that I love you, my darling. The sultan of the Ottomans lays his heart at your slim, white feet, beloved, and humbly asks that you be the mother of his sons. I would fight with you no longer. Let me plant my seed deep with-in your fertile garden. Let me cherish you—and the new life that will grow within you."

She was silent a moment. Then she asked "And if I said 'No,' my lord—what then?"

"I would send you from me, my dove, probably back to Constantinople. For I cannot remain near you and not want to make love to you."

"You will not grow angry with me, as your father did, because I like to study and read?"

"No."

"Then come, my beloved lord. The spring is almost upon us, and if we are to harvest a good crop before the year is out, we must begin."

He was stunned by her frankness. Her laughter was mischievous. "Oh, Murad, you great fool! I love you! I admit to it, though I am not at all sure I should. I have always loved you. You were my first love, and now it seems you are to be my last. My now and for-ever love. And so it was written in the stars before either of us even took root in our mothers' wombs. So Ali Yahya assures me."

His eager lips found her equally eager ones and soon his mouth was scorching hers, then moving down her body, tasting of breast and belly. When finally he entered her she was but half-conscious: never, never had she known such sweetness. She cried with joy in his possession of her, and again as he released his seed within her. And in that single blazing moment before pleasure claimed her completely, she knew she had conceived a son.

Chapter 17

AFTER TWO YEARS, THE CITY OF ADRIANOPLE HAD fallen to the Turks. There had been virtually no help from Constantinople. The emperor, being a vassal of the sultan, had simply not dared to send his troops.

The wealthiest of Constantinople's merchants had raised a troop of cavalry and two troops of foot soldiers. Having outfitted them and paid them a year's wages in advance, they sent them off to protect their vast investments in the Thracian city's factories and export houses. Once within the city, however, the mercenaries were trapped, along with the inhabitants. The latter were not delighted by having to feed several hundred additional mouths.

Adrianople was one of the last real jewels in Byzantium's crown. One hundred and thirty-seven miles northwest of Constantinople, it was set on the banks of the Tunja River where it met with the Maritsa River. Located in the center of the Thracian coastal plain, it was surrounded by fertile, well-watered valleys and a surprisingly barren upland. It was said to be located on the site of the ancient city of Uskadame. Certainly something had been there when Hadrian rebuilt the city in the year 125 B.C. Two hundred fifty-three years later the Roman emperor, Valens, lost the city to the Goths. They later lost it to the Bulgars, who lost it to the Byzantines, who lost it to the Crusaders, who lost it back to Byzantium. Byzantium had now lost it forever to the Turks.

There were several reasons for the desirability of possessing Adrianople. It was the marketplace for the entire agricultural region surrounding it, a region that grew fruits and vegetables of every kind, wine grapes, cotton, flax, mulberry bushes, and flowers—especially roses and poppies. The people produced silk, finished cotton cloth, linen of every grade, woolen goods, leather articles, and exquisite silk tapestries. Also produced and exported were rose water, attar of roses, wax, opium, and a red dye that was to be known as "turkey red."

It was here that the Turks intended to move their capital from Bursa. Adrianople, soon to be renamed Edirne, was to be the Ottomans, first capital city in Europe. Those sections of the city which had surrendered without a fight were spared the conqueror's vengeance.

Those sections which had resisted once the Turks breached the city walls were subjected to the traditional three days of pillage and rape. The aged and useless were slaughtered or left to starve, unless they had relatives who could ransom them and remove them from the city. Pregnant and nursing women were the first to be sold into slavery, for a healthy, fertile female slave was a valuable possession. Stripped naked on the block, the way they carried their unborn was discussed knowledgeably by the interested buyers. The space between their hipbones was thought to be a good indication of how easily they would bear their young. Good breeders were welcome in a man's house. Their unborn, especially sons, were an added bonus to the sale.

Those women who had already borne their babies and now suckled them, were examined for the heaviness of their breasts and even manually milked by the prospective buyers to check the richness of their milk. A woman with more rich milk than her own baby needed could suckle an orphan or the child of a dry mother. The weeping that issued forth from this particular slave market was piteous. But none of the crowds paid a great deal of attention. Such were the fortunes of war.

The children were the next to be sold. The prettier ones, both boys and girls, went quickly in the fast and furious bidding. Next came the young men, beauty and strength being the most obvious assets. Many young men were purchased by their relatives from other parts of the city They were desperate to retain the young male members of their families who were responsible for breeding the next generation and keeping alive the family name. There were tragedies here too. Twin brothers were auctioned separately, and the family could only afford to retrieve one. The remaining brother was sold to an Arab trader who hoped to make a fortune on the blond boy further south. The identical brothers were torn apart to the sound of awful sobs.

The sisters and female cousins of these young men were less fortunate. Most of the young girls caught by the Turkish soldiers had been raped. Placed last on the slave block as part of the legitimate booty, their youth and their beauty brought good prices from everyone except their families, who were not eager to regain their dishonored daughters. Many a sobbing girl was led away before the stony faces of her own parents.

The sultan, of course, was offered the pick of the captives. But Ali Yahya chose the artisans and craftsmen because Murad intended building a new palace.

The site he had chosen was a large island in the Maritsa River. On one side of the island the view was towards the city, on the other toward the distant, forested mountains. The island was well-treed with a large hill upon the crest of which the palace was to be located. The design was similar to the Alhambra's, and indeed its architect was a young Moor. There would be courts and fountains, and the entire palace would be surrounded by a carefully cultivated, terraced parkland of gardens, meadow, and woodland. There would be dockage facilities on either side of the island.

The work began immediately, for Murad hoped to have it finished in time for the birth of Adora's child. Giant blocks of marble were quarried and brought from the Marmara islands. Other pieces were taken from nearby Roman ruins to be cleaned, polished, and recut. Great logs of oak and beech were hauled from the mountains, and several shiploads of cedar from the Mideast arrived at the mouth of the Tunja to be reloaded onto barges and taken upriver to Adrianople.

The finest craftsmen, both free and slave, were

brought to work on the palace. There were simple car-
penters as well as master builders and carvers. There
were plumbers to lay the copper piping for the baths,
kitchens, and fountains; painters and gilders; men to
lay roof tiles; men to set the wall and floor tiles. In the
cities of Bursa and Adrianople the weavers spent long
hours at their looms turning out silks, satins, gauzes,
and wools. These fabrics were then turned over to the
master weavers and seamstresses to be turned into
tapestries, rugs, draperies, and other hangings.

Murad drove his architect, who in turn drove his
craftsmen and workers as hard as he could. But he
dared not tell the sultan that the palace would not be
finished in time for the child's birth. It was finally
Theadora who solved the dilemma by suggesting to
the architect that he concentrate his men's efforts into
completing her part of the palace first.

Hers was one of six courts. It was to be called The
Court of the Beloved.

The Court of the Sun faced southwest and was tiled
in red, yellow, gold, and orange. All the flowers in this
court were gaily colored. The Court of the Stars and
the Moon was done in blue- and cream-colored tiles.
Here were planted heavily fragrant nightblooming
flowers such as sweet nicotiana, lilies, and moon-
flower vines. About the deep-blue tiled fountain were
set twelve silver plaques, each one representing a sign
of the zodiac. There would also be the Court of the
Olive Trees, the Court of the Blue Dolphins, and the
Court of the Jeweled Fountains.

Adora's private court faced south and west. It contained her own kitchen and dining room, a complete

bath, a nursery for her expected child, her own spa-cious bedroom, a small library, three reception rooms, and sleeping quarters for her slaves. The open court-yard was large and boasted several small reflecting pools and a beautiful fountain, the water spouting forth from a golden lily. There were dwarfed flower-ing trees—cherry, apple, almond, and peach. In the spring there would be pink and white blossoms, blue and white hyacinths, yellow, gold and white narcis-sus, and all varieties of Persian tulips. In the summer the garden would bloom with multi-colored roses, windflowers, and lilies—Adora's favorite. In the autumn the apple trees would offer their fruits to the inhabitants of the Court of the Beloved exclusively.

Adora told Murad that the entire palace would not be finished in time for their child's birth. But before he could complain she explained that the baby would still be birthed in the palace, for her own court was to be finished first. The child she carried would be the first Ottoman to be born in Europe.

Adora soothed Murad gently. "You are not," she told him, "putting up a tent, my lord. Palaces take time to build if they are built to endure. When you and I have long since disappeared from men's memories, I would have those walking the earth then point to your palace and say 'and that is the Island Serai, built by Sultan Murad, son of Orkhan Ghazi. It was the first royal residence built by the Ottomans in Europe, and in it was born the first European Ottoman sultan.' If your palace is well built, my lord, it will endure for-ever, a monument to you. But if you force the work-men to build quickly, your palace will not endure longer than your own life span."

He smiled lovingly at her. "Being full with my seed has not dulled your clever Greek powers of reasoning."

"I had not heard that carrying a child in the womb shut off the brain, my lord." Damn! Would he *never* learn?

He laughed. "Your pretty tongue is as always, my dove, over-saucy."

She laughed back. "Would you truly have me be as those vapid creatures who populate your bed these nights?" She lowered her eyes and slipped awkwardly to her knees. "Yeth, my lord," she lisped in a brutally stunning imitation of one of his favorites, "whatever my lord sath. Each word from hith mouth ith a dewdrop of withdom, my lord."

Murad pulled Adora up and made a wry face. "How can I fault Ali Yahya?" he asked. "Every girl in my harem is exquisite. One is lovelier than the other. But, Allah! They are as stupid as a flock of sheep!"

She teased him without mercy. "But surely that is what you want, my lord. You are always faulting me for my intelligence, saying it is not suitable to a beautiful woman. Now you fault these lovely girls because they lack brains. You are a fickle man, my lord. There is no pleasing you."

"If you were not so fat with my son, impudent slave, I should beat you," he growled. But his eyes were merry and his hand on her rounded belly was gentle. Then his voice roughened, and he said, "You are misshapen with the child. Your nose is too long, your mouth too small. Your hair is lank. And yet, you are the most beautiful, exciting woman I have ever seen! What sorcery is this that you practice on me, Theadora of Byzantium?"

Her violet eyes glittered, and he was not sure she wasn't holding back tears. This touched him, for she was such a proud little creature. "I practice no sorcery, my lord," she said softly, "unless there is something magical in my love for you."

"Little witch," he said low, catching her hand and kissing the palm.

Her marvelous violet eyes caught his, and for the briefest, eeriest second he believed she could read his thoughts. But then she took his hand and placed it on her belly. "The child moves, my love. Can you feel him?"

Beneath his fingers he felt first what seemed a gentle fluttering, but then suddenly the center of his palm was kicked hard. He started, staring down at his hand in wonder, almost as if he expected to see a footprint. She laughed happily.

"He is surely your headstrong son," she said.

He tenderly drew her into his, arms and stroked her swollen breasts.

"Don't!"

He looked sharply at her, and she blushingly confessed, "It makes me hunger for you, my lord, and you know that it is now forbidden me."

"I hunger for you too, Adora," he answered gravely "Be patient, my dove, and soon we will share a bed again." And he held her close until, safe in the warmth of his arms, she fell asleep. Only then did he lower her carefully to the pillows. Rising, he pulled the coverlet over her.

He stood for a moment gazing down at her. Then he walked slowly from the room and sought the spyhole that looked down into the common room of the harem. It was early, and his maidens were still up and chattering. They were, he mused, a nice collection. He must remember to compliment Ali Yahya's good taste. His eye fell on two girls in particular. One was a lovely, fair-skinned, little blond from northern Greece with large sky blue eyes. Her pretty, round breasts had saucy pink nipples. The other was a tall, dark-skinned beauty from beyond the Sahara Desert.

Watching his women secretly amused him, and he wondered what they would say if they knew he observed them. Nothing, he answered himself. They would say absolutely nothing. They would giggle, pose, and preen, but they would say nothing for there was not half an intelligent thought among them. Their main aim in life was to attract his attention first, and then please him. Why that did not delight him he did not understand.

A beautiful, complacent female offered no challenge. Adora had certainly spoiled him for other women! He had, he chuckled to himself, grown quite used to being fought with—verbally, mentally, and physically—even up to the very moment of surrender. And he found it far more exciting than mere sexual skill. The maidens of his harem cared if they pleased him, fearing not to. Adora loved him, but she feared him not a whit.

He felt a familiar stirring, and acknowledged his need for a woman. No, by Allah! No simple woman but Adora satisfied him any more. He would send for *two* maidens, the black maiden and the golden Greek girl. Perhaps together they could quench the fire in his aching loins.

He signaled a slave and commanded him to fetch Ali Yahya. The chief eunuch arrived quickly, and the sultan instructed him. Face impassive, the eunuch bowed low from the waist

"It shall be as you wish, my lord," he said. All the while he chuckled inwardly, knowing his plan to gain power was working. Murad was unhappy because the princess was denied him, and he sought to sate himself with two women. Ali Yahya entered the harem knowing full well that, above him, the sultan observed him through the spyhole.

Murad watched carefully, observing the reactions of the two women he had chosen. Their reactions would give him an indication of their characters. The blond, as he had guessed, was shy. She blushed a pretty pink, her hands flying up to her cheeks, her small mouth making a little "O" of surprised delight, and her blue eyes widening with just a touch of fear.

The dark girl, on the other hand, looked haughtily up at Ali Yahya and smiled seductively Flicking a scornful glance at the Greek, she said something that caused the other to flush beet red. The chief eunuch tapped the dark one lightly on the cheek in an admonishing gesture, but the black girl simply laughed.

The sultan's lips drew back in a wolfish smile. A soft kitten and a fierce tigress, he mused to himself. Perhaps the evening would not prove disappointing after all.

The two maidens were brought to him, and the eunuch disrobed them so he might gaze upon them. Side by side they were magnificent—ebony and ivory together.

He looked to the dark girl. "Pleasure me, Leila." Lying back among the cushions of the bed he allowed her to open his robe and fondle him. The dark girl bent her head and took him in her mouth, her tongue tracing sensual patterns until his root began to swell and fill her mouth.

"Aisha!" The little blond started. "Come!" And the Greek girl lay near him. He spoke again. Leaning over him, she placed a full breast in his open mouth. Sucking on the soft flesh, conscious of the pleasure the dark girl was giving him, he willfully pushed all thought of Theadora from his troubled mind. It was her duty and her privilege to bear his child. It was his right to sate his desires with other women. It was the way of their world, had been since the beginning of that world, and would be until the end of time.

Chapter 18

THE COURT OF THE BELOVED WAS FINISHED, AND Theadora's bedroom was the most talked about room in the entire harem. Every woman envied the princess her quarters, her pregnancy, and the sultan's love.

The bedchamber was paneled half-way up the wall in squares of dark wood. Above the paneling the wall was painted a deep yellow-gold color, and topped with a plaster molding of flowers painted in scarlet, blue and gold. The floors were highly-polished wide boards of dark-stained oak. The ceilings were beamed, the beams painted to match the moldings.

Centered on one wall was a large yellow- and blue-tiled fireplace topped with an enormous conical copper hood covered in sheets of beaten gold. The tiled fireplace apron was raised and extended several feet out into the room. The walls on either side of the hearth were hung with beautiful silk hangings, one of which depicted the flowers of spring and early summer, the other the flowers of late summer and autumn.

The wall facing the fireplace contained a raised, carpeted platform holding a large bed. The bed had carved and gilded posts and was hung with coral silk hangings, all embroidered with flowers, leaves, and vines. The embroidery was done in gold thread, seed pearls, and jade. There was a matching coverlet.

To the right of the head of the bed the wall was windowed with long, tall, mullioned casement windows. The glass had been blown by six Venetian glassblowers unfortunate enough to have been in a section of Adrianople that resisted the Turks. The sultan had promised them full pardon and coveted Turkish citizenship as well if they blew the window glass and decorative glass for his palace. Until then, they remained in bondage to him. The windows in Adora's bedroom had a very faint golden hue. They looked out onto her private garden. The draperies were the same coral silk as the bed-hangings.

The thick, luxurious rugs had gold, blue, and white medallion designs. The wardrobes that were cleverly incorporated into the walls of the room were lined with cedar and held sliding trays for her clothes.

There were large round tables of beaten brass on ebony stands; a thronelike chair with carved arms, legs, and back, and a gold brocade cushion; small ebony side tables inlaid in mother-of-pearl; and stools of velvet and of brocade. Hanging lamps swung from silver chains, casting amber, ruby, and sapphire shadows and scenting the room with perfumed oil. Pure white beeswax candles burned in gold candlesticks. It was a room of beauty and serenity—perfect for lovers.

Now, however, the time had come for Theodora Cantacuzene to give birth to Sultan Murad's child, and before the walls of the bedchamber would hear the soft voices of lovers it would hear the agony of the childbearing woman who was restlessly pacing the floor.

"Lie down and rest, my princess," fussed Iris. "You behave as if this were your first child."

"Halil was important only to me, Iris. He had older brothers. This baby is very important to the entire empire. He will be the next sultan."

"*If* you bear a son, my princess."

Theadora shot her a venomous look. "It is a son I birth, old witch," she said, gritting her teeth at the contraction that tore through her. "Fetch the midwife now!" As Iris hurried off, Theadora lay down on the bed and rubbed her belly with her fingers, using quick little circular motions. This, the midwife had told her, would ease the pain.

The midwife was a Moor, and Moors knew more about medicine than anyone else did. Theadora had personally chosen Fatima for her skill, her excellent reputation—she had never been known to lose a mother—and because she was clean. Fatima now entered the room and made her way to the bed.

"Well, my lady," she said cheerfully. "How goes it?" And washing her hands quickly in a basin held by a slave, she pushed Theadora's caftan above her raised knees and examined her patient. "Hmm. Yes. Yes. You're doing very nicely. Anyone can see you're meant to be a breeder. We have almost full dilation."

She glanced up and saw the look of grim determination on the princess's face. "Don't push yet, Highness! Pant like a dog. Ah, that's it! Now! Push! Yes! Yes! You are completely dilated, and I can see the babe's head. Iris! Get some slaves to bring the birthing stool in—and place it in front of the windows so my patient can look out."

Within a few short minutes Adora had had another contraction and had been settled on the birthing stool. She was soaked with perspiration and her legs trembled.

The birthing stool was of hard, aged oak, gilded with gold leaf and inlaid with semiprecious stones. It had a high, straight back with a lattice-work carving atop it, wide arms partially padded in red leather, and straight legs which ended in carved lion's feet. The seat was flat and open so the midwife could catch the infant easily.

Now, as Adora reached the final stages of labor, the women of the harem were allowed in to witness the birth. There must be no doubt as to the child's authenticity and parentage. They crowded about the birthing stool, their faces reflecting envy, sympathy, fear, and concern. Theadora gripped the padded arms of the chair and shut out their nervous chatter. The room was stiflingly hot, and the many scents of the women's perfumes were overpowering and made her stomach roll with nausea.

She focused her eyes on the garden beyond the leaded golden windows. It was a brilliant afternoon with a cloudless, bright blue sky. A clear sun reflected off the blindingly white snow covering the garden. For a brief moment, a small grey-brown bird wrestling with a red berry on a nearby evergreen bush distracted Adora and she laughed at its comic antics.

The women about her were aghast. Did the princess feel no pain? What kind of creature was she that she laughed at the height of her travail? Collectively they shivered, remembering Adora's amethyst-colored eyes. Witches were known to have odd-colored eyes.

Another contraction tore through her and, obeying Fatima's instructions, Adora panted first and then bore down hard. She made no outcry but the pain was fierce, and perspiration poured over her body, running down her legs, making the seat slippery. Iris mopped her face with a cool, scented cloth. Fatima knelt below, her equipment spread out next to her on a clean linen towel.

"The next contraction will give us the head, princess."

"It's coming!" gasped Adora from between clenched teeth.

"Pant, Highness! Pant!" A pause. "Now, Highness! Now! *Push!* Push hard! Ah, I have the mite's head. Very good, my princess!"

Adora sank back, exhausted, smiling gratefully as a young slavegirl held a cool, sweet drink to her lips. She sipped almost greedily, then lay her head back, breathing deeply and slowly.

"You are doing very, very well, my lady," said Fatima encouragingly. "The shoulders next, then the rest of the little body, and we'll soon be done."

"*You* will be done," chuckled Adora. "For me it will begin again, Fatima."

The midwife looked up, smiling. "True, Highness," she said, "and with your radiant beauty, I expect to be serving you on quite a regular basis if the sultan is the stallion they say he is."

The women of the harem tittered. Adora would have laughed at the midwife's ribald humor but for the next pain. It seemed to be ripping her in half. Pant.

Pant. Pant. Push. Push. Push.

"The shoulders! I have the shoulders, and good broad shoulders they are!" cried Fatima.

The child was beginning to whimper now, a whimper that turned into a howl of anger as the next contraction pushed it completely from its mother's body. Laying the outraged infant on a linen, Fatima cut the cord and bound it tightly. Next, she quickly cleaned the mucus from the child's nose, mouth, and throat. "A son!" she cried excitedly "The princess has been delivered of a son! Praise be to Allah! Sultan Murad has a fine, strong male heir!" Standing, she lifted the bloodied, shrieking infant for its mother and the others to see.

The boy was fair with enormous dark-blue eyes and a headful of tight, damp, black curls. He was long, with big hands and feet, and his lungs were quite powerful. A slavewoman took the child from Fatima and laying it gently on a table cleaned the birthing blood from it with a soft cotton cloth and warm olive oil. This done, the baby was tightly swaddled and wrapped in a satin quilt.

Theadora had already delivered the afterbirth. Having examined, cleaned, and packed her patient's female area, Fatima allowed Adora to be stripped of her soaking garment and sponged with warm, scented water before being toweled dry. She was then redressed in a quilted garnet-red robe and tucked into her bed. Proudly Iris brushed her mistress's long dark hair until it glistened.

The women of the harem clustered excitedly about the foot of Adora's bed. The sultan was coming! Here was a chance, thought the foolish younger maidens, to be noticed by the master. The more experienced women resigned themselves to being ignored. Adora and her son were powerful competition. But . . . another time . . . another place . . . they would be noticed.

They fell to their knees, heads touching the floor, as the sultan swept into the room. So filled were his eyes with Adora and the child she cradled, that he did not even see them. His deep voice vibrated with emotion in the hushed quiet of the room.

"Show me the child, Adora."

She carefully unwrapped the baby's blanket and handed him the swaddled infant. For a long moment he looked down at the child who, strangely quiet, looked back with unblinking eyes. Then a wide smile split Murad's face. He laughed aloud. "This is indeed my son! I, Murad, son of Orkhan, recognize this child as my son and my heir. Here is your next sultan!"

"So be it! We hear and obey" came the murmuring voices. Then, rising as one, the harem women filed from the room. Iris quickly drew up a chair for the sultan. Taking the infant from its mother, she also left.

For a moment they looked long at each other. Then he caught her hands and, looking deep into her eyes, said, "Thank you, Adora. Thank you for my first son."

"I have only done my proper duty by you, my lord," she answered mischievously.

His laughter had a warm sound to it. "Fresh from childbirth, and yet still impudent. Will it always be so between us, Adora?"

"Would you have me any other way, my lord?" she countered.

"No, my love, I would not," he admitted. "Never become as the other women of my harem. Then you would bore me."

"Never fear, my Murad. I may do many things in my lifetime, but one thing I shall never do is bore you." And then before her words could register fully, she quickly asked, "And does your son please you, my lord? He is a fine, strong boy."

"He pleases me beyond measure, and I have already chosen a name for him. I hope it will please you. I intend calling him Bajazet after our great general."

"The one who beat my Byzantine ancestors so badly in battle?" Her voice was shaking with laughter as he nodded. "God in heaven, Murad, how you insult my family! John, of course, will see the humor in it. No one else will."

"You do," he said quietly.

"Yes," she answered. "I do see the humor in it. I also see the implied threat. But I know that my city's future lies with the Ottomans, not the Greeks. Since the city must eventually fall, I would just as soon it fell to you, or to our son whom I will teach to love and respect what is good in both cultures."

His hand cupped her chin and he leaned over and gently brushed her lips. "You are wise beyond your years, my dove. How fortunate it was that I was passing that convent orchard those many years ago."

She smiled a smile of incredible sweetness. "I love you, my lord Murad."

"Yet you still chafe, my pet, do you not?"

She sighed deeply. "I cannot help it. It is my nature. It is simply not enough for me to be Murad's favorite and Bajazet's mother. If history remembers me, that is how they will remember me. But what it is I do want, even I do not know."

He stood up and laughed. "At least you are honest, my Adora." Then be bent and kissed her lightly. "Get some rest, my beloved. It cannot have been easy work giving birth to my son. You must be exhausted."

She caught at the sleeve of his brocade robe. "Give me a proper kiss before you leave me, my love. I will not shatter now if you kiss me."

He chuckled, pleased. "So you are eager for my kisses, eh? I never thought to hear you admit that." He sat on the edge of the bed and drew her into the warm loving half-circle of his arm. Then his mouth closed over hers, and the depth and passion of his kiss left her breathless and trembling. His free hand slipped past the opening of her robe to cup a plump breast. He teasingly rubbed the nipple hard with his thumb. His voice was husky as he said, "In six weeks you will be purified. See the boy has a wet nurse by then. I will not share you, not even with my son." Their eyes met briefly, and she felt a stab of desire race through her. She wondered at the attraction between them. She yearned for him but an hour past childbirth!

He stood suddenly and left the room. Adora lay back on her pillows. She was not one bit sleepy yet. She was far too excited for sleep. She had done it! She had given Murad his first son! She would give him other sons too, for she would have no others usurping her position. Legally she was his slave, but that mattered not. Her position now was strong. And the best part of all was that he still wanted her.

The child was beautiful with his dark hair and blue eyes, though she was sure the eyes would soon become black like his father's. Then suddenly she thought of Alexander, and of their golden child. The tears slid down her cheeks. Why? Why should she think of *him* now after all these months? She could only suppose that the shock of his death followed so quickly by her sister's treachery was finally catching up with her. She let herself cry until she could cry no more. It was, she knew, better that way.

She relaxed and finally slept, secure in her position with Murad, secure in her motherhood.

Chapter 19

WHEN THE EMPEROR JOHN HEARD WHAT HIS NEPHEW had been named he saw, as Adora had predicted, the humor of it. He laughed. His wife, Helena, was not amused.

"She deliberately insults us, and you laugh!" she stormed at her husband.

"You can hardly expect her to have any love for Byzantium, my dear," observed the emperor dryly.

"She was born here! She is a daughter of one of Byzantium's oldest families! She is *my* sister! She was married to the Despot of Mesembria!"

"Whom you poisoned, my dear. After that you sold its queen, your own sister, into slavery"

The empress looked frightened. "How do you know that? You cannot prove such terrible charges!"

John Paleaologi laughed again. "I do not have to prove them, my dear. When poor Julian Tzimisces realized whom his poison had slain he came to me and confessed all. He was afraid you might be trying to kill me also."

Helena's eyes were wide with fear. "Why have you said nothing to me before?" she asked. "Why have you not punished me?"

"And let Thea know how Alexander died? Let her know that her own sister killed the man she loved? No, Helena, you have hurt her enough. Understand, however, that should she *ever* find out the full extent of your cruelty, I will kill you. I will kill you myself and take pleasure in doing it." He reached out and caressed her neck gently, sensually. Helena shivered. "Thea has made her peace with Murad," continued the emperor. "She is the sultan's wife and the mother of his only son."

"She is no wife to Murad," snarled Helena. "She is his slave and his concubine. He has not even elevated her to the status of kadin."

"Neither has he elevated anyone else, my dear. He has, however, publicly acknowledged Thea's son as *his son* and *his heir.* That, my dear, is the greatest public declaration of his love for her that he can make. She is well aware of that and is content. You have lost, Helena. By merely being herself, Theadora has won. Cease this war on your sister. You have done enough. You tried to murder her and her oldest son, Halil, but the pirates of Phocaea held them for ransom. When the sultan learned of your involvement, the ransom cost me money I could not afford. Far worse, it cost me our beloved daughter, prestige, territory, and soldiers' lives.

"When Thea came to us after Alexander's death you violated our family's honor by betraying her and selling her into slavery. *When* will you stop? When, Helena?"

"Never! Will you not understand, John? Thea and her sons are a terrible threat to us! They can even claim your throne through her!"

The emperor laughed heartily. "No, Helena, they cannot. Nor would Murad ever resort to such a silly ploy. My empire is in its decline. I know that. But it will not fall yet, not in my lifetime. I will do whatever I must to see to its continuation. As to our sons, only time will tell their strength as rulers.

"Helena, in our lifetime together, I have rarely forbidden you anything. I have turned a blind eye to your many lovers. Now, however, I do forbid you! Cease this vendetta against your sister. I have sent our new nephew a large two-handled gold cup encrusted with diamonds and turquoises, his birthstone. I had to levy a special tax on the churches of the city in order to raise the money for it. So poor is the royal credit that the goldsmiths would not make the cup without being paid in advance."

"It's disgusting," said Helena. "Poor Sultan Orkhan dead so short a time, and his grieving widow marries once, has twins, is widowed yet a second time, becomes the sultan's whore, and spawns yet *another* man's bastard."

"At least Thea confines herself to one man at a time, my love," said John Paleaologi softly.

Helena's sky blue eyes widened in shock as her husband continued, "Is one young stud at a time not enough for you, Helena? Playing the bitch in heat to an entire pack of young officers, even in the privacy of your own apartments, isn't wise. Gossip spreads faster from six mouths than from one, and you must have performed remarkably. The accolades you received were truly marvelous."

The empress swallowed hard. And John Paleaologi chuckled at her obvious discomfort.

"Why don't you divorce me?" she whispered.

"Because, my dear, I prefer the known quantity. Like my father, I am lazy by nature. You have all the attributes of a good empress, my dear. You've given me sons who I know are mine. You are beautiful. And though you nag me constantly, you do not interfere in my government. I am not a man who adapts easily to change, and so I would prefer that you remain my wife. But if you cause any further scandal, Helena, I will dispose of you. You do understand that, don't you, my dear?"

She nodded slowly, as surprised as she always was when he was masterful with her. Still, she would have the last word. "I know you have a mistress," she said.

"Of course I do, Helena. You can hardly deny me my little diversion. She is a nice, quiet woman whose discretion I value highly. You could learn from her, my dear. Now remember what I have told you. Stop your battles with Theadora. Murad loves her—make no mistake about that—and her new son is the joy of his life."

Helena said nothing further, but her mind was busy. Theadora was like a damned cat, emerging whole and with another life each time Helena struck at her. The empress of Byzantium valued her position highly, and for years her dreams had been haunted by a childish voice saying, "If I marry the infidel, I shall see he brings his army to capture the city. Then *I* shall be its empress, not *you*!"

That Theadora's threat had been made in a fit of

ADORA

childish pique, and had been long forgotten by its
originator, did not occur to the empress. In her tortured mind she could see only that, as the boundaries
of the sultan's empire widened, the boundaries of her
empire shrank. The sultan's beloved was Thea. So
Helena, who had never been particularly bright,
believed that if she could destroy Theadora, the
Ottoman advance would stop.

In the short time Murad had been sultan, the Turks
had gained effective control of Thrace, its key
fortresses, and its rich plain which spread to the very
foot of the Balkan mountain range. They had spread
terror of the Ottomans throughout southeastern
Europe by their deliberate massacre of the Chorlu
garrison, whose commandant had been publicly
beheaded. Adrianople had then fallen and was now
the Turkish capital.

The Ottoman armies next moved westward. They
bypassed Constantinople, but their emissaries were
already with the emperor. Once again, John Paleaologi
was forced to sign a treaty that bound him to refrain
from regaining his losses in Thrace. He could not support his fellow Christians, the Serbians and the
Bulgars, in their resistance against the advancing
Turks. And he must support Murad militarily against
his Muslim rivals in Asia Minor.

And though his own church condemned him, his
ministers wailed, and his wife raged at him, John
knew that he had bought more time for his city. He
realized that Murad could probably take
Constantinople. By acquiescing to his brother-in-law's
demands he saved the city. The Turks now went on to

tougher challenges, thus allowing John the opportunity to secretly seek help elsewhere.

But he could not seem to convince the rulers of western Europe that if Constantinople fell, they themselves would be in grave danger. The old and foolish rivalry between the Roman and the Greek churches was partly at the bottom of western Europe's reluctance to aid Byzantium. Then too, the Latin Christians fought among themselves. The great Italian banking houses which had financed everything from trade with the East to religious crusades began to fail. Recession and social crisis followed in Europe. The peasants revolted against their landlords whether these were feudal or monastic. Workers disputed with their merchant masters. The bubonic plague appeared from the East to ravage all of Europe. Discovery of the new world turned the youth of the old world westward, leaving Europe open to the Ottoman conqueror.

Murad's armies penetrated deeper into Europe, to Bulgaria, Macedonia, Serbia. Then, suddenly, they appeared in Hungary, a stronghold of the Roman Church. Pope Urban V made several desperate attempts to unite the various Christian powers under his banner, even going so far as to include the Greeks, in his effort to defend Christendom. A mounted force of Serbs and Hungarians foolishly crossed the Maritza River heading towards Adrianople. They were swiftly wiped out. Further combined efforts were hampered by the conflict between the Greek and the Latin Churches.

"The Osmanlis are merely enemies," wrote Petrarch to the Pope, "but the schismatic Greeks are worse than enemies."

"Better a sultan's hat than a cardinal's hat," was the Greek reply.

Murad moved back and forth between the various battle fronts and his capital, Adrianople. He had planned his expansion carefully and had several competent generals who followed his orders to the letter—thus, he had the freedom to pursue his goal of building a carefully chosen and disciplined infantry force which would serve the sultan alone. Recruited from among his young Christian subjects, they were to become the Corp of Janissaries, began first by his father.

Murad now developed and enlarged this force, begun by Orkhan as a personal bodyguard. It became a small army designed to maintain his law and order and to defend his newly conquered European territories. They were loyal to Murad alone.

In each area held by the Ottomans the non-Moslems were offered the opportunity to convert. Those who did were granted all the privileges of Turkish citizenship, including the right to exempt their sons from military duty by the payment of a one-time head tax. Those who retained their original faith might gain Turkish citizenship, but their sons between the ages of six and twelve were liable to be drafted into the Janissaries. Twice yearly the Ottoman authorities selected Christian boys from among the available recruits. Once chosen, the boys were immediately taken away from their families and brought up as Moslems.

Hand-picked for intelligence and physical beauty, they were trained strictly and disciplined harshly.

They were heedless of hardships of any kind. Their duty was to serve the sultan alone and to depend on him personally, to dedicate their lives to his military service. Like monks, they were forbidden to marry or to own property. For all this, they were paid on a scale higher than any other military unit in any army.

The great religious sheikh, Haji Bektash, gave the Janissaries his blessing and presented them with their standard. It was the crescent moon and the double-bladed sword of Osman emblazoned on scarlet silk. Predicting the Janissaries' future, the elderly sheikh said, "Your visage shall be bright and shining, its arm strong, it sword keen, its arrow sharp-pointed. You will be victorious in every battle and will never return except in triumph." He then presented the new force with their white-felt caps, each of which was adorned with a wooden spoon instead of a pom-pom.

The spoon, along with a big stew pot, symbolized the higher standard of living of the Janissaries compared with other military units. The titles of their officers were taken from the kitchen. First Maker of Soup, First Cook, First Carrier of Water. The great black pot was not to be used only for cooking. In later centuries the pot was turned over and drummed upon when the elite corps was displeased with the sultan. It was also used to measure the Janissaries' share of booty.

In western Europe there arose great indignation that the Turks would impose on their Christian subjects what in effect amounted to a blood tax. It was immoral to tear young boys from their families, forcing them to follow an alien religion and to serve a barbaric master.

Murad laughed at the outcry. His Christian counterparts were often far crueler to their Moslem or, for that matter, their Christian captives. His new contingent amounted to fewer than five hundred fighting men and perhaps that same number of young trainees. He had larger units of *hired* Christian mercenaries now fighting against their fellow Christians in the Balkans! At no time were his armies without large numbers of Christians fighting for him against other Christians. The Corp of Janissaries would grow, but eventually the Christian peasants would embrace Islam rather than lose their sturdy sons who were needed to help work the land.

Murad and his people were now faced with an enormous challenge. The Ottomans were a nomadic people who had come out of the dawn of time to wander the steppes of non-Moslem central Asia. As they had moved westward they had assimilated other cultures, had even been enslaved and converted to Islam under the Abbasid caliphate. In Baghdad they had been trained as soldiers and administrators, raised far above the common domestic slave. Hence they felt neither shame nor fear of slavery as did the Christians. The power of the Ottomans grew until they overthrew their masters and replaced them with a slave dynasty of their own. Still, they were nomads. And again they moved west, conquering everything in their path.

Now, however, they had begun to think of settling down. Now they must become rulers of men rather than shepherds of sheep. Other nomadic groups had tried and failed: the Avars, the Huns, the Mongols.

The mistake these others had made had been in believing that by leaving the conquered on their own land to remain economically productive they would cooperate with their conquerers. The conquered did not cooperate. They instead became unproductive parasites. This resulted in the rapid decline and fall of most nomad empires.

The Ottomans were not going to be flimflammed by a wily peasantry. Already they had evolved the practice of training human watchdogs to keep their human cattle obedient and their enemies at bay. The enslaved Janissaries were the beginning. Now there rose a vast civil service made up of superior slaves loyal to the sultan alone. The Christian subjects of the sultan found their lives being administered by men who were almost all Christians. Those who did not produce, from the level of the peasantry on upwards, were quickly replaced. And Murad was free to pursue his military conquests and enjoy his growing family.

Though he kept a harem and was not averse to using other women, his tendency was to remain relatively monogamous. He was true to Adora. She did not begrudge him his other women, provided his interest in the harem remained mild.

Five months after Bajazet's birth, Murad's seed again took root in the fertile soil of Adora's womb. And when their son was but two months past his first birthday he was joined in his nursery by twin brothers, Osman and Orkhan. The sultan was jubilant. He had three healthy sons! Surely Allah had showered him with blessings.

Thrice-secure, Adora sought out Ali Yahya and

asked to be free from pregnancy for a time. The master of the sultan's household agreed with the princess that to retain Murad's interest now she must again become more the lover and less the mother. As her sons were all outrageously strong and healthy, he saw no reason for her to bear children until she wanted to.

To amuse her lord, Adora learned the sensual oriental dances currently being done by a troupe of Egyptian dancers who were performing in the city. Each day she practiced with her teacher, Leila, a full-breasted, full-hipped woman with almond-shaped gold eyes. After a few weeks, Leila said, "You could earn your living at this, Highness, and have not one, but half a dozen sultans at your feet."

Theadora laughed. "I desire no one but my lord Murad, Leila. For him alone will I dance."

"He should be honored, Highness, for never have I seen anyone perform with such grace, such passion. How well you feel the music! Dance for him tomorrow as you have danced today and it is he who will be *your* slave! You will rouse his desire as no woman ever has! I can teach you no more."

Theadora was pleased. On the morrow Murad would return from two months at the front, and Adora had planned his homecoming in meticulous detail. When he arrived at the nearly completed Island Serai she greeted him lovingly, her three sons about her like chicks about a hen, the twins just barely able to stand. This reminded him, should he chance to have forgotten, of her position in his life.

The children were taken by their nurses and Adora escorted her lord to his own quarters and helped remove his travel-stained garments. "Your bath awaits you, my lord," she said. "I have prepared an evening which I hope will please you. I have a small surprise."

Before he could answer, she was gone. And he found himself in his bath, attended by six of the most exquisite, nubile young girls he had ever seen, all completely naked. They went calmly about the job of washing and shaving him. He was gently patted dry with fluffy towels and then massaged with sweet oils. His natural lust began to exhibit itself in a delicious tingling. But, before he could take advantage of the delights around him, the skillful fingers of the pretty masseuse put him to sleep.

An hour later he awakened, delightfully refreshed, to find a fully garbed older woman offering him a tiny cup of hot sweet coffee. He gulped it down. Standing up, he was quickly surrounded by slaves who anointed his body with musk and then dressed him in a deep-blue velvet robe embroidered at the hem, wrists, and collar in silver thread, turquoises and pearls. The robe was closed with silver frogs over turquoise buttons. It was lined inside in alternating bands of silk and soft fur. The effect on his naked skin was sensuous and delightful. His slippers were of lambskin, dyed blue to match his robe and lined with lambswool. A gold chain with a jeweled medallion was put over his neck. Several rings—a large baroque pearl, a sapphire, and a turquoise—were slipped on his fingers.

The older woman who had given him the coffee seemed to be supervising, and when he was dressed she said, "If my lord will follow me, his meal and the entertainment await him."

"Where is the Lady Theadora?"

"She will join you eventually, master. In the meantime she asks that you eat and pleasure yourself as it pleases you, my lord."

The woman led him into his salon where a low table had been set up. He seated himself amid the brightly-colored cushions and was immediately joined by two beautiful girls. One speared raw oysters and placed them in his waiting mouth. The other carefully touched the side of his mouth with a linen napkin, stopping the juices before they ran.

Never had any Ottoman been served in such a luxurious manner. These were Byzantine customs, and Murad decided he liked them very much. The girls who served him were nude from the waist up, and their pink silk trousers were so sheer that nothing was left to imagination. Both were blue-eyed blonds. Their hair had been braided into single thick braids, their heads topped with thin gold chains. A single tear-drop pearl lay in the center of each of their foreheads.

A tass kebab followed the oysters: tender chunks of baby lamb with cooked onion and love apples on a bed of rice pilaf. Now the other girl fed him while the first girl plied the napkin. She mopped the juices of the meal up with pieces of soft, flat bread which she then fed him. Honeyed yogurt and coffee ended his meal. Murad was enjoying himself hugely. He was clean, warm, relaxed, and well-fed. He was beginning to feel quite mellow.

The dishes were cleared away and the entertainment began. Sprawled back amid the pillows, each arm cradling a girl, he chuckled as a group of small dogs was put through their paces by their elderly trainer. He very much enjoyed the three female jugglers who also did acrobatics.

Then, from behind a carved screen, music began. Six maidens in red and gold skirts and blouses began to dance for him.

They danced well, but suddenly the tempo of the music shifted subtly and the six girls disappeared. One veiled dancer appeared, swathed in black, silver, and gold silks. She clicked her brass finger tals in a challenge to the hidden musicians. Slowly and sensually, the woman's body weaved to the music. The sultan realized, as the woman discarded the first silk, that she was about to do the dance of the veils.

The first veil had covered her hair which was in itself a long, dark, shining veil. The second and third veils bared her back and then her breasts. Snowy, coral-tipped cones of firm flesh moved provocatively as she danced.

The sultan's breath caught in his throat as he watched the twin temptations and he leaned forward, completely unaware that his hands were hungrily kneading a breast belonging to each of his companions. As the dancer excited him further he felt his manhood rising hard and throbbing beneath his luxurious robe. He cruelly pinched the nipples of the breasts, but the young slavegirls dared not cry out for fear of displeasing their master.

The music became more insinuating, and the dancer writhed her beautiful body in an obvious imitation of aroused passion. Beneath the shimmering veils that were falling one by one, her legs were becoming visible.

As his desire mounted, he wondered who she was and why she had never danced for him before. She must be new in the harem. Was the face as fair as the body? Releasing his two companions from his cruel grasp and sitting cross-legged, he allowed his hunger to take complete possession of him. The two maidens were dismissed with a wave of his hand, and he was alone with the mysterious dancer.

The music began to mount in intensity. The dancer whirled, the remaining silks billowing out like the petals of a flower about its stem. The woman moved nearer, teasingly brushing him with the nipples of her full breasts. He could feel the heat of her lovely body, and smell her scent. It was hauntingly familiar. Her eyes above the black veil glittered like jewels in the flickering lamplight and he reached for her. With a low laugh, she eluded him.

His black eyes narrowed dangerously, but then his mouth twisted in a smile. He would let her finish her performance. But then . . . The woman's lush body weaved the taunting final movements of the dance. Suddenly all the remaining veils but the one that hid her face were gone. She stood proudly naked above him for a moment before sinking to the floor in a gesture of submission.

He rose, his whole body throbbing with lust. Walking over to the dancer, he raised her and tore the dark veil from her face.

"Adora!" His ragged voice was incredulous.

"Did I please you, my lord?"

He pushed her to the cushions and, tearing his robe open, flung himself on her. Her warm hands caught at his aching organ, and guided it home. He drove deep, his hands beneath her buttocks, kneading them. "Bitch! Sweet! Tempting! Little! Bitch!" he murmured, thrusting into her again and again.

She opened herself wide to him, reveling in the bigness, the hardness, of him. She had been too long without him, and if he were hungry for her, she easily matched his passion. From deep within her she felt the cry well up and, sobbing his name, she yielded herself totally.

Aware of her surrender but completely lost in the warmth and sweetness of her, he groaned his delight and set about to reach his peak. They were both so keyed-up that the blazing climax left them drained and shaken.

They lay, exhausted, breathing heavily. Finally Murad managed to find his voice. "Woman!" he said fiercely, "You are a never ending source of wonder to me. Is there no end to your variety, Adora? When, in Allah's name, did you learn to dance like that?"

She laughed shakily. "There has been a troupe of Egyptian dancers in the city for some weeks now. The lead dancer, Leila, taught me here in the palace. She says I have a natural talent. Did I truly please you, my lord?"

"Allah! Could you not tell?"

"Do you ravish all the dancers who please you so?" she teased.

"No woman ever danced for me as you have, beloved. I will allow you to dance for no one else. Not even the most honored guests will ever see you perform." He drew her into his arms and kissed her, his tongue gently thrusting between her teeth to caress, to rouse, to stoke the fires of her passion. She sighed deeply and returned the kiss, her mouth soft and yielding, provocatively sucking on his tongue.

When at last they breathlessly ceased their kissing, he murmured into her little ear, "There is no one like you in the world, Adora. You are unique among women, a priceless jewel among the many grains of worthless sand. The others I desire occasionally, for a man requires variety. But I love you, my darling. I must never be without you."

She was trembling with joy, though she hid it from him. He must never know how vital he was to her very existence. She now loved him as she had never loved any man, even her beloved Alexander. But he must never know, lest he use that special power to control her. She rose from the tumbled pillows and held out her hand to him. "Come to bed, my lord," she said softly. "Come to my couch, my love. The night is young."

His dark eyes burning like live coals, he swept her up into his arms, burying his hot face in the scented tangle of her silken hair. "Woman!" he whispered huskily. He carried her through the short hallway that connected their courts, "Woman! The memory of this night will haunt me if I live to one hundred years!"

Chapter 20

HELENA, EMPRESS OF BYZANTIUM, LOOKED WITH hidden glee at the woman before her. The creature was short with large, pendulous breasts. Helena had secretly observed her in the bath and knew that beneath the rich robes were heavy thighs, a sagging belly, and enormous hips. Both the woman's very white skin, and her dull, brown hair were coarse. And though her eyes were a rather fine topaz color they were made small and piglike by her plump cheeks which had been reddened in an attempt at youthful color. She was gowned in purple brocade, trimmed with brown martin fur at the neck and sleeves. The sleeves were slashed and cloth of gold showed through.

She was Mara, daughter of a Greek priest named Sergius. Mara was the mother of Murad's first son, Cuntuz. It had taken Helena some time to trace Mara for, though she was the daughter of a holy man, she was also a whore—by nature and by profession. Murad had not been her first lover, though she had always maintained that he was the father of her son.

Forced from her village on the Gallipoli peninsula by her angry parents, she had become a camp follower of the Turkish army, servicing any man who would pay the price. Her child had remained with his grandparents who, though embarrassed by their daughter's morals, housed her child.

Cuntuz had been continually reminded of his mother's evil ways, of his wicked infidel father, and of his own bastardy. The children of the village had been merciless. His grandparents, no more thoughtful than others, were forever telling him how lucky he was to have their charity He was forced to spend a great deal of time in the church praying that God would overlook the shame of his very existence, would burn his vile parents in eternal hellfire, and would bless his wonderful grandparents who had taken him into their home.

Cuntuz was now twelve and a half. Suddenly, his mother—richly dressed and with a full purse— appeared to claim him. He could remember seeing her only three times in his life, the last time four years ago. He barely knew her, and he didn't like her. But faced with the choice of remaining with his carping grandparents who pleaded with him to remember his immortal soul and remain with them, or go with his mother who promised him that he would be a prince, the choice was easy. It was made especially easy, when his mother, her eyes knowing, said slyly, "Soon you will be a man, my son, and I will see that you have many fine girls to satisfy you." He had lately felt urges and longings strange to him and had taken to spying on the village maidens when they bathed in a nearby stream.

He and his mother had gone to Constantinople

where they remained for several months in a small palace, guests of the empress. Cuntuz had been coached in elementary manners, the rough, country edge worn off his tongue by a diction teacher. And he had made a friend, the first he had ever had. This was Prince Andronicus, the empress's oldest son, fifteen.

The boys became inseparable, much to the irritation of the empress, who was forced to grit her teeth and accept the situation. Only the fact that she would soon be sending Cuntuz and his mother to his father in Adrianople prevented Helena from taking firmer action. She did not feel that Cuntuz was a fit companion for her son.

Andronicus was very much like Cuntuz. Being older, and having been brought up in the city, Andronicus had had better opportunities to develop the unpleasant side of his nature. He was nothing like his handsome and charming younger brother, Manuel, who made friends easily. Andronicus had been virtually friendless. The open admiration of the new boy won him over.

On Cuntuz's thirteenth birthday Prince Andronicus took his new friend to an exclusive brothel. There, the boy became a man. A man who, like his royal friend, had an appetite for cruelty and perversion. The boys began spending more and more time in the whorehouses of the city. Singly, each was obnoxious; together they were dangerous, for their cruelty knew no bounds. Their arrival each evening at a house of pleasure was apt to set the madame fretting nervously, wondering if she would lose any of her girls. Andronicus and Cuntuz made life unbearable torture for the young prostitutes of Constantinople, for they never patronized the same house two nights in a row and no one ever knew where they would strike next. Fortunately, before they could kill anyone, the time came for Cuntuz to go to Adrianople.

Now he stood with his mother before the empress. He thought to himself that Helena had fine, big tits. He wondered how it would feel to suck on those breasts and then bite down hard on the nipples, causing her to scream with the terrible pain he would inflict. He stood silently, mentally stripping his royal benefactress naked, wondering if what they said about her was true. He imagined her bent over, begging for mercy while he raised red welts on her round, soft bottom with a horse crop. Then when her plump, pretty cheeks blushed rosy red for him he would ass-fuck her! Beneath his elegant robe he grew hard and erect.

Looking at the unconcealed lust on the boy's face, Helena knew roughly what he was thinking and wondered whether he would be worth the risk. There would be hell to pay if John found out. But if she were very, very careful he would not find out. In this very palace was a secret, windowless room outfitted with a couch for such occasions. The boy and his mother would be leaving in the morning. Perhaps—No! Yes! Later this afternoon she would have the boy brought to her for a few hours. She had heard he was insatiable. She forced her mind back to what the boy's idiot mother was saying.

"You're sure," Mara quavered, "that Murad will welcome us in Adrianople?"

"Of course!" snapped Helena. God, the woman was driving her crazy "How many times must I tell you he will be delighted to have Cuntuz by his side. His other sons are but babies. As a warrior, Murad is in constant danger of being killed. Do you think if that happened the Ottomans would welcome my sister's mewling infants as Murad's heirs? They would far prefer Cuntuz, who is virtually a grown man. Your son could then protect his own succession in the Ottoman fashion by strangling his half-brothers. You, dear Mara, will be a most powerful woman when your son succeeds to his father's throne."

Mara licked her lips nervously. "Sultan Murad has never seen my son. When I told him I was pregnant he gave me gold, but I never saw him again. He never even acknowledged the boy."

"Neither has he ever denied him," said Helena. "Rest assured, my dear Mara. All will be well. If, heaven forfend, Murad sends you away, there is always a place for you among my ladies. You have my protection." It was a promise easily given for Helena didn't believe the sultan would send them back. If he did, it would be with an income. And the damage to Theadora would have been done. Her sister would not feel so inviolate then!

Rising, the empress smiled down on the fat woman. "I will bid you good-bye now, my friend, for you will be leaving early in the morning. Prince Cuntuz, if you will attend me in an hour's time I will give you your final instructions on how to deal with Ottoman court customs." And Helena glided from the room.

When she had gone, Mara turned to her son. "You

know, of course, that the bitch lusts for a quick tumble with you."

He grinned. "I'll give her a ride she'll not soon forget, mother dear. She'll be groveling for mercy by the time I'm through with her. Be sure you are as kind to my friend, Andronicus. He swears you are the best piece he has ever had. He tells me your mouth does wonderful things that can drive a man mad with delight."

"Small praise from a lad of fifteen," returned Mara sourly. "Don't burn all your bridges with the empress, Cuntuz. Despite what she says, we may need to return here. I do not really believe that the sultan will welcome us. I will try for your sake though, for I owe you that."

"Am I really his son?"

"I believe so. When a man kept me as he did, I fucked only him. I even fancied myself in love with Murad. Ah, Cuntuz, you should have seen me then. I was a tiny little thing with fine breasts and skin like the best white Bursa silk! A man could span my waist with his hands!"

He looked unbelieving. He could not imagine this mountain of flesh petite and desirable. But then, she must have had something other than an open and willing hole to attract his father even for so short a time. He disliked her less now than when they had first joined forces. He realized that she had tried, even as she was trying now, to do her best for him. Awkwardly he patted the beringed hand.

"We had best go now, mother, lest we be late for our appointments."

A week later Sultan Murad found himself face to

face with an almost-grown son and that son's mother. He had not even remembered their existence. The peasant girl he had kept for his pleasure in the Gallipoli Peninsula had been of no importance to him. She had attracted him with her golden eyes and big breasts. She had been no stranger to men, and he hadn't known or cared if she was faithful to him. She was simply available when he wanted her. That had been enough, for he had ached with the terrible loss of Adora to his father. When Mara announced her impending motherhood he hadn't questioned it but had given her gold and ridden off for less involved company. He had not even known the child's sex, or whether it had lived or died. He hadn't cared enough to find out.

From the beginning, there was antipathy between the man and the boy. Murad looked at Cuntuz. The lad was soft, uneducated. His mouth already showed signs of dissipation. The eyes were cruel and shifty. Cuntuz looked at his "father" and saw a hard, successful man whose feats he could never hope to equal. He hated Murad for this.

The sultan would neither confirm nor deny his paternity. Nor would he make Cuntuz his legal heir. That position belonged to four-year-old Prince Bajazet, to be followed by his twin brothers. To solidify his decision, Murad called in the ulemas, the Muslim lawgivers, to debate his judgement, and to confirm or deny it. He would abide by their decision. After long and careful consideration, the ulemas agreed with the sultan. They had no wish to cast doubts upon an innocent boy's birth, but Mara's reputation was poor. No one, not even his mother, could be absolutely certain of Cuntuz's paternity. And where the descent of Osman's line was concerned, there could be no doubt whatever. Prince Bajazet was confirmed as his father's heir.

The sultan agreed to settle an allowance on Mara—but she must return to Constantinople. There was no place for her in Adrianople. Murad laughed to himself. Adora and his harem were solidly united for the first time since he had become sultan. Adora was well aware who had sent Mara and Cuntuz to Murad. And she was outraged that her own sister would try to replace her beautiful and bright little Bajazet with that horrible boy whose eyes had undressed her on the two occasions that they had met. Adora refused to believe that Murad had fathered such a son.

The other women of the harem simply wanted no additional competition. Adora was quite enough.

Cuntuz was to remain in Adrianople. There was always the possibility that he was Murad's son, and Murad felt he owed the boy something if that were true. Cuntuz was to be educated in both academic and martial subjects. If he had talents, then perhaps the boy could be of use to the empire.

Cuntuz did not wish to remain. He wanted to return to Constantinople and pick up his life of drinking and wenching with his friend, Prince Andronicus. His mother quickly disabused him of the notion. "With the money your father is settling on me I can open my own house of pleasure," Mara told her son. "I know what the rich men and women of Byzantium like, and I will cater to their lusts. There is no further place for you in my life. Remain with the sultan and your fortune is made. If you do not wish to do that you may return to your grandparents. I do not think you would enjoy it."

"I can stay with Andronicus," replied the boy. "He is my friend."

"Do not be a fool!" replied his mother. "Do you think the empress will allow that association to continue if you are of no use to her? You have already served her purposes by coming here. It is either stay here or return to your grandparents."

It was no real choice. Cuntuz remained. He hated it, for the sultan had given orders that he was to be treated like any boy in the Palace School. Thus, he was beaten for his errors, which were many. There rose in the already warped boy a blazing hatred for Sultan Murad and for the sultan's acknowledged sons.

Cuntuz was forced to bide his time. He was young. But eventually he would have his vengeance.

Chapter 21

THE TSAR OF THE BULGARS HAD DIED AT A VAST OLD AGE, leaving his three grown sons to squabble among themselves over his kingdom. To the northwest, Prince Lazar held sway. To the south, Prince Vukashin. Caught between them was their eldest brother, Ivan, who believed it should all belong to him.

On the other side of the Balkan mountains the sultan waited to see which of them would come to him for aid. When they all did, he carefully evaluated the positions of each and decided that when the time came for choosing he would side with the eldest, Prince Ivan. Vukashin was a poor general. Murad defeated him and quickly annexed the southern part of the late tsar's kingdom.

Prince Lazar now found himself besieged by an army of Hungarian crusaders who, with the Pope's blessing, sought to take over his kingdom. Two hundred thousand Bulgarians were forcibly converted by the Franciscans from the Orthodox to the Latin rite. The sultan marched and was welcomed by the persecuted Bulgarians as the savior who would restore their freedom of worship. And he did—under his usual conditions. The Bulgarians were too happy to be rid of the minions of the Latin Church to care that their sons were now open to the Janissary draft.

Tsar Ivan now found himself free of his rivals but faced with a formidable opponent. He would continue to rule—but only on Sultan Murad's terms. Following the example of the emperors of Byzantium, Ivan became the Ottoman's vassal. His daughter, Thamar, joined the sultan's harem.

Knowing Murad's devotion to Adora, Ivan took a leaf from the Byzantine's book. Thamar's dowry would be paid in gold, but only when the union bore fruit. There was always the possibility that his daughter might supplant Theodora. But failing that, she would at least have a child to console her.

Theodora was furious when she heard that Murad had agreed to the terms of the Bulgarian tsar, but she tried to hide her anger. The girl had the potential to become a serious rival. This was no ordinary harem maiden but a princess, like herself.

Adora looked into the Venetian-glass mirror that Murad had given her when the twins were born. Her hair was still lustrously dark with its reddish-gold lights, her eyes their beautiful amethyst-purple, her fair skin clear and unlined. Still, she sighed, she was twenty-nine and the Princess Thamar was just fifteen. Dear God! Her rival was the same age as her son, Halil!

She could only hope that the girl was ill-favored. How else could she compete with youth? Adora had doubts. Murad, in his mid-forties, was approaching a dangerous age. Would he still love her after the nights he spent in the younger woman's bed? She felt the tears splash down her cheeks.

Coming up behind her Murad saw the tears and surmised the reason. "No, my dove," he said, turning her so that she was cradled against him. She protested faintly, trying to hide her wet face from him. "Adora," the sound of his deep voice caressing her name sent a shiver through her. "It is a political arrangement. Tsar Ivan hopes to keep me at bay by using his daughter. I could hardly refuse the girl once she was offered."

"Why not?" she muttered tearfully. "You have a harem full of women. Did you really need another?"

He laughed. "It would have been most ungallant of me to refuse the tsar's daughter!"

"Is she beautiful?"

"Yes," he said honestly. "She is very young and very lovely. But she is not to my taste, nor is she my love. You are my only love, Adora.

"Nevertheless, I shall keep my word. I will take this maiden to my bed and I will keep her there until she swells with my seed. Then I will collect her dowry. We need all the gold we can gather, Adora. Building an empire costs money.

"I will need your help too, my dove. Do not make yourself Thamar's enemy You need not be her friend if you do not wish it, but be in a position to watch her for me, for I do not trust the tsar. I believe he sends his daughter to spy for him.

"So there will be no doubt about your position in my life or in my house, I have prepared a decree to be released on the day I accept Thamar into my house. It elevates you to the position of bas-kadin. I have already named your sons my heirs."

She flung her arms about his neck and kissed him passionately. "Thank you, my lord! Oh, thank you! I do love you so, Murad!"

He grinned boyishly at her. "And I love you too, my dove," he said. And he did. He had enslaved her, yet she would not be humbled. Like a flower after a storm, she always rose to bloom anew. She was his magnificently proud princess, and he wanted no mate but her.

Still, he was the Ottoman, and he would take Thamar of Bulgaria to his bed. Though he would return to Adora, Thamar would be a delightful diversion. His mind wandered back to the day he first saw her. He had entered Tsar Ivan's capital city of Veliko Türnovo at the head of a large force. The message to the Bulgarians was clear.

It was during that visit that Ivan offered his daughter. Murad sat with Ivan in a small room in the tsar's castle. The room was lit by pure wax candles that gave off a soft, flattering golden light. A girl entered, followed by an old woman. At first Murad could not see her face for her head was modestly lowered. They stood silently before the two men, and the tsar nodded. The old woman reached out and drew the velvet cloak from the girl. Thamar stood naked before her father and her prospective lord.

"She is flawless," said the tsar roughly.

Murad's eyes widened just enough to show his interest, but he said nothing. He was surprised that the tsar would hawk his daughter's charms in such a manner. Obviously, Ivan wanted to place her in Murad's house very badly.

"Look up, girl, and let the sultan see your face!" snapped Ivan.

Thamar raised her head, and Murad was suitably impressed. The girl's face was oval in shape and fair in coloring, with rose-pink cheeks. Her eyes, fringed with thick dark-gold lashes beneath delicately arched golden-brown brows, were large and brown-gold. There was no expression in them. It was as if the girl had divorced herself from all that was happening to her. The nose was small and straight. The chin had a dainty cleft. The red mouth was generous and well-shaped.

She held her head high, and he followed the swan-like neck down to the small round breasts with their little pink nipples, hard and tight in the chill of the room, like closed buds. The navel was just faintly rounded, the waist tiny, the hips broad, the legs slim and well-shaped with slender, high-arched feet. Without spoken instruction the girl now slowly turned until her back faced him. It was a beautiful, long, smooth back that ended in small, plump, dimpled buttocks.

The old crone who attended the maiden loosened the girl's hair, and it fell down her back to the floor. Now Murad was truly impressed. Thamar's hair was the color of April sunshine, and the sultan had never seen anything like it before. It was thick and shining and fell in rippling waves. Unable to contain himself, Murad rose and walked over to the girl. He reached out and stroked the lustrous mass. Catching it between his fingers, he felt the incredible texture of it. It was as soft as thistledown, yet not too fine.

Damn! The tsar was a sly old fox! He would certainly never love the girl, but he now lusted to possess her and that fabulous hair. He heard himself say, "The girl is a virgin?"

Smiling, the tsar nodded. Irritated by Ivan's show of superiority, Murad said brutally, "I shall require proof of my own. Just before I bed with the girl my own Moorish physician will decide the matter. Rest assured that I can tell a real virgin. No amount of weeping and feigning pain will fool me. So be sure, Ivan, that you deal honestly with me. If you or your daughter are lying to me, I will give her to my soldiers when I have finished with her."

The girl paled, gasped, and swayed. Catching her before she fell, Murad was unable to resist caressing a small breast. Thamar shivered first and then reddened with embarrassment. It told Murad what he wanted to know. Though he would still have the physician check, he was certain the girl was innocent.

Now the day had come for Thamar to enter the harem of Sultan Murad. Since she came as a concubine, not a wife, her arrival was a subdued one. When she stepped from her litter she was greeted, not by the sultan, as she had expected, but by a beautiful, richly clad young woman.

"Welcome to the Island Serai, Thamar of the Bulgars. I am Theadora of Byzantium, the sultan's bas-kadin."

"I expected the sultan to greet me," replied Thamar ungraciously.

"And so he would have if he were a Christian prince, or *if* you came as his wife. Alas, Moslem sul-

ADORA

tans learn different manners and we poor Christian
princesses who are sent into political concubinage
must learn to cope." Laughing, she put an arm about
the girl. "Come, my dear. I will wager you are tired,
hungry, and perhaps even a little frightened. You are
to have a beautiful, spacious apartment of your own
in the harem. But first a bath to wash the dust of your
journey from you and then a hot meal and a good
night's rest."

Thamar shook the friendly arm off. "Where is Lord
Murad? When will I see him? I demand that you tell
me!"

Theadora took the girl firmly by the hand and half
pulled, half dragged her to the privacy of her own
salon in the Court of the Beloved. Releasing Thamar's
hand, she faced her and said firmly, "I think it is time
you faced your situation honestly, my dear. You are
not to be the sultan's wife. You will be one of many
concubines. Sultan Murad has no wife, nor will he
ever have. He has a harem of women to suit his varied
moods. And he has one kadin. A kadin, Thamar, is a
maiden who has borne him sons and whom the sultan
wishes to honor.

"I am my lord's kadin. His *only* kadin. My sons,
Bajazet, Osman, and Orkhan are Murad's heirs. I
would like to be your friend, for my lord's happiness
is my first duty. Make no mistake, however, Thamar,
in the harem only the sultan's word supplants mine.

"You will see our lord Murad when *he* so desires
and not before. *You* may demand nothing. Only the
sultan demands. My lord thought you would be
weary and has ordered that you rest tonight."

370

When the girl frowned in obvious annoyance, Theadora's patience came to an abrupt end. "I had been told you were a virgin, but I have never known a virgin to be so eager for her lord's bed," she said cruelly.

The girl flushed with embarrassment. "I am not eager," she whispered. "I did not expect to be greeted in such a manner. Is it always so here?"

"What were you told of the harem?"

Again Thamar flushed. "I was told that whatever happened I must remember it was for my country. That the peasants would revere me as a saint."

Adora swallowed her laughter. The girl would be horribly offended. "They also, I am sure, made veiled references to unbridled licentiousness and orgies. I am afraid we will disappoint you, Thamar. The sultan is a very moral man. The Christian nobleman has a legal wife, an openly flaunted mistress, several secret mistresses, and exercises the *droit de seigneur* on every available virgin. The sultan is far more honest. He keeps a harem of women. The mothers of his children are honored, for the Moslems revere motherhood. Girls who don't attract his favor are married off to those the sultan wishes to favor. Older women are pensioned. Is such decency as this practiced in the Christian world?"

"Are you a Moslem, my lady?" asked the girl fearfully.

"No, Thamar, I am as faithful a member of the Eastern Church as you are. Father Lucas says the mass each day in my private chapel. You are welcome to join me in my devotions. Now, however, I suggest we return to our schedule: a bath, a meal, and a good night's sleep."

Adora escorted the subdued girl to the harem which was located in the Court of the Jeweled Fountains. Thamar attempted to be aloof, but the sight of a room full of beautiful women was both fascinating and unnerving. Her father had instructed her to gain the sultan's affection so that he might confide in her. She was then to pass on to her father all the information she had gathered. How, thought Thamar ruefully, was she supposed to gain the sultan's confidence when she would have trouble even gaining his attention?

Not only that, but her father's information regarding the princess Theadora was obviously incorrect also. Tsar Ivan had assured his daughter that the Byzantine princess was only one of the women in the harem. She had no authority or special place in the sultan's life. And she was a much older woman, practically elderly. Had she not been Sultan Orkhan's wife? Thamar was already composing in her mind a strongly worded letter to her sire. Casting a final glance about the harem salon, she realized she had nothing to offer Murad that the other women didn't have, except possibly her lovely hair.

Adora settled the girl as comfortably as possible, and then left her to her slaves. She could understand Murad's temptation. The maiden was indeed lovely—lovely enough to hold him it she had any sense at all. Her earlier show of temperament gave Adora cause for concern. She was not sure if it stemmed from strength of character or from stubbornness. She hoped it was the latter.

Back in the main salon of the harem the other women clustered in small groups, talking. This new princess was lovely and as different from Princess Theadora as dawn is from dusk. Would she supplant the favorite? Should they become Thamar's new friends now and thus be in line for her favors when she overcame Theadora?

A lovely Italian girl who was an occasional favorite of Murad's laughed mockingly at the others. "You are a pack of fools," she said, "to even contemplate choosing this new girl over the lady Theadora. Most of you have not even yet been in the sultan's bed. I have, and I can tell you that there is no one who will ever replace Princess Theadora in our lord Murad's heart. He is like a great lion who enjoys the company of many young lionesses but is truly mated to only one."

"But he must give this Thamar a child or her dowry will not be paid," said another girl. "When a man has a child by a woman he is always more attentive to her."

"Attentive, perhaps. In love with, no," came the Italian's reply. "The babe will be for Princess Thamar's amusement. And let us pray to Allah she conceives a girl child, for Prince Bajazet and his brothers are our lord Murad's heirs and Princess Theadora will brook no interference in the succession. Choose sides if you would be so foolish. But if you do, be sure you choose the right side. At least with our princess Adora we have a predictable quantity."

The women of the harem were strangely silent. They did not see Thamar until the next day when the entire harem, led by Theadora, participated in the ritual bridal bath. Thamar would go to the sultan's bed that night. Seeing the Bulgarian's nude, youthful beauty lost Thamar most of her support. The bored young beauties of the harem spent every waking hour working to entice the sultan. Here came a princess who would have no greater position than they had, yet she was being rushed to the sultan's bed. Had it not been for Adora's kindness, they would have turned on their new rival and torn her to pieces.

Adora, however, could afford to be generous. She was pregnant again. When she had learned that Murad intended taking the Bulgarian into his harem she had decided to forgo her previous precautions. As she knew that Murad would continue to bed with Thamar until he got her with child, Adora intended to make her own condition known quite soon. Nevertheless, she felt a stab of jealousy as she escorted the girl to Murad's apartment in the Court of the Sun.

So frightened was Thamar that she had to be practically pushed into the room. Ali Yahya stepped from the shadows, removed her plain white silk robe, and departed. Before her loomed a large, velvet hung bed. Thamar reluctantly stumbled forward. Remembering what she had been taught that afternoon, she kissed the embroidered hem of the coverlet and then crawled up from the foot of the bed to the sultan's side.

He watched her progress with amused, narrowed eyes. She had a deliciously provocative bottom. He sat cross-legged, his lower body hidden by the coverlet. As his chest was bare, she suspected the rest of him was too.

"Good evening, my little one. Are you well rested from your journey?" he queried pleasantly.

"Yes, my lord."

"And Adora has made you feel comfortable, and welcome?"

"Adora?"

"My kadin Theadora," he said. "I have always called her Adora."

"Oh, yes," said Thamar. She felt a twinge of resentment. She also felt very self-conscious in her nudity. She flushed and the sultan laughed low.

He reached out and pulled the pins from her hair which tumbled down to cover her. "Exquisite," he murmured. "Utterly exquisite." Lifting the coverlet he invited, "Come under and be warm."

Sliding beneath the rich robe, she saw that he was indeed nude. She lay still and straight and as far away from him as she dared. He reached over and pulled her closer. She was too afraid to protest.

"Do you know what I am going to do to you?" he asked her.

"Yes. You are to fuck me for that is how babies are made," she answered him.

"Do you know what that means, Thamar?" He strongly suspected that she did not. These Christian girls were always so poorly prepared for a man. "Have you ever seen the animals mate?"

"No, my lord. I was raised in a castle, not a farm-yard. Such indelicate sights are not meant for my eyes. My brothers' wives did tell me that, even though I was only to be your leman, I was to submit to you in all things as if you were really my husband. They said what men and women did to make babies was called 'fucking,' but I know not what they meant and they would not tell me. They said my husband would explain all things."

He sighed. "You have heard of the manroot?"

"Yes."

"Good!" He took her hand, and put it between his legs. "Touch it, sweet," he commanded her. "Fondle it gently. That is the manroot. At the moment it is soft and at rest, but as my desire for you grows it will increase in size. Through it flows my seed."

Hesitantly, she let her fingers close around him. For a few moments she did nothing more than hold him. Then, as her touch grew surer, she caressed him boldly. The warm touch began to rouse him, and as he grew harder and bigger in her hand, she gasped with surprise. Dropping the manroot, she drew back.

He laughed delightedly. "Fear not, little virgin, it is not yet time for us to be joined. Lesson Two involves where the manroot goes to plant my seed." He reached down and touched the soft, sensitive area between her legs. She gasped again and tried to pull away. But the sultan held her firmly with one arm while a finger gently explored her most intimate places. "There is where I will enter you," he said softly, then withdrew his hand. "It is too soon. First I would have a kiss from you, Thamar, and then I will explore all of your lovely body."

He shifted her so that she was beneath him and, bending down, found the wide, generous mouth. His first taste told him that she had never been kissed. It reminded him of Adora's lips when they had stolen kisses in the orchard of St. Catherine's so long ago. He pressed his mouth down harder against the girl beneath him, forcing the lips to part, then plunged his tongue into her mouth. To his surprise, her tongue fenced skillfully with his, which increased his ardor.

His hands found her little breasts and he squeezed, enjoying the feel of them. Then he bent his head to cover the small globes with hot kisses. His mouth sucked each nipple long and lovingly, and Thamar moaned with a sense of growing pleasure.

Allah, but she was sweet flesh, this royal virgin! His hands slid over her satiny, trembling body This was how it should have been with Adora, he thought. Murad let his lips wander down the smooth torso, feeling her pulse jump under his seeking mouth. She quivered and squirmed with passion.

Murad pulled himself up and found her mouth again, placing little kisses at the corners, pleased when she caught his head in her hands and forced his lips back to hers for another kiss. She sighed, whispering his name when he nuzzled at her little ear. "Thamar, my little virgin, I will not take you until you feel ready. But you must tell me," he murmured in her golden hair.

"Oh, now, my lord! Please now."

Pleased with her eagerness, he separated her thighs with his knee and, guiding his manhood with a hand, found her. Beneath him, Thamar tensed. The throbbing urgency between her legs was driving her almost mad with longing. She had no idea what it was she sought, but she knew it had to do with this man who was now her lord and master.

She could feel him enter her, filling her with his bulk. Then something blocked his passage. Disappointed, she moaned petulantly, "It is not enough! Not enough!"

Murad laughed in the heat of his lust. "There is more, eager, greedy one. First there will be pain, Thamar, then sweet delight. And never again will there be pain."

"Oh, yes!" she panted, straining against him.

Slowly he moved within the girl, driving her to a fever pitch. Then suddenly Thamar felt a terrible and unbearable burning pain spreading throughout her belly. Frightened, she cried out and tried to twist away from him, but he held her firmly, driving deeper and harder into her. Then the pain began to recede, leaving only delight. It was as he had promised. No longer fearful, she moved with him until he brought her to a perfect climax. Satisfied that she was fulfilled in her first sexual encounter, he went on to find his own pleasure.

Thamar was still floating with delight as Murad sought his own perfection. The sisters had never told her how delicious this fucking really was. They had tried to frighten her, the bitches! Thamar tenderly held the man laboring over her, rubbing the small of his back with innocently skillful little fingertips, thrusting her hips up to meet his downward motion. Oh, heaven! It was sweet! Sweet!

Then suddenly the hardness of the manroot within her broke and she was flooded with warm wetness. The man above her collapsed, sobbing "Adora! My own, sweet Adora!"

Thamar stiffened. She could not have heard it. *She did not hear it!* But once again Murad murmured into Thamar's hair, "Adora, my own!" Then he rolled from her onto his side and fell into a sound sleep.

Thamar lay rigid with anger. It was bad enough to have been forced into a harem, a harem ruled by an exquisitely beautiful woman who obviously held the sultan's heart. Here she stifled a sob. Not even to be free of that woman in the most intimate of moments! It was unforgivable! He was an unfeeling brute, and as for Theadora—The worst vengeance Thamar could. think of was not enough.

Adora! Thamar felt a sour taste rise in the back of her throat. Adora! She was so beautiful, so assured, so safe in Murad's love. There was nothing left for anyone else. The Byzantine had spoiled the sultan for anyone else. Thamar ached, for she too wanted to be loved.

The sultan would continue to bed with her until his seed found root in her womb. Then he would return to his beloved Adora, who was obviously never out of his thoughts even when he coupled with other women. A black and bitter hatred for Theadora was born in the Bulgarian girl. She knew not how she would do it, but someday she would be revenged.

Chapter 22

WITHIN A SHORT TIME OF HER INITIAL BEDDING THAMAR was sure she was pregnant. Shortly, she was proved correct. But even here she was not to be the center of attention for Adora was also with child. This reminded Thamar that she was just one of the harem. She was resentful of the other women. At first they put this down to her nervous condition, but later they realized it was her true attitude. Those who might have been her friends faded quickly away. Thamar was left alone.

Adora understood the younger girl's apparent misery for she had once been in a similar situation. She asked Murad to give Thamar the Court of the Blue Dolphins for her own. This was the smallest of the Island Serai's six courts, but it would be Thamar's own domain. Perhaps this mark of distinction would cheer her. Adora remembered well her own early days in the Bursa Palace with the unkind Anastatia sniping at her in an effort to make her miscarry Halil. She had been as frightened, unhappy, and miserable as young Thamar seemed to be.

For her show of kindness Adora was treated to a temper tantrum.

"Are you trying to isolate me?" snarled Thamar.

"I merely thought you would enjoy having your own private court, as I do," replied Adora. "If you would prefer to remain in your apartment in the harem you are welcome to do so."

"You need not have bothered to speak to my lord Murad on my behalf, but if this is truly my own domain then get out! I do not want you here! If this is mine I don't have to have you here! Get out!"

The attending slaves were shocked. They waited, frightened, to see what would happen next. But Adora dismissed them with a wave of her hand. Then she turned to face her young antagonist. "Sit down, Thamar," she commanded.

"I prefer to stand," muttered the girl.

"*Sit down!*" Seeing the fury of Adora's face, Thamar obeyed. "Now, Thamar, I think it is time we discussed this situation. From the moment you entered our lord Murad's house I have treated you with kindness. I have offered my friendship. Perhaps there is something about me that prevents our being friends but there is no excuse for this hostility and rudeness. Tell me what it is that troubles you. Perhaps together we can ease your misery."

"You would not understand."

"You cannot know that unless you tell me." Adora smiled encouragingly

Thamar shot her an angry look, and then the words burst forth. "I was raised to be the *wife* of a Christian lord. To love him. To support him in all things. To bear his children. To be his only chatelaine. Instead I am sent to an infidel's harem. Very well, I told myself, it is

God's will and I will accept it meekly as a good Christian daughter. What I cannot accept, however, is that on my wedding night, at the height of *our* passion Murad cried out *your* name! Not only once! I will never forgive either of you for that! *Never!"*

Oh, God! thought Adora, her heart constricting painfully. Thamar had been so needlessly hurt. And Murad was apparently still preoccupied by her virginity. That it had been lost to another man was still hurting him. She reached out and touched the girl's arm. Wet-eyed, Thamar looked angrily at her. "It will not help," said Adora softly, "but I am truly sorry you have suffered on my account. But you must forgive Murad, Thamar. He is, it seems, haunted by the ghost of something that cannot be changed, but he is a good man, and he would be grieved to know that he has hurt you."

"You are right," said Thamar bitterly. "Your words do not help. I can understand his loving you. You are so beautiful, and so assured. But why can he not love me a little also?" she wailed. "I carry his child too!"

"Perhaps if you will stop snarling at everyone, he will. Give him time, Thamar. I have known my lord Murad since I was younger than you. I was the last and the youngest of his father's wives. I left Byzantium when I was but a little maid. I had been married to Sultan Orkhan by proxy in Constantinople. Like you, I was not required to renounce my religion. And until I was old enough, and the sultan took me to his bed, I lived in the Convent of St. Catherine in Bursa. Murad's younger brother, Prince Halil, is my son. After Sultan Orkhan died I was remarried to the lord of Mesembria, and when he died Sultan Murad offered me his favor."

"Having been a wife, you became a concubine?" Thamar was incredulous.

"Yes.""But why? Surely if Emperor John had insisted, Sultan Murad would have married you."

Adora laughed gently "No, Thamar, he would not. He did not have to, you see. In the beginning the Ottomans wed legally with Christian royalty in order to further their cause. Now, however, the Ottoman is stronger than the Christians around him, and though he may take their daughters into his bed as a bribe, he feels he need no longer formally wed with them.

"My brother-in-law, Emperor John, is as much a vassal to my lord Murad as is your father, Tsar Ivan."

Thamar looked discomfited. "How did you reconcile yourself to this situation?" she asked.

"Firstly," answered Adora, "I love my lord Murad. Secondly, I daily practice my faith, which gives me strength. I accept the fact that I am still nought but a woman, and 'tis the men who rule this world. I do not believe God will hold either of us responsible for the situation our families have placed us in. By obeying them, we are only being good Christian daughters. If what they have done is wrong, then it is they who will suffer—not us."

"But should we enjoy our situation, Adora?"

"I do not see why not, Thamar. After all, if we are not pleasant and loving we will displease the sultan who is a very intuitive man. This will make him unhappy with our families who have sent us to him to please him. It is our duty to enjoy our life in our lord Murad's house."

If the sultan had heard Adora's conversation with Thamar he would have laughed at first, and then he would have accused her of being a devious Greek. If there was one thing Adora did *not* accept it was the fact that women were the inferiors of men.

Though Murad did not hear the conversation, he did benefit from it. Thamar had taken Adora's words very much to heart, and the young Bulgarian took on a very different attitude.

She was brighter than the harem beauties, but she had very little wit and was therefore a natural foil for the clever Murad. He delighted in teasing her just so he might see her cheeks turn rosy in pretty confusion. She took to treating the sultan as a demigod. This attitude soothed Murad, but infuriated Adora, especially when Murad began referring to Thamar as his "kitten" and to Adora as his "tigress."

Then too, as Adora's pregnancy advanced she became pear-shaped while Thamar barely showed her condition.

"She looks as if she has swallowed an olive," said Adora petulantly to her son, Halil, "while I appear to have consumed a giant melon!"

He laughed. "I don't suppose, then, that this is the time to tell you that you are to become a grandmother."

"Halil! *How could you*? You are only sixteen!"

"But Alexis is almost eighteen, mother, and very eager to begin our family. She is such an adorable creature that I could not refuse her. And," his eyes twinkled, "quite frankly, I enjoyed filling her request by filling her belly." He ducked as she swatted at him. "Besides, I was Bajazet's age when you were eighteen."

Theadora winced. "Try," she said through clenched teeth, "not to crow too loudly to your half-brother about your wife's state. Your place in life is still partially dependent on my favor with Murad. It is difficult enough to cope with a silly girl of sixteen without you telling my lord that I am to be a grandmother! My God, Halil! I am not yet thirty. My little sons are but five and three-and-a-half. Thank heavens you are in Nicea and not here in Adrianople. At least I need not be reminded daily of your perfidy." Then, seeing her son's woebegone expression, she relented. "Oh, very well, Halil! When is the child due?"

"Not for seven months, mother."

"Good! By that time I shall have borne my lord another one. I shall tell him of your child while I nurse my own. It will not seem so bad then."

Halil laughed again. "So you carry another lad, eh?"

"Yes! I birth only sons," she said proudly.

It was not to be, however. This time Adora gave birth on an unusually cold and rainy summer's dawn. It was a daughter. Worse, the child came feet first, and only the skill of Fatima the Moor saved both mother and baby. The birth was, as usual, witnessed by the women of the harem. When the sex of the child finally was announced Thamar smiled triumphantly and folded her hands complacently over her belly. Weak as she was, Adora felt the strong urge to rise from her bed and rake her fingernails down her face.

Afterward, they tucked her into her bed and

brought her daughter to her, but she would not even look at the baby. "Get a wetnurse for it," she commanded. "I give suck only to princes, not female brats!" The infant whimpered as if sensing the rejection. Theadora's face softened. Slowly she lifted the blanket and gazed on the face of her new daughter. It was a smooth, heart-shaped face with two large and beautiful blue eyes fringed in thick lashes. The child had a headful of thick, shining dark-brown curls, a rosebud mouth, and high on her left cheekbone an unusual birthmark: a tiny dark crescent above which rode a little star mole.

Iris, Fatima, and the other slaves watched Adora expectantly.

"She may have given a bit of trouble in the birthing," said the midwife quietly, "but she's the loveliest babe I've seen in many a day, my lady. Your three boys will spoil her terribly."

"And so will her proud father." Murad had entered the room unobserved. He bent and kissed Adora. "Once again you have done the thing that pleases me the most. I wanted a daughter!"

"But I wanted to give you a son," she said softly.

"You have already given me three, my dove. I wanted something of you, and now I have it. My daughter will be called Janfeda. Only the noblest Moslem prince will be good enough for her when I finally bestow her hand, many years from now."

"You are not displeased then?"

"No, my dove, I am delighted."

When he had left she wept with relief, and there was no wetnurse for Janfeda until after her mother's time of purification, as it had been with Theadora's sons.

Almost three months later Thamar bore a healthy son who was named Yakub. Called from the sultan's bed to be a witness to the birth, Adora had her small revenge on her rival. Her body had regained its youthful form and she had a delicious, flushed, and tousled look about her. Her amethyst eyes were languorous, and her mouth softly bruised from Murad's kisses. All this was quite obvious to the women of the harem.

Thamar was not having an easy time. She was small, and her baby was big. She had refused to have the midwife, Fatima the Moor, because she was Adora's "minion." She could not, Thamar claimed, feel safe under such circumstances. The insult was uncalled for and Murad was angered. But Adora shrugged and sighed.

"She may be endangering not only herself but the child also, my lord. But if you force Fatima upon her, the result of the fear might be worse. She is young and healthy. She should do well." Theadora did not believe for one minute that Thamar was afraid of her. This was probably the start of a campaign on the Bulgarian's part.

The result of Thamar's attitude was that, in the end, Fatima had to be called to save both mother and child. The midwife pulled the baby from the exhausted girl's body, but the delay cost Thamar further children. She was badly torn. Only Fatima's skill prevented her reluctant patient from bleeding to death.

Following the birth, the Court of the Blue Dolphins

became an armed camp with entry practically impossible. Thamar had taken some of her bridal allowance and bought herself two dozen fighting eunuchs who allowed only the sultan free access to the Bulgarian. Those serving Thamar had either come with her from Bulgaria or were newly purchased. They were allowed no contact with the rest of the inhabitants of the Island Serai. Food for the court was purchased daily by the old crone who had been Thamar's nurse.

Three days after the birth Adora arrived at the Court of the Blue Dolphins laden with gifts for the new mother and her child. The gifts were taken from the sultan's bas-kadin, but Adora was refused admittance to the court. Furious, she sought out Murad. "She is attempting to make it appear that I would harm her or her child," said Adora. "It is a terrible insult to cast such suspicion on my good name!"

The sultan agreed. There had been peace in his house until Thamar had come. He now regretted having been overcome with lust. He did not intend to allow her to harm his beloved Adora by innuendo. Taking his favorite by the hand, he walked with her to the Court of the Blue Dolphins. The eunuchs quickly opened ranks to admit them.

They found Thamar settled comfortably on a couch in her garden, the child in his cradle by her side. Her look of joy at seeing Murad quickly disappeared when she saw Adora.

"How dare you refuse admittance to the woman who rules this harem?" he thundered.

"I am your kadin too," quavered Thamar, "and this is my court."

"No, you are not a kadin. I have not given you that honor. I am the master in this house, and I have made Adora the mistress here. She has been more than kind, even begging this court for you. In return you attempt to slander her unjustly."

"It is not unjust! Because of her I can have no other children. Her evil Moor saw to that! No doubt the witch would have strangled my son as well had not the entire harem been present!"

"My God!" gasped Adora, whitening. "You are mad, Thamar! The birth has addled her wits, Murad."

"No," said the sultan, his black eyes narrowing, "she knows exactly what she says. Now hear me, Thamar! Your own stupidity and stubbornness has rendered you sterile. It was a miracle you did not kill the child. Fatima saved your life. Your child is my fourth acknowledged son. There is very little possibility of his ever ruling. Adora has no reason to fear you or your child and is no danger to either of you. To suggest such a thing is slanderous and unforgivable. If you persist in this charade I will remove Yakub from your care. My kadin will always be allowed immediate entry to this court. Do you understand me?"

"Y—y—yes my lord."

"Good," said Murad firmly. "Come, Adora. We will leave Thamar to rest now."

But the battle lines had been drawn, and Adora now faced two enemies within the house of Osman: Thamar and the evil Prince Cuntuz. For the present, she left the Bulgarian alone. She hoped a time of quiet would alleviate Thamar's fear. Thamar was not devious, so her fear was real enough, though unjustified.

Prince Cuntuz was a different matter. He learned to read and write in the prince's school, but higher learning escaped him. The one thing he had inherited from his father was his ability with weapons. He quickly became skilled with knife and dagger, sword and scimitar, lance and bow. He swam and wrestled well and was an excellent horseman. But his lack of intellect prevented his ever being a commander, for he could not grasp tactics. It was yet another cause for bitterness in Cuntuz, who did not mellow as the years passed.

Though he was treated like a prince, though he was reputedly the oldest of Murad's sons, his mother's reputation was costing him his rightful place in history. Or so be believed. If his four younger brothers were out of the way, his father would have to turn to him. There would be no other choice.

Cuntuz set about to make friends with Adora's sons, who were now ten and nine.

Generously he helped to teach his younger siblings horsemanship and weaponry. Adora watched Bajazet, Osman, and Orkhan nervously, for some instinct warned her against Cuntuz. But as she had no proof to back up her fears, she pushed them away. Tall, slender boys with dark hair, fair skin, and black eyes like Murad's, her sons were so handsome. If only they weren't so enamored of Cuntuz! But with nothing to put her finger on, she had no grounds to destroy the relationship. Murad was pleased that Cuntuz finally seemed at home. The sultan even began including him in family evenings.

Here was the one area where Adora and Thamar

agreed; neither liked Cuntuz. Once when Murad had been momentarily called away by a messenger, Adora turned back into her dimly lit antechamber and found Cuntuz blocking her way. When he made no move to step aside, she said quietly, "I would pass, Cuntuz."

"You must pay me a toll," he leered.

Adora felt the anger well up in her. "Step aside!" she hissed.

He reached out and grasped her right breast, squeezing at so tightly that she winced. Adora's eyes narrowed dangerously. "Take your hand from me," she said coldly, forcing herself to remain still and straight, "else I tell your father of this incident."

"Your sister, Helena, liked it when I did this to her," he murmured low. "In fact, she liked it when I . . ." and here Cuntuz began a catalogue of perversions so foul that Adora almost fainted. Instead she made herself stand very still. And when he had finished, inquiring lasciviously, "Would you not like to taste such delights?" she fixed him with a cold stare. For a moment their eyes remained locked. Then Cuntuz released her.

"You will not tell my father," he said smugly, "if you do I will deny the incident and say you seek to discredit me."

"Rest assured, Cuntuz," she said calmly, "that if I tell my lord Murad, he will believe me." Then she brushed past him. Behind her, his eyes blazed hatred, but she did not see.

Several days later Adora sought for her sons late in the afternoon. They had, she was told, gone riding with Cuntuz. A prickle of apprehension ran through her, and she hurried to find Ali Yahya. A troop of Janissaries was sent after the princes. An hour into the hills they met with Cuntuz who claimed that they had been attacked by bandits. His three younger half-brothers had been taken captive, though he had managed to escape. The trail was clear, he claimed, so he would return to the Island Serai to get more aid. Having no real reason to doubt him, they let him go.

The trail was clear. And because it was late spring, the light remained. At no point could the Janissaries find the tracks of more than four horses. And when they found all three of the younger princes' horses wandering, the soldiers became suspicious.

"Do you think he's killed them?" asked the second-in-command.

"Probably," said the captain grimly, "but we must find them before we return. We cannot go back without the bodies as proof."

It was growing dark, and they stopped to make torches so that they might continue to follow the trail. Eventually the flickering torchlights led them up a small hill into a rock-strewn clearing. There they found the boys. They had been stripped naked and staked out in the cold night air. Their young bodies had been lashed with a metal-tipped whip, opening several bloody stripes which eventually would have attracted wolves. They had been doused with icy water from a nearby stream.

Young Osman was dead. Orkhan, his twin, was unconscious. But Bajazet was conscious, shivering, and furious with himself for having been taken in by his older half-brother.

The Janissaries built a huge fire and, finding the boys' clothes, dressed them quickly Bringing them to the roaring blaze, they rubbed their hands and feet in an effort to stimulate their circulation. Orkhan remained unconscious, despite their efforts. But Bajazet couldn't stop talking, and when one Janissary remarked that the deceased prince had a bruise on the side of his head, the boy burst out, "Cuntuz kicked him there when Osman cursed him for what he was doing to us. My brother never spoke again. That accursed spawn of a Greek whore boasted that with us dead, he would next poison little Yakub, and see that our mother was blamed! He said our father would have no choice but to make him his heir. We must get back to the Island Serai!"

"Dare we move Prince Orkhan, Highness?" questioned the Janissary captain.

"We must! You cannot possibly get him warm here. He needs our mother's touch."

It was well past midnight when they returned to the Island Serai. Five-year-old Prince Yakub was safe: Prince Cuntuz had never returned to the palace to carry out his plans. Adora's grief over the dead Osman had to wait while she attended to his twin. But at dawn Orkhan opened his eyes, smiled at his parents and Bajazet, and said, "I have to go now, mother. Osman is calling me." And before any of them could say a word, the boy died.

For a moment all was silent. Then Adora began to wail. Clutching the bodies of her twin sons, she wept until she thought she could weep no more—but wept again. Murad had never felt so helpless in his life.

They had been his sons too, but he had not nurtured them within his own body or suckled them.

"I will avenge them, I swear it," he promised her.

"Yes," she sobbed, "avenge them. It will not bring my babies back to me, but avenge them!"

And when he had left her she called her surviving son to her. "Listen to me, Bajazet. This tragedy could encourage Thamar to act against you, but I will see you are protected. Someday you will be sultan, and when that time comes you will not allow sentiment to overrule you. You will instantly destroy your rivals, whoever they may be. Do you understand me, Bajazet? Never again must you be threatened!"

"I understand, mother. On the day I become sultan, Yakub will die before he can act against me. This empire will never be divided!"

Clasping the boy in her arms, Theadora began weeping afresh. Bajazet looked grimly over her shoulder at the bodies of his twin brothers. Slowly, silently, the tears ran down the boy's face. No, he vowed silently, he would not forget.

Chapter 23

Prince Cuntuz fled to Constantinople where he begged asylum of the empress. Her cold blue eyes took in the boy who had briefly been her lover. In the years away he had become a man, and had probably learned many an interesting trick. The Turks were known for their licentiousness.

"Why should I take you under my protection?" she demanded of him.

"Because I have done something that should please you greatly."

"What?" She was not particularly interested.

"I have killed your sister's sons."

"You lie! Did you really? How could you?"

He told her, and Helena mused aloud. "The sultan will most certainly demand your return."

"But you will not give me up," he said, softly caressing the tender inside of her arm. "You will hide me, and protect me."

"Why on earth would I do that, Cuntuz?"

"Because I can do things for you that no other man can. You know that well, my wicked Byzantine whore. Don't you?"

"Tell me," she teased provocatively, and so he did.

Smiling, she nodded and agreed to hide him.

John Paleaologi was furious. But for once, Helena correctly understood the situation. "The sultan has bigger things to do than besiege this city to obtain his wayward son," she said. "Cuntuz has behaved badly. But his mother is my friend, and Murad would be overly harsh with the boy."

The emperor turned purple with anger and choked. "Either I am mad," he said, "or you are! Cuntuz has behaved badly? Cuntuz is responsible for the brutal, premeditated murders of two nine-year-old boys and the attempted murder of a ten-year-old boy. His own half-brothers! *If* Mara is correct about her son's paternity."

"They are not all dead?"

"No, my dear. Bajazet, the eldest, survived. He is as filled with plans for revenge as is his father. Cuntuz is not even safe within the walls of this city. I will certainly not protect him from Murad. Where is he?"

"He is under the protection of the Church," she answered smugly. "He never gave up his religion, and his grandparents raised him in our true faith. You cannot violate the laws of sanctuary, John."

Boxed in by the Church, the emperor wrote his overlord an apologetic letter filled with his personal sympathy, explaining the difficulty of his situation. Murad wrote back absolving his vassal, but warning him to keep Cuntuz under constant observation, and not allow him to leave Constantinople. Thus the renegade prince—-drinking, gambling, and wenching about the city with his boon companion, Prince Andronicus—thought himself quite safe.

As Murad began a new western advance, Thamar's father, Tsar Ivan, launched a campaign against him. Joining with the Serbians, he attacked the Ottoman forces and was quickly and soundly defeated at Samakov. Ivan fled to the mountains leaving the passes to the Plain of Sofia open to the Turks. And he left his unfortunate daughter, Thamar, very much in disfavor with her lord.

Murad was in no hurry to take the city of Sofia. He was no longer a tribesman on a swift raid for quick booty. He was an empire builder, and as such he moved to secure his left flank. The valleys of the Struma and the Vardar were to be occupied as quickly as possible.

The Struma River Valley was part of Serbia. The Vardar was in Macedonia. Both areas were as torn with internal troubles as Bulgaria had been. The Serbian army marched to the Maritza River to engage the Ottoman forces. They were defeated at Cernomen and three of their princes were killed.

Thus the Serbians were conquered as easily as the Thracians had been some ten years earlier. The two major cities of Serres and Drama were swiftly colonized, the main churches turned into mosques. The smaller cities and villages of the Struma Valley accepted and acknowledged the sultan's sovereignty. The mountain chieftains became Ottoman vassals.

The following year Murad's armies crossed the Vardar River and took the eastern end of its valley. Now Murad paused in his campaign of western expansion, and turned his eyes back to Anatolia.

By this time, John Paleaologi had decided that the

time was right to seek aid from western Europe. Murad was far too occupied to notice his scholarly brother-in-law, so John traveled quietly to Italy to warn of the growing Ottoman menace.

Once before the emperor had sought aid of his western neighbors. He had made a secret visit to Hungary two years prior and, by swearing the submission of the Greek Church to the Latin, he was promised aid against the Turks. On his return home, however, he was captured and held by the Bulgarians who objected to what they considered the emperor's betrayal. This gave a fine excuse to John's Catholic cousin, Amedeo of Savoy, to invade Gallipoli. Having captured it, he sailed into the Black Sea to fight the Bulgarians, and gained his cousin's release.

Freed, John Paleaologi made for Constantinople. When his cousin insisted on his acceptance to Rome, John refused. Angered, Amedeo fought the Greeks.

Now, John ventured to Rome where he once again foreswore the Orthodox faith in favor of the Roman Church. In exchange he was to receive military aid from his fellow Catholic princes. When the aid was not forthcoming, John sadly departed for home. In Venice he was detained for "debt" and forced to send to his elder son for the ransom. Andronicus had been left as regent in his father's absence.

Helena saw an opportunity to be free of her husband, and Andronicus saw his opportunity to be emperor. He refused to aid his father. But John's younger son, Manuel, saw his opportunity to get into his father's favor, thus supplanting his older sibling. Manuel raised the ransom and personally brought his father home to Constantinople.

John Paleaologi faced the sad truth. The city of his ancestors was doomed to fall to the Turks. Perhaps not today, or tomorrow, but sometime in the near future the city would change hands. Those who worshiped in the Greek Church were in the minority, and would get no help from their Catholic brethren.

Wiser and wearier than he had ever been, the emperor of Byzantium reaffirmed his oath of vassalage to his brother-in-law, the sultan. Never again would he seek aid against the Ottoman whom he found to be a better friend than his Christian associates.

Though the Pope and the princes of western Christendom were not aware of it, their shabby treatment of Byzantium's ruler would one day have far-reaching effects. It meant that each eastern-European grouping—Greek, Serb, Slav, or Bulgar—would prefer the rule of the Ottoman Moslems who offered them religious freedom to that of the western-European Catholic Christians who tried to force them to the Latin Church.

John Paleaologi settled down to what he hoped would now be a quiet life. His wife, involved as usual in her many love affairs, was being discreet and offered him no current trouble. His older son, Andronicus, in total disgrace and sulking, spent all of his time with Prince Cuntuz, following his unpleasant nature. Manuel had been elevated to the position of co-emperor as reward for his aid. John Paleaologi knew Manuel's motives, but at least the boy had brains, really loved his father, and was eager to learn the business of ruling. Unlike Andronicus, Manuel understood that leadership involved responsibility as well as privilege.

For a short time all was quiet in the Byzantine Empire. And then one day the emperor and his younger son awoke to find that Andronicus and Cuntuz were leading a rebellion against their respective fathers. Where they had gotten the money to finance such a venture was a puzzle to everyone but the emperor.

The emperor's spies were swift and thorough. The money had come originally from the papacy which had tithed the rulers of western Europe to pay for their meddling. It was next transferred to the Hungarians who passed it on to the two renegade princes. These two had both foresworn the Greek Church in favor of the Latin and had promised to bring their subjects to Catholicism, once they overcame their fathers.

Neither John nor Murad could believe that the leaders of the West actually expected two such inept fools as Andronicus and Cuntuz to deliver what they promised. The real reason they had been set to rebellion was probably the hope of stirring dissension between Constantinople and the sultan.

Murad's response to the plot was characteristically swift.

He trapped the two miscreants and their ragtag army in the town of Demotika. The townspeople were hardly overjoyed to find themselves caught in the midst of this siege. They had no interest in the rebellion. They smuggled out a message to the sultan, disclaiming any responsibility for the plot and begging the sultan to free them of Andronicus and Cuntuz.

Murad quickly complied with the wishes of his loyal subjects: he took the town with a minimum of bloodshed and damage. The Greek rebels who had aided Andronicus and Cuntuz were bound together and flung living from the city walls to drown in the Maritza River below. The sultan ordered the young Turks involved to be executed by their own fathers.

Now the two rulers turned to their own offspring. Looking on Cuntuz with contempt, Murad said, "This is not the first time you have earned my anger. The last time you fled rather than face the consequences of your terrible crime. You will not flee me now, Cuntuz. If it were up to me I know the punishment I should inflict on you, but judgement belongs to the mother of my dead sons and my living heir."

Cuntuz's composure slipped. He could face a swift death, but the vengeance of a mother for the murder of her young sons was a frightening thing. The Byzantines were noted for particularly exquisite tortures.

From behind the sultan's throne stepped Theadora and Bajazet. The boy had grown in the last four years. He was almost a man, and there had been talk of an alliance with the heiress-princess of Germiyan. Suddenly the sultan's voice boomed, "Theadora of Byzantium, what sentence will you pronounce on this man for the murder of your sons, Osman and Orkhan?"

"Death, my lord, preceded by blinding," came the reply.

"So be it," said the sultan. "On you Cuntuz of

Gallipoli I pronounce the sentence of death by beheading for your rebellion against me. First, however, your hands will be cut off, and you will be blinded for your crime of fratricide. This is my judgement."

"A boon, my lord!"

"Yes, Theadora?"

"I would blind him myself. And my son, Bajazet, would perform the beheading."

"The law forbids the taking of a brother's life by another brother."

"Do not the prophets say an eye for an eye, my lord? And, too, this man's mother was a known whore. The mullahs and ulemas forbade his inclusion on the list of your legal heirs. I see nothing of you in him, and I do not recognize him as either your son or a half-brother to Prince Bajazet. If by wildest chance your blood does flow in his veins, then his fratricide and his rebellion against you negate any relationship between the Ottoman and him. Therefore my son breaks no law."

A very faint smile touched the sultan's lips, and he leaned over to his brother-in-law. "Does she not reason like a Greek advocate?" he asked softly.

"She is her father's daughter," said John, "knowing when to press the advantage and when to retreat."

Murad turned back to his favorite. "It will be as you wish, Adora. But are you sure you wish to blind this renegade yourself?"

Her amethyst eyes darkened and grew hard. "For four years my children have cried daily to me from their graves to avenge them. They will not rest until I do—and neither will I. Having someone else perform the deed is not enough. Bajazet and I must do it our-selves, else we condemn Osman and Orkhan to wan-der forever in the half-world between life and death."

"So be it," pronounced Murad, and the mullahs and ulemas sitting cross-legged about the judgement hall nodded their agreement. Vengeance was something they could understand. That Theadora and her son wished to perform this act of vengeance they approved. Bajazet had already shown his courage by fighting with his father against the rebels. It was good to know that his mother, female though she was, also possessed courage.

Now all eyes turned to the emperor of Byzantium to see what judgment he would pass on his own son. John could do no less than his overlord, and so Andronicus was also condemned to mutilation, blind-ing, and beheading. First, however, he would watch his friend die.

A small, flat brass brazier was brought forth by a slave. It glowed red with burning coals. Seeing it forced Cuntuz to reality, and he tried to run. Two young Janissaries leapt forward and dragged him back. He pulled away from them with the superhu-man strength of a desperate man and threw himself at Adora's feet.

"Mercy, lady," he babbled. "My life I forfeit, but blind me not!"

She drew back as if his very touch would contami-nate her. Her voice was icy, toneless. "Did you show my babies mercy when you brutally murdered them? They trusted you. You were a man to whom they looked up, and they were but impressionable little boys. If I had my way, Cuntuz of Gallipoli, I should have you flayed alive and then thrown to the dogs!"

A block and a kettle of boiling pitch were added to the brazier. Cuntuz was dragged screaming to his knees by the brawny Janissaries. His hands were forced onto the block and, before he could scream again, they were removed from his body by the swift blade of a sword. The stumps were thrust into the hot pitch to prevent bleeding. Shocked into silence he could only stare in horror at his arms. Now he was dragged backward, his handless arms pinioned to his sides, his body straddled, his head held in the iron grip of a large Janissary.

A slave handed Adora a small pair of iron pincers. Seeing her hand tremble slightly, the sultan moved to her side. "You do not have to do this yourself," he said softly. Her face was very pale.

She looked up, her violet eyes tearing. "When he murdered my children he was not content to simply leave them to die on the mountain. He opened bloody wounds on them to attract wild beasts. Had the Janissaries not arrived in time, they might have been torn to pieces. What a terrible death for anyone, let alone little boys! Not satisfied, he poured icy water on them and they nearly froze in the night air. Bajazet still catches cold easily because of that."

"My lord Murad, I cringe at the thought of causing anyone pain, but I will be revenged! My children, both living and dead, demand it!"

And before anyone realized what she was doing, Adora took a live coal from the pan with the pincers and touched it to Cuntuz's right eye. He made no outcry for he had fainted. She repeated her action on the left eye when it was opened by the Janissary.

No sound was heard except a pitiful whimpering from the throat of Prince Andronicus. Adora lay the pincers carefully on the side of the pan. Heedless of the roomful of people, Murad put an arm about her and led her to a stool.

"You are a brave woman," he said softly.

"I did what must be done," she answered. Then, in a low voice, "Reprieve the death sentence and the mutilation for my nephew, my lord. Have his blinding done with boiling vinegar. That will make it only a temporary condition."

"Why?"

"Because then Andronicus will remain capable of continuing to quarrel and scheme against his father and brother. That will keep them so well occupied that Byzantium will not bother us further. Your vengeance here has been swift and fair. We need not the death of an unimportant princeling. It accomplishes nothing."

He nodded. "Very well, but I will not announce my clemency until after Prince Andronicus has seen his partner beheaded. Let him be thoroughly frightened by this lesson." He rose from her side. "Revive the prisoner, Cuntuz, and prepare him for his execution. Bring a selection of well-honed swords for Prince Bajazet, and bring a lined basket. I would not have the floor bloodied."

Conscious now, Cuntuz wept from sightless eyes as around him he heard the preparations being made for his death. The sultan turned to the other rebel. "Prince Andronicus! You will hold the basket to catch the head." And before the terrified man could protest, he was prodded forward and forced to his knees. The basket, lined in large green leaves, was shoved into his arms.

The blind man was now led forth and helped down. His blackened eye sockets stared straight at Andronicus. "I'll be waiting in hell for you, *my friend*," he said venomously.

"Don't talk to me!" returned Andronicus, hysteria in his voice. "This is all *your fault*! All I had to do was wait for my father to grow old and die. But you wanted the money those damned Hungarians offered us. We never even got to spend it! I hate you!"

"Coward," sneered Cuntuz. Then he grew silent as he heard behind him the swish of a sword being tested. "Bajazet? Are you there, boy?"

"Yes, Cuntuz."

"Remember what I taught you. Pick a sword that is light, but has a firm feel to it. Then strike swiftly."

Bajazet laughed mirthlessly. "Fear not, dog! My aim will be true. Bend your neck so I may see the target." Then he said haughtily, "You, my brave Byzantine cousin! Hold the basket higher unless you wish your friend's head in your lap." And Bajazet raised his sword, calling, "Farewell, dog!" He brought it down swiftly and Cuntuz's head tumbled into the basket face up.

Prince Andronicus looked into his friend's face and vomited before dropping the basket, fainting. Bajazet handed his sword to a Janissary and looked with disgust upon his relation. "*That* led a rebellion against you?" he asked his father scornfully

Murad nodded. "Neither under nor overestimate your enemies, my son. The rankest coward has moments of bravery or defiance." He turned to the emperor. "It is not necessary that your son die, John. His death would serve no purpose. Blind him with boiling vinegar, and what comes after is Allah's will."

Fully comprehending the mercy shown his son, the emperor of Byzantium knelt and kissed Murad's hand. Then he stood and, taking a basin of the vinegar, he faced his son. "You have been granted your life. Your punishment will give you time to contemplate your sins and to reform," he said sternly, and then he threw the contents of the basin in his son's eyes.

Andronicus shrieked and tried to shield himself, but he was held firmly by the soldiers. "I am blind!" he cried frantically. "Papa! Papa? Where are you? Do not leave me! Do not leave your 'droni!'"

"I will not leave you, my son," replied the emperor sadly, and the mullahs and ulemas seated about the room nodded, marveling at the sultan's fairness.

Chapter 24

THE EMIR OF GERMIYAN WAS GIVING HIS ELDEST daughter to Prince Bajazet. Her name was Zubedya, and she was very fair. The emirs of both Karamania and Aydin had made offers for this princess. They did not, however, present the same potential threat to Germiyan as did the Ottoman sultan. In accepting Zubedya for his son, Murad also accepted the responsibility of protecting a new possession. Zubedya's younger sister, Zenobia, would be given to one of Murad's generals with a large dowry, ending any threat from that quarter.

The sultan had had to make a concession to the emir of Germiyan, a concession that enraged both Adora and Thamar. Nothing could make the emir send his daughter to Prince Bajazet except a formal ceremony of marriage. If Aydin and Karamania offered marriage, the royal Ottoman could do no less. Without marriage, Princess Zubedya and her sister would go elsewhere, and Murad would find himself having to go to war not only with Germiyan, but with Aydin and Karamania as well.

The emir of Germiyan loved his daughters. Eventually they might be replaced in their husbands' affections by other women, but they would be wives and as such they would at least retain their rank and privileges. The other women would be mere concubines.

The wedding would be celebrated in Bursa, and the Ottoman court removed from their new capital in Europe back to the old one in Asia. In an effort to soothe his angry favorite, Murad ordered a small, exquisite palace known as the Mountain Serai be prepared for her, but Adora was adamant.

She stormed furiously at him, "The daughter of a half-savage Asiatic emir, got on the body of an unknown slavegirl! This is what you *marry* to my son? You dare to raise this chit above me? I am Theodora Cantacuzene, a princess of Byzantium! Allah in his paradise—even Thamar of the Bulgars is better bred than the Germiyan wench. And yet the girl is to *wed* with your heir while I, his mother, must continue to hide my shame at being nothing but your concubine!" Her face was a study in fury. But inside Adora laughed. She had waited years for this opportunity, and the look on Murad's face told her he knew he was trapped.

"You are my beloved," he answered her.

She looked coldly at him. "I am not a simple maiden to be swayed by romantic drivel, my lord Murad."

"You were never a 'simple' maiden, my dove," he chuckled. "I told you when I first took you that I had no need to make dynastic marriages. My antecedents needed their marriages. I do not."

"Perhaps you had no 'need' once, my lord Murad, but you have a 'need' now," she answered him silkenly.

He recognized the tone. It was her battle-cry voice, and he asked quietly, "Explain your words, woman."

She smiled sweetly at him. "It is quite simple, my lord. You cannot in fairness or good conscience raise Zubedya of Germiyan above Thamar and me. The girl is already overproud of her position as heiress to her father's lands. She will have no respect for us, though we be much better bred than she. If you do not wed with Thamar and me, Bajazet will not wed with Zubedya. And think not to threaten us with Yakub for your younger son is as determined as the older that you wed with his mother."

"I can have you beaten for this impertinence," he threatened grimly.

"I will die before I ask your mercy," she returned, and he knew it to be true. "You claim to love me, Murad. For years you have poured forth a torrent of words proclaiming your passion for me. I have borne you three sons and a daughter, upon whom you dote. Will you give Janfeda to some man as concubine when she is old enough, or will you see her properly wed? No, my lord Murad. You need make no dynastic marriages, but if you truly love me you will wed with me before our son takes his wife."

"And Thamar also, Adora?"

She sighed. "Yes, Thamar also."

"Why?" he demanded. "You don't like each other, yet you would raise her to your level."

"She too is the mother of your child, and though Bulgaria at its height can scarcely compare with Byzantium even at its lowest point, Thamar is still of a royal house—as I am." She put her slender hand on his brawny arm and looked up at him. "It has not been easy for her, Murad. At least I have your love. Even as wives we would not really be equals, but it would soothe Thamar's pride. She has given you a son, and is worthy of it."

"I have not said I would marry either of you," he grumbled.

"But you will, my lord, for you know what I say is true."

"Damn me, woman, do not nag at me!"

She knelt quietly, eyes lowered, hands folded quietly. The perfect picture of the submissive wife, which he knew she was not and would never be. She had a point. A wife always commanded far more respect in the harem than did a favorite. And when he was gone a widow wielded more power than an ex-favorite.

"I will have no fanfare," he said. "It will be done quietly. Tonight." He clapped his hands and told the attending slave, "Have Ali Yahya fetch the chief mullah of Adrianople." The slave departed, and the sultan turned to Adora. "My sons will witness this act. Send them to me, and tell Thamar of my decision."

She rose from her kneeling position. "Thank you, my lord."

"You are at least gracious in victory," he said wryly. "Well, woman, what will you have for your bride's price?"

"Constantinople!" she answered calmly.

He burst out laughing. "You put a high price on yourself, Adora, but damn me, you're well worth it! For now, however, I will settle an amount of gold on you. Return it to me when I give you the city."

"With interest, my lord, for I shall invest it with the Venetians." She moved to the door. Then, turning, she said simply, "I love you, Murad. I always have."

He pulled her roughly into his arms and buried his face in her hair. For a moment they stood silently, and she could feel the even beat of his heart. "I am not a romantic prince such as are spoken of by the Persian poets," he said. "*I* know how I feel, but sometimes I have trouble with the words. I am a man of war, not love."

"You are my prince of love," she interrupted him.

He held her away from him so he might look into her face. "Woman," he said huskily, "you are a part of me. If I lost you I should be as one half dead."

Her violet eyes shone with joy. He was encouraged to go on. "I love you, Adora." And then abruptly turning away from her, he said, "Send my sons to me."

A few hours later Adora and Thamar stood quietly hidden in a small room above the sultan's private salon. They secretly watched and listened through a carved lattice as the sultan dictated their marriage contracts to the scribes. This was followed by the brief Moslem wedding ceremony, witnessed by Prince Bajazet and his half-brother, Prince Yakub. The brides did not participate in the ceremony. Murad united himself first with Theadora, then with Thamar. When it was over, neither woman said a word to the other, but went her own way back to her own court.

The following day the court began its trip to Bursa, traveling overland to the coast within sight of Constantinople. Before they embarked across the Sea of Marmora, Adora sent a verbal message to her sister,

Helena, via the Byzantine guards sent by the emperor to honor his overlord. "Tell the empress that her sister, the sultan's *wife*, sends her greetings."

"She gives herself airs," sniffed Helena after the message had been delivered.

"She only speaks the truth," said John Paleaologi with a happy chuckle. He fingered the parchment he was holding and looked down at it again. "He married her several days ago."

The look on his wife's face was extremely gratifying to the emperor, and he did not temper her disappointment by telling her that Murad also had taken Thamar to wife. Let Helena stew in her own venom! And with that happy thought, the emperor left his wife and Constantinople to join the festivities in Bursa.

The emir of Germiyan's daughter was to be wed with a pomp unlike anything yet seen in the Ottoman court. The sultan enjoyed the more elegant of Byzantine customs, and so did his sons. So while the younger Germiyan princess, Zenobia, who was but ten, was quietly wed to Murad's loyal general and sent to live with her husband's mother, her older sister was married amid general rejoicing and great festivities.

Throughout the city, whole sheep were roasted over open fires, and the sultan's slaves moved through the crowds offering freshly baked cakes of chopped almonds and honey. Murad gave each of his noble visitors his own palace with a staff of well-trained servants, and a harem of half a dozen beautiful virgins. The rulers of Germiyan, Tekke, Hamid, Karamania, Sarakhan, Aydin, and Byzantium were so honored.

There were wrestlers, acrobats, and jongleurs, puppet shows and trained animals performing all about the city. Byzantium's elegant customs and love of display were creeping into the Ottoman way of life, and the Ottomans liked it.

While Murad hosted the wedding feast for the bridegroom and his guests, Adora entertained the bride and the other women. The feasting and festivities went on for nine days. On the evening of the ninth day, Zubedya of Germiyan was carried in a closed litter to her husband's house where she met Bajazet for the first time. She was accompanied by Adora and Thamar.

When they had prepared the girl for bed, Adora said, "I will inform your lord and master that you await his pleasure."

"No, my lady mother," said Zubedya. "The custom of my land is that the husband of a princess of Germiyan must wait upon *her* on their wedding night. The marriage contract between my father, the emir, and Prince Bajazet's father, the sultan, permits me to retain my own customs." Thamar looked shocked, but Adora laughed. "I think that neither my lord Murad nor my son is aware of this custom. It is truth and not fear?"

"Truth, madame. I swear it."

Adora laughed again. "A very good custom," she said, "and one we shall take for our own. From this day forth it will be thus for all Ottoman princesses." She looked at Zubedya. "You will not keep Bajazet waiting long, child? He is proud, as are all men, and I would have you happy with him. Do not begin on the wrong foot."

The girl shook her head. Adora kissed her on the cheek. "I wish you joy," she said. Thamar followed Adora's example and then the two women left the bride.

"If the chit were married to my son I would not allow such a thing," snapped Thamar as they hurried to greet the bridegroom and his party.

"But she is not married to your son. She is married to mine."

"I don't know why Murad could not have arranged for my Yakub to wed with Germiyan," complained Thamar. "Then at least Yakub would have had his own kingdom when the old emir died."

"Murad is not interested in Yakub having his own kingdom. He is building an empire for the future generations of Ottoman sultans who will follow him. One day we will rule from Constantinople to Belgrade to Baghdad."

"You are mad!" sneered Thamar.

"No, I have vision, as did my ancestors. They were empire-builders too. But I cannot expect the daughter of a man little more than a tribal chieftain to understand such a thing."

And before Thamar could reply, they entered the atrium of the house to greet the bridegroom and his party. Adora looked at her two sons with a feeling of amazement. Halil was a handsome replica of her own father, a tall, dark, blue-eyed man with curly black hair and a full beard. His cleverly built-up boot made the limp barely visible. He was an invaluable advisor to his half-brother Murad.

At eighteen, Bajazet was his father's son. He was a tall man, with a long prominent nose, large, expressive black eyes, and Murad's sensual mouth. From his mother he had inherited his fair skin which he now kept smoothly shaven. As he grew older he would grow a magnificent black beard like his older half-brother, Halil.

From both his parents he had inherited intelligence, and he was already showing himself to be a brilliant military commander. The soldiers had nicknamed him "Yiderim," or "thunderbolt." Though bright, Bajazet was impulsive. His parents hoped this trait would diminish as he grew older.

Adora kissed her younger son, and he asked, "My bride awaits me?"

Adora turned to the emir of Germiyan. "Tell me, my lord emir, is there in your country a custom that permits your daughter to keep the bridegroom waiting upon her?"

For a moment the elderly ruler of Germiyan looked puzzled. Then, as comprehension dawned, he looked embarrassed. "I had forgotten!" he exclaimed. "Trust that minx Zubedya to remember the ancient custom"

"Do you mean," asked Murad, "that according to this custom Bajazet may not enter the bridal chamber until he is given leave?" When Adora nodded, the sultan chuckled. "It seems, my son, that you have married a spirited maiden," and when Bajazet's face darkened with anger, his father clapped him on the shoulder and laughed. "We have promised that Zubedya may retain her own customs. Let the girl have her moment. By morning she will have no doubt about who is cock and who is hen in your household."

"That is right, little brother," said Prince Halil, "but be sure that the girl understands who is the real master, else your married life will be one long battle. Beat her, if necessary."

"Halil!" Adora glowered at her older son. But the men chuckled. She turned to Bajazet and kissed him. "I wish you joy, my darling." A tear slid down her cheek and he kissed it away, a tender smile on his lips. "You grew too fast for me," she explained softly and then quickly left the house to return to her own serai.

"My mother has a tender heart," observed the prince.

"Your mother is priceless above all women," said the sultan. "There is no other woman like her in this world."

When Bajazet finally had been admitted to the bridal chamber, Murad wished his important guests goodnight and rode to the Mountain Serai. He dismounted in the courtyard and was escorted to the baths. An hour later, feeling relaxed and pampered, he entered his favorite wife's bedchamber to find her brewing him coffee. Near the little burner was a large bowl of honeyed yogurt and a plate of tiny cakes. Clad in a loose white silk robe, he stretched out on the pillows to watch her.

The girl in Adora was finally gone, but in its place was a magnificent woman who set his pulses racing. He smiled wryly to himself. His harem was full of nubile beauties. Even his second wife was not yet thirty. Yet, as always, he wanted only this beautiful woman. She was forty-one now but her hair was still dark, her eyes and skin clear.

She turned those eyes on him now. "What do you think about, my lord?"

"I think of how lovely you are. Of tonight at our son's house how the eyes of the princelings could not keep away from you. The emir of Karamania had heard you were but a slave, and he offered me a king's ransom for you. He was greatly disappointed to learn that you are my beloved wife. He could not resist asking if I were not tired of you, and if I might not divorce you and sell you to him!"

"And what did you tell him?"

"That all the gold in the world would be but a thousandth of your value."

"You are extravagant, my lord," she teased him.

"And you are irreplaceable in my heart," he answered, drawing her into his arms.

"Your coffee," she protested faintly, then gave herself over to his kisses.

Afterward, when they lay content beside each other, she thought it was time to speak of something she very much desired. She had rarely asked him for anything. She shifted so that she reclined on her side. Looking down on him, she said, "You have betrothed our daughter, Janfeda, to the young caliph of Baghdad. When will she go from us?"

"Shortly, my dove. I want her safe in Baghdad before the winter storms. I thought to send her by ship as far as Trebizond, and then overland from there to Baghdad."

"And what will you do then, my lord?"

"Go off on campaign!" he said enthusiastically.

She nodded. "And what am I to do, my lord?"

"Do? What do you mean, my dove?"

"What am I to do? My sons are both grown and married. My daughter goes to wed the caliph soon. There is nothing left for me. I am not a woman content to sit idly in the harem, painting my toenails."

He nodded gravely. "What would you do, Adora? For I know you well enough to know you have hatched a plot in that beautiful head of yours."

"I would come with you, my lord. On campaign. Many women travel with their men in the army."

His face registered delight. "I have never thought to ask you, my dove. Would you truly enjoy it?"

"I do not know, my lord, but I would rather be with you than left behind. Thamar will enjoy being the queen bee in the harem, but I will be with you!" She wrapped her arms about his neck and kissed him lingeringly. "Say yes, my lord! Please say yes!"

He enjoyed her pretty plea and slid his hands beneath her robe to caress the warm, silken skin. He felt her shiver with pleasure, and his own desire flamed.

"Say yes," she whispered against his ear, biting it gently.

"Yes," he answered, pulling her into his arms. "Yes, you deliciously sensual witch!" And he kissed her cool, soft mouth with an ardor she eagerly returned. The years had not dimmed their passion for one another.

Chapter 25

THE EMPEROR'S YOUNGER SON, MANUEL, HAD BEEN made governor of Salonika. Had he been content to govern, John would have been pleased, for Manuel was a skillful ruler. But Manuel's mistress, from a wealthy Christian family in Serres, managed to involve Manuel in a plot to overthrow Murad's government in Serres.

Manuel found himself besieged by the Ottoman troops and in a great deal of trouble with the sultan. He fled home to his parents in Constantinople. But for once John and Helena were in agreement: officially, they would not acknowledge him. When, at their weekly audience of supplicants, the chamberlain announced, "Prince Manuel Paleaologi, royal governor of Salonika," the emperor said loudly, "We will not receive him." Then he and Helena rose and left the hall together. There was a stunned silence, then a buzz of amazement from the hall.

They saw their son privately, however.

"Fool!" screamed the empress. "There was no harm in rutting with that she-devil of Serres, but to be led by her into direct opposition with Sultan Murad! Did you really expect to overthrow his rule?! Christos! Do not tell me you actually believed that?" She whirled about to face her husband. "This is as much your fault as his! You would place Manuel above his older brother, your rightful heir. He has done no better than Andronicus!"

Manuel Paleaologi looked at his mother with distaste. There was a pouch beneath her chin, powder clung to the wrinkles about her eyes, she dyed her hair. Yet she still attracted lovers like a bitch in heat. Her escapades had always been a source of embarrassment to him, especially as a child. His brother, who was her favorite child, found it amusing.

"Why do you stare at me like that?" she demanded of Manuel.

"I was thinking," he said slowly, with satisfaction, "that you are getting old." Then he fell back, reeling from the force of her blow.

"Leave us, Helena," said the emperor sharply, and she stormed from the room. John Paleaologi turned back to his younger son. "Sit down, Manuel." When the prince obeyed, John asked, "Why, my son? I went against custom and placed you above your brother because you deserved it. You are a natural ruler. Now you have behaved as foolishly as Andronicus. I cannot protect you from the folly you have committed. Surely you knew that when you came to me."

Manuel nodded, shamefaced.

"Was she worth it, my son? Was this temptress of Serres worth your disgrace?"

"No, father," came the low reply.

The emperor let a little smile touch his lips. Then he said, "Well, Manuel, you have learned a hard lesson. I will elaborate upon it for you. Your mistress was not worth the trouble she has caused you. No woman ever is."

"Not even a woman like my aunt Theadora?"

The emperor smiled. "Your aunt Thea would *never* ask the impossible of a man. She is far too wise," said the emperor.

"What must I do, father? Where can I go now?"

"Have you courage, my son? For you will need courage to do what must be done."

"If I do not have it, father, I will find it somehow."

"You must go to Sultan Murad and throw yourself on his mercy."

Manuel whitened. "He will kill me," he whispered fearfully.

"No," said the emperor, "he will not kill you, Manuel. That would defeat his purpose. I see Thea's subtle mind in all this. Murad is playing us against each other. If he kills us off, he cannot do that any longer. Go to Bursa. He is there now. Beg his pardon. He will forgive you."

"That is easy for you to say, father. It is not your life you play with."

"No!" thundered the emperor. "It is not my life, but a life far dearer to me! It is the life of my favorite son: the only man fit to rule Byzantium when I am gone. You have said you would find the courage, Manuel. You must. You have no other choice. I will not receive you publicly or privately again. Nor will I allow you sanctuary here in the city. You endanger us all, everyone from the lowliest beggar to the emperor is in danger from Murad's vengeance if we defy him. Where is your conscience?"

"Our walls are unbreachable," protested the prince.

"No longer, not completely. There are places where they are weakened, and when I tried to refortify them recently, the sultan forced us to tear down what we had rebuilt."

Manuel sighed and drew a deep breath. "I will go, father."

"Good, my son!" said the emperor, clapping his son on his shoulder. "I will see that word is sent to Bursa ahead of you." He stood up. The audience was at in end. The emperor clasped his son to his breast. "Go with God, my son," he said quietly.

Manuel left the Imperial Palace to find an escort awaiting him. They rode to the yacht basin at the Boucoleon Harbor. His escort left him after putting him aboard a waiting ship. The ship arrived several hours later at the port of Scutari on the Asian side of the Marmora. The captain gave Manuel a fine stallion which had made the voyage stabled in the stern of the ship.

"With your father's compliments, Highness. Godspeed."

Manuel Paleaologi rode off alone. His fear was not of the journey, for the sultan's roads were safe. He feared what awaited him in Bursa.

His father was sure the sultan would forgive him, but Manuel remembered the massacred garrison at Chorlu and the seige of Demotika when sons were ordered executed by their own fathers. He also remembered that the two fathers who had refused to kill their sons had been executed themselves. Manuel recalled that his cousin, Bajazet, had beheaded the rebellious Cuntuz. If the sultan could be that cold with a rebellious son, what chance did he have?

He stopped at a small caravansary that night and got drunk on fermented fruit juice. The following afternoon he rode into the palace courtyard at Bursa. His monumental headache, made worse by several hours ride in the bright sunlight, was punishment enough. He was escorted courteously to a small apartment and attended by soft-spoken slaves who saw to his bath and steamed and massaged his headache away. He was brought a light lunch for which he found he had appetite. But he saw no one but the slaves, and they could not answer his questions. His nerves were beginning to fail him.

Finally, after supper had been served him that evening, a palace official came to tell him that the sultan would see him in the morning. Manuel was more nervous now than he had been when he arrived. Then the thought struck him that if Murad had intended to kill him he would have been housed in the palace dungeons rather than a comfortable suite. Perhaps his father was right. He dozed fitfully throughout the night.

In the morning he was taken before his uncle. Murad looked enormously imposing sitting on a throne of black marble, clad in a jeweled robe of cloth of gold. He wore a gold turban with a pigeon's-blood ruby in its center. Looking down on Manuel, Murad said sternly, "Well, nephew?"

Manuel flung himself flat. He was unable to stand now, for his legs were trembling terribly. "Mercy, my lord uncle! I have wronged you, but your reputation for fairness is well known. Forgive me! I will not err again!"

The corners of the sultan's mouth twitched. "That is an enormous vow you make, Prince Manuel. To never err again . . ."

"My lord, I only meant—"

"I know what you meant, you young fool! You swore to be my liegeman, and you have broken that vow. I should have you beheaded and get the matter over with.

"However, I am informed that the cause of your disgrace was a woman. I can do no more than Allah himself did when the father of us all, Adam, was led astray by the woman, Eve. So it has been, down through the ages. Normally intelligent men being led into a folly by a pretty smile and a pair of plump tits." He laughed mirthlessly. "Your father informs me that you are ordinarily level-headed, and that you have a talent for governing. Very well. I will spare you, *this* time. But betray me again, nephew . . ." He let the thought hang between them. Then he said, "You will return to Constantinople and co-govern again, under your father's guidance. I have arranged a marriage for you with the young daughter of the last despot of Nicea. Her name is Julia. I am told she is virtuous and has a sweet nature. We can make sure of the first. But as for the second, nephew, you will have to take your chances like the rest of us."

Manuel felt the sweat running down his back and legs. He was weak with relief. Slowly he pulled himself up. "Sire," he said, and his voice broke. He gulped back his tears. "Sire, my grateful thanks. I swear I will not fail you again."

"See you do not," said the sultan sternly. "Now go and see your aunt and thank her for your life. She pleaded very prettily for you."

Manuel backed from the audience chamber, and followed the slave who led him to Theadora. As he entered the room, she rose and came toward him with her hands outstretched. Giving him a hug and a kiss on his cheek, she said, "So, Manuel, you have met with the lion in his own den and you have emerged alive."

"Barely, aunt." God! She was lovelier than ever! Nothing at all like his mother! How could two sisters be so completely different?

"Sit down, my dear. You look exhausted. Iris, see to refreshments. My nephew appears in need of sustenance. How is your father, Manuel? And, of course, my dear sister?"

"My father is well. My mother is as usual." He saw the twinkle in her eye. "I understand," he continued, "that I have your silver tongue to thank for my life."

She nodded smilingly. "An old debt I owed your father, Manuel. But now it is paid. Betray my lord Murad ever again, and I myself will wield the sword that executes you."

"I understand, aunt. I will not be disloyal again."

"Now, tell me what you think of your impending marriage."

"I suppose," he said, "it is time I settled down and bred some sons."

"No curiosity about your bride?"

"Do I have a choice, aunt?"

"No," she laughed, "but do not look so doleful. The

maiden is lovely."

"You have seen her?"

"Yes. She lives here in the Bursa Palace. She is a hostage for her family's good behavior. This marriage between you two will bind them closer to us when they learn how well we have settled her. I think they expected she would be put in some emir's harem. They did not think to see her become empress of Byzantium someday."

"What is she like?"

"Fair, with reddish-blond hair and bright blue eyes. Her mother was a Greek. She reads, writes, and speaks Greek. And she reads and speaks Turkish as well. She is soft-spoken, has been taught all the house-wifely virtues, and is faithful in her devotions. She has spent part of her time with us learning the Eastern way of pleasing a husband. I feel you will find her most accomplished." Theadora's eyes were sparkling mischievously.

"Am I allowed a glimpse of this paragon, aunt?"

"Go to the window, Manuel, and look out into my garden. The two maidens tossing the ball are your cousin, Janfeda, and your betrothed, Julia."

"Janfeda, here? I had heard she was to go to Baghdad."

"She goes soon."

Manuel Paleaologi studied the girl who played with his pretty cousin. Julia was a pretty little thing. She laughed easily and was good-natured when she missed a catch. His good fortune suddenly over-whelmed him. He had ridden into Bursa expecting not to leave it alive. Instead, he was forgiven his sins and presented with a beautiful bride.

A lesser man might have made the mistake of considering this a sign of weakness on the sultan's part. Manuel Paleaologi did not make that mistake. His father had been right: Murad was playing the Paleaologi family against one another. It suited him that Manuel take young Julia of Nicea for a wife. A stupid man might have resented this. But Manuel, like his father, saw that the once-great empire of Byzantium had shrunk to nothing. He knew that sooner or later what was left would fall to the Ottoman Turks. In the meantime, he and John would do what they could to preserve what remained of Byzantium. He was his father's son, and John Paleaologi could be proud of him. If peace with the Turks meant a wedding with that adorable creature running about the lawn, then Manuel would certainly wed with her.

"When your eyes narrow like that," came the aunt's voice, "you look like your father, and I know you are thinking."

He laughed with good grace. "I was thinking I am a fortunate man. I am alive, and I have a beautiful bride. When am I to wed with the maid?"

"Tomorrow. My lord Murad has brought the metropolitan of Nicea here to Bursa, and he will perform the ceremony at noon."

"Does the bride know yet?" asked Manuel dryly.

"She will be told this evening," replied Adora smoothly. "And now, nephew, I will allow you to return to your own quarters. You will want to spend time in prayer and meditation prior to your marriage."

Her tone was serious, but her eyes teased. He stood, kissed her soft cheek, and left the room. Adora sat for a few minutes, pleased with the day's work. She liked Manuel. He was so much like his gentle father. When John Paleaologi told his son he would send word ahead, it had been to Adora he had written, not the sultan. The sultan's favorite wife was not well-acquainted with Manuel, but John had not been half so eloquent when he had spoken of his older son. Manuel's record as governor was a good one, and his love and loyalty to his father were genuine. Adora had been impressed enough to chance pleading for the young man. Now, having spoken with him, she believed her faith in John's judgement had been justified.

"Ahh, you are thinking again," teased Murad as he entered the room. "You will get wrinkles. Too much thought is not good for a woman."

"Then your harem should be wrinkle-free," she shot back at him. "There isn't one whole thought among them all."

Roaring his laughter, he scooped her up and carried her to her bed. He dumped her on it. Flinging himself down next to her, he kissed her. "Your mouth tastes of grapes, Adora," he said, loosening her hair from its elegant coronet. The dark, silken mantle fell about her shoulders. Taking a handful, he crushed it between his fingers and sniffed its fragrance. "I have pardoned your nephew, woman. And I have given him a beautiful bride."

She pressed her cheek against his chest and felt his strong heartbeat. "I am aware of all this, my lord Murad."

"Am I not entitled to a reward for my most generous behavior?"

"Yes, my lord, you are. I have almost finished embroidering your new slippers with seed pearls," she replied gravely.

"*Seed pearls? On my slippers?*" He was incredulous.

"Yes, my lord," she answered demurely, but her voice held a funny tremor and her eyes were lowered. "I have pricked my poor fingers most dreadfully, but 'tis a fine reward for my lord's generosity."

He pinioned her beneath him with a smothered oath. "Look at me, woman!"

His command was met by a burst of silvery laughter as she raised her lovely eyes to him. "Do you not want the slippers, my lord?" she asked innocently.

"No! I want you!" he answered fiercely.

She slid her arms around his neck. "Have me then, my lord! I await you!" And she placed a sweet, burning kiss on his mouth.

Her sheer robe melted away under his quick hands, and she was naked to his soft, sure touch.

His own brocade robe opened beneath her skillful fingers. She returned his caresses, running her hands down his long back, cupping the hard roundness of his buttocks in her warm hands.

"Woman," he murmured against her throat, "if the houris assigned to me in Paradise have hands half as soft, half as clever as yours I shall consider myself blessed."

She laughed softly and reached down to fondle his manhood. Gently she roused a passion in him so great that only the fierce and swift possession of her body could satisfy it.

Now it was he who was the master, leading her on, holding her back, making her cry out with pleasure. He kissed her again and again until she was almost swooning, and she returned the kisses with a depth and ardor that only increased his passion. Frantically he whispered her name against her ear. *"Adora! Adora! Adora!"* and she answered him softly, "Murad, my beloved!"

Then suddenly he could no longer control his desires. He felt her body reaching the same blazing climax. She shuddered violently several times. Her skin was almost burning to the touch. Groaning, he spilled his milky seed into her soft body and, in a burst of clarity, she realized again that in this constant battle between men and women, it was the woman who emerged victorious in the end. Tenderly she cradled him against her, crooning soft little love words to him.

When she awoke in the morning he was still asleep beside her, looking boyish despite his years. For a moment she lay quietly watching him. Then she dropped a kiss on his brow. The dark eyes that opened and looked upon her were for the briefest moment so filled with love that she was astounded. She knew he loved her but he was not a man given to saying so often. The emotion she had glimpsed made her feel humble. She understood why he hid it from her. Murad would always consider love a weakness. He believed that showing such weakness to a woman lessened him and gave the woman an unfair advantage.

She smothered a chuckle. Would he never trust her

love for him? "Arise, my lord, my love! The sun is already up, and this is the day we wed my nephew with the little heiress of Nicea."

How lovely she still is, he thought, gazing on her camellia-skinned nudity, her long dark hair swirling about her. "Have we not even a moment to ourselves?" he growled, kissing her round shoulder.

"No," she teased, rising from their bed. "Would you have the marketplace gossips say that Sultan Murad has grown soft, and lingers within a woman's arms once the sun is up?"

Laughing, he leapt from the bed and delivered a well-aimed smack to her tempting backside. He was rewarded with a shriek of outrage. "You, my lady Adora, have a wicked tongue."

Rubbing her injured part, she pouted, "And you, my lord slug-a-bed, have a hard hand." And catching up a gauze robe she fled to her bath, his appreciative chuckle echoing behind her.

The witch must always have the last word, he thought.

Murad left her suite for his own. He wanted young Manuel bedded as quickly as possible. Although the emperor could have no objection to the girl, he would probably be irritated to find that the sultan had usurped his paternal authority. Murad wanted the little Julia pregnant quickly so there could be no chance of annulment. The girl's mother had been an excellent breeder. Murad hoped Julia would prove just as fecund, but the girl's slenderness worried him somewhat.

Murad was not officially part of the religious ceremony. He stood behind a carved screen as the patriarch of Nicea united the young couple. The sultan was amused to see the wide-eyed girl sneaking looks at the stranger to whom she was being married.

Afterward, he joined the newlyweds in a small celebration in Adora's apartments. Thamar was also there, but more to lobby for her own son than to wish the bride and groom well. Isolating Murad in a corner, she complained, "First your son, Bajazet, is wed to Zubedya of Germiyan. Now you wed your nephew, Manuel, to Julia of Nicea. What of our son, Yakub? Have you no noble bride. for him? Is only Theadora's family dear to you?"

He fixed her with a hard look. She was no longer the slender beauty with the gorgeous golden hair who had fascinated him. She was heavier, her skin had coarsened, her hair was faded. It never occurred to Murad that his absence from her life and her bed were responsible for these changes. He had never been particularly fond of her, and right now she was an irritant.

"Yakub is my younger son. He is not my choice to succeed me. Yakub's fate rests with his older brother, Bajazet. My father's choice was my brother, Suleiman, and therefore I took no fertile favorites, nor spawned children until after his death. It is possible that Yakub will not survive my death by more than a few hours. If such is to be his fate, none of his sons would survive either."

Her eyes were wide with shock. "What is it you say to me?" she whispered.

"There can be only one sultan," he said quietly.

"But your own father made his brother Al-addin, his vizir."

"And I deposed a half-brother who was my elder, for there were those who would have put Ibrahim before me and ruled through him."

"You would condone your own son's murder?" She was horrified.

"Yes!" he answered her fiercely. "You are a Christian, Thamar, and were raised in a world where mounting a crusade against the 'infidel' Turk was daily talk. Your Christian brothers would love nothing better than to cause dissension between two heirs to my kingdom. Therefore, when I die, it is probable that Yakub will follow me shortly. There can be only one sultan. Let us have no more talk of this, or of brides for Yakub."

"Why then was your half-brother, Halil, spared when you became sultan? Was not Theadora's son by your father a danger to you also? Or perhaps," she suggested unpleasantly, "he is really your son and not Orkhan's child."

He wanted to hit her, but he would not spoil the party. Instead he fixed her with a look of intense dislike. "My half-brother is a cripple. Certainly you know that deformity of any kind is not permitted an Ottoman sultan. And never again abuse Adora by foul innuendo, Thamar, else I will tear your tongue from your head. Her life with my father was an unhappy one."

"Something like my life with you," she taunted.

"Your own bitterness is what makes your unhappiness. You became my second wife knowing full well that Theadora claimed all my heart."

"Did I have any choice?"

"No," he admitted. "You were bound to obey your father."

"And you might have refused my father's offer, but you lusted after me!"

"You could have been happy, Thamar. Adora welcomed you as a sister and tried to smooth your way. You brushed her kindness aside and behaved like a spoiled child."

"And at the height of your passion on our wedding night you whispered *her* name over and over again like a prayer!"

"I did?" He was shocked by the hatred in her eyes as well as the knowledge she had just imparted. She turned and stalked slowly from the room.

Only Theadora had witnessed the exchange. She had not, of course, heard the words spoken between them, but she had seen Thamar's hatred. She now sent Murad a puzzled look. But he merely smiled and joined her. She soon forgot the strange scene.

Thamar, however, did not forget. The bitterness that had been growing hidden in her over the years now took a turn toward revenge. Returning to her apartments, she dismissed her women and flung herself on her bed, weeping. Suddenly she knew she was not alone. Sitting up, she saw a eunuch standing quietly in the corner.

"What are you doing here?" she demanded furiously.

"I thought I might be of service, my lady. It breaks my heart to hear you weep so."

"Why should you care?" she muttered.

In answer he crossed the room and knelt before her. "Because I dare to love you, my lady," he murmured.

Shocked, Thamar looked closely at the kneeling eunuch. He was unbelievably beautiful with liquid brown eyes fringed in thick dark lashes, and curly black hair. He was tall and, unlike most eunuchs, muscular and firm.

"I have not seen you before," she said.

"Yet I was assigned to your service over a year ago," he answered. "I have seen the look of sadness grow on you, my lady, and I have longed to erase it."

Thamar was beginning to feel better. This outrageous young eunuch was talking to her as if he truly cared. "What is your name?" she asked at last.

"Demetrios, my lovely lady."

She hid a smile, trying to sound bored. "Once I was lovely, Demetrios, but no longer."

"A bit of exercise, a special rinse to return the gold to your hair . . . and of course, someone to love you."

"The first two are easily done," she said, "but the third is impossible."

"I," and he lowered his voice, "could love you, my dearest lady." He let his meltingly beautiful brown eyes sweep over her. Thamar felt a flush run from her toes to her head.

"You are a eunuch," she whispered. Then, fearfully, "Aren't you?"

"My sweet, innocent lady," he murmured, taking her hand in his and caressing it. "There are two ways to geld a male. With little boys, all is removed—but with older boys and young men as myself only the sac containing the seeds of life are taken. The mortality rate is less that way." He stood and dropped his pantaloons. The rod of his manhood hung flaccid. "Caress me, my lady," he begged. Fascinated, Thamar complied.

Within moments he was as hard and as big as any normal man. Gently he pushed her back amid the pillows of her couch. "Please, sweet mistress, give your Demetrios permission to make you happy again."

If they were caught, she thought for a brief moment, if— "Oh, yes," she breathed eagerly. And she tore away her robe in eagerness. He caught at her hands. "Slowly, my lady. Let me." And he carefully removed the silken underdrawers and chemises. Gazing at her longingly, he thought what a fine figure of a woman she was. A bit flabby in places now, but he would soon take care of that. Ali Yahya had been correct about her. She was eager for a lover.

Kneeling beside her couch, he took her little foot in his hands, tenderly kissing each toe, then the sole, the heel, the ankle. His lips slid up one leg and then over and down the other. Still kneeling, his mouth moved across her navel and up to her breasts. Gently he bit at her nipples, then teased them with his hot tongue. She was panting quickly, her eyes closed, a look of bliss on her face. He moved to enter her bed, and she gasped, "The door! Bolt the door!"

Returning, he mounted quickly and drove into her. She spent too quickly, sobbing with eagerness, and cursed in frustration.

"No, no, sweet lady," Demetrios reassured her. "I am like a bull and will pleasure you long and slowly."

It was a promise not lightly made, and it was the beginning of the most incredible night of Thamar's life. The eunuch serviced his mistress again and again until she was so exhausted that she could not raise her head from the pillows. At this point Demetrios deemed it wise to stop, though Thamar protested.

"You will come to me tomorrow night?"

"As my princess wishes," he replied, smiling down at her.

"Yes! God, yes!"

"Then I must obey."

"You must become my chief eunuch," she said.

"You have a chief eunuch."

"Dispose of him somehow," she murmured, and instantly fell asleep.

Demetrios slipped from the room and went immediately to Ali Yahya's quarters. As he grew older, Ali Yahya had discovered he needed less and less sleep. Consequently, except for about three hours in the deepest part of the night, he was always awake.

"You have finally succeeded?" he asked as Demetrios entered, a look of triumph on his face.

"I have succeeded completely, master. I caught her in a weak moment. She returned from the wedding in very low spirits. She was so busy dismissing her women she did not even see me. When she thought herself alone, she wept. Making my presence known, I comforted her."

"Fully?"

"Fully, master. I am now her lover. She has already begged me to return tomorrow. She wishes me to be her chief eunuch and has told me to dispose of Paulus."

"Indeed," said Ali Yahya dryly. "You must be well worth the outrageous price I paid for you. I will see that Paulus is sent to Prince Halil's house in Nicea. You have done very well, Demetrios. Now, you must gain Princess Thamar's complete confidence, and you must keep it. From now on your contact with me must always be a secret and made only when absolutely necessary. You know what you must do. I now give you control of Princess Thamar's household. You will answer to no one but me."

"I hear and obey, master," said the young eunuch, bowing.

Ali Yahya nodded slowly, then spoke again. "Remember where your true loyalties lie, Demetrios. If you become ambitious and attempt to betray me, your death will be a very long and extremely unpleasant one. Serve me well, and you will be a rich and a free man some day."

"I hear and obey, master," replied Demetrios. He left the room.

Ali Yahya sat back, well-satisfied. He trusted the younger man. He had picked him most carefully.

He had observed, as the sultan ignored his second wife over the years, that the only outlet for Thamar's love was her son. Yakub had been taken from his mother at the age of six and brought up in his own court, a strict Moslem one. He respected his mother and even harbored an affection for her, but he did not understand her. She was too intense, and her plots to advance him in the eyes of his father were embarrassing.

Ali Yahya worried about Thamar. Allah only knew what the lonely, embittered, and frustrated woman might do. He had decided to give her a new interest, one who would not only involve her attention, but who would keep him fully informed of her plots.

He had looked for several months for the right person. Thamar was suspicious by nature. He had needed a young man, but not too young. Someone moderately intelligent and trustworthy, but not ambitious.

By chance he had heard of Demetrios, the slave of a wealthy merchant. As his master had aged and grown feeble, Demetrios had taken over his business and run it at a profit for his master. Unfortunately he had also gotten involved with his master's two bored young wives, for Demetrios hated to see a pretty woman unhappy. When one of the wives discovered that the other was also enjoying the eunuch's services, she revenged herself by crying "rape" the next time Demetrios visited her. Demetrios was flogged and sent to the slave market by his outraged master. He was to be re-gelded, and then sold.

Fortunately, the slavemaster was taken by Demetrios's beauty. Re-gelding was seldom successful. If the young man died, which was likely, a handsome profit would be lost. The risk was to the slavemaster, not to the slave owner. The slavemaster had remembered that his old friend, Ali Yahya, was looking for a young eunuch. Ali Yahya came, was impressed, and the bargain was made. Demetrios was so grateful for the gift of his life that he swore to obey Ali Yahya unquestioningly. The sultan's chief eunuch knew he could trust this new addition to his staff.

Prince Bajazet must be protected at all costs for he was his father's choice. Prince Yakub, though loyal to his father and older brother, might be tempted by his unhappy mother's plots. Thamar must be side-tracked. Demetrios was chosen to do the job.

Paulus was replaced by Demetrios. And, one day, the few female slaves Thamar kept were all replaced by new women. Knowing no differently, these women gave their loyalty to Demetrios.

The sultan's second wife began to change. The extra pounds she had gained melted away, and her hair became soft and shining again. Demetrios satisfied her physical needs each night.

Though she grew calmer and more content, she could not refrain from plotting. But Demetrios managed to confine Thamar's schemes to the talk stages. He was worried by her extreme hatred of the sultan's favorite wife. Thamar could become completely irrational if Theadora's name were even mentioned. She would rant on and on about her plans to make Adora suffer as she had suffered. Demetrios did not understand this, for Thamar quite frankly admitted that she had never loved Sultan Murad. Why then, this unreasonable hatred for Theadora? This was one thing Demetrios did not report to Ali Yahya.

The young eunuch was truly fond of his mistress. If a humble former fisherman from the province of Morea could dare to love a princess, then Demetrios did. Though Thamar might be her own worst enemy, she now had someone who would protect her from herself.

Chapter 26

Prince Andronicus had been imprisoned for several years in the Marble Tower, which was located at the far western end of the city. After his temporary blinding, he had been returned there to languish. His wife was dead, and his one son, John, was being raised in the palace.

He lived comfortably, his servants were pleasant, and he was denied nothing . . . except women, and his freedom. His world consisted of the rooms in which he lived, though the tower windows gave him a panoramic view of the city, the countryside beyond it, and the sea of Marmora.

He was allowed no visitors for fear he would begin plotting again. No one came in any case, for none of his former friends wished to be identified with a convicted traitor. Andronicus was quite surprised, therefore, to see his mother arrive one afternoon, heavily cloaked, and paying lavish bribes to his guards.

She embraced him excitedly. "The hour of your deliverance is near, my darling son," she gushed. "Your brother has disgraced himself at last!" And she quickly filled him in on the events of the past few months. "Your foolish father has sent Manuel to Bursa to beg Murad's pardon. Poor Manuel will not, of course, return alive. Your father will then have to free you!"

"I shall be his co-emperor!" Then Andronicus's eyes narrowed. "Perhaps I shall be the only emperor," he said softly.

"Oh, yes, my darling!" cried Helena. "Whatever you want, I will help you to get. You shall have it. I swear it!"

But Prince Manuel did return from Bursa. He was forgiven his sins by the sultan, and he had a bride who was already with child. The emperor was relieved to see his favorite son, though he was at first a trifle put out that his paternal rights had been assumed by Murad. However, within a few days John had to admit that Murad's choice of a bride for Manuel had been perfect. She was sweet-natured, obedient, and very much in love with her husband. Manuel returned her affection equally. The emperor could wish no more for his son.

The empress was not pleased. Not only was Julia everything Helena wasn't, she was also very pretty. Quiet spoken, but firm of character, Julia moved in to fill the gap left by the empress's constant absences. The emperor and his younger son had more of a feeling of family than they had had in years, and John prepared to name young Julia co-empress when her child was born.

The baby was a girl. It was the kind of disappointment that Manuel and his father might have borne with good grace had young Julia not sickened and died of a milk fever almost immediately thereafter.

Manuel was heartbroken. He had his infant daughter moved into his own bedroom so he might watch over her at night, and he swore never to wed again.

"Andronicus's son, John, can follow me," he told his father sadly. "He is a good lad, and more like us than like his father."

So the matter was settled for the time being. Julia's daughter was baptized Theadora, after her father's aunt. The empress, her grandmother, was enraged.

Helena began to plot again. Though her beauty had coarsened, she was still attractive, and she exuded a primitive sensuality that attracted men.

Now Helena decided to marshall support among her influential friends in the interests of her older son, Andronicus. He should be co-emperor with his father, not Manuel. She chose as her co-conspirators General Justin Dukas, one of the empire's finest soldiers; Basil Phocas, a leading banker and merchant; and Alexius Commenus, the premier nobleman of the empire. The general would bring military support to Helena's cause, the merchant-banker financial aid. Commenus would bring the nobility, who all followed his lead. It was often said that if Alexius Commenus shaved his head and painted it crimson, so would most of Constantinople's noblemen.

Although Justin Dukas could guarantee certain regiments of the Byzantine army, additional support would be needed. Basil Phocas's money bought Genoese and Ottoman troops who waited discreetly outside the city for Andronicus to join them.

In Bursa, Murad laughed 'til his sides ached at Helena's machinations. Adora was concerned for the safety of John and Manuel.

"They will not be harmed, my dove;" he assured her. "The banker, Phocas, is in my service. He will see that neither John nor Manuel is harmed."

Comprehension dawned. "Then it is really *you* who finances the Ottoman troops Helena bought?"

"Oh, no!" chuckled Murad. "Phocas is footing the bill, but no Ottoman troops fight without my permission. It suits me to keep Byzantium in an internal uproar for now. That way they cannot plot against me while I plan my next campaign for expansion."

"Is the city included in this new expansion?" she asked. "Do not forget that you owe me my bridal price."

"Someday," said Murad quietly and seriously, "we will rule our empire from there. But the time is not yet ripe. I must first conquer all of Anatolia so there is no one at my back. Germiyan has been absorbed into our family, but the emirates of Aydin and Karamania remain a threat. And there is yet one Byzantine city left near us. I must have Philadelphia!"

"Do not forget," she reminded him, "that when you have removed the Paleaologi from your path, there are still the Commenii of Trebizond. They, too, are heirs to the Caesars."

"If all else in Anatolia is mine, what chance has Trebizond against me? It will be surrounded by a Moslem world on three sides, and a Moslem sea on the fourth side."

His strategy was, as always, correct. Murad securely planned his next campaign while the Paleaologi family were kept busy fighting with each other for the right to govern a dying empire.

Andronicus escaped the Marble Tower and joined his troops outside the walls. The population of Constantinople was pulled back and forth in their loyalties by daily rumors. The yearly advent of the plague was said to be God's way of showing the people that Andronicus was in the right and John and Manuel in the wrong.

In no time at all General Dukas had swayed the remaining military units over to Andronicus's side. The city's Golden Gate was deliberately opened early one dawn to Andronicus and his mercenaries. They marched down the Triumphal Way to the cheers of the populace. Emperor John and his younger son, Manuel, were spared only by the intervention of Basil Phocas, who threatened to withdraw his financial support if they were harmed. Since Andronicus needed the continued financial aid of the merchant-banking community to pay his troops, he had no choice but to accede.

Basil Phocas heaved a secret sigh of relief. His continued wealth in these difficult times was due to the fact that his caravans traveled in safety throughout Asia. This was due to Ottoman protection. In return, Phocas spied for Murad and did his bidding discreetly. He had promised the sultan that neither of the deposed co-emperors would be harmed. But he had not counted on the viciousness of the empress. Helena wanted her spouse and younger son dead.

Fortunately, the other chief conspirators agreed with Phocas. John and Manuel were imprisoned in the Marble Tower that had held Andronicus. Basil Phocas personally paid the Ottoman soldiers who guarded the prisoners and the servants who waited on them. The soldiers and servants were told that Sultan Murad wanted the two men kept alive. If anyone offered them a bribe to visit the prisoners or to poison them, they were to accept the money and then immediately report to Phocas. In this manner the two men were kept safe.

Inspired by Helena's success, Thamar decided to try her hand at intrigue. She entered into secret negotiations with the wife of Murad's deadly enemy, the emir of Aydin. Her objective, as always, was a kingdom for her son, Prince Yakub. He, of course, knew nothing of his mother's plans.

The emir's fourth wife was the heiress of Tekke. She had but one child, a daughter of thirteen. It was this girl—and Tekke—that Thamar sought for her son. Even her beloved Demetrios was kept unaware of her plans and it was only by chance that he learned of the plot before it could be completed.

One night he awoke to hear her talking in her sleep. He debated shaking her awake. But he realized that, if he did so and her plans were later foiled, she would know who had betrayed her.

Having heard enough to give him an idea of what she was up to, he rose quietly and sought for the small ebony and mother-of-pearl box in which she kept her correspondence. Sure enough within he found not only copies of her letters, but the letters from Aydin's fourth wife as well. Shaking his head at the foolishness of keeping such incriminating letters, he slipped from the room with the box.

When Ali Yahya had read the letters he said, "Return the box to its hiding place, Demetrios. Say nothing, of course, but continue to serve your lady well." Then, he handed the younger man an exquisite sapphire ring.

Demetrios slipped the ring on his finger and did as he was bid. He wondered how Ali Yahya would circumvent Thamar's plans. But he did not have long to wait before finding out. Several weeks later there came word that the emir of Aydin's fourth wife and her daughter had been drowned in a boating accident.

Though Thamar kept her own council, he knew the reason for her unhappy mood and he strove harder to please her. He was touchingly tender and understood one day when, for no apparent reason, she burst into tears.

Dismissing her women, he held her in his arms while she wept. "Why do you cry, my beloved?" he encouraged her. To his surprise she admitted, "I *must* have a kingdom for Yakub! He will never follow Murad while Bajazet lives. And though his older brother is fond of him, he will kill him before their father's body is cold. If I can find another kingdom for him, then he is no threat to them."

Demetrios felt a terrible sadness sweep over him. "Oh, my dear one," he said gently. "You do not understand, and I do not know if you ever will. There is no other kingdom for your son. The sultan means to eventually rule all of Asia and Europe. Perhaps the Ottoman will not succeed in Sultan Murad's lifetime, but surely in the lifetime of his descendants. Your son is too fine a man and too good a soldier to remain alive when the present sultan dies. You must accept this, my beloved, though it breaks your heart. If Prince Bajazet does not die before his father does, it is he who will rule next. Your son will die. There is no other way Bajazet can be safe. You must accept it."

"I did not bear and raise my son to be slaughtered like a sacrificial lamb!" she screamed.

"Hush, mistress," he comforted her. "It is the way of the world. You must steel yourself. God willing, it will be many years before you lose your son. He might even die a natural death."

She quieted, but the look in her eye warned him that she would not accept her son's fate without a fight. He would have to watch her carefully from now on. What, he wondered, would she do?

In the meantime Andronicus had had himself crowned the fourth emperor of that name. At first he had been very popular for he talked convincingly about lifting the Turkish yoke and of restoring the city's prosperity. He could, of course, do neither. Soon there were rumblings of discontent. Andronicus levied new taxes to pay for his diversions.

Helena, too, was disappointed in her eldest son. She was no longer accorded the respect due her position as she had been with her husband. Worse, her allowance had not been paid. When she demanded to know why, the emperor's new bursar told her that Andronicus had given no orders that she receive money.

Angrily she sought out her son. He was, as usual, surrounded by courtesans and hangers-on. "Could we not speak privately?" she asked.

"There is nothing you cannot say in front of my friends," he answered rudely.

Helena gritted her teeth. There was nothing for it but to speak. "The money due me to run my household this quarter has not been paid, and your bursar tells me he has no order to pay me."

"I need all my money myself," answered Andronicus.

"The empress always received an allowance."

"You are not my empress, mother. You are my father's empress. Get your money from your lovers. Or will they not pay any more for what has been so well used?"

The women about Andronicus giggled at the outraged look on Helena's face; the men smirked. But she was not so easily bested.

"I cannot imagine why you need all the money, Andronicus. Women of the streets, such as these," and she waved her hand to include those clustered about her son, "can usually be had for a few coppers. Or a crust of bread. Or nothing." Then she turned and regally departed the room, pleased with the gasps of outrage behind her.

She was beginning to realize her mistake in favoring her elder son over her husband and Manuel. He had no real interest in the city, or the remainder of the empire. Helena had expected a share of the power when Andronicus took over. She was worse off now than she had been before.

Returning to her apartment, she found it being searched and her servants in an uproar. A young captain was in possession of her jewel cases.

"What is going on?" she demanded, trying hard to keep her voice calm.

"Orders of the emperor," said the young officer. "We are to seize and confiscate the state jewels in your possession."

Helena's wild burst of laughter startled everyone in the room. "State jewels? There are *no* state jewels, captain! The state jewels of Byzantium were sold or stolen during the Latin reign years ago. The jewels worn by me on state occasions are paste imitations!"

"And what are these, madame?" He held out the lacquered jewel cases.

"Those are my private property, captain. Each piece of jewelry in those boxes was a gift to me. They are mine alone."

"I must take them all, madame. The emperor's orders made no distinctions."

Helena stared, and her china-blue eyes widened further to see her silver and gold plate and her vessels being carried away. The captain looked away, embarrassed.

"Fetch General Dukas," she ordered one of her maids.

The captain barred the woman's way. "No one will be allowed to leave or enter this apartment without the emperor's written permission," he said. "You are under house arrest, madame."

"How are we to get food?" Helena asked with a calm she was far from feeling.

"It will be brought to you twice daily, madame." Then, as if it was an afterthought, he said, "I am sorry, madame." And signaling his men to gather up the empress's property, he left.

The evening meal turned out to be a disgusting mess of peas, beans, and lentils, a loaf of coarse, brown bread, and a pitcher of inferior wine. Helena and her servants looked at the tray with disgust. There was not enough food to feed more than three people, and the empress had fourteen servants. Angrily she shoved the tray over, and her little dogs rushed to lap up the mess. Within minutes they were all dead.

"The ungrateful bastard," the empress said furiously. Then she announced, "All but two of you will have to go. The fairest way to decide will be to draw lots."

"Sara and I will stay, my lady," said her tiring woman, Irene. "It is our right, as we have been with you the longest."

"Use the secret passage," said Helena. "I have nothing left with which to bribe the guards in any case. That way they will not know you are gone. One of you can bring us food and drink daily."

"Come with us, madame," begged her chief eunuch.

"And leave my son and his friends in complete control of the palace? Never! But you, Constans, go to Basil Phocas and tell him what has happened here. Tell him—tell him—that I have made a mistake in judgement."

The empress's servants escaped safely, and several days later Basil Phocas arrived via the secret passage. Sara and Irene kept watch while Helena and her former lover talked.

"What exactly do you want me to do?" asked the banker.

"John and Manuel must be restored. Andronicus is utterly impossible."

"It will take some time, my dear."

"But it can be done?"

"I believe so."

"Then see to it! I cannot stay penned up here forever."

The banker smiled and departed. The empress, imprisoned in her own rooms, waited and waited. And waited. After many months word was smuggled into her that her husband and younger son had escaped and were safe in Bursa with Sultan Murad.

Murad was now confident that he could continue to manipulate both sides in the Paleaologi's dynastic struggles. Andronicus was dethroned, pardoned, and sent to his brother's old city of Salonika to be governor. John and Manuel were restored to Constantinople as co-emperors. The price was high. A larger annual cash tribute, a substantial contingent of Byzantine soldiers to serve in the Ottoman's army, and the city of Philadelphia. Philadelphia had been the last remaining bastion of Byzantium in Asia Minor.

The Philadelphians objected to being ceded to the Ottoman empire. Thus Adora had her first chance to go on campaign. In this instance, Murad would lead his armies personally. Fighting in the ranks of the Ottoman army were the two Byzantine co-emperors who now openly admitted to ruling only by the grace and favor of the Turkish sultan.

The Ottoman army marched from Bursa in early spring, crossing mountains whose tops were still covered with snow. Adora did not intend being shaken to death in a heaving palanquin, so she devised a costume that was both practical and modest. Murad at first was offended at the thought of his wife riding astride. He changed his mind when she modeled her costume for him.

It was all white and consisted of wide light wool pantaloons, a high necked, long-sleeved silk shirt which was tight at the wrists, a silk sash at the waist, and a fur-lined white wool cape with a gold and turquoise buckle. She wore high boots of Cordoba leather with a low heel, and matching warm brown riding gloves. There was also a small turban with long side drapes in the manner of the tribesmen of the steppe. This could cover her face, should she choose to veil herself.

"Do you approve, my lord?" she pirouetted for him. She was so excited, so gay with the prospect of accompanying him.

He couldn't resist smiling back at her, and he did approve her choice of clothing for her public appearance. He had never, in fact, seen her so well clothed. There was barely an inch of skin showing. Had she been younger he would not have allowed it, but maturity had given her a youthful dignity. There would be no familiarity among his men.

"I do approve, my dove. You have, as always, been clever in your choice of clothing. I understand from Ali Yahya that you have also been learning to ride. I have a surprise for you. Come!" And he led her to the windows overlooking the courtyard.

There, standing quietly with its groom, was a coal black palfrey, caparisoned with an azure and silver silken throw, and a saddle and bridle. Adora gave a squeal of excitement. "Is she mine? Oh, Murad! She is beautiful! What is her name?"

"She is called Wind Song. If I had known that such a simple gift would please you so, I could have saved a fortune in jewels all these years."

She turned, and the sunlight lit one side of her face. He caught his breath at her beauty, astounded at how lovely she still was. Or was it because he loved her so much? Her arms slid around his neck, and standing on her toes, she kissed him.

"Thank you, my lord," she said simply. He felt an ache in his throat he couldn't explain.

When they rode out from Bursa, Adora rode by his side. Wind Song matched the elegant prancing steps of Murad's great white Arabian stallion, Ivory. It was not unusual for a sultan's wife to accompany her lord on campaign, but it was unusual for her to ride with him. The effect of Adora's unorthodox behavior was favorable. The Ottoman troops were impressed that Prince Bajazet's mother rode with them. It enhanced the heir's position greatly.

When they reached Philadelphia, she watched the battle from a hillside opposite the town's main gates. By rights the city now belonged to Murad. But the population had been stirred up by its governor, who feared to lose his place, and by its clergy, who hated the sultan. The people refused to accept the new overlord.

The emperor John entered the city under a flag of truce and pleaded with the inhabitants to accept their new master. If they accepted Murad willingly, there would be no destruction. Philadelphians would face only what other Christian inhabitants of the Ottoman Empire faced. They would pay a yearly head tax, and their sons between the ages of six and twelve would be eligible for a draft into the Corps of Janissaries. Other than that their lives would go on as before. They might, of course, convert to Islam in which case they would escape the head tax and the Janissaries.

The governor and the clergy were insulting when John suggested that they played lightly with the lives of Philadelphia's citizens. "You cannot hope to win," he pleaded. "You are surrounded by Islam. Have you told the people the truth, or have you filled them full of foolishness about resisting the infidel? Murad is generous, but he did not march all the way from Bursa to be denied. He will take the city."

"Then it will be over our dead bodies," pronounced the governor pompously.

"I never knew a governor to lead an army or to die in the fighting," said the emperor scathingly. "Be well advised that when the sultan enters the city I will seek you out myself."

"Our people will be martyrs in God's holy war against the infidel," intoned the city's patriarch.

The emperor looked on the priest pityingly. "My poor people will suffer fire and the sword because of your vanity, father. I do not think God will reward you for all the souls who will be on your conscience when this battle is over."

But they would not listen. They hustled him out of the city before he could talk to the populace. Murad was disappointed. He would have preferred a peaceful entry. Now Philadelphia must be made an example, so that other cities would think twice before resisting the Ottoman.

In less than a week Philadelphia fell to Murad. The Sultan's soldiers, both Christian and Moslem, were allowed the traditional three days of pillage before order was restored.

Those caught with weapons, soldiers and citizens alike, were immediately put to the sword. The first night the city rang with screams as every woman and girl, ferreted out by the sultan's soldiers, was raped again and again. Neither age nor vocation nor status was any protection. Little girls as young as six suffered, as did nuns, who were dragged from their convents to satisfy the furious lust of battle-weary soldiers.

By morning of the fourth day there wasn't a woman in the city who had escaped the sultan's army. They and the children and the other survivors were herded into the marketplace to be sold into slavery. Eager bidders had arrived from the surrounding Moslem territories.

It was each soldier's right to sell any captive he had caught unless that person converted to Islam. There were few conversions. Not all the captives were sold, as many of the soldiers who had fought with Murad would now bring their families to recolonize the city. They would need slaves.

A percentage of each sale went into the sultan's coffers. The remainder was split between the soldier and the merchant who conducted the sale.

All the valuables found within the city were confiscated for the sultan's treasury. The churches were emptied, purified, and turned into mosques. Both the governor and the religious patriarch who had so boldly defied the emperor and the sultan were beheaded for causing Murad trouble and for inciting *his* city to rebellion. Thus the last Christian city left in Asia Minor, except Trebizon, fell to the Ottomans.

Adora had viewed the battle for Philadelphia and the ensuing pillage with a stoic interest that fascinated Murad. Finally, unable to control his curiosity, he asked her her thoughts on the campaign. She toyed with a pillow before answering.

"You were more than fair, my lord," she answered.

"Have you no feeling for your people, mother?" asked Bajazet.

Murad stifled a smile at Adora's frown of annoyance. "My dear son," she replied, her voice dripping sarcasm, "though I am but an infidel dog, and a lowly female at that, I am still an Ottoman. Your uncle John legally ceded Philadelphia to your father for certain aid and favors. Its governor chose not to obey his overlord, and incited the people to resistance. They have only reaped the rewards of their disobedience. If we had chosen to let them defy us until they chose to stop, it would have cost many Ottoman lives in the future. Though it is not so, many people believe that to show mercy is a sign of weakness. Therefore we can rarely allow ourselves that gentle luxury. Remember, Bajazet, always strike quickly, before your enemies have a chance to think, else they defeat you.

Murad nodded. She had learned a great deal of battle strategy from him, he thought. He was surprised and flattered. "Listen to your mother, my son," he said, and his eyes twinkled teasingly, "for though she is but a woman, she is a clever Greek. And her words are given weight by virtue of her vast age." And he laughed as she launched herself at him.

Prince Bajazet looked horrified as his parents wrestled together amid the pillows. He was a grown man with a pregnant wife and did not think of his mother, and father as being physical with each other. To be sure, his father kept a harem, and his mother was yet young, but—they were his parents!

"Scoundrel!" hissed Adora, yanking at Murad's thick silver-black hair.

"Witch," murmured the sultan, "how is it you still have the ability to inflame me?"

"My *vast age* has given me the power to stir the watery blood of an older man!" she retorted wickedly.

He laughed again. Then he found her angry mouth and kissed it thoroughly before moving on to more interesting parts of her anatomy. Adora began to make soft, contented noises. Flushing crimson, Prince Bajazet fled the room. His parents never noticed that he had gone.

Chapter 27

THE OTTOMANS NOW RULED ASIA MINOR, EXCEPT FOR the emirate of Karamania and the small Greek Christian kingdom of Trebizond. Murad now turned his eyes back to Europe. He saw that he needed three additional cities if he were to secure his position in the Balkans. These were Sofia in northern Bulgaria, which would extend his rule to the Danube; and Serbian Nish and Monastir, to establish his rule west of the Vardar River. Murad and his entire household returned to his European capital, Adrianople, from there to direct the new campaigns.

While he occupied himself with his campaigns, Adora occupied herself with their growing family. Zubedya had quickly produced four sons who were named Suleiman, Isa, Musa, and Kasim. Adora did not like the Germiyan. The closeness she had hoped would develop between them had not. The Germiyan was a proud, cold woman who gave only what she had to and no more. She did not love her husband. In fact, Adora did not believe she had any affection at all for Bajazet.

Her son was a brilliant, mercurial man very much like his maternal grandfather, John Cantacuzene, but with a dangerous streak of pride and rashness that worried Adora. He had, she knew, never felt anything but the mildest affection for any woman. Yet she knew that he had never had a man for a lover, either. There had never been any grand passion in Bajazet's life. And Adora felt that he needed the stabilizing influence of a beloved woman. Neither Zubedya nor the few silly girls he kept in his small harem filled this need.

It seemed that, unlike his parents, Bajazet was not a sensual man. He did not seem to feel the lack of a passionate love. His life was completely taken up by the military.

This did not bother his wife. She seemed to have no interest in anything having to do with Bajazet, and that lack of interest applied to his sons. No sooner had she produced them than they were turned over to wetnurses and slaves.

Bajazet returned to Asia on his father's orders in order to help Murad take Karamania. Germiyan had been Zubedya's dowry. Hamid had been purchased from its ruler who preferred gold and peace of mind to the nervous strain of having the Ottoman Empire on his doorstep. To the south, the emir of Tekke had fathered a son in his old age. He fought hard with the sultan to retain his lands. The result was that Murad gained Tekke's uplands and lake region, leaving the emir, for the present, with the southern valleys and the lowlands between the Taurus mountains and the Mediterranean.

Only Karamania stood in Murad's way. Despite his large army, the left wing of which was under

Prince Bajazet's command, the battle of Konya ended in a draw. Both sides claimed victory. Murad had gained neither territory nor booty, tribute nor military aid. The emir of Karamania kissed his hand in a public gesture of reconciliation, but that was all Murad achieved.

Murad had fought his war on two fronts, and had been generally victorious. But he had met his match in one Moslem ruler, and could not extend his dominion any further into Asia. He had, however, gained his objective in Europe: Sofia, Nish, and Monastir, along with the city of Prilep to its north, were now Ottoman strongholds.

Back in Asia Minor, Murad had trouble with his army. In an effort not to irritate the Asian Moslems, he ordered his troops to refrain from looting the countryside about the city of Konya. The Serbian troops fighting with Prince Bajazet were furious. They considered themselves cheated, as looting and rape were a soldier's reward. They disobeyed the sultan. Murad could not allow such a breach of discipline in his ranks. The Serbian contingent was lined up, and every sixth man executed on the spot. The rest returned to Serbia raging over what they considered unjust treatment.

Never one to miss an opportunity, Thamar's uncle, Prince Lazar, emerged from hiding. Using the incident at Konya, Lazar fomented Serbian resistance against Murad. With the Ottomans in control of Nish, upper Serbia and Bosnia were now threatened. Lazar and the prince of Bosnia formed the Pan-Serbian Alliance.

Murad's younger son, Yakub, had been left in

charge of the Ottoman troops in Europe. His answer to Lazar was to take his army across the Vadar and invade Bosnia. Unfortunately, the majority of the Ottoman army was in Asia with the sultan. Prince Yakub, badly outnumbered, was defeated at Plochnik. He lost four-fifths of his men.

There was wild rejoicing among the Serbs, Bosnians, Albanians, Bulgarians, and Hungarians. The invincible Turks had finally been defeated! Immediately the Balkan Slavs rallied about Lazar's banner, determined to drive the Ottomans from Europe.

Murad showed no great haste to avenge Plochnik.

"How long will they remain united?" he asked Adora. "They have never before been able to stay together. Soon one of them will be insulted by another, or else they will start fighting over religion."

"But you cannot ignore the insult these Slavs have given us," she fumed.

He smiled. "I shall not be idle, my dove. Thamar's father grows old. I think before his sons get any ideas about ruling and join the Pan-Serbian alliance, I must relieve Ivan of his territory."

At the first sign of Ottoman troops Tsar Ivan withdrew to his castle-fortress on the Danube and sued for peace. Then, suddenly, he changed his mind and attempted a last, desperate resistance. One of his two sons died in the fighting. The survivor was strangled by Janissaries at the sultan's victory. Murad was now content to leave his father-in-law as his governor in the new territory. Ivan was a broken man, and in no position to aid his fellow Slavs in their new alliance.

Thamar, wild with grief over her brothers' deaths, privately vowed vengeance on Murad. Over the last few years the eunuch, Demetrios, had held her complete confidence. But now she shut even him out of her thoughts. Demetrios worried. Though he reported his mistress's actions to Ali Yahya, he loved the Bulgarian princess greatly. She was, he knew, her own worst enemy. On several occasions he had stepped in just in time to prevent her from destroying herself in some futile plot.

Thamar, with the slyness of the half-mad, managed to enter into another secret correspondence. This time it was with her uncle, Prince Lazar, head of the Pan-Serbian Alliance. The letters flew between them. Murad and Bajazet would die, assassinated by some means. Prince Yakub was to be the next sultan. Her son would, Thamar promised, be converted to Christianity. He would lead his people out of darkness and into the true faith. Islam would soon be wiped out.

The time, of course, was not right yet, Prince Lazar wrote to his demented niece. He would tell her when it was. Lazar was pleased by this chink in the sultan's camp. He wanted the deaths of the sultan and both his sons. Leaderless, the Ottomans could be destroyed. Thamar's madness was the key to success here. Yes, Lazar was delighted.

Thamar hugged her secret to herself, occasionally breaking into a wild laughter that frightened her slaves. Frantic, knowing that something was seriously wrong, Demetrios tried to find out what she hid. He applied to Ali Yahya for aid, but the chief eunuch was busy making preparations for Adora to accompany Murad on his campaign against the Pan-Serbian Alliance.

"Your mistress is merely suffering shock over her brothers' deaths," he told the anxious Demetrios.

"No! No! It is more than simply her old bitterness. She is plotting something, but I cannot find out what. She says her actions will elevate her to sainthood, and be the ruin of Islam."

Ali Yahya made an impatient noise. "*What* can she possibly do, Demetrios? She never leaves her apartments except to travel between palaces. She hasn't had a visitor in years. Rest easy. The lady Thamar babbles with frustration. She is helpless." And he dismissed his worried slave.

Several weeks later the armies of the Pan-Serbian alliance faced the sultan's armies across a desolate mountain field known as the Plain of the Blackbirds. Above the tents at the western end flew the flags of Serbia, Bosnia, Albania, Hungary, Herzegovina, and Wallachia. Flags of the Papacy and of the Orthodox Churches could also be seen.

At the eastern end flew the flags of the Ottoman sultan. The sultan was outnumbered, but the morale and confidence of his men were great. Murad was so sure of victory that he gave orders that no castles, cities, or villages in the territory be destroyed. It was a rich land he was fighting over, and it was not in his interest to ravage it.

Hearing of this Prince Lazar felt his confidence draining away. He began to panic. Why, he asked himself, did Murad feel so confident when he was so badly outnumbered? There was treachery within his own camp! He sensed it. But who would betray him? His glance fell upon one of his sons-in-law, Milosh Obravitch, who had recently criticized him. Of course!

"Traitor!" Lazar shouted at the startled young man. "It is you who has betrayed us!"

Amazed, Milosh Obravitch protested his innocence. He was hustled out of Prince Lazar's tent by his brother-in-law, Vuk Brankovitch. Brankovitch's heart was pounding. He had come as close to fainting a few minutes back as ever in his life. When Lazar had shouted "traitor," he had thought his game was up, but had kept his calm long enough to realize it was the hapless Milosh who was being accused. Brankovitch rushed Milosh from the tent and Lazar's wrath before his denials could be believed. He did not want Lazar turning his suspicions elsewhere. For Brankovitch knew that tomorrow, when the battle began, he would be withdrawing his twelve thousand men from the fighting, mortally weakening the Pan-Serbian Alliance.

Vuk Brankovitch did not believe that the Pan-Serbian Alliance would prevail over the Ottoman Turks. After several years of marriage and eight daughters, Brankovitch finally had a healthy, infant son. The prearranged withdrawal of his troops would guarantee that his lands would remain his. Thus, they would pass to his son.

In the Ottoman camp the sultan worried, for the wind was blowing strongly from the west. Come morning, his troops would be at a disadvantage, fighting with dust in their eyes. He must pray to Allah for a change in the wind.

Murad sat cross-legged in his luxurious tent, eating supper with his two sons. Behind them Adora directed the slaves and nibbled a bit when she could. Three musicians played quietly. When the meal had been cleared away, the sultan motioned to his favorite wife to sit with him. Placing two small bowls of sugared almonds on nearby tables she settled herself by his side to watch the dancing.

His arm slid around her, and he leaned over to kiss her. "Your mother," he told Bajazet and Yakub, "used to dance for me alone." He chuckled. "She was extremely skillful, as I remember."

Adora laughed. "I am surprised you do remember, my lord, since you rarely allowed me to finish a dance."

"Do you still dance for father?" Bajazet enquired politely.

"Occasionally," she answered, and laughed at his surprised look.

Murad was slightly disgruntled. "If you would ask my harem," growled Murad to Bajazet, "you would find out that I am not quite dead, boy!"

"Peace, my lords," Adora interposed between them. "Bajazet, Yakub, see that your troops are comfortable for the night, and pray with them for Allah's blessing on us. Your father and I bid you both a good night."

The two princes rose, kissed her, bid their father a good evening, and left the tent. She dismissed the musicians and the two dancers. "Would you be alone, my lord?"

"For now, my dove. Go to our bed. I will join you later."

She left. For a while Murad sat in silence listening to the wind howling about the tent. The lamps flickered eerily. The camp was very quiet but for that wind. He *must* win tomorrow! And he would! Then he would return to Asia Minor and *finally* subdue the irritating emir of Karamania.

Slowly Murad rose and moved to his prayer rug. Kneeling, he touched his forehead to the ground three times. He prayed for heaven's protection of his cause and for all the men who made up his army whether they were Christian or Moslem. He prayed that those of his men who would die tomorrow would die in the true faith of Islam. Murad then stood up and joined his wife.

She awaited him with a steaming wooden bathtub. Swiftly disrobing him, she helped him into the hot water and gently bathed him. Then she wrapped him in a large, warm towel. When he was dry, she slipped a silk robe on him.

Murad stretched out on their bed and gave himself over to the pleasure of watching her as she bathed. He marveled at the firm beauty of her body. As he gazed at his beloved Adora he felt his need for her growing, though he seldom indulged in sexual games before a battle.

Clean and dry, she reached for her robe. "Don't!" he said.

"As my lord wishes," she answered and lay down,

naked, next to him.

"Why is it woman, that you still managed to please me?" he muttered, pulling her into his arms.

"Perhaps it is my familiarity."

"In other words, I am getting old and do not like new experiences," he teased, nibbling on her plump shoulder.

"We both grow old, my dear lord."

"Not *that* old!" he answered, taking her with a suddenness that surprised her. When she gasped softly, he stopped her mouth with a burning kiss, then murmured against her ear, "Woman of my heart, I love you. I would lose myself in you this night."

And when he finally slept, content, she lay awake keeping watch over him, feeling strangely protective of this man who was her whole life. Only when the sky began to lighten and turn gray with the coming dawn did she fall asleep.

When she awoke the sun was up, and she could hear the battle trumpets sounding. There was great activity outside her tent. Murad was gone, and the pillow where his head had so lately lain was cold. She scrambled to her feet, calling to her slaves.

"Has the sultan gone? Is the battle begun?"

"No, and no, my lady," said Iris. "There is time yet."

Adora dressed quickly and hurried outside. Messengers rushed back and forth between the sections of the army. She noted that the wind was gone. The day was warm and quite clear. Catching the cloak of a young Janissary she said, "Take me to the sultan." She was immediately led to Murad, who was with his generals.

They had all grown so used to seeing her with him on campaign that her presence was barely noticed. The sultan casually put an arm about her, and continued giving orders. He, with his cavalry guard and his Janissaries, would occupy the center position. Prince Bajazet would command the newly reorganized European troops on the right flank. Prince Yakub, reassigned to command the Asian troops, would be on the left flank.

With the other officers now dismissed, Adora wished both her son and Yakub good fortune and a safe return. Both young men knelt for her blessing. Then she and Murad were alone for a few minutes.

"The wind went with the night," he said.

"I know. Why did you not wake me before you left the tent? I had hoped to break my fast with you. Some friendly peasants brought a basket of newly-ripened peaches for us."

He smiled. "Peaches! Always your weakness, eh, my dove?" Then he sobered. "I did not awake you, Adora, because I know how these last minute preparations for battle always worry you. I had hoped to be away before you awoke."

"And what, Allah forbid, if something had happened to you?" she said reproachfully.

"It is not my fate to die in battle, Adora. I shall always come home to you reeking of blood, sweat, and dirt, and you will scold me as you do our children, overlooking the fact that one cannot stay clean in battle. Am I not right, my dove?" He held her gently against him, and she could feel the sure beat of his heart beneath her hot cheek.

"You make me sound like a foolish maid," she protested.

"Never foolish, but always my naughty maiden, stealing peaches from the convent orchard."

She chuckled, somewhat mollified. "What on earth made you think of that?" she asked. But before he could answer, the trumpets sounded and the armorer hurried in with the sultan's breastplate. With nimble fingers she helped him close the fastenings, then buckled on his great sword. The armorer and his assistant stood waiting with the sultan's helmet, shield, and heavy mace.

The sultan put his arm about his wife and kissed her deeply. He held her for a moment. "May Allah guard you and bring you safely back to me, my lord," she said softly. He smiled a quick smile at her, then walked swiftly from the tent.

For a moment she stood quietly. Then she called out, "Ali Yahya! Come! We will go and watch the battle." The eunuch approached silently from a room within the tent. He draped a light silk cloak about her shoulders. Together they walked through the nearly deserted camp, and ascended a small hill overlooking the plain of Kossovo, the Plain of the Blackbirds.

Below them, in perfect formation and facing each other, were the armies of the Pan-Serbian Alliance and the Ottoman Empire. She saw Murad give the signal to attack, and an advance guard of two thousand archers loosed their arrows. The enemy foot soldiers raised their shield in what appeared to be a single motion. There were few casualties, and they parted to allow their cavalry through. The Serbs charged, shouting wildly, and broke through the Turks' left flank. Prince Bajazet came to Yakub's rescue with a massive counterstroke. He fought valiantly, using his great mace with deadly accuracy. Adora, watching from her hill, thought that her son seemed almost invincible. She was not able to see that he bled from several small wounds.

The battle remained in doubt. The hours flew by, and the Ottomans were still on the defensive. Then suddenly a great shout went up from the Serbian side as Vuk Brankovitch and his twelve thousand men withdrew from the battlefield. Badly weakened by this defection, the remaining members of the Pan-Serbian Alliance broke their ranks and fled. With a whoop of triumph the Ottoman soldiers tore after them.

Murad had been correct about the Serbs. They could not remain united, even under dire circumstances. Satisfied that his armies could finish without him, the sultan withdrew from the field. Adora and Ali Yahya hurried down the hill to meet him. As the little group returned to camp, slaves ran to meet their master. They took his armor and weapons from him and seated him to draw off his boots. They brought him a basin of warm, scented water, and he washed his hands and face.

"You see," he grinned up at Adora, "it is not my fate to die in battle."

"Praise Allah!" she murmured, sitting on a stool by his feet and laying her head against his knee. He reached down and stroked her hair. A slave placed a bowl of peaches at his elbow, and Murad handed her one before biting into one himself. The sultan's *aid-de-camp* entered the tent, prostrated himself, and then said, "We have a deserter of high rank from the enemy side, my padishah. One of Prince Lazar's sons-in-law. He asks to see you."

"My lord," protested Adora, "the battle has exhausted you. See this princeling tomorrow."

Murad looked irritated by the interruption. But assuming it was Vuk Brankovitch, he sighed and said, "I will see him now and get it over with. Then we will spend a few quiet hours together before my generals come to give me their reports."

Adora got up, and moved back into the shadows of the tent. The *aide-de-camp* left and returned quickly with a richly dressed young man who knelt in submission before the seated Murad. The man was not Brankovitch.

"Your name?" demanded the sultan.

"Milosh Obravitch, infidel dog!" cried the young man, jumping forward, his hand raised.

Adora screamed and leapt from the shadows, flinging herself in the direction of Murad. The *aide-de-camp* and the guards were as quick. It was too late. Milosh Obravitch twice plunged his dagger into the sultan's chest, so hard that both times it went through his back. The Janissaries, streaming into the tent, grabbed the assassin. Spread-eagling him, they lopped off his head. Blood from the man's severed neck gushed onto the rugs.

Heedless, Adora cradled her husband in her arms.

"Murad! Oh, my love!" she sobbed.

He struggled to speak, his face white, the light in his eyes fading rapidly. "Forgive . . . the cruelties. I love you . . . Adora . . ."

"I know, my love! I know! Do not speak. The physician is coming." Oh, God! She felt so cold! Why was she so cold?

A sad smile flickered on his face, and he shook his head. "Kiss me farewell, dove."

She bent her wet face and touched his cooling lips with hers.

"Peaches," he said weakly. "You smell of peaches," and then he fell back in her arms, his black eyes open and sightless.

For a moment she thought her heart would stop and that she might be granted the mercy of following him. Then she heard her own voice saying, "The sultan is dead. Notify Prince—notify Sultan Bajazet. *No one else! No one must know yet!*"

The Janissary captain stepped forward. "Prince Yakub?"

"See to it immediately after the battle," she ordered. "Prince Yakub is not to return. Do not wait for word from my son. I will not have this decision on him. It is my responsibility."

"To hear is to obey, Highness."

"Ali Yahya!"

"Madame?"

"No one enters this tent until my son comes. Tell them the sultan rests with his wife after a hard battle and cannot be disturbed."

"It will be as my lady says."

Then she was alone, still cradling Murad's body. Gently she drew his eyelids closed. He looked so relaxed, asleep. Slowly her tears fell on him. She made no sound. In the heat of the tent she could smell the nearby bowl of peaches, and she recalled his last words to her. "Peaches! You smell of peaches." They had begun together with peaches stolen from St. Catherine's orchard. Now it was ended in a tent smelling of peaches on a battlefield called Kossovo.

Throughout the rest of the day Theadora of Byzantium sat on the floor of the sultan's tent holding her husband's dead body. And while she sat, her numbed mind remembered their years together. It had not always been as easy between them as it had been in these last years. He had not always understood the passionate, intelligent woman whom he had moved heaven and earth to possess; and she had rarely been able to hide the woman she really was. But there had always, from their first moment, been love between them. Always, even during their fierce battles.

I have been blessed, she thought, in having such love. Then she thought again, but what will I do now? Bajazet respects me, but I do not think he knows how to love, even me. Zubedya certainly does not care for me, nor do her four sons, my grandsons. Once again I am alone. Murad! Murad! Why have you left me? She wailed her grief silently, and she rocked back and forth with her precious burden.

It was thus that Bajazet found her, her eyes swollen almost shut from weeping. He silently surveyed her. Her robe was covered with dried and blackened blood, her face puffy and streaked with tears. A wave of pity swept over him. He had never seen her other than elegant and beautiful. Bajazet had not yet found love, and did not understand the emotion, but he knew how his parents had loved one another. She was going to be lost.

"Mother."

She looked up at him. "My lord sultan?"

He was amazed at her calm, her correct behavior in the face of her tragedy. "It is time to let him go, mother." Bajazet held out his hand to her.

"He wanted to be buried in Bursa," she said quietly.

"So be it," answered Bajazet.

Slowly she released her hold on Murad's body, and allowed her son to help her up. He led her from the tent. "Yakub?" she asked him.

"My half-brother died in the battle, they tell me. He will be buried with honor, along with our father. He was a fine soldier and a good man."

"It is good," she said to him. "There can be only one sultan."

"I have already avenged my father, mother. We have slain almost all of the Serbian nobility. I have allowed only one of Prince Lazar's sons to live. The Serbs are no longer a threat to us, and it will be better if one of their own governs them. I will need their troops to defend the Danube Valley against the Hungarians."

"Which of Prince Lazar's sons is it, and what terms have you made with him?"

"Stephen Bulcovitz. He is but sixteen. He will pay us as an annual tribute 65 percent of the yearly revenues from the Serbian silver mines. He must command a contingent in my army, and send me Serbian troops whenever and wherever I need them."

She nodded. "You have done well, my son."

"There is more," he said. "Stephen Bulcovitz has a sister. Her name is Despina, and I will take her to wife."

"Prince Lazar's daughter? Thamar's cousin? Are you mad? You would marry the offspring of the man responsible for your father's death?"

"I need the alliance, mother! Zubedya binds me with Asia, but I need a European wife as well. The Serbs will trouble us no longer, and Despina will serve my purpose. Father would have approved."

"Do not speak to me of your father! He is not cold yet, and you would wed with his murderer's daughter!" He tried to comfort her, but she pulled away from him. "Dear God! I am surely cursed! Your father loved me, but *you* do not love me, and neither does your wife, or your children. Now you will wed with Thamar's cousin, and once again I will be alone."

"Meet with the girl, my mother. I do not have to wed with her if she displeases you. You are a fine judge of character, and I trust your opinion. If you feel that this Despina is not suitable then I will look elsewhere for a European bride. After today there will be plenty of noble Christian widows seeking to placate me with their nubile daughters."

Prince Lazar had been married twice, and it was his second wife, a Macedonian noblewoman, who had produced his youngest son, Stephen, and his youngest daughter, Despina, who was fourteen. The girl was spirited, but she was not proud, and she had an open and sweet nature. Her features were fine. Her skin was fair, and her long hair dark auburn. She had a small waist, nicely rounded hips, and came just to Bajazet's shoulder. Though Theadora had expected to dislike the girl, she could not.

Despina was shy with Theadora for awhile, but as her confidence grew, her concern for the older woman's loss became paramount. "You have had your own loss," said the sultan's mother.

A shadow passed over the girl's face, and then she said quietly, "I loved my father, madame. He was always good to me, and there will never be another like him in my life. However, God has blessed me in my grief by sending me your son to love. Though I am but his second wife, I shall endeavor to make him happy."

Deeply moved, Theadora put her arms about the girl. "I think, my child, that it is my son who is blessed."

To Adora's delight, there was true love between the two young people. The wedding was celebrated quickly and quietly as they were all in mourning. Bajazet was content to stay with his beloved bride much of the time. And within less than a year, Despina had given him a son. He was called Mohammed.

Bajazet then went back to war. Adora approved her son's return to the battlefield, for Murad had left his plans for conquest written down in several parchment scrolls. These were now in Bajazet's possession. The new sultan had only to follow his father's plans and success would be his.

Despina, with a wisdom and generosity far beyond her years, understood how desperately Theadora needed someone to love. Recognizing, too, her mother-in-law's superior knowledge in all things involving the raising of rulers-to-be, the girl stepped aside, leaving the care of her son to Theadora.

Despina concentrated all her energies on Bajazet; Theadora gave all of herself to Mohammed.

Seeing the baby's alert black eyes and broad brow, Theadora envisioned Murad. She saw her own renewed purpose in living. It would never be as it had been with Murad, but this life would afford her much. Theadora prayed that the boy would be the Ottoman to finally take Constantinople, and she recalled the prophecy, "And Mohammed shall take Constantinople."

Theadora of Byzantium was delighted. She had plans again, visions of the future. She would not be just another widow, honored but entirely forgotten. She was still in the center of history.

EPILOGUE

Bursa

December 1427

Epilogue

THE ORCHARDS OF ST. CATHERINE'S CONVENT LAY QUIET in the cool December sun. The bare branches of the trees rustled softly in a faint breeze. Though the original convent and its orchards had been destroyed when Tamerlane the Tartar took the city some twenty-five years before, they had been rebuilt by Princess Theadora, matriarch of the Ottoman family. In the center of the new orchard there had been built a small marble tomb. This would hold the old woman when she finally released her firm grip on life.

She was now ninety years old. She had outlived Orkhan, Alexander, and Murad. She had outlived her children, all of them, and even her grandson, Mohammed. She had made peace with herself and with her memories, except for the memory of her son Bajazet. For Bajazet had, in his growing arrogance, destroyed the empire Murad had so carefully assembled. Bajazet had been responsible for many deaths, including the death of the gentle Despina and even his own at the hands of the great Tartar warlord, Tamerlane, who had conquered the young sultan and his armies.

Theadora remembered all too well the day

Tamerlane and his army had entered Bursa. They pillaged, looted, raped, and burned their way through the city. They had stabled their horses in the mosques! Tamerlane had not cared for public opinion. He would show them who their new master was.

He had divided the empire as he saw fit, and had surprised Theadora by applying to her family the same logical measures Murad had once used to control the Paleaologis. The khan had laughed at her anger, saying, "Let Bajazet's cubs fight one another for their empire. It will keep them out of real mischief, and I can return to Samarkand knowing there is no knife at my back."

Theadora could not allow him a victory over her. "*You* have set the empire back fifty years," she said, "but *we* will triumph in the end. In ages to come our empire will endure and thrive. But Tamerlane, *if* he is remembered at all, will be recalled only as one of many troublesome Mongol raiders."

The barb found its mark.

"Woman, you have the tongue of an adder," he said. "It is no wonder you have outlived most of your family. It is your own poison that keeps you alive." Then, grudgingly, he admitted, "You are not like any female I have ever known. You are too strong to be a mere woman. Who are you, really?"

Theadora walked to the door of the room. Turning slowly, she said, "You have never known my like before, nor will you again." Her glance was a proud and mocking one.

"I am Theadora Cantacuzene, a princess of Byzantium. Farewell, Tartar."

And then she was gone.

The old woman sighed. There had been so many years of strife, of civil war. She had heartened when her grandson, Mohammed, took over and restored the government to a firm and stable one. Then he had died suddenly, and his son Murad II had been forced to meet his younger brother in battle and kill him before he could begin to organize his lands. Like his namesake, the young Murad II had brought his empire together. Peace now reigned in that empire. The fact was that, once again, the Ottomans were ready to move toward Constantinople.

Theadora was removed from the workings of government now. She had left the Bursa Palace when Mohammed died. All her old friends were long gone, including Iris and Ali Yahya. So she had returned to her little house within the walls of St. Catherine's. She was deferred to, of course, and greatly respected, but she was lonely. There was nothing left for her but memories, and she wanted to be where those memories were strongest.

This afternoon she walked slowly through the silent orchards. Though her hair was silver, her carriage was still proud. She had shrunk a little with the years, but her violet eyes had not faded. Behind her walked two young nuns whose job it was to help care for her. She resented their presence, but the sultan had ordered it.

She would not, however, allow them to intrude on her memories. Since they were both meek creatures they spoke only when spoken to by their crusty mistress. To them, the orchards were a barren winter place. Shivering, they pulled their black cloaks about them.

To Theadora it was mid-summer, and the trees were heavy with ripening golden peaches.

"Adora!"

She stopped and looked up, startled by the sound of his voice after all these years. He stood before her as she had first known him, tall and young and handsome. His black eyes twinkling, he laughed at her surprise.

"Murad!"

"Come, dove," he smiled, holding out his hands to her. *"It is time for you to go."*

Her eyes filled with tears. *"I have waited so long for you to come for me,"* she said. Reaching out, she took his hand.

"I know, dove. It has been a long time, but I shall never leave you again. Come now. It is not far."

And without question she went with him, pausing only a moment to gaze back at the two nuns who, with fluttering cries, were now bent over the crumpled body of the silver-haired old woman.

Author's Note

ON MAY 29, 1453, CONSTANTINOPLE FELL TO Mohammed II, son of Murad II.

About the Author

ADORA is the third novel of Bertrice Small, *New York Times* bestselling author. It was originally published as a mass market paperback in May 1980.